# Securely Insecure

## A STORY OF LOVE, LOSS, AND UNBREAKABLE FRIENDSHIP

### DONNA LYNN LITO

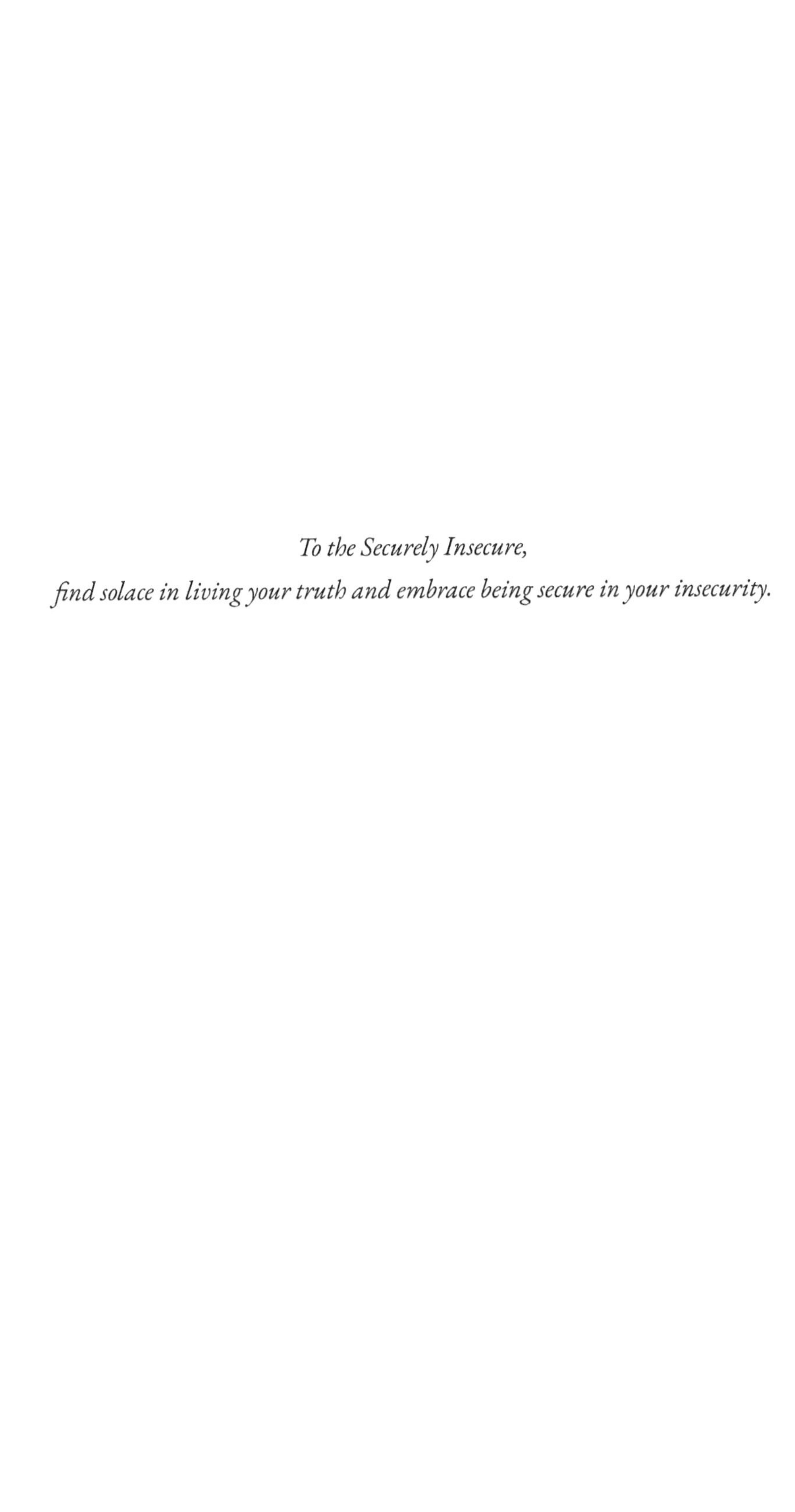

*To the Securely Insecure,*
*find solace in living your truth and embrace being secure in your insecurity.*

# PART I

# CHAPTER ONE

*Lynnie: South Oaks Nursing Home.*

"Lynnie, how are you today, baby?" A woman gently nudges the arm of the petite body lying peacefully, a frail, huddled shape beneath blankets of off-white crochet.

It takes Lynnie more than a moment to recognize Helen, the attending nurse, but a flash of recollection shoots through the wrinkled eyes of the old woman who watches her aide intently.

Helen is a large woman, appearing almost too outsized to be nimble on her toes in the many tasks she has to do. She has caring eyes, approaching the bedside gingerly, careful to move slowly. "Looking good, baby girl," she says with a chuckle as she pats the soft hand emerging from the warmth of the sheets to lift itself to her own. "Nice warm skin, today, honey."

Helen gives an earnest smile; the hands before her have lived a lifetime of memories, and now, they receive respect. The nod of the elderly woman acknowledges the warmth of her smile, appreciating her care, though uncertain how her surroundings have come to be.

"Sit yourself up, baby," Helen says with a sweep of one cool hand beneath the elderly woman's shoulders, aiding her to become upright perhaps faster than her mind can keep pace.

Helen now guides the woman gently to her reading chair, where a stack of journals lies on the table. "What are these?" she asks in a tone of sincere interest.

The silence of Lynnie indicates uncertainty in how to answer. Confused, her small voice whispers at last, "I don't know where they came from, but there are some fascinating stories in those books. Someone brings them. *I* don't know who. A young man."

Helen lifts one, and Lynnie tenses, unreasonably anxious about her handling these 'books'.

"Ahhh, your journals from your youth, are they, Lynnie? How wonderful! Yes, your son brought them in a couple of weeks ago. He thinks they might help you to remember."

The look of confusion occupies Lynnie's eyes again. Each time the young polite man comes to visit, she is trying desperately to understand why he comes.

"Lynnie, your sons come to see you every Tuesday," ventures Helen. "That's nice, isn't it? Those twin boys of yours are hard to tell apart. I don't know how you were able to manage them when they were babies. What did you do, Lynnie, stick labels on them?"

Helen smiles. "And your eldest—is it Blake—is very protective of you, Lynnie. He visits three times a week and keeps us nurses on our toes. Dear child, he sure does love his mama."

Lynnie sits momentarily with this information, trying to place the three men, seemingly confused about why they dote on her so fiercely. "Well, I don't know either!" she responds.

Helen's mouth turns down for a moment. Lynnie feels so lost these days, unable to recall for half the time. As for the other half, she mostly sleeps the days away.

Despite all Helen's best efforts, Lynnie hasn't the slightest idea why those men fuss so much.

"Helen, these ladies in these journals, can I talk to them? I have so many questions," Lynnie asks. She places her hands into her lap, fidgeting with her fingers. "They'll know the answers."

Helen continued her routine, humming as Lynnie sat by the window, staring at the birds chirping a sweet song. Though Lynnie cannot remember when, she is certain that there must have been a time when she moved with ease, a time when she knew everyone's names and who they were supposed to be. Soon bored, Lynnie rises, moving with care and a deliberate steadiness as she makes her way from the chair to the bathroom. Every step is calculated and deliberate.

Lynnie approaches the sink to wash her hands, pressing on the hygiene soap dispenser.

"Who is that?" she asks at first, eyeing herself in the mirror.

Helen turns. "It's you, honey bun. We talk about this every day. It's a mirror, see?"

Lynnie taps the silvered wall, staring curiously at the reflection.

"Oh, I remember," she says, her lips upturning as delicate fingers trace the outline of her own shape. "Yes, I believe that's me."

The lines on her face are deep now, creviced with age and wisdom.

Each one tells its story, a tale of a time when life was easier to maneuver. A time when she had tenacity and vigor, a time when she was young and filled with energy.

She glances at her gray hair, knowing she has earned each sparkling streak. A few whispers of hair fall on her cheek, and she gently waves them off her face. Her hands are veiny now, skinny, the skin saggy, filled with age spots. Although brittle, her nails are perfectly manicured thanks to sweet little Alice, a volunteer who visits once a week.

Lynnie's eyes are still the same as ever, a shade of hazel that can be mistaken for brown.

She stares again, tracing the once youthful, bright and hopeful face.

*Life has made me harder yet kinder, stronger yet empathetic, and wiser but more forgiving. This is the benefit of age; you can open your heart wider because you have learned that we are all a bit broken. With grace and empathy, we are redeemable and worthy.*

*Age allows for great knowledge and the understanding that nothing is permanent, especially life. This knowledge is the gift of death. In our youth, we are clouded by ego and self-righteousness. At the end of life, we have the unique view only age can provide, becoming fervently aware of the bends and cracks of each person walking this earth; it is what makes us human. Isn't the human experience supposed to be tumultuous and challenging?*

*What would be the point if it wasn't?*

*We are put on this earth to learn, grow, falter, and forgive; if we are lucky, we embrace the love and joy surrounding us. I know this now. I have learned this. Because I have lived it.*

General noise sounds emanate from outside the bathroom, and Lynnie jolts back from her thoughts, returned to the present by the young staff bustling around, talking loudly. Giggling.

Lynnie's time to go home is approaching. But for what exactly?

To live her life? Or to die?

She is grateful for the life she has lived that made her become resilient, brave, bold, and confident. The little girl inside no longer begs to fit in, for she has aged into a soul with purpose and meaning, a woman who has overcome obstacles and heartbreak. A mother, wife, and friend who was reliable and loving to a fault. At eighty-nine years old and having lived an entire life, she is neither scared nor sad about death. It is an inevitable component of life's beauty.

Suddenly, a bright red cardinal bird flutters toward the window, and Lynnie's eyes widen. The creature lingers close to the glass as if staring peculiarly before taking flight. The small joys of watching birds freely explore is something Lynnie has known over the last couple of years.

Youth often finds these morning visits from birds horribly intrusive and disturbing. No doubt their incessant song intrudes on their hung-over reverie.

It is not wasted on Lynnie how only as you age, the wonder of a bird in flight becomes magical. Memories flood back on reaching the twilight years, so many details long forgotten making a reappearance. Suddenly, the aroma of a particular time of life is poignant, the colors vibrant, the associated feelings—buried deep—arising again. Some memories bring a sense of reveling in happiness. Times of excitement, youth, and curiosity are intoxicating to the old. Other memories only fit to leave behind lie too far in the subconscious, lingering despite a desperate suppression of their pain. The elderly remember all they wish to forget but long to relive.

The end of life is funny like that.

Later that day, Lynnie finds herself back in her reading chair and picks up the top journal. Her long fingers and arthritic knuckles brush the cover of the book. She studies it, noticing its faded wording written in purple pen sprawled out in a cursive hand: *New Beginnings!*

It seems familiar but again, Lynnie cannot quite place why.

⚬⬥⚬

JOURNAL

IT IS THE END OF AUGUST, AND THE BEGINNING OF A COOL BREEZE IS TAKING OVER THE ONCE WARM AIR OF THE SEASON. THE FRAGRANCE OF SUMMER BLOSSOMS BEGINS TO FADE AS THE SMELL OF FALLEN LEAVES EMANATES FROM THE EARTH. MUCH HAS ALREADY CHANGED SINCE SUMMER!

Another season of my life is upon me, and climate change reminds me how life is ever-shifting. High school is a distant memory now, and college life is just beginning. While my tan is still apparent, it's starting to fade, just like everything. But I still have fond memories of the summer; it was 'eventful' to say the least!

We spent six weeks at my best friend Stacy's grandparents' summer home on Long Island, New York, in the Hamptons, making our grand entrance into adulthood. Stacy had met a man a whole ten years older! He was (in her words) wealthy and worldly, so we spent the summer on his yacht, in fancy restaurants, and rubbing elbows with the Hamptons' most elite, pretentious, shallow people. It felt like a movie, but we knew we didn't belong amongst this caliber of people.

Well, at eighteen years old and with our entire lives ahead of us, of course, we were more than willing to spend endless summer nights underage drinking and being arm candy to handsome bachelors. We flirted with disaster all summer. After all, Stacy and I would soon go our separate ways to different universities and start new chapters of our lives. While we were excited, we were also a bit sad that

THE DISTANCE WOULD CHANGE OUR RELATIONSHIP. WE VOWED WE WOULD NEVER FIND ANOTHER FRIENDSHIP LIKE OURS, BUT THAT STATEMENT BECAME PAINFULLY UNTRUE IN THE MONTHS AHEAD.

Lynnie sits back, her eyes sparkling with reminiscences. Despite what those doctors may think, there are times when Lynnie remembers way more than she lets on.

# CHAPTER TWO

*Lynnie: August in Ohio, the Summer before College.*

She can vaguely recall her childhood home as a ranch-style house set mid-block with gray shutters and a blue door, also a mat at the front that said 'WELCOME'. That was ironic at best because even the home's occupants never felt welcomed. Everyone was an imposition there.

When she was younger, the tall oak trees seemed especially grand, and during the fall, the orange and red leaves crunched at her feet as she walked up the walkway, giving her comfort; it was something she was sure to miss—maybe one of the few things, though.

Even though Lynnie was packing her physical belongings in crates ready to go off to school, she had mentally escaped from her childhood home ages ago. She had willfully detached from it, a conscious effort, disconnecting and always looking to the future in search of acceptance.

Being an only child and the daughter of two narcissistic parents, it was no wonder they'd stopped having children after Lynnie. Both Mom and Dad were self-loathing and deranged in their own way. Frankly, neither had any business having children at all or even staying married, for that matter. From the beginning, their arrangement was anything but ideal, and the years had only made them grow increasingly impatient with one another and even more bitter about how life had treated them, or perhaps how they treated life. Children had no place in this mess.

In comparison to others, Lynnie's parents had little to complain about, but despite that, they somehow lived with a great sense of entitlement and little, if any, gratitude. The air of arrogance and hostility had always embarrassed Lynnie and made her cringe. Once, when she'd dared to comment about how her parents had treated the waiter, they'd laughed it off.

"Grow up, Lynnie," her mom had said. "You don't know anything. Wait till you're my age."

It was evident from the beginning that she wasn't like them and never would be, going out of her way to avoid being anything like either of them. God help her if she were to turn out even remotely like them. No, Lynnie was certain she would forge her own path from an early age.

Although she longed for parents who doted on her, she knew image and perfection were first and foremost in their minds. They never even tried to hide that fact.

Lynnie knew her parents differed from others in her younger years but never really understood its depth. Specifically, her mother would act a certain way in public, showing fake interest, but behind closed doors, she would treat Lynnie as invisible. The child was always underfoot, in the way, unwelcome. She would stride right past her and never say a word as if the girl were a ghost.

So, needless to say, Lynnie was surprised to see her mother in the audience at a school play one day. At first, seeing her mother there alongside everyone else's parents, Lynnie's heart swelled at last. Maybe there was hope after all. "There's my girl," her mother enthused to one of the other moms in a show of affected fake fondness and pride. "Bless her; she makes me proud every single day. Very talented, my Lynnie, she is."

*Yeah, sure,* thought Lynnie. *That's not what you usually say to me, is it?*

And she watched as her mother clapped and hollered when her daughter came on stage.

*I don't know why you bother, Mom. It's obvious you don't like me at all.*

Watching her mother exaggerate her devotion to her, Lynnie was disgusted by the scene.

"Oh, yes, my daughter makes us proud for sure," Marylou boasted as loudly as possible.

Lynnie was mortified and embarrassed by the exasperating and embarrassing show to the community that they were the perfect family, the scenes confusing and hurtful. She would overhear parents gushing about how lucky Marylou was to be so close to her teenage daughter.

"I wish I could be so close to my Suze," one said. "At this age, they're so awkward, aren't they? So damn argumentative. Well, there's no chance we'll get closer now, not now that my girl's your Lynnie's age. It's too late to start trying to build anything now."

Then, wistfully, the woman had eyed Lynnie and said, "You're so lucky, Lynnie. You and your mom have something really special. You know, you should cherish your mom."

It was nauseating at best, but Lynnie had been trained to smile politely, never letting on that the doting mother act was all a revolting sham. Oh, they were 'close' all right, because Marylou never let Lynnie out of her sight so she could shame and chastise her for whatever she was doing, dawn till dusk, daily. "Lynnie, you're so stupid," she would say, or, "Lynnie, get a grip."

Inside the home, the hateful words of Marylou criticizing Lynnie were intense and perpetual.

"Lynnie, goddammit, why are you walking like a truck driver? Straighten your back and lift your chin like you have some class, will ya? And try wearing a dress for a change."

Then when Lynnie did wear a dress, her mother had fired, "Jesus, do you look like a whore."

Lynnie wanted to abide by the purported rules of her latest scolding, but no matter how hard she tried, there would always be something new to criticize. Gracefully—so she believed—she would walk into the kitchen for a snack, but she could feel her mother's eyes on her from her desk. "How can you look in the mirror without being bothered by those fat thighs? I mean, really, Lynnie, I would be embarrassed if I were you. Lay off the snacks and for fuck sake, drink more water and get some exercise. Before you know it, there'll be no turning back."

*I should be sticking up for myself,* Lynnie thought in a reproach to her timid self, but the words just wouldn't come out. But this was not the first time nor the last, was it? Mother would always have something else to say, and something else, and then something else... The abuse was endless. Why would it make a difference if she argued back? There would always be more to come. So she remained silent, the easiest thing she could do in the face of all this.

The *only* thing.

One day, Lynnie came downstairs wearing a wrinkled shirt and messy bun.

Her mother silently rose from her seat to raise her hand, pulling back her shirt sleeve as if preparing for something before smacking her daughter—hard—across the side of her head.

"You are a fucking embarrassment. Look at you. I mean, Jesus. What I'd have done at your age to have the opportunities we've provided for you. But it all goes over your head, don't it? Now go upstairs and change into something appropriate, you fucking fat slob! Waste of space!"

The sting of that hand on Lynnie's face would last longer than any tears. It was then she knew she had to escape her mother's toxic behavior before losing what was left of her self-esteem.

The constant criticism, severe insecurities, and harsh treatment of her childhood set Lynnie out for a lifetime of emotional trauma. She would never be sophisticated enough, never intelligent enough, never hardworking or beautiful enough for her mother's liking.

These thoughts magnified every insecurity. She saw her flaws in the bright sunshine of the days, but also dreamed of them in the depths of the dark nights. There was no escape.

Living with her mother was similar to living with a bully who would observe her from dawn till dusk, terrorizing her every move and making notes on all the badness in her, except there was no respite because the bully was, in fact, her mother and they lived under the same roof.

This unrealistic expectation of perfection was overwhelming. When it was time to look at colleges, Lynnie searched as far away from her as possible, in no way tethered to her hometown.

Most of her classmates would soon be moving on as well, making a move even easier. It wasn't as if she was having to make a big move that no one else was making. It was exciting.

In writing each college essay and filling out every application, the hope of a new beginning was finally becoming possible. But would it work? Would any college accept Lynnie?

They did. One morning, when Lynnie ran to the mailbox at the end of the drive before her mother was up, she found a letter addressed to her in typed black ink. Her heart thrummed in her chest and quietly, quickly, she slipped into the kitchen for a sharp knife to slit the envelope open.

'Dear Lynne,' it began. 'We are delighted to tell you...'

And so it went on. Acceptance letters started pouring in, bringing her a step closer to freedom.

Lynnie waited daily for the mail to come, searching through the mail, hoping for yet another envelope addressed to her. Some days, Marylou would watch as Lynnie demanded to see the mail every day, growing impatient by her daughter's eagerness.

She must have wondered, what was so amazing about the prospect of moving away?

Then perhaps it dawned on Marylou that there was a way to spoil Lynnie's prospects.

On a rainy summer afternoon, Lynnie was looking for ChapStick on her mom's desk. Then ...

*What's that? I swear that envelope is addressed to me!*

Sure enough, it was. It was an envelope addressed to her from the University of Delaware and it lay right there, part crumpled, badly concealed under her mother's stack of papers.

She ripped the envelope open, not considering that her mother had intentionally hidden it.

She was pleased to find her acceptance to the University of Delaware.

Lynnie's scream of elation was a sign of relief and excitement.

"Stop being so fucking desperate," her mother scolded. "I knew I should have just thrown away that junk mail when I received it, and I've told you before about snooping around my desk." She added it for good measure, but Lynnie was unfazed, clutching her potential way out.

"You shouldn't have taken it, Mom," she said, but rode over the feelings; there was just no sense in commencing a bitter argument in the face of the news that soon, she'd be out of here. The sooner it came to pass, the better! And from that moment on, if Lynnie wasn't shut away in her room packing boxes and bags for her departure, she was reading prospectuses and books.

Even well before leaving for the Hamptons, Lynnie had started packing her belongings, unable to withhold her excitement to move out. While her friends enjoyed their last summer in the quaint town and counted down with misery, she counted the days until she left for college.

Lynnie barely saw any classmates. There was only her friend Stacy, but she too was busy making plans for the future, even though Stacy had no intention of moving away.

So, Lynnie spent most of her time meticulously packing up her room, relishing knowing she would never be living at 120, Birch Street again.

"Wow, you're already packed!" cried Stacy when they finally managed to get together again.

She could sense the disappointment in Stacy's voice.

"Yup, and I can't wait to get the fuck out of here," Lynnie said more aggressively than intended. Lynnie noticed Stacy look away but forced a smile.

"I'm happy for you, but promise you will come back to visit," Stacy said.

Lynnie bit into her bottom lip, not saying anything in response as she taped up another box.

Stacy had decided to stay home from school and attend a community college. "I don't want to be too far away, and money's tight at our house," Stacy said. "Plus, mom's already really stressed about the finances. It's just cheaper if I stay local."

So, she'd surrendered to the idea of attending a local community school.

But she swore she would visit and keep in touch regularly. Despite that, she still wanted Lynnie to keep returning home; that way, they could keep in touch more often.

But it wasn't in Lynnie's mind to come anywhere near this godforsaken town anymore.

After their trip to the Hamptons, Lynnie retreated from Stacy.

It was just something necessary something vital for her own mental wellbeing. This was the end of an era, the beginning of something new and exciting—something that could help her to grow and free her from the past with all its vile elements and unpleasant criticisms.

Lynnie often spoke about never returning again once she left for college, in fact.

Stacy still could not—or would not—accept it.

"Lynnie, you just can't mean it. We've been friends forever, and now you're just planning to go away and disappear? That's not fair."

And Stacy's lips had trembled and her voice quaked, and it all had the cumulative effect of making Lynnie obstinate. It was a revelation, too, that all of her life, it had been Marylou's criticizing that had made her feel low. But now,

Stacy showed how good things could bring negative feelings too. Stacy loved her, yet this love of a best friend was making her feel so bad.

Stacy's upset voice went on and on.

"Surely, you'll at least come home for Christmas, won't you? You won't just ... go."

Then her pleading, tear-filled eyes had bored into Lynnie's own.

Lynnie didn't have the heart to come out and say no, but they were both aware of Lynnie's home life and desperation to escape her mother's controlling abuse. Lynnie just looked away, hoping this moment would pass and stop making her feel responsible for another's happiness.

As the day approached to leave for school, Marylou became more belligerent. Her drinking and prescription medicine use was at an all-time high. Lynnie knew that the more she drank, the nastier she would get, but eventually, if she were lucky, Marylou would pass out entirely.

Was it even possible that the spike in her alcohol consumption was because of the realization that her only child would soon be gone? Was it celebratory or sad? She couldn't know for sure.

Whatever it was, Marylou had to get it out of her system because her drinking caused her father to disappear for weeks and for Lynnie to retreat inside herself.

Soon, her mother would be left with her own self-loathing of being alone, though occasionally, Lynnie could have sworn she had noticed her mother's face soften.

She'd tried to meet her gaze, but she would quickly retreat, disappearing into her angry soul.

The day had finally come, August 15th, a day Lynnie had dreamt about for months, and after meticulously packing the last of the crates of belongings into an old beat-up maroon Toyota Corolla, Lynnie was ready to finally set off to Delaware. Between the chipped paint and fading color, the dents and scratches of that beat-up old car were barely noticeable. Yes, Lynnie was proud of it, having bought it for herself last summer, despite all her parents' objections.

Her parents had *offered* to buy her a brand-new car; why that was, Lynnie hadn't been able to understand, but most likely it was to save them the embarrassment of knowing their neighbors could see that *maroon thing, that monstrosity,* as her mother had called it, on their driveway.

Anyway, Lynnie would have none of it, and the purchase of the dilapidated vehicle was a reminder that represented independence and freedom.

It was apparent they only offered to buy the car for the appearance of it, and Lynnie longed for a separate identity. To them, going to the trouble and expense of buying a car would have been just another thing to wave over her head, and Lynnie would no longer participate in that facade.

Her mother consistently called the part-time job at *Matt's Mart* frivolous and immature, and she would be horrified if any of her local friends dared to mention that they saw Lynnie bagging groceries. While most parents would have taken pride in the fact that their child would acquire a job in high school to save money to help pay expenses, this only made her mother fume.

"Lynnie," she would reproach. "I'm beyond embarrassed that *my* daughter will be seen by everyone, bagging groceries in a low-end store! It is truly unbelievable and shameful."

Marylou saw her family as prestigious.

Lynnie saw her parents as deluded.

Without a doubt, that was one of the many reasons she had taken the job and kept it. Besides, just as she said to her mother, "I wouldn't be seen if they didn't shop there, Mother!"

It was true, too; how would they even spot her bagging groceries if these snooty folk didn't visit Matt's Mart themselves? So, what was supposed to be so shameful about it?

If it was good enough for her mother's friends and neighbors to shop there, then it made no sense to say that Lynnie shouldn't lower herself to working there. Mom had to be crazy ...

So, not only was the job an excuse to be out of the house, but it was also a way to embarrass Marylou to the point of torment. Lynnie wasted no opportunity to do that whenever she could.

"Hello, Mrs. McGrogor," Lynnie would say, seeing the familiar woman looking through the produce. She made a point to seek out her mother's friends and greet them with a wave and smile, knowing they would report back to her the next time they gathered at the country club. "I didn't know you shopped here, Mrs. McGrogor. Nice and cheap, isn't it? Cheap and cheerful."

And she always expected the women to dash out, feigning that this had never happened. But oddly, they did not, and it soon became apparent that only Marylou had a problem with the store.

This only escalated the tension at home, but it was her only power over her mother.

And it felt so good, too.

Lynnie spent the rest of the summer happily bagging groceries, saving every dime for the great escape she called 'the Toxic Terminator.'

*This is it,* thought Lynnie. *You have been waiting for this your entire life.*

⚊⚊◆⚊⚊

Now that the day had come, it all was quite overwhelming—it was finally time.

She had packed up her car and was ready to set off. She grabbed a bottle of water and the last of her bags and holding a pack of potato chips for the ride, she looked around and headed toward her car. Her father walked her to the driver's side and gave her a tight squeeze.

In a soft whisper, he said, "Go live, my beautiful daughter. I love you."

Lynnie looked at her mother, who had a tear in her eye, and said, "Take care of yourself."

She gave Lynnie a quick nod and a small wave. It looked as if she was about to say something, but Lynnie quickly started her car's engine, not to linger too long in her presence.

As she pulled away from everything and everyone she knew, she waved goodbye to her childhood home, friends, and parents. And as the car slowly trundled off down the street, an immense wave of relief and freedom overcame Lynnie, settling across her like a warm blanket.

She turned the corner and headed southeast to college in Delaware.

The long drive would give her a chance to think about everything. And think she did.

She wondered how her parents would manage, worried that the deafening silence of the house would eat away at her parents' already brittle marriage. As much as she hated her mother, she would never wish for them to separate and to become unhappy. Dad deserved better, anyway.

She snapped out of the thought, turning the radio louder. There was no point in looking into the past; she would never return here, having awaited this day for as long as she could remember.

Now, there was a slight twinge of sadness. *What was that about?* she wondered, but quickly dismissed the emotion, excited to begin the next chapter of life at the University of Delaware.

Mile by mile, she drove farther away from the person she was forced to be, feeling more relief as the miles faded, traveling closer to a clean start. The eight-hour ride gave her so much time to fantasize, too, about how she would portray herself at college, finally leaving the lonely, insecure, timid Lynnie behind, creating whoever she wanted to become.

She was excited and petrified, all at the same time.

The fear came from imagining that people would see right through her, deeming her a fraud, a fake. Yet to leave behind her past and become the person she longed to be, the risk was worth it.

As Lynnie drove, she imagined a day without her mother nitpicking her outfit, posture, or hair. Until now, she had never been fully aware of how much her mother's voice played relentlessly inside her head, making her insecure, awkward, and fragile. She never quite planted her feet on solid ground, always looking for footing, like a newborn giraffe stumbling in random directions.

Lynnie vowed to change and evolve into the person she had longed to be throughout her childhood, no longer allowing her mother to steal any more thoughts or kill her aspirations.

Lynnie breathed easier as the distance from *home* became greater; she held her own power now, finally realizing she'd had it in her possession all along but had been too fearful.

Little did she know that the chains of her past were invisible, the control unspoken.

Her mother's hold taunted her, enraging Lynnie. For one thing, how could her father have just disregarded the treatment? He had always been kind and gentle to Lynnie, and she used to dream about him taking her away and leaving her mother behind, but it never happened.

At best, her father would look up from his computer and try to give a smile of encouragement but say nothing. Year in, year out, he looked on and saw how much abuse his daughter took, and year in and year out, he still sat there, empathizing but doing not a single thing to stop it.

His lack of support or protection from her mother's cruelty only fueled her insecurity. It was clear that her mother loathed herself even more than the rest of them but that was no excuse.

As those thoughts came into her head, tears blurred Lynnie's eyes as she drove along.

Her hand slammed repeatedly on the steering wheel as if trying to hurt her palm to distract herself. It worked. She quickly dismissed the hidden rage inside.

Eventually, signs for South College Drive came in sight, offering a welcomed distraction.

*New life, here I come*, she thought.

As the cars zoomed past, she sang along with the radio to pass the time, remembering the words to every song on the playlist. Fresh air consumed her as the wind hit her face, feelings of freedom and peace relaxing Lynnie's shoulders as she belted out the lyrics.

Time passed, her throat aching from singing so much and so loudly.

Soon, her exit approached, a feeling of relief and anxiety consuming her though she mustered up courage, intent on staying focused on the directions.

When she finally approached the school entrance, the buildings looked tall and clustered together in a row, surrounded by a courtyard filled with trees. This was the campus, a place so alien and yet it already felt like coming home. Driving through the campus, she saw unfamiliar faces, many with a look of excitement, though also many with a strange look of hesitation.

An empty parking spot made her grateful, and soon, she was leaning across the passenger seat, gathering the paperwork needed to check in to her dormitory.

Inhaling deeply, she was filled with an emotion not felt in a very long time: Hope.

Hope of becoming free from the lack of love.

Hope of making a life for herself, away from her mother's judgmental eye, and finally feel peace from within.

Hope.

She would keep this word as her mantra for many years to come.

JOURNAL

THE DRIVE HERE WAS LONG BUT SO WORTH IT.

LEAVING MY PARENTS BACK IN OHIO WAS EXCITING AND PETRIFYING, BUT I'M READY FOR A NEW START. I AM EXCITED TO BE HERE AND SURROUNDED BY SO MANY NEW PEOPLE.

CAN'T WAIT TO SEE WHAT THE FUTURE HOLDS HERE AT COLLEGE!

# CHAPTER THREE

*Lynnie: Freshman Year, University of Delaware.*

Lynnie parked in the unloading zone, the hauling of crates and an array of suitcases crowding the walkway to the entrance. Upperclassmen were ready to acclimate all newcomers to the campus. The sun shone, and a slight breeze made the trees rustle above. She took a moment to look around at the enthusiastic helpers while the apprehensive freshmen introduced themselves.

She stumbled to the line, then stood nervously, unable to make eye contact with the other students. Frustrated, her awkward mannerisms caused her to doubt her decision.

*Breathe,* she thought. *You have been waiting for this opportunity for years. Don't you dare blow it.*

Too insecure to initiate conversation herself, she forced a small smile at the girl behind, who was busy looking for something in an oversized purse. Lynnie was hoping the stranger would make eye contact. But she did not. Lynnie looked at the others, taking note of their faces.

After that, she quickly looked away, kicking herself for being so pathetic and cowardly.

*Dammit,* Lynnie thought, knowing her mother's voice was echoing in her head.

*'See, Lynnie; you made another mistake coming here, and now you'll soon see what happens when you make bad decisions! If you think I or your father are going to come and fetch you home, you're wrong. You made your decision, and now, you have to live with it.'*

Her sweaty palms only made her panic and squirm with shame. Quick breaths overcame Lynnie, her pounding heart making her anxiety rise. It had only happened one other time and on that occasion, it landed her in the hospital. Frightened of having another terrible panic attack, Lynnie quickly excused herself, got out of line, and walked toward the campus arboretum.

There, the bright flowers and the sweet smell of their essence helped slow her breath, and the vibrant colors of the green life captured her senses as her heart slowed.

To her right, she noticed a small pond filled with Koi fish.

She walked over, reveling in the orange glow of the fish swimming freely in their enclosure.

Trapped in an artificial pond yet swimming happily, she understood the metaphor of the Kois' circumstances; after fifteen minutes, she was able to compose herself, returning to the line of students and the frenzy of people she had left behind earlier. It all seemed so overwhelming, still.

A petite blonde-haired girl with a southern drawl eyed Lynnie as she approached.

"Hi, how are you?" she asked. Lynnie just smiled, giving no answer but it was nice to have been acknowledged. For years, her mother had made her feel invisible on many days, as if nothing she did was noticeable—or if it was seen, then it would be for all the wrong reasons.

That girl's bright smile already made the escape to college so worthwhile.

She was friendly with kind eyes, but Lynnie just hoped she appreciated the long drive was making the students impatient and anxious to enter their dorms and unpack before dark.

She did not want to ignore the girl's warm greeting, but sometimes, she just felt so ... awkward. Anyway, there was an urgency to keep the line moving.

She smiled again at the girl, giving a slight and uncertain wave. And then, Lynnie moved on.

Soon, all the freshmen would begin wishing their tearful parents and envious younger siblings goodbye and begin making new friends and memories.

Good for them, but Lynnie had cast off her abysmal past years ago.

She was ready to soak in her freedom.

After receiving the keys to her dorm room and completing the necessary paperwork, Lynnie realized she was alone. *I can't let that get on top of me,* she reprimanded herself. *It's only like being in the Hamptons. Surrounded by people, yes, but still ever so lonely!*

With that thought, she set about gathering the filled crates with her belongings.

Unloading the car, her pulse raced, her heart singing to itself; she was filled with excitement and couldn't wait to explore the campus and meet new friends. Hopefully, the next time, she would muster up the courage to actually respond beyond a timid wave and a smile.

When the last of her crates were empty, and all the items had been placed haphazardly in her dorm room, Lynnie returned and parked her car in the long-term student parking lot.

Walking back, she took in the scenery. Her feet seemed to almost know the way already, walking leisurely through campus, watching unfamiliar faces pass by; the vast diversity was inspiring Lynnie to expand her knowledge beyond her small hometown.

The chatter of students throughout the dorm excited Lynnie to settle into her new space.

Despite all efforts to be brave, however, she was more nervous and insecure than anticipated.

A pile of spilled pretzels from the shake of her hands made her stomach lurch. Strangers hurriedly passed by, never noticing the insecure newcomer hoping for a sense of belonging.

Her stomach was grumbling from hunger, but the thought of finding the cafeteria seemed overwhelming. Not only would it be hard to locate, possibly, but also, maybe it would be full of people and she would have to get in line and fight her way through, not something Lynnie relished. Instead, she found a small snack shack and grabbed some French fries, eating them en route back to the dorm. The campus was massive, and she was already having second thoughts about choosing such a large school. *Why did I decide to come here? It's insanely big and busy.*

*Not really the kind of place I like. But I'm here now and stuck with it.*

She had toured smaller universities but a larger school would surely bring more opportunities, wouldn't it, and this had partly driven the decision to choose this place.

Besides, coming from such a small town, she constantly felt under a microscope in a tiny place where everyone watched everyone else, reporting on everything a person did.

The autonomy of a larger school had been so enticing, plus there'd be more people from diverse backgrounds. Childhood had been boring, and Lynnie had never really fitted in. This place meant a brand-new fresh start, and before coming, she'd vowed to join in everything, to make lots of friends and to learn a whole heap of new skills and hobbies.

Now she was here, she only wished to hide. *So much for dreams then,* Lynnie thought.

Eating French fries on her own on her way back to the dorm, she felt so alone. She dunked the crispy French fry in ketchup and glanced around, knowing this was her opportunity—and her own responsibility—to make the next four years worthwhile. After all the days alone in her bedroom back home, lonely and isolated, she had the chance to change life's trajectory.

She'd have to force herself out of her comfort zone, embracing all that was on offer.

The days meshed, Lynnie becoming acclimated on campus. She settled into classes right away, nestling into her dorm room but still hadn't socially branched out.

She sighed. "I should have requested a dorm mate," she said to herself, but under her mother's influence, being an only child and then abruptly sharing a room with a stranger would have felt like too much of a change at once. Plus, her mother had never wanted any stranger inside her own living space, especially one she couldn't vet before her arrival, so having friends over and having people to stay was still an alien concept. Lynnie now knew she should have insisted on a roommate, quietly regretting the decision she had made. And it was all too late now. Everyone else had been given their rooms, and no one was looking out for one anymore.

But why did everyone else seem to make new friendships so quickly and effortlessly? What was so wrong with her that she could barely say hi to anyone, even if they smiled?

Lynnie was still avoiding the cafeteria, spending most of her meals alone at the snack shack, but French fries and Cokes were getting old. Sooner or later, she would be getting sick too.

She would have to find her way into the cafeteria at some point.

"Why is it so difficult for me to fit in?" Lynnie mumbled. Around her, acquaintances quickly became friends, cliques were formed, and she was still finding herself awkwardly lingering outside all these groups, hoping to fit in somewhere. She was discouraged that her meekness had followed her to college, even though she was determined not to succumb to insecurities.

Her big plans of reinvention were riddled with insecurity and doubt, and she was feeling more alone than ever but hopeful of finally connecting, given the vast number of people around.

For one thing, there had to be other girls just like her; not everyone here would be outgoing.

There was no one to complain to, anyway, and her parents never called to check, which frankly was a blessing. Weeks still went by with little connection with the other students and even when she tried initiating conversations with others, it was always forced and awkward.

Would life here ever get better than it had been in her hometown?

Could she ever form the friendships she saw blossoming around her?

There were no definite answers, only a strong likelihood of years of loneliness, and with this knowledge, she would have to make the best of it since there seemed to be no other options. So, Lynnie stayed focused on her studies, though still hoping to create a social life on campus.

Passing the snack shack, the aroma of sizzling fries reminded her of the promise she had made to herself weeks ago to leave her lack of confidence behind. There came the reminder that she was the same old insecure creature walking the campus, and that her idle attempts were still always littered with excuses and fear. She kept having the same conversations in her head but didn't change her actions; although her intentions were good, her resolve was weak. Lynnie knew she was at a crossroads and it was time for her to step into her new life without hesitation.

Lynnie was lost in thought when she mindlessly walked in the opposite direction of the library, ending up mistakenly at the corner of the gymnasium. Trying to redirect herself back toward the library, she noticed a group of girls chatting excitedly.

From the bits she could overhear, it seemed they were enthusiastic about joining the swim team.

Although curious about the excitement, she wouldn't dare to approach the girls, but she lingered from afar. There was chatter, chiding, and laughter among some girls, others waiting patiently in the back to have a look at the flier. Staring at them looking at a sign-up sheet, she carelessly walked straight into another student passing by. With that, her books and bags flew, causing chaos. *Real smooth,* she thought. That was when and how she had met Amanda.

Amanda had soft green eyes, light brown hair, and blonde highlights that Lynnie suspected were from many days of sitting out in the sun.

Embarrassed, Lynnie hurried to gather her belongings to get out of the way, but those feelings came flooding back from home, those sensations of only ever being in the way again.

Had it not been for her existence, her parents would have divorced long ago and perhaps even found happiness apart. But there she was, 'in the way,' or at least that was how it felt.

As Lynnie frantically gathered her belongings to leave, Amanda graciously made her blunder seem like no big deal. "Don't worry, the hall is narrow," she explained. "And I almost did the same thing fifteen minutes ago. In fact, I'm always doing it!"

"I'm sorry. Jeez, I apologize," Lynnie clumsily said as she introduced herself. "I'll start again. Hi, I'm Lynnie. Do you swim competitively?" she awkwardly blurted out. Proud to have initiated a conversation, albeit a really painful one, Lynnie waited patiently for a response.

Amanda explained that she had made the nationals at her high school but had to cut her season short because of some medical issues. Before signing her name on the sign-up sheet for the intramural swim team, she hesitated a moment and glanced over at Lynnie. "I'll do it if you do."

Well, that seemed like a challenge, and one thing Lynnie liked was a challenge. "You're on," she exclaimed.

Immediately, regret washed over Lynnie as the words slipped past her lips. Desperate as ever for human contact, agreeing to join the swim team spontaneously had seemed a good idea. But just in the same way as she often said yes to things, only to regret it later and then not show up, this was causing a turmoil of regret in Lynnie's gut. *I wish I'd kept my mouth shut!*

She had swum in the Long Island oceans and a few pools, but she had never been part of an actual swim team. Frankly, she had never been on any team of any kind, for that matter.

*I hope my desperation to adhere to a group is to try something new, and not because I'm falling back into portraying my old people-pleasing habits,* Lynnie thought, but quickly dismissed these anxieties. *Oh well. I'll have to do it now; it's my one chance to make friends.*

She excitedly focused on her new adventure before considering her decision further, and talking herself out of a potential friendship.

Because Lynnie's parents had busy work schedules, she had never participated in organized school teams, so she didn't know the first thing about swimming or being a teammate.

*What did I just get myself into?* she wondered. *I must really be pathetically desperate to make new friends if I've gone and joined a swim team! What a stupid decision. I'll look a fool.*

As she put it, however, Amanda was 'super-stoked'!

"Tell you what, Lynnie! Why don't you come and meet up with a couple of my friends for lunch later today?"

Lynnie was excited and terrified, both of this new unintentional sport she had just joined, and of the prospect of meeting several new girls at once if she took up Amanda's suggestion.

But at the same time, she was smiling ear to ear; college was promising to bring new opportunities, new friendships, and new adventures and she was open to all of it, despite the jitters in her belly. *I can only hope the girls go easy on me; they'll probably see I'm weird.*

She felt insecure, lonely, and depressed when she returned to her dorm. Unworthiness overwhelmed her. *Maybe I'll just not show up to meet with Amanda.*

It was that old familiar pattern setting in again, the one in which she said yes to something and was momentarily riding high on a cloud before plummeting back to earth, canceling the plan.

Walking through the campus later that day, she felt slightly nervous about meeting the group. Her cell phone rang before she could process those thoughts, disrupting her from overthinking.

"Hey there, Lynnie." Stacy's familiar voice was on the other end.

"Oh, hi. What's up? I was just on my way to meet some friends."

"Wow, go you! I'm happy for you and glad to see you settling in. I just wanted to let you know I was thinking of coming to see—"

Before Stacy could continue, Lynnie interrupted, "Listen, thanks for the call. I got to run, I'm already running late. Chat to you soon. Bye."

It was rude, and Lynnie felt guilty ending the call abruptly, but Stacy was the last thing she could worry about now. Coming from a small town, she hadn't had the chance of making any new friends since kindergarten. Not that she had a lot of friends anyway.

In fact, besides Stacy, Lynnie didn't have any at all.

She hadn't ever been invited to many parties, her parents not being involved in many school functions, leaving Stacy as the only viable companion.

Stacy's mom was a single parent working two jobs just to make ends meet, so she, too, was an outcast in their suburban town. The two fit together like twins, leeching onto each other initially, primarily out of loneliness but eventually, forming a tight friendship through many years.

Thinking back, Lynnie suspected their friendship had chiefly been based on convenience and on having at least one person in their snobby town to count on.

Frankly, Stacy and Lynnie had very little in common besides that desperate need to belong.

As it was, their daily phone conversations were becoming briefer, and soon, daily calls became weekly ones, and then weeks would go by. By now, Lynnie was barely hearing from Stacy at all.

And Lynnie, for her part, was making no effort at all to contact Stacy herself. It must have been sending out a clear signal: 'I have moved on, leaving the small town behind'.

Fear of starting over stifled Lynnie, but fighting through her insecurity, she soon found herself in front of the café. Inside, she could see where the wall cracks had all started forming a web from where the paint had been chipping away. She stared momentarily, thinking how the cracked paint on the wall reminded her of her parents' marriage.

When exactly was it that everything had changed?

Tension and sadness had taken up residence in their home for as long as she could remember, negative vibes occupying their living space. Standing frozen and panicked, staring at chipped paint in a small café, unable to feel her legs, she knew that the time was now to make a change.

*Move,* she demanded her stiff body.

Nervously, she forced her limbs to move past the entranceway and into the dining room.

The pale-yellow wallpaper in the dining area made the café seem quaint and old and there was something charming about the big windows in the café making you feel immediately at home. The old, cozy café made her feel the way she envisioned her own home might feel one day.

The aroma of the biscuits and butter buzzing around her reminded her of the growing hunger pangs. Approaching the girls sitting in the far-left corner, she could see immediate smiles amongst all the girls' faces, her heart beating faster the closer she came to the table.

Lynnie's mind jumbled, and her palms were sweaty.

All she could muster up at that moment was a casual, awkward, "Hey there, all." Her voice trembled softly, and she could barely recognize the escaping sound.

They looked up momentarily, then carried on chatting. Was she invisible to these girls as well?

Were they never going to respond to her greeting?

But it seemed as if they had just been caught in the middle of a conversation, maybe. They had something to discuss, something to finish off before they could turn to the newcomer.

She hoped it was that anyway. Meanwhile, she hung around, hopping from foot to foot.

Lynnie watched in awe of how the group dressed casually, like most college students, but with an air of sophistication, something she had no idea how to achieve. It wouldn't have been any more difficult to dress like a catwalk model than it was to look so casually perfect as these girls.

They dressed differently from one another, but all seemed to be kindred spirits.

It seemed unusual to witness the ease of the conversation and friendship, such a foreign experience. It made her think back to her high school years, reminiscing the times when kids would congregate at lunch and after school. It had come so easily to them all.

By college, many of the kids here had already experienced the insecure dilemmas of the lunchroom. Where to sit. With whom. The self-consciousness of every move. That had been high school life, something these girls had been exposed to as well and had worked through by now.

Now in college, the atmosphere was far more relaxed anyway, and people were more confident although Lynnie was the clear exception. Having lived in a tormenting state of nagging insecurity her entire life, from the looks of things, it wouldn't be ending anytime soon.

*Why am I always so awkward and insecure?*

This same question kept ringing in her mind continuously.

Lynnie would have blamed this too on her mother and sometimes did, but it wasn't entirely her fault. It was Lynnie's own inability to fit in because of low confidence about everything. She needed to be confident and better, but it wasn't taught, unlike algebra.

Small changes in habits would help her, but where should she start?

She watched as the girls still continued with their conversation, observing them pausing, taking turns sharing, laughing, just finding it natural being in one another's company, as if they each knew instinctively what to do, so relaxed and at ease with one another.

Their confidence as they sat around, sharing stories openly, seemed amazing.

How close these girls seemed to have become in just a few weeks since they'd started school!

It seemed far too easy for them to welcome new friendships, something for which Lynnie longed but could never accomplish.

She had always been a bit socially awkward, envying casual conversations and openness. Still, she forged toward the group of girls again, hoping to avoid another awful blunder. She noticed Amanda gazing up at her now and then, never saying a word, but casting a slightly awkward smile. Should Lynnie go away? But after all, hadn't Amanda invited her to come along?

So, Lynnie sheepishly approached the table, venturing closer, fearful to interrupt their lunch.

Perhaps they hadn't heard her say hello and in that case, they would have thought she was rude, hanging about and listening in like that. So, what now?

Was she supposed to say hello a second time?

*What's even the point? They're deliberately ignoring me.*

She was about to turn around before they could chide her for clumsily lingering.

Before she could turn away, Amanda clapped her hands and jumped up. "Hey there, I'm so thrilled you came," she said, her voice earnest and cheerful. "Please, let me introduce you to some of my friends. Sorry we couldn't say anything right away; we were just in a discussion."

The small chatter between the other girls quieted, and they became attentive too.

Lynnie stood self-consciously as the group turned their heads to acknowledge her presence.

They were pretty, cheerful, and immediately just as welcoming as Amanda.

Jessica was eager to include her as her new friend and unexpectedly hugged Lynnie with delight. "Lynnie, so pleased to meet you! I've heard so much about you!"

Jessica's bright smile and cheerful demeanor made her feel welcomed.

Just as Lynnie's shoulders relaxed, her relief was interrupted by the harsh sound of a girl's thick upstate New York accent. "Yeah, we heard how clumsy you are."

Her edge was both intriguing and a little intimidating. At first, Lynnie felt embarrassed by the joke but—wait! Wasn't that warmth in her eyes and her voice? Sure, she was making fun of Lynnie but in an oddly nice way. *Hell, even I can live with that.* After all, she had seen teens teasing one another before. Sometimes, it could be rough, but they'd laugh it off, and it all seemed to be an essential part of being in a group. *Bring it on,* Lynnie thought.

"Don't mind her," Jessica graciously chimed in. "She's just playing with you. She has that New York edge, you know, but like the rest of us, you'll get used to it."

"Yeah, I'm just messing with you. My name's Myra. You'll get used to my sarcasm. It's what keeps me sane," she revealed.

"Hi Myra, I vacationed in the Hamptons this past summer. Do you live near there?" Lynnie asked, trying to make any kind of a connection with this slightly intimidating woman.

"Oh, so a rich snob then," Myra quipped. "Whoa, girls, she's got loads of money! Right, all our nights out are on Lynnie!" She winked at Lynnie. "Again, just kidding, Lynnie. You look worried." She started chuckling. Then she finally answered the question—did she live near the Hamptons? "No, I live in upstate

New York. Never even been to Long Island but have gone to New York City a couple of times with my mother."

Myra seemed strangely pensive about it.

Amanda seemed to be looking around nervously. Her plate was still full of food, and she moved it around from one side of her plate to the other as if unwilling to eat it.

Amanda offered, "Myra's from New York but way upstate near Plattsburgh, practically in Canada. 'Upstaters' don't consider themselves New Yorkers, instead saying they come from the State of New York."

Myra nodded. "There's a big difference between where I live and other parts of New York."

Lynnie nodded in agreement, although she had never been further north than New York City, and that was when she was around six, when her parents went to see a musical on Broadway.

Jessica seemed the most proper out of the bunch, her pearl necklace and flat blue shoes perfectly matching her eyes, fashion scarf, and purse.

Lynnie observed that Jessica's mannerisms matched those of a woman of the 1920s, with her soft, elegant grace. She was stunning and full of poise, also a dash of nervous energy.

*She's trying to portray perfection and conceal who she is, but who am I to judge?*

Softly, she said, "Lovely to meet you. I hear you're joining the swim team with Amanda."

Lynnie gave a hesitant smile. "I guess I am," she said, her enthusiasm only a little false.

"More like I challenged her into it, and it seems like our new friend doesn't shy away from challenges," said Amanda.

*If only you knew the real me,* Lynnie thought.

Lynnie's eye was drawn to Amanda. How thin she seemed! How could she swim, being so frail looking? It was more a sport for stronger, more robust women, with big shoulders and plenty of body strength; she just couldn't envisage little Amanda pushing aside the water.

But it was not her place to ask or to comment, still cowering inside her own skin.

Little did the new friends know she was terrified of almost everything, mainly things where she could fail. Failure was not a familiar emotion for Lynnie and one that made her uneasy.

She would only do a thing if she could be good at it, taking pride in making sure that in everything she did, she strived for perfection. But this leap of faith in swimming was pushing her limits. As proud as she was to take the chance of failure, how could she handle it if she failed?

After the brief introductions, the ladies sat down again, chatting as if they'd known each other for ages although it had only been weeks since they had met. And for Lynnie, the first time.

For the first time, Lynnie was at ease with the other students.

*Is this what other people regularly experience? This is how it feels to be normal? Wow.*

It was her first experience like this, and she couldn't believe it had taken this long to enjoy social normality. Lynnie's shoulders relaxed and she tucked herself closer into the group of her newly found friends. The joy from these emotions had her carefully optimistic.

As much as she tried not to allow herself to become hopeful, she knew it was already too late.

She had never met girls like this, and although overwhelmed by the interaction, she was excited to explore these new relationships.

The conversation continued for hours, laughing, joking, gossiping, exchanging make-up tips, and debating the best burger joints in town, the ones with the cutest guys on campus.

There was never a lull in the discussion, and not once did she feel like a burden.

These were new emotions, ones that she hadn't enjoyed in her childhood. Though grateful and excited for their openness, however, she was still reserved. This had been a big step, and as they said their goodbyes, she looked forward to having lunch with them again tomorrow.

Lynnie left the café elated, prancing back to her dormitory as if on cloud nine.

Once inside, she breathed gratitude, feeling a true sense of belonging for the first time, maybe ever. Her clumsiness had, for once, been beneficial!

She didn't want to get her hopes up but could these be the girls she had been destined to meet? During her lonely teenage years alone in her bedroom, she had dreamed of having friends with whom she could have lunch, becoming part of something more than herself.

Perhaps it was her desperation for companionship, but she badly wanted to believe that her days of cold French fries at the shack were over. She was so excited about her day.

Suddenly, a thought came, and she voiced it aloud. "I'm dying to tell Stacy!"

But picking up the phone to dial the number, something inside told her not to call.

Without dialing, she hung up, knowing that this news would not make Stacy share in the happiness. How could it? After all, she had not only left Stacy behind lately, but she had also cut off their last call and not once had Lynnie initiated another. Lynnie shook off the feeling of shame, focusing only on the present and unwilling to dwell on the past.

The following week, Lynnie showed up to swim practice awkwardly, in a pale blue swimsuit that was snug at the bottom. Wearing a swim cap made her nose look big, the goggles on her face also tight against her skin. This outfit wasn't pretty, but she embraced the experience, deciding to put forth the effort for the team. It was far more complicated than she had ever anticipated, nowhere near as enjoyable as she had hoped. Still, she stayed steadfast.

Soon, she was competing and improving every week, enjoying it more at one point, getting comfortable in the water. The sound of it splashing and the feel of her body gliding through the water became a way to gain confidence. She felt her body getting stronger and her determination more persistent, but there were downsides. The chlorine dried out her already brittle hair, while her skin became itchy from the hours spent underwater. It had become irritating, annoying.

The social aspect had been the only thing that kept Lynnie participating, but after pulling her calf muscle halfway through the season, she hung up her goggles; the swim team wasn't for her.

Frankly, she hadn't thought swimming was ever really for her, but she had wanted to fit in somewhere at this massive institution. Although she didn't gain the swimmer's physique she had hoped for, she had gained some genuine new friends and was grateful for that opportunity.

She reasoned it had been worth her still sore calf if it meant meeting new people.

Amanda stayed on the team, even competing. Lynnie and the others would cheer her on regularly, impressed by her natural skill, her speed and grace leaving them collectively in awe.

Amanda and Lynnie developed a close friendship; she was always the first one Lynnie sought out in the group, its voice and energy, helping to keep Lynnie's social anxiety at bay. Often, they would spend late nights walking the grounds of campus, talking. Amanda seemed to be holding back an essential part of her life, but Lynnie didn't pry. She spoke to Amanda about her complicated relationship with her mother and her desire to break free from her disapproval.

One evening as they discussed the upcoming week's swim meet, Lynnie felt an intense chill.

"Doesn't the air feel really cold to you?" she asked Amanda.

Glancing at Amanda, she saw her looking in the distance as if she had something to say.

There was an awkward silence for a moment, then Amanda laughed, yelling, "Skunk! Run!" They ran back to the dorms, giggling the entire time.

That night when Lynnie lay in bed, she thought about what Amanda had been on the verge of saying, but she dismissed it, rolling over to fall asleep.

---

JOURNAL

I'M SO PROUD OF MYSELF FOR BEING ON THE SWIM TEAM, ALTHOUGH MY SEASON WAS CUT SHORT. BUT I DO ENJOY WATCHING AMANDA COMPETE. THERE IS SOMETHING ABOUT HER THAT I CAN'T QUITE PUT MY FINGER ON THOUGH, ALWAYS MAKING ME FEEL LIKE SHE'S HIDING SOMETHING.

MAYBE I'M JUST BEING PARANOID BECAUSE HAVING FRIENDS IS A NEW THING FOR ME.

EITHER WAY, I'M HAPPY TO BE PART OF THIS GROUP. SOME DAYS, IT SEEMS ALMOST TOO GOOD TO BE TRUE AND I KEEP RUBBING AT MY EYES, EXPECTING TO WAKE UP.

---

# Chapter Four



*Lynnie: College Life.*

As the months passed, the four became inseparable, barely noticing the rest of the thousands of other students on campus. They were submerged in their own friendships, enjoyed experiencing college life together. Day by day, their bond and friendship became closer.

Their new friendship carried a significant meaning within their existence.

Majoring in different things, they didn't have classes together but studied collectively whenever possible, arranging work and school schedules around one another, rarely missing having dinner together. On an off day, when one had to study, they would meet up later in the evening for coffee and a chat. Their codependency was fierce, but they took it for charm.

At times, having friends was such a new experience that Lynnie had to force herself to engage. It still seemed as if it would never come quite naturally, as if she would always feel 'on the periphery' despite how much the others might welcome and value her.

Feeling unworthy, also beyond surprised to have a group of people voluntarily wanting to include her in their lives left Lynnie in awe. She knew that these feelings of shame stemmed from childhood, but she often would get overwhelmed, succumbing to her insecurities.

At times like this, she would withdraw from the group, quietly talking herself out of the unease, later apologizing for her shady behavior.

For the most part, she was at ease with them and could be herself, the timid, shy girl slowly transforming into a more vibrant woman. Her effort to gain confidence was finally succeeding, feeling herself starting to bloom into a new and improved version. Lynnie became more confident and outgoing, feeling overall happier than she had ever been.

As fall became winter, Lynnie found she had settled into college and her newfound friendships. While the experience was new, she was finally enjoying life and felt content.

With their different personalities came diverse connections.

For the first time, Lynnie no longer felt a sense of loneliness but now allowed herself to believe she belonged. In the short months since her arrival at the university, she had learned how to trust, understanding that friendship and companionship were essential parts of life.

No longer in her mother's toxic surroundings, Lynnie was thriving, becoming more social, more vibrant, and confident, feeling a true sense of happiness.

Over the months, the once casual friendship was only growing more robust, and their discussions becoming more profound and correspondingly personal.

The young women became an intricate part of Lynnie's life, their strong emotional attachment to each other sincere, their loyalty to each other fierce, their bond unbreakable. Had Lynnie known that life in Delaware would have healed her, she wouldn't have dreaded life back home quite as much. A part of her had known there was more, something bigger coming her way.

Finally, she felt as though she had arrived, ready to live, excited to be exactly where she was for the first time. Yet as with everything in life, nothing could be perfect.

Soon, life as she knew it was about to change.

One late night while drinking hot cocoa, Amanda seemed distant.

"Everything OK, Amanda?"

At first, the other girl seemed not to register that Lynnie was talking to her.

"Amanda?"

"Oh yes, I'm sorry; I'm so distracted. I have a lot on my mind."

Lynnie noticed Amanda had that same look the night walking on campus.

"Spill the tea. We don't have all day," chimed Jessica.

Usually, Jessica's impatience would cause chuckles between them, but Myra looked sternly at her.

"Enough," scolded Myra.

She gently nudged Amanda.

"C'mon, Amanda. You've been off all day. What's going on with you?"

The room became silent as they watched Amanda's shoulders slump, her eyes filling with tears. The air in the room seemed to have dissipated, Amanda breaking down without any more hesitation. The three girls looked around at one another, unsure what to do next.

This was new territory, one about which they were uncertain. Lynnie wondered if Amanda had a boyfriend back home that she hadn't mentioned, and they'd broken up, or if it was something more. None of the girls could have been ready or expecting the night to unfold the way it had, and once Amanda's words started spilling out, they were all headed into uncharted territory.

⸎❖⸎

JOURNAL

I CAN'T SHAKE THE FEELING THAT AMANDA IS DISTRACTED BY SOMETHING.

IT'S ODD BECAUSE I OFTEN WATCH HER STARE OFF ALMOST OBLIVIOUS TO HER SURROUNDINGS. THERE SEEMS TO BE A PLEXIGLASS BETWEEN HER AND THE REST OF THE WORLD.

⸻ ❧ ⸻

# Chapter Five

*Amanda: A Truth Untold.*

A call home from her family had her frazzled to the point that she could barely function.

The overwhelming feeling of shame was consuming her to the point of utter distress.

The girls kept badgering her, and all she wanted was for everyone to leave her alone.

She finally exploded, "I'm better off on my own. I don't need any of you."

It was wholly out of character, sending her friends reeling, exchanging glances of confusion.

Before she could stop herself, she reached into her dresser, taking a long sip from the small flask hidden beneath her soft pink pajamas. Amanda could tell the others were stunned and they all must have known that it was a lie, that really, she did care and was simply hurting—reeling from something terrible. Now, she had no choice but to tell them what her real family life was like. She had resisted for so long, but the anxiety of holding onto this secret was boiling inside.

They would be shocked by the truth but it was time to tell them about her family's challenges.

Up until now, she hadn't talked too much about her family, steadfastly refusing, the fear of judgment keeping Amanda from disclosing her past.

They crowded around her, Jessica giving her a hug, and Lynnie following suit. Myra was the only one who did not, just resting a warm hand on her friend's shoulder.

"We know you don't want us to go away," voiced Myra.

"And we're not going, even if you do want it," said Jessica.

Amanda looked downcast, ashamed at what she had said to the people who loved her.

"I don't want you to go," she said. "And I'm definitely not better off alone."

She caught her breath, then began to speak in a low tone.

"This is really hard for me to talk about, guys. In high school, a lot of stuff happened, and I wanted to leave it all back at home. You know how it is ... Frankly, I never wanted to tell anyone, but I can't keep this inside anymore. My older brother, Tommy, was in a terrible football accident and became addicted to his pain medicine. Which also led to my own troubles."

Amanda paused for a moment, gazing around the room, seeing the confused and concerned faces of her friends.

"Jeez, Amanda, you are just telling us this now?" Myra said. "You should've relied on us."

"Go on, Amanda, what happened to you and your brother?" Jessica said softly.

"As you know, Tommy was a star quarterback of our varsity high school team. He was good-looking, charismatic, intelligent, funny, and everything you would imagine of a perfect all-American teen. Tommy was the life of our family, always ready for a laugh, a smile, and one of his well-known massive bear hugs. He would squeeze me so hard that I could feel all the stress and anxiety leave my body, comforted by his strong arms holding me tight."

Amanda watched as her friends listened attentively.

"Go on," encouraged Jessica.

"Our entire community knew the Young family and was proud of Tommy's accomplishments. Honestly, I never felt like I could measure up to my 6'3" older brother. Not only was his size enormous but so was his personality. My brother was carefree and funny, and everyone around admired his zest for life. And I do mean everyone. From being the star quarterback often written up in the local papers, winning numerous awards for his athletic abilities, to being top of his class and homecoming king, Tommy was every parent's dream child. To Tommy's credit, he never came off as over-confident or arrogant, always kind and loving. He didn't think that much of himself. In fact, that's what he would say. But everything changed after the accident."

Myra asked, "Tommy was involved in an accident? What sort of accident? Car crash?"

Diplomacy was not Myra's strong point, but her heart was in the right place.

Amanda hesitated as her voice quivered.

"It was the last game of the season, and the Tomahawks were due to be playing their rival, the Generals. It was the fourth quarter, and the game was close. Tommy had just intercepted a play and was running full speed to score a touchdown. From what seemed to be out of nowhere, he got hit by another player who tackled him with immense force. The sound of gasps filled the air.

"The crowd immediately fell silent as I watched Tommy go down like a ton of bricks. I looked over at my mother, who had her hand covering her mouth, afraid to breathe. Under her breath, I heard her whisper, 'Dear God, help him, no, no, no ... Oh Tommy, oh Tommy ...'

"She fell silent as my father grasped for her hand, both looking ahead in shock. As he lay there, I couldn't help but think the worst. We watched as he descended to the ground, instantly knowing by how his head jerked back that the injury was severe. I assumed that he would have a terrible concussion but would recover. I mean, that's what you'd naturally think, right?"

Amanda wiped a tear from her eye.

"The silence in the stadium was eerie, and the vibe was suspenseful, so still and quiet. What seemed like forever passed as we sat there awaiting the paramedics, staring at Tommy, willing him, but he didn't move. His body just lay still. I had to wonder, was he even alive? There were the medics crowded around, people even coming in from the crowd, doctors ...

"But no one would move him. 'Neck, it's his neck!' one medic called to another across the expanse. And we just knew it was bad, really bad, and Tommy might not even make it. Because it looked as if there were half a dozen doctors around him, but although they could monitor him, the looks they passed one to the other were terrible. No one was daring to say how bad it was.

"We were so far away but we could just tell how things were. The crowd was solemnly silent, and the fate of my brother was unknown. Finally, the paramedics from the air ambulance arrived to urgently put him on a spinal board and haul my brother off, with my parents and me chasing behind. So much of the night was a blur, but I kept praying ... You know, just praying that my brother hadn't sustained a fatal injury."

Amanda took another swig from the flask, holding Jessica's hand.

"The drive to the hospital was endless. Dad was speeding, my mother was silent, and I was in the backseat in total shock, just saying nothing because they needed quietness. It was surreal, and time seemed to drag on as we hurried to get to my brother. As we rushed into the emergency room, we watched my brother getting wheeled into an examination room as doctors ran in there as well. He didn't move, so the nurses were frantically making notes, checking all his vitals.

"At that moment, I just knew that Tommy's injury had to be really bad, really substantial. I mean, I knew that this was the kind of injury he couldn't come back from. The look of intensity of the doctors and nurses frightened me. It was then that I knew our lives were about to change."

Amanda's voice became angry as the sadness in her eyes remained.

"The doctors wouldn't tell us anything, but one nurse said, 'Hold tight. He's going to be all right. We are doing everything we can.' Those words rang in the air for a moment until my mother fell to the ground sobbing. My father ran to my mother, crouching beside her, whispering something into her ear. After a few minutes, they disappeared into the waiting room corner, leaving me alone to process what was happening. And I just couldn't. Couldn't think at all."

Amanda stood to grab a tissue as the girls looked concerned at one another, then she continued, "Tommy was in a coma for twelve long grueling days. Time seemed to stand still as we sat by his bedside, declaring our love, praying for him to return to us, singing to him, playing his favorite music and getting his friends in to take turns by his bed.

"The community gathered, bringing casseroles and pastries to the hospital. The school organized a candlelit vigil at the football field, which was so sweet, sending love and hope to our family. We couldn't have asked for a more supportive or loving community, and were grateful to our friends and family who held us up during our darkest time. But it lasted a long, long while."

"This must have been so difficult," Jessica said gently. "So horrible."

"It was, it still is," Amanda said. "The days were long and arduous. We didn't know when and if Tommy would wake to make it all the more painful. We were emotionally exhausted, taking turns going home, trying to catch some sleep. But once we were home, it was impossible.

"We couldn't sleep or think or eat, and we'd only want to rush back to be by Tommy's side again, to start the whole thing over again. Every day seemed like an eternity. The waiting, praying to a God we'd spent most of our lives ignoring. We were hoping for answers, begging for them from everywhere and everyone. It was torturous, you know? Still, we just had to keep on believing, showing up to be by his side for when and if he did wake up and need us.

"I wanted to escape from the chaos in my mind. I knew people cared about my family and loved Tommy, but my life was at a standstill, making me feel annihilated with guilt, shame, and worry. I was longing for normality, but my family life was forever altered. Obviously, it was.

"And what right did I even have to be demanding things for *me* in all this? Tommy was going to be crippled or stay in a coma, or we would have to turn off his life support and he'd die. And there was I, in the middle of it all, wanting to be noticed, to be seen, wanting to cry for myself.

"All of this took a massive toll on my well-being. I was just a teenager myself, and carrying the burden of a serious injury every day became too much for me to handle. I would wake from nightmares of sirens, unable to distinguish between reality and dreams. In my confusion, I would run toward Tommy's door for comfort, unable to reconcile with him not being there. My heart would be pounding, my head spinning, and I'd collapse onto his bed, inhaling any remembrance of my older brother, realizing then that he was still at the hospital. I kept withdrawing from social events, unable to find a place for my grief. My life was consumed with his recovery."

Myra interrupted, "Amanda, you shouldn't feel guilty that you wanted to have a normal high school experience. This must have been very traumatic for your entire family."

"It was, and the guilt of enjoying any high school function would linger in my mind, causing me to feel immense shame. Knowing that Tommy should be enjoying the last of his high school days and not be in a hospital bed made me want to shrink inside myself. My parents encouraged me to return to normalcy, but I felt lost without my brother by my side. The insistence that I return to school only made the anxiety more profound. The crowded hallways filled with endless chatter made me so annoyed, causing resentment toward the people I once admired. Well, you can imagine that because you saw it for yourselves when I told you to leave me alone.

"Life went on for everyone else, but I couldn't accept my new reality. The daily life of high school seemed ridiculous to me now. The excitement that high school had once brought was now a dreaded nightmare. I wanted my old life back but felt guilty about complaining.

"I would daydream of life, imagining how it would be if Tommy were healthy again, my parents united, my life back to normal. I miss it—my old life—every day."

"So, when did he wake up?" Lynnie asked, only hoping against hope that he had.

"By the sixth day, we were restless and running out of hope. The doctor assured us he would wake, insisting we had to be patient. We weren't at all convinced that the doctors even believed this, but we had no choice but to have hope and faith in the doctors caring for my brother. Watching my brother lying in a hospital bed with no movement was odd. The beeping sounds of the machines filled me with anxiety, not knowing if he would wake up at all. And if he even did wake up, would there be anything of our Tommy remaining? The doctors had gone through all the details of how much people changed when they had a spinal or brain injury.

"They warned us to be ready for a different version of Tommy, especially an angry one.

"After such a long time, slow movements in my brother's fingers started around noon on the twelfth day. His fluttering eyes were erratic and spontaneous. My mother was the first to notice his hand jolt, quickly grabbing it. Softly, she spoke his name, reassuring him she was by his side.

"I just remember her saying, 'Tommy, we're all here. Me, your dad, Amanda ...' Then nothing. We were unsure what to make of the sudden movements, but I suppose at least it gave us hope. Hours later, there was more movement in his fingers, his eyes fluttering open.

"He looked around, confused, not saying a word. As he finally awoke, we were relieved but skeptical about his recovery, almost expecting him to just be the Tommy we all knew and wanted him to be despite everything the doctors had warned us about. It's like we were playing make believe. But his eyes were telling us a very different story. They were all over the place and staring past us most of the time. He looked so ... weird. Nurses and doctors came rushing in at my mother's screams of desperation. She excitedly called out, 'Tommy's up. My son is back.' We were ushered out of the room as the doctors ran tests, carefully examining him.

"The doctors came out to speak with us. I'll never forget the term one used. He said he was 'cautiously optimistic'. What did that mean? I—we—didn't fully understand his prognosis.

"Tommy had suffered such a severe concussion that he didn't even remember the accident at all. We only found out much later that his last memory of that day was when they were all in the locker room getting dressed for the game. 'I never played, Mom,' he said, insisting that he had never even left that locker room. We still didn't know what the future would hold for him, and the stress of the unknown was probably the most challenging time of our lives. Even the doctors couldn't give us any concrete information because of Tommy's specific type of injury.

"It took three months of physical therapy and intense rehabilitation until Tommy was ready to come home. He was still a lot slower mentally than I remembered, but the doctors assured us that his brain was still healing and could fully recover over time. The community was supportive, filled with love for Tommy, which kept our family going. However, time passed, and people became busy, all the visitors starting to dwindle. Their patience with us was running out, I guess.

"Our family's daily activities had changed drastically as well. Where there were once busy practice schedules, we substituted them with doctor visits, second opinions, and possible surgery scheduling. Tommy's recovery eventually took over the family to a point where the rest of us didn't even exist anymore, but we weren't supposed to feel upset about the fact it was all Tommy, Tommy, Tommy … completely out of control. It was like some heavy freight train rolling down the tracks on a hill, and no one could stop it or slow it, or handle it.

"It just went the way it would go, and we all had to just go along with it. Our goal and mission were to get Tommy well, but now he was changing as well. His head and his neck were healing physically, but his mind ... he just wasn't anything like the boy we had known before.

"This wasn't our Tommy. Frustration and depression were something we hadn't even considered as part of his care, despite all the warnings that it would probably move toward anger and resentment. He used to scream at us, lash out at us, and we just weren't allowed to live unless every spare minute was spent doing something for Tommy. It wasn't his fault, of course.

"But Tommy, a soft-spoken, easy-going kid, had become frustrated, dark, and rageful.

"At first, my parents were optimistic and determined to get Tommy stronger than ever and back on the field, and they were putting up with everything he threw at them, saying nothing, just helping him 24/7. They hoped and hoped. If they were better at caring for him, he'd get back to his old self; that was what they thought. But Tommy would never play ball again, and so now, it was becoming all too clear that he never would be 'back to his old self'. Because without the game, he was nothing like the Tommy we knew, and never could be. We needed a new goal.

"The goal now was to get him to function better in his mind and body. It was exhausting for everyone, and the medical bills were also becoming more overwhelming as time passed.

"The spirit and energy of the house had changed. My secure home became a house full of tension. We all praised Tommy's small achievements at home, and while I celebrated along with Tommy, I felt defeated by the humble victories, like the day Tommy ate a boiled egg with a spoon, the egg dropping everywhere and the spoon looked so awkward in his hand, and we were supposed to cheer him on for that, and we did, but it was hollow. Tommy was making gradual progress, and the prognosis was favorable, but the momentum of life was increasingly slow.

"I looked to my future at college, where it would be a fresh start—no longer tethered to my past as the family who'd endured—well, were still enduring—so much heartache. I felt guilty as I scanned college brochures, knowing Tommy would no longer attend Ohio State University on a full scholarship. Instead, he was still undergoing physical therapy, his brain often getting tired before his body did. It was frustrating to watch and even more frustrating for Tommy.

"Although he was getting better and stronger each day, he still suffered from broken bones and neurological deficits and was in a lot of pain. The doctors carefully prescribed pain medication to Tommy with specific instructions. I noticed that my parents weren't fully monitoring his pain medication, and slowly, there was a strange shift within the family. Tommy grew even more frustrated and impatient while my parents began to tire of their pair of moody teenagers.

"They tuned out, so we kids now had to grow up without them. Tommy was by now doing lots of things for himself, but he was always fulltime at home, and he was watching TV and playing computer games, and moody and sullen, and taking those damn pain meds all the time.

"In an instant, our parents' own marriage was starting to fall apart. Being only thirteen months younger than Tommy, I was also lost without him. We weren't just siblings. We were friends. After the accident, there'd been a void in my life, and I was lonelier than I had ever felt. My life was spiraling out of control, my once happy family in turmoil and despair. It broke my heart to see the demise of my relatively mundane life. It became something I no longer recognized.

"Where there were once family dinners that consisted of homemade meals, noisy chatter, and a house full of love, empty takeout boxes now filled our kitchen counters, a deafening silence and exhaustion taking its place. The mood was tense, and I was scared, frustrated, confused."

"Were you able to talk to anyone about what was happening?" Myra asked.

"No. I think everyone was just trying to make it through another day, to be honest," said Amanda. "Anyway, for me, my insecurities about not being good enough started eating away at my soul. I would find comfort in food late at night when the house went quiet.

"I would sneak into the kitchen, go to the back of the pantry, unwrapping an enormous number of snacks. I'd stand there, consuming them all in one hit without a thought, ingesting thousands of calories within minutes. Every morsel of the crunchy granola bars lit up my taste buds. From that, I would gobble up candy, cookies, and pastries until I couldn't eat another bite.

"As I sat there depressed, embarrassed, and empty, I would convince myself of the comfort and love I felt from food. Within minutes, I'd start feeling immense guilt and severe disgust, so I'd force all that food back up into the toilet, sticking my fingers in my throat. The water splashing in the bathroom made me feel reborn, washing away all my imaginary unrelenting sins.

"Binge eating had become my security, a new companion during the lonely nights. The force of vomiting would be the control I needed over what was happening around me.

"This went on for weeks, then months. What started as an occasional habit became a regular, consistent occurrence controlling and consuming my life."

Amanda looked around at her friends' mouths agape, but it all made sense to Lynnie.

She remembered Amanda telling her about a medical issue and her not swimming competitively for one year. The thinness of her body, her small food portions, her constant need to exercise and burn calories all began threading together the missing pieces.

"My beautiful light brown curls, big smile, and flawless complexion became shallow, my green eyes became vacant, my bones became weak, and my frail, wispy hair became like hay. I started shrinking, then was beginning to hear whispers in my high school hallways. I had no desire to be around people, withdrawing from the swim team, spending most weekends alone, locked in my room. I was so disengaged at school with my friends and studies that eventually, there was a meeting with the school psychologist, guidance counselor, teachers, and my parents.

"When the loudspeaker came on and called my name, I immediately knew it wouldn't be good. I feared the walk to the main office, really worried about my brother, causing my stomach to turn in anticipation of what else could go wrong for my family. In the conference room, it was somber. Had I not known better, I would've thought someone had died.

"My parents sat with tears in their eyes, lumps in their throats, pure desperation in their hearts. Immediately, I became defensive, demanding to know what was going on, why we were here.

"The high school principal, Mr. Collins, sternly suggested I take a seat, and without any more words, everyone in the room turned to a small screen in the corner of the conference room table.

"The video started playing, and a grainy image, almost too dark to make out, appeared on the screen. Although I barely recognized myself, it was an image of me sprawled out with Tommy's pills in one hand, grossly tearing through bags of Doritos, potato chips, soda, cold canned beans, frozen corn, and cereal boxes. While I never took any of Tommy's pills, I used to just hold them while gorging myself with food as a way to stand against all that had happened to my family.

"I kept the drugs in anger, knowing what my parents had yet to figure out.

"Tommy was becoming more reliant on the pain pills as well; they were his crutch too. I saw how he would sneak extra medication when no one noticed, escaping into his room quietly.

"In my mind, the medicine Tommy was becoming more dependent on went ignored, the medical bills becoming the focus as if there was nothing to think about other than those, you know? Which was stupid because behind the pills was a boy who needed more than that.

"At night, I would hear hushed voices between my parents, trying to figure out how they could manage the expense of the next medical bill. Of course, it would turn into a blame game.

"Mom would say Dad had spent too much when they were younger, on frivolous things. If they'd saved some money, she would say, then they wouldn't be in this mess.

"Dad would say he was sorry, but he'd never envisaged having a crippled son! Soon, their voices grew louder until I heard a door slam, then silence. That was the awful part, how angry they had become at one another, the realization that my parents had lost their former lives too.

"During my food binges, I would replay those arguments between my parents, holding those damn pills in my hand as if they were some sort of a shield against my life's new reality.

"I know it sounds crazy, but I felt that if I could shield myself from the pills, in some way, it would protect my brother from his addiction to them as well. No idea how that made any sense!

"As I watched the remainder of the video, time stood still. No one moved or spoke for what seemed like an eternity. I only vaguely recognized my image; maybe I just didn't want to, didn't want to admit this was me. I couldn't believe my parents had set me up. Staging a secret camera to catch my binging seemed extreme at the time. Especially since Tommy was becoming more addicted to his pain medicine by the day, had they not realized that they had a bigger problem at hand than whether I ate cereal and cookies and pastries until I made myself vomit it all back up?

"Plus, didn't they see that if they only focused again on Tommy, if they could only help Tommy with his pain and his medications, that was also going to help me? But it was like they just wanted to shut us both out, or to shout at us and tell us how hopeless we were these days, that we weren't trying hard enough to pull ourselves out of our godforsaken mess.

"I was both infuriated and relieved at this revelation that they had been videoing me in secret, and they were angry at me that they'd 'had to do it'. The invisible daughter was now seen.

"Despite everything, I felt a loyalty to Tommy not to tell his secret. I naively believed that Tommy would move past this phase in his life, knowing I was taking the fall for my brother, hoping that my allegiance to him would somehow repair our relationship if not our health.

"Mostly, I felt violated, embarrassed, beginning to starve myself and binge eat to take control of my out-of-control family life. Slamming doors, quiet middle-of-the-night sobbing, drained beings resided where once vibrant middle-aged parents had thrived. And I couldn't blame them for any of this any more than they could honestly have blamed Tommy for *his* injuries.

"We were all the victims in this. None of us had asked for this misery, this loss of control.

"The process of eating, starving, binging was the only thing I had actual control over.

"And now, I was exposed, so vulnerable, but I at least agreed to therapy and treatment immediately. My brother, however, just carried on doing what he did, becoming more and more reliant on his pain medicine. When my parents finally realized what I already knew, they just monitored his medication, becoming even more controlling and paranoid. They failed to realize that Tommy had a drug dealer on the side, feeding him whatever he wanted to numb his pain.

"Our relationship hasn't been the same since. Tommy still struggles with addiction, and I just found out that he had yet another relapse and he's back in our local rehab center. That football accident took so much from our family, its consequences so detrimental and traumatic for us all."

Amanda was unsure what her friends were thinking.

Before they could say anything, she continued, "I chose to live and get better. Never looked back." Amanda paused momentarily, realizing her 'truth' wasn't exactly true.

"The truth was that I still had those same feelings from the past but tried burying them so that I could function like everyone else. I just wanted to be 'normal.' My feelings of sadness stuffed deep inside—as I tried desperately to be the 'good girl' and the quiet girl everyone hoped and expected me to be during this time—were exhausting. In the dark, quiet moments at night, I still felt the strong urge to purge. It never really goes away. But I would convince myself to plow through another day. Outwardly, I was happy; inside, I was silently dying."

Amanda looked around the room, starting to feel uneasy.

"My family assumed after I got help that I was better; they never asked, you know? But it felt like I had no choice but to pretend to *be* better, even though I was sure I wasn't free of it.

"I would lie awake in bed with anxiety on many long nights, wishing my mom would come in, asking how I felt. She didn't, of course, and I don't blame her. Her plate was already full of Tommy. They, too, just wanted to move on from that awful night. They needed to find themselves again, to have the permission and freedom from us to try and make some sort of life.

"So, I stayed quiet but my mind raced with thoughts of the night of the accident. Visions of my brother lying on the field motionless would replay in my mind. Replaying the sound of the crowd, the gasps in the air, and the looks on spectators' faces consumed the night hours.

"My stomach would turn as I reluctantly recounted the first day seeing my brother at the hospital. The smell of the third floor still lingers in my mind. *Beep, beep, beep,* the sound of the machines would march on, ringing uncertainty in my ear."

Looking down, Amanda noticed she was trembling. Her breath was short; she needed a moment to get her thoughts in order as the girls patiently waited for her to continue.

"As time passed, life in my small suburban town became mundane for my family and me. Thankfully, my parents' relationship improved when Tommy, although never able to play football again, enrolled in a local college, studying sports injury science.

"I became healthy mentally, physically, and emotionally. It wasn't without struggle, but finally, I began to see the future as a new beginning and adventure. I was ready for college, and my experience of addiction and depression were helping to make my decision to study social work an easy one. I knew firsthand how addiction could change a person and a family, and with proper care, I would provide hope and guidance on how many people at the clinic had helped me. And I really am confident I can make a difference, helping others with addiction."

Amanda felt good to be releasing the shame, opening up about the truth of her past. She was exhausted after it but her shoulders relaxed, relief sweeping over her face.

The girls sat silent, listening until she finished, Amanda feeling the embrace of her friends and the comfort that they cared. Amanda had started with her life story; it was the beginning of all the tales the friends had yet to hear and had yet to comment on.

"Amanda," Lynnie said quietly. "You are very brave. We all have stuff that we're trying to forget. You're not alone, not ever. Perhaps that's why we bonded so quickly with one another. The heart often needs to find security in the most insecure, which may be the magic of healing."

❖

JOURNAL

TONIGHT, AMANDA TOLD US ABOUT HER FAMILY PROBLEMS AND HER STRUGGLE WITH ADDICTION. IT MAKES SENSE NOW HOW FRAIL SHE LOOKS. A HEAVINESS WEIGHS ON HER; I UNDERSTAND WHY. AMANDA HAS DEALT WITH A LOT, AND I JUST HOPE SHE FINDS COMFORT IN KNOWING THAT WE ALL HAVE OUR SECRETS.

MY GUT WAS TELLING ME THAT THERE WAS MORE TO AMANDA THAN SHE WAS SAYING. I NEED TO START TRUSTING MY INSTINCTS INSTEAD OF BRUSHING OFF WARNING SIGNS. I HOPE AMANDA IS BEING TRUTHFUL

ABOUT HER RECOVERY. I REALLY, REALLY HOPE SO FOR HER SAKE.

THERE IS A DARKNESS ABOUT HER BUT MAYBE I'M JUST BEING PARANOID.

AND I AM PROUD OF HER, NO MATTER WHAT.

# Chapter Six

*Myra: The Revelations.*

No one mentioned again the sensitive and soul-revealing information that Amanda had just voiced to everyone so bravely, treating her with the same warmth as prior to knowing it.

"Thanks for listening, guys," Amanda said, peeling a banana.

Myra grabbed Amanda's hand, saying, "No, thank you, Amanda. That was brave of you to talk to us. I wish I had even a fraction of the courage you do."

"Hey," Amanda said. "Ladies, we need to be honest with one another or what's the point?"

Lynnie glanced at Myra, knowing she now wanted to say something.

"You are right. I have a feeling we do all have something to share. Let's go grab some ice cream and meet back at my dorm," Myra said. There was a strangeness to her tone; it was as if perhaps even she had something to share, something to impart that might help her.

Twenty minutes and four pints of ice cream later, the ladies gathered on bean bags sprawled around the room. Myra glanced around, nervously considering divulging her secrets.

She fiddled with her hands as she softly began.

"I would like to share some things about my past as well."

Jessica was biting her lip, uncomfortable with what might also be discussed.

Clearing her throat, Myra said, "Well, no doubt you've all guessed that I have something I'd like to speak about."

The girls nodded, all quiet, Jessica resting a hand on her friend's knee, and everyone rapt.

"My mother, Karen, loved alcohol more than she loved breathing air. The burning feeling that went down her throat as the alcohol splashed from the glass to her lips was euphoria and there was no hiding it; you could just see it in her eyes and on her lips, the smile, the way her eyes rolled sometimes. She never even tried, never pretended that she wasn't an alcoholic, you know?

"She never feigned that the demon drink wasn't more important to her than anything else. The release of tension, pain, and the undeniable sense of solitude that alcohol gave her was a reckless companionship. Sometimes, Karen would dabble a bit with cocaine, but coke was a rich man's drug. She didn't have anywhere near the funds to support that expensive and inescapable habit.

"She also didn't have the intellect or the energy to go out robbing people or doing all those nefarious things other coke addicts knew how to do to keep on fueling their next fix!"

Myra laughed; only Myra could giggle at something like that, forever making light of the most intense of situations. "No, alcohol was her drug of choice and the destruction it caused, she simply ignored despite my well-being. So, you can probably already write how this goes.

"You know what happens to alcoholics and the families of them. I would beg my mother to stop, often finding her staggering into my bedroom at night, climbing under my sheets, lying close to me. I hated the smell of her breath but loved the warmth of her skin, loved her closeness near to me, which went a little way to making up for the fact that she was never really there if you get what I mean. Karen would whisper, 'I'm sorry,' and although she meant the words, she would never change her actions. That was what hurt me the most, that I was never worth it.

"But my mother would never change, *couldn't* ever change and there was no sense in expecting it. Alcohol had eaten away at her soul and taken possession of her being, owning her."

Lynnie paced the room looking for a hair tie.

Myra continued, "The cold winter of upstate New York often seemed less brutal than living in the house I was forced to call home. The winters there were dreadfully long, I mean really bitterly cold inside and out, the wind seeming even harsher these last few years. I started to notice the temperature more now than when I was a child. In actuality, I'm startlingly aware of *everything* now. My mother was a child herself, who had a child, counting on me to raise her.

"It was an exhausting and unreasonable expectation. As early as five o'clock, I would get up for school, eat an overflowing bowl of Crunch cereal and begin a half-a-mile walk, all the way down the long, lonely roads of upstate New York, my little legs bowing under the weight.

"By that, I mean the weight of all the stuff I was carrying in my big school bag that was slung over my shoulders but also, there was the sheer *emotional* weight of it all. But it was just what I had to do. As a seven-year-old, I was unaware of my unclean body, my mismatched clothes, or lack of lunch. Time and time again, the teachers would ask to speak to my mother, but Karen never followed up with their calls or meetings, and eventually, the school gave up trying.

"Once I exhausted all my lame excuses for why my parents couldn't be contacted, I stopped trying to keep up the image I had created in my imagination. From then on, I no longer made excuses for my life or my mother, no longer hiding that I was a child raising my own mom.

"I stopped pretending that my father was away on business, beginning to admit to myself that my mother was a liability and embarrassment to me in many ways. But I loved her despite her faults. I loved how her unbrushed hair fell on her dark brown eyes, or how her drunken stumble made her look like a clumsy dancer, and that somehow, she always managed to get up again.

"Of course, I worried for my mother's safety, trying on numerous occasions to get my mother some help, but I was just a kid. I'm not sure if she *could* not or *would* not stop drinking."

Myra looked off into the distance, surprised at her own unexpected emotional vulnerability. Myra's palms were sweaty as she inhaled large gulps of water. "I felt guilty for not getting her to stop drinking, like at some stage, probably like all kids of all addicts, it had become my fault.

"I felt I was supposed to be able to get her to stop this destructive behavior, that I failed her.

"Also, I was beginning to feel something else too, something new, which was the rage toward her for not loving me enough to want to stop, not enough to even give it a go. The internal struggle was something that I couldn't reconcile with, and it's still haunting me even now."

Sitting silently, eyebrows furrowed, the girls listened.

Myra could feel her face softening now. It was a cathartic feeling to be unburdening.

"To be fair, there were good times too. Karen would bake brownies with me, always letting me lick the bowl clean of uncooked batter. She taught me about measuring ingredients, the importance of mixing the batter, and the enjoyment of the aroma that a homemade treat could bring. Sometimes, my mom and I would hold hands, skipping on the grass until we were so tired, we'd just collapse on the soft green ground. We would take turns looking up at the clouds, deciphering the shapes into objects, laughing at the thought of a dinosaur eating an apple.

"At night, Karen would snuggle up in bed with me, holding me close. The smell of my mother was a mix of stale booze and old perfume, but it comforted me. I felt safe and happy on those days. The following day though, I would find her passed out and still in the same stinking clothes from the night before, an empty bottle not too far from her. I would gaze at her, willing her to stop, but she didn't. Karen was never violent or unkind to me, just neglectful and absent."

Myra laughed at the memory, and for a moment, tears formed as she quickly took a breath. "One day, we were making homemade macaroni and cheese together. I looked forward to the feast I would later devour, being sure not to eat anything all day to save my appetite.

"It took hours to grate the cheese, to make the fresh pasta, boil the water. My taste buds were soaring in anticipation. We carefully constructed our cheesy masterpiece into a pan, smothered it with even more cheese, placing it in the oven to marry the ingredients together.

"My mother instructed me to play outside for a little while. She cleaned up, preparing for supper. Soon after that, I heard a noise coming from the place. The fire alarm was going off, and I saw smoke billowing from the kitchen window. Panicked, I took off toward the house to check on my mother. I found the kitchen still as messy as when I'd left before going outside to play.

"As I frantically made my way through the kitchen, I saw no flames, just heavy smoke. The smoke was actually filling the house, my lungs consuming my senses. I flung open every window and door of the house to clear out some of the stench and the thick smoky fog."

Without taking a moment to breathe, Myra kept talking. "When I could finally see, I found my mother slumped over at the table, her hair wet from the spilled drink beside her.

"I screamed her name, and when she came to, I immediately realized that she must have passed out, forgetting all about the macaroni and cheese in the oven. Later, we tried to salvage our dinner, but it was ruined. I went to bed that night hungry and disappointed. I desperately wanted a sober mother, at least for more than a couple of days at a time. At least long enough to care to put a paltry meal on the table for us both, making sure we were fed. I hated to watch her stumbling through the house carelessly, knocking over picture frames on the coffee table.

"One picture was of me swinging on a swing at the park, smiling broadly with pure joy in my eyes. I vividly remember the day the photo had been taken. My mom was sitting on a bench nearby, talking with a stranger in a black coat. He handed her a bag full of something white in exchange for a couple of dollars, quickly walking away. I didn't understand the transaction then.

"And of course, I never mentioned it to anyone. One day though, after a couple of encounters with the same man in the black coat, I got curious, starting to ask my mother about it, and Karen quickly dismissed my inquiry and yelled from afar, 'Hey Myra, smile, silly!' I was far from the ground, giggling at the birds flying overhead. I let out a loud giggle, hearing the sound of the camera snap with delight. It was a good memory, and I have plenty of them despite it all."

Myra stretched her arms out wide, trying to make light of the situation, but the boiling up anger was taking control. Myra sighed. "Karen had good intentions, but her disease was worsening. The more I longed for my mother to be someone else, the more resentful I grew.

"I was so desperately trying to keep my rage inside, but one day it became unbearable, the pent-up anger overflowing. I walked home from school, the neighborhood kids teasing me all the way about my dirty, smelly, stained clothes. I tried to ignore the taunts, beginning to walk faster. Two boys started catching up to me, approaching at a faster pace than I anticipated.

"The insults became more personal. They chanted in unison, 'Myra, Myra, her mother is a drunk; she makes her money giving strangers fucks.' My stomach turned, my face burning, and my mind racing with rage. I bent down, found an enormous rock, pegging it at that boy who stood at least six inches taller than me. I threw that rock as hard as possible, frightened by how much rage was within me. It hit him right on the side of the head, and I just stood there for a minute, watching the blood drip from the boy's eye with a weird kind of self-satisfied pleasure.

"Stunned, he stared at me as his white t-shirt started turning red. 'Fuck you, Myra; you're just as psycho as your mother!' he shouted. 'Everyone *knows* she's psycho!' I motioned as if I would lob another rock at him, but he had run away before I could bend down to get one.

"Once I was alone again, I sobbed all the rest of the way home. If people had known how kind and caring my mother could be without alcohol, I imagine she would have been well-liked around our small town. I always knew my mother had a reputation, but getting teased for it was the part that was most traumatizing. I'd heard people whisper when we went to the market, and I'd seen—well, couldn't help seeing—the way people stared at us in judgment and contempt.

"When I was younger, I naively greeted the other customers, watching their smiles fade as they recognized us. I didn't meet their gazes. My cheeks were burning when I asked my mother why people were rude in this town. I never realized they were only rude to us, that they were mostly delightful to everyone else. And my mother replied defiantly, 'Myra baby, they're like that to us because they think their shit doesn't stink. Half of these people have bigger problems than ours, but they pretend to be all high and mighty for show.'

"She said, 'Pay no mind to them, my sweet angel. We do what we must to get by in this world. We will always be OK if we have each other, won't we? We will always be OK. You and me.'"

Myra's head was down, staring at the floor, but she liked the thought of them being a team, sticking together against the rest of the town. "It made me feel like we were secret superheroes. I even told my mama so. She smiled, saying, 'I suppose we are, baby girl, I suppose we are.'

"Generally, I didn't let those whispers get to me and you know, maybe that's partly why people think I can be a bit hard, like I have this outer shell, always making jokes and not taking things as seriously as others do. It's because I had to learn to put on this 'I don't care' face.

"I stayed to myself, and my mother never cared much about others' thoughts either. But hearing that boy relentlessly taunting me that afternoon sent me into a tizzy. I crumbled the entire way home, tears dripping down my cheeks and bitterness consuming me down to my belly. My anger got caught in my throat as I tried to scream. It had really broken me that day.

"The shame was immense, and my secret rage toward Mom made me feel guilty and mean. I knew my mother was sick and poor, that she didn't know how to be any other way than how she was. She didn't have any real life skills and selling her body to the locals was how she put food on the table and alcohol in her hand. She would say, 'No shame in a day's work, Myra. Don't let anyone tell you differently. And everything can be *a day's work* if someone will pay you for it.'

"I didn't understand what kind of *day's work* she did, nor did I ask. It was common knowledge to everyone in town except me. Until now. It was confirmation of what I'd suspected all along."

Despite Myra's efforts to keep herself hidden and out of the spotlight, things came to a head when she went to school with head lice. The school deemed Karen unfit, and Myra was sent to foster care when the school could no longer ignore the foul smell and the fact that young Myra was constantly getting caught stealing food from the cafeteria's garbage.

By that point, the school could no longer disregard Karen's neglect. They called a meeting, and Karen denied any wrongdoing. Well, she really didn't see any alternatives.

Karen's fists were tight and her voice tense when she shouted, 'She's my baby. Leave us alone!' as the two police officers pried Myra off her leg. Karen and Myra sobbed, trying to get to one another, but the authorities had decided, and there was nothing either of them could do.

⸙

"At night, I would wonder if my mother was still alive and, during the morning hours, would fear for her, wondering who would be there for her, who'd wipe the vomit off her face, also making sure she had some dry toast and tea to help with the expected daily hangover.

"I had such anxiety being away from her, spending most of my time reading the obituaries, wondering if my mother was in them. I was more scared for her than for me, because like I said, I was responsible for her, I was raising her because she couldn't even care for her own self.

"I missed her as well like any kid misses her mom, just wanting to be safe back home with her. The authorities had removed me from my mother, but I was in far more danger in foster care.

"Late at night, under the dirty sheets, I would talk to my mother, hoping she would hear my cries for her from afar," she explained tearfully to the girls. "I would imagine the smell of her skin close to me as I drifted off to sleep, sometimes hearing her voice in my dreams.

"Each day away from her made me resent and yet love her more if that makes sense. I grew angrier with my mother for letting me be taken away, forcing me to live with strangers. Although she was unpredictable, living with my mother was tolerable, and it was all I had known. Being with people without connection or genuine care for me was more unbearable and frightening."

⸺⸺◦❦◦⸺⸺

It took nearly a year apart, but the state finally awarded custody back to Karen. The Children's Protective Service people, however, were still making those unwelcome monthly welfare visits.

When the child was finally reunited with Karen, who had quit drinking, they both changed. Myra was less patient, more guarded, and angrier than Karen remembered. Karen was more religious and apologetic with a new sense of being, making Myra uncomfortable and confused.

The change in Karen was what Myra had long since hoped for, but now a new, unfamiliar sense of anxiety consumed Myra because life again had become unpredictable. The fear of the unknown and when the next binge would happen made her feel insecure about the future.

Plus, this version of Karen was not quite the same; she wasn't as carefree and funny, appearing more anxious, more stressed about the small things she would have ignored when she was drunk.

But in no way did Myra hope for her mother to revert to the old ways. Sober was better.

*Sober* meant being responsible and somewhat more reliable. It meant not falling asleep when there was something cooking in the oven, and it meant asking Myra if she was OK and if she had had a good day, and to tell her what was on her mind. In short, sobriety meant 'fairly normal'.

But it still brought its own form of unpredictability, as odd as that sounded. Myra didn't know how to understand this new mother, the one who no longer was reaching for the bottle.

When Myra's mother would drink, the outcome had always been that she would pass out and be hungover in the morning. Myra was still spending her days expecting the worst, and when it didn't happen, she was cautiously optimistic but simultaneously miserably skeptical. Myra had spent most of her life caring for her mother, which felt oddly normal, making her feel useful too.

Their relationship had been built on dysfunction, and having a mother who had become responsible and somewhat motherly was excruciatingly unpredictable.

Myra wanted to believe in her present life changes, but life had made her skeptical and bitter.

⬥⬥⬥

As Myra continued talking, she could see how uncomfortable Lynnie, Jessica, and Amanda were by the way they fidgeted with their hands. She continued despite their discomfort.

If she didn't, she would never talk about it again.

"Having my belongings stuffed in large garbage bags and having to drag them from house to house, being an unwanted stranger in other people's homes, and having no place to belong broke my spirit. But I was grateful to be in a stable home with my mother for now. It was comforting to sleep without fearing any unwelcome guests intruding into my room, forcing me to 'earn my keep' in the most brutal, vile way."

Myra saw Lynnie's mouth open wide, realizing that her friend had been abused. Still, Myra somehow continued, "At first, I resisted the advances of the older men, intentionally wearing the most oversized, ugliest clothes. Despite my efforts, the advances never stopped."

Myra's eyes filled with tears. "The door opening night after night was relentless. My muffled cries went unheard, and the burning sensation between my legs was unbearable. I became numb, even feeling I was losing a piece of myself during that time. I couldn't help resenting my mother because her negligence had allowed so many attacks on my body or soul. Still, even now, I feel dirty, used, and unworthy of happiness. I'm not sure I will ever feel clean again. I was supposed to trust the adults to protect me, but I quickly discovered I only had myself to rely on." The warmth of the girls embracing Myra made her feel something she hadn't in a long time, safety.

"You are safe now," Jessica said softly, stroking Myra's cheek to wipe away her tears.

"We will never tell anyone. Myra, you can trust us. We promise," Amanda said with a smile.

Suddenly, the feeling of safety disappeared, leaving Myra feeling only embarrassed. She had to just carry on telling her story; in opening up and revealing horrible truths, there was strength.

"In some ways, it made me stronger, knowing that I was responsible for my future, committed to living a life in which I could have power and independence. I'd spent years stuffing these memories deep inside, never able to talk about it with anyone, until now," Myra whispered.

"I swore I would never allow anyone to break my spirit again, hence it appears that I'm tough and have this air of defiance. It's a coping mechanism. I was never sure if my mother would relapse, leaving me to care for her again. Anyway, I knew I would constantly fend for myself despite my mother's sobriety. I had been suspicious of her promises, learning long ago that the one thing I could count on was broken promises. The bottom line is that although she loved me, she couldn't control her love for alcohol, her bad choices with men, and poor financial decisions.

"I knew that my life would be what I made of it. Despite my upbringing, I loved my mother but I refused to ever become like her. My mother's flaws made me more determined to thrive and succeed. I took nothing for granted at school, relied on no one, just working hard."

One teacher found her way into Myra's guarded heart and head.

Mrs. Nali took a particular interest in Myra almost immediately, often buying the girl new pencils and notebooks, encouraging her to read as many novels as she could by the author Brene Brown, fine books about empowerment, determination, and courage.

Mrs. Nali recognized something that, from afar, many could have easily missed. Without fully disclosing her childhood, Mrs. Nali often referred to them as 'us girls', proclaiming she knew what it was like to be strong survivors. Mrs. Nali was beautiful with her straight black hair and big blue eyes. At first glance, she was stunning and perfect-looking. But if you took the time to focus on her eyes, you would notice a deep sadness.

Outwardly, Mrs. Nali was happy and friendly, although sometimes, Myra would catch her staring out of her window with a pained look of hurt, a look that was unmistakable.

She knew without asking what had happened, and it was probably her story too.

Mrs. Nali consistently checked in with Myra throughout high school, asking about her plans and academic achievements, introducing her to local science clubs and competitions, and helping her enter creative writing contests.

She ensured Myra was on track for a full scholarship to whatever university she chose.

"In many ways, Mrs. Nali was the mother I never had, the friend I had always hoped for, and the mentor I was lucky and grateful enough to have on my side. I began believing in my abilities, and in living a life full of promise. By 11th grade, I was at the top of my class, and universities were already looking to offer me generous scholarships. The influence of Mrs. Nali was the one thing I relied on, and I was determined to make her proud."

After years of heartbreak and uncertainty, Myra finally felt worthy of the chance for a future; however, she was still a scared little girl longing for a typical family life filled with special memories from holidays, warm hugs upon arrival from school, or proud parents who gloated about their daughter's achievements at cocktail parties. The hole in her heart was from the lack of genuine love and family; it would always be a piece of her, yet she learned to live despite it.

"Knowing me as you do, you probably never imagined I have loneliness, mistrust, and inner sadness buried deep inside. They're all still there, every day. I just learned to keep them in.

"The motive for my academic achievements was my way of taking control of my future. I became so competitive that I wouldn't accept anything but academic perfection at school.

"As a little girl, I would observe other mothers doting on their daughters, playing with their hair, or meticulously dressing them in perfectly matched outfits. I always carried a noticeable ache in my heart, longing to be someone's daughter. Although the hurt and insecurities were present, I developed a stiff upper lip and a rugged exterior. Watching my mother pass out on a stained green couch in a dingy rented house that smelled of mildew and vomit and stale alcohol was a stench I would never forget but one I became used to. That was my normality."

As Myra's senior year ended, she was excited to leave her old life behind, never looking back. She was looking forward to the prospect of starting at college with a new identity.

"I could leave town, leaving behind the shame I had endured because of my mother. I took a deep breath at the possibility of this new beginning. College afforded me a chance to be free of my past. I will forever be grateful to Mrs. Nali for steering me in the right direction.

"In some ways, though, I'm thankful to my mother for showing me the harsh truth of the world. The hardships, despair, poverty, and abuse I endured throughout childhood made my future exciting. I would no longer recognize myself as the poor girl from the wrong side of town. Soon, I would begin the next chapter of my life, and nothing could be sweeter. I knew Karen would drink herself to death one day, though I hadn't suspected it would be this way ..."

For a brief moment, Myra looked lost, gazing downward, playing with her fingers. She sucked in a tremendous intake of breath, then her watery eyes looked up again, and she carried on.

"I instinctively knew she was gone when I walked up the driveway. I called her name anyway, learning through those drunken days to always check the bathroom first. Walking down the hallway to the bathroom, it was eerily quiet. Usually, the television would be blaring in the background, the intense smell of cigarette smoke greeting me at the door. Not today though.

"Today was different. I knew that something was amiss by the silence and only the faint scent of nicotine. Slowly, I continued to walk down the narrow hallway, carefully looking around for any sign of her. There was none, not a thing; I carried on calling to her anyway, and no answer came. The stillness in the house was frightening, and it said it all. I wanted to believe that my mother was off on a job interview at the five and dime down the road, the way she had promised.

"We had spoken earlier about her getting a safer, stabler job. She seemed hopeful about it, even asking me what she should wear for the interview, modeling two outfits. I'd prayed that this job interview would lead to a job and that her life would finally get on track properly.

"I thought it odd as I passed her bedroom, noticing the bed neatly made. I couldn't remember the last time my mother had even made a bed. Like, she just wasn't capable of it because keeping a house nice and worrying about unmade beds didn't enter her realm of existence.

"Still, I was hopeful. I told myself she'd been making great strides, becoming sober and more of a mother, so why wouldn't she have taken it upon herself to make a bed for once in her life?

"My satisfied smile faded. The bathroom light was on, and the door open, and then I saw my mother's legs dangling out of the bathtub as I got closer. Upon further inspection, she was dressed in the outfit she had chosen for that interview. As I inched closer, her face was beautifully made up with blue eyeshadow, rose lip gloss, and a subtle hint of mascara. Her hair was blown out, the faint smell of her favorite perfume still lingering in the air.

"Confused, I started screaming her name. This couldn't be. It just couldn't, not now, not after she had tried so hard and was finally fighting her way out of that squalid, downbeat, broken life.

"But it was true. My mother lay still on the bathroom floor, blood trailing from her skull, lying in a massive pool of it that had started to knit and congeal; she must have been there for ages because of the knitting of the blood and how cold she already was. There was no evident smell of alcohol, but I couldn't be sure if she had been drinking. Countless times before, I had discovered her on the bathroom floor, passed out drunk, motionless. This time, it was for good.

"I later learned from the autopsy report that her official cause of death was a heart attack, which came as a huge relief. It could have been drugs. It could have been alcohol. It was neither of those, just that her poor sad heart had been through so much and couldn't take it anymore.

"My mother had made fundamental changes, turning her life around leading up to the day of her death, and the God she'd only just begun to believe in had to come along and torn her away before she could even get herself a respectable job. Honestly, I don't know what the sense was in believing in this so-called God. He was horrible and cruel … None of it added up."

Myra felt an urge of rage at the reality of saying this all out loud.

"I felt so cheated, that I had never gotten to know my mother sober, only the alcoholic town whore who was always misunderstood," she said as the finally unrestrainable tears appeared.

"I didn't care much what people thought, especially now. At the time, when I'd been going through all this turmoil with her, I guess I'd never seen just how many life lessons she actually taught me. We had always been so caught up in the 'badness' of everything that we couldn't—well, I couldn't—see the good. For one thing, from my mother, I had learned that it didn't matter who thought what about you; the only one who had to accept you was yourself.

"But despite that, a small part of me was still wanting to show the local townies how amazing my mother could have been if given the opportunity. Watching her leave our house for the last time on a gurney with a white sheet draped over her still body, I had never felt so alone. I was unsure what to do, knowing we had very few savings for a burial and I wanted the best for her.

"She, in my mind, deserved the best too. Despite her appalling life, she'd loved me so much.

"Anyway, as my mom was being transferred into the ambulance, I demanded they stop because I couldn't let the last image of my mother be of her lying like that on the bathroom floor.

"A short, heavy-set man stopped, looking on sympathetically, obviously seeing the awful state I was in. So they slowed, and I took that opportunity and ran up to her stiff body and held her, inhaling for the last time my mother's essence, my new mother, the one who had been clean and wholesome at last despite her slight smell of nicotine. I slipped the gold necklace with the eagle charm off her neck, snatching one last look at the woman who had birthed me, given me life.

"Despite everything, I was broken-hearted and walked back into the house. The quiet inside was deafening. I had no idea what would become of me now. I was genuinely lost, bereft.

"Not that my mother had been the most present or reliable parental figure, but it was just pleasant and made me feel warm in my heart to have someone in this world who cared about me.

"With all her faults, I'd never doubted for one moment that my mother loved me unconditionally, that there was nothing I could ever have done to make her say she disliked me or was ashamed of me, or that I should stop pestering her the way some parents behaved toward their adult children. The only problem was that she loved alcohol more than she loved herself."

Between quiet, reluctant sobs, Myra added, "I always wear the necklace I removed from her neck the day she died. When worried or stressed, I hold the small eagle charm in my palm, and I think of her, trying to be really still and quiet, asking for her presence again, feeling her. It makes me feel connected to her even though I want to leave the past behind. But I don't run from my past anymore. Instead, I celebrate the little girl who made it through a painful childhood."

Myra felt a sense of relief and embarrassment upon realizing she had been talking nonstop for over an hour. She had one secret fewer to tell, and it left her feeling lighter, emotionally.

"I guess I should tell you my birth name too, while I'm confessing all!"

Her humor was making a reappearance, making all the girls smile and finally believe they could breathe again. "Go on, what was it?" Amanda demanded to know. "Is it really bad?"

Everyone snickered.

"No! I was born Michelle Nelson. But when I turned eighteen, I was so determined to leave my past behind that I legally changed my name to Myra Nali. *Myra* means sweet-smelling, and since I'd spent my childhood taunted by other kids for smelling dirty and neglected, I chose that name, vowing never to be seen as undesirable again because of the neglect I'd endured.

"And as for my last name, Nali, well you know that was the name of my old teacher and mentor who'd kindly taken me under her wing, allowing me to thrive for the first time in my life.

"I didn't know what my future held, but never wanted my old name and old life to be associated with the new one I was sure to make for myself. I worked hard to create a life for myself, to leave my past behind ..."

Myra looked momentarily a little uncomfortable, awkward, struggling with something.

Everyone waited patiently. "... So I need to insist that this story never leave this room. I mean I'm sorry to say it and everything because there's no one I trust in the world more than you."

She eyed everyone as if slightly ashamed she was asking such a thing from the girls she trusted anyway. Did she really have to put it in words? But being her usual bold self, she did.

The girls nodded in agreement, knowing they had just been privy to a lot of pain and growth, swearing never to speak a word of it again, just the same respect as for Amanda's story.

⸙

JOURNAL

I AM BLOWN AWAY BY MYRA'S PAST.

SHE IS SO LOYAL AND STRONG, AND I HAVE SUCH RESPECT FOR HER FORTITUDE NOW. I LOVE THAT SHE WEARS HER

MOTHER'S NECKLACE EVEN TODAY, AND THAT SHE WASN'T ASHAMED OF HER MOTHER AND DIDN'T DISTANCE HERSELF FROM HER OR ALIENATE HER, NO MATTER THE PAIN HER MOM WAS INFLICTING ON HER.

THAT'S TRULY BIG-HEARTED, GENEROUS IN A WAY MOST OF US CAN'T EVER ACHIEVE.

TONIGHT, IT MUST HAVE BEEN HARD FOR MYRA TO TALK ABOUT ALL THAT. BUT I'M GLAD SHE DID.

IT MAKES ME KNOW HER MORE DEEPLY. HER DETERMINATION TO SUCCEED IS ADMIRABLE.

MYRA WILL ALWAYS PROTECT THE ONES SHE LOVES. I HOPE THAT INCLUDES ME.

# CHAPTER SEVEN

*Jessica: The All-American Girl.*

A week passed, one in which Jessica had been quite distracted. After dinner one night, she asked if they could all meet at the student union to grab coffee before heading back to watch a movie at her dorm. So, that was what they did.

"These last couple of weeks, I've been feeling closer to you guys than ever. You have no idea how much I appreciate you—Myra and Amanda—for revealing your lives. But it makes me feel guilty for not being transparent myself," she said, twirling her hair nervously. "I'd like to share."

Before speaking again, Jessica looked around the room, a little embarrassed by her seemingly small secret in comparison to Myra's.

She wasn't one to dwell on the negative, also feeling uncertain she wanted to share her story of immense heartbreak that had taken her such efforts to overcome. Was it a good thing to talk about herself so openly, and for the length of time it would take to get the full story out?

She hesitated for a moment, thinking. But what was there to lose?

"Well, here goes," she began. "I was the typical all-American girl. I was even prom queen, so it should come as no surprise that I was easily liked and admired."

She said it with a chuckle.

"I know you guys know David as my father, but the truth is he's actually not my biological father. David raised me, so I just always considered him Dad. When I was five, my birth father, Ed, had been killed in a motorcycle accident, and being an only child left my mother a lot of room to adore me, dedicating much of her attention solely to me. I guess I … I was just lucky."

After Jessica said that, she quickly cringed and glanced over to Myra.

Not wanting to hurt Myra for being loved, she squeezed Myra's arm lightly. Myra just nodded, encouraging her to continue with no ill feelings toward the love she'd been fortunate to receive.

"From what I was told, my biological father, Ed, was a gentleman with a big heart and a contagious laugh. He always said he was proud of having me as a daughter, showing me off to everyone around town. His friends, even now, still reminisce about how he would be caught joyfully singing with his nails painted pink, wearing a tiara, all because he was proud of me painting him up that way, not having any sisters to 'make beautiful'!

"On the outside, Ed was a tattooed tough guy, but inside, he was as sweet as could be, with a very big heart. Everyone says he would have done anything to see me smile and laugh, even at his own expense. He didn't put himself first. Happiness for us was all my father cared about.

"He was still just as in love with my mother from the day they'd met until the day of the accident. So, everyone liked Ed and I was cherished too throughout the small town. People cheerfully smiled at me, the townies often telling me that my presence was a blessing to them.

"The stories I had heard about my father made others' memories feel like my own too, because they would speak of him as if he was truly someone special, someone they had adored. I learned that he'd spent countless hours taking me to the park, and off to picnics, and reading to me at night. His absence was noticed, but I felt his presence with me throughout my life.

"Whenever I missed him, I would sit in his beloved armchair, soaking up his essence. I still could faintly smell the scent of his wretched Old Spice aftershave—that was pleasant only if he was the one wearing it, whereas on anyone else, I thought it was putrid—and I never forgot the warmth of his arms holding me on his lap. Something had broken within our universe, smashed to fragments alongside his broken body when my father died. My mom tried to be brave for me, but she was heartbroken too, beyond belief. At night, I would hear her cry for hours, and innocently, I would go into my mother's room; I'd lie next to her, rigid as a board because even if I tried snuggling up, she would never respond to my presence at all during those nights.

"In retrospect, I'm sure she was hurting too much, still trying to process everything and needing time alone to grieve since she spent her days caring for me.

"The nights were her only times alone to deal with her loss and pain. And I was a kid, just craving to stay beside my mom to feel safe again and to try to make her feel better.

"It became a habit that I would sleep with her at night in my father's spot. Eventually, she didn't seem to mind me being there and I didn't have to lie there like a wooden post anymore. We would be holding hands in silence, knowing how much we were both missing the man who had brought such joy to both our worlds. I felt scared and helpless during the nights, hearing her sobbing from my bedroom. It was then that I'd go creeping into her bed to keep her company."

Ed and Marie had met in grade school, and from the time they were ten years old, they had been constants in one another's lives. Marie knew she would marry Ed the day she saw him.

She came home that day from school, screaming to her mother that she had met the boy of her dreams. Her mother just giggled, thinking it was a childhood crush, never believing that her daughter really had been so lucky as to find the love of her life at ten years old.

As the years passed, they both had other childish relationships but stayed in touch, not starting to connect again in earnest until their senior year in high school.

Ed left for the army, Marie going off to pursue a two-year course at business school.

Before departing, they had both been at a party, when Marie joked about the first time she had set eyes on him. "I ran home to tell my mother that I'd found the boy of my dreams!"

Ed's eyes flickered with delight and a sweet smile. 'And how do you know you haven't?'

Nervously, Marie laughed at his arrogance in asking her out for a proper date to the movies. She, of course, said yes, and they had been a couple since.

Ed stayed in the army beyond boot camp, Marie eventually completing her degree. Now, they were keeping in touch daily by letters, and when Ed returned after that time, he immediately proposed. Two years later, he was discharged from the army, and they wed on a fall day outside in the park, in the same spot where they had met on the playground.

Their wedding pictures were epic, him pushing her on the swing, then playing tag on the grass. They had come full circle, their love true, and unique, and enduring.

When Ed died, Marie's world was shattered. Who even was she without him?

Though trying to be brave for Jessica, she relied on friends and family to watch over her young daughter. Marie had a hard time getting out of bed until she went to seek help from a bereavement counselor. Eventually, Marie went to the doctor, being prescribed antidepressants for her debilitating lows. As time went on, she began living again.

Jessica and Marie grew to have an unbreakable bond.

The years went on, and Marie would often sit quietly, staring at a picture of Ed and giving a sad smile. Ed was still the love of her life, even far beyond death, and she never forgot him or allowed anyone else to, either.

Jessica looked at the girls as she clutched her pant leg, "She told me so many stories about him that it almost felt like he was still with us. One of my favorite recollections was on my mother's birthday when he decorated the entire backyard with lights, then put soft music on to resemble a makeshift dance floor, and strung flowers everywhere around our yard.

"He blindfolded my mother, leading her into the yard where I was waiting with a perfectly wrapped gift. He dressed me in a bright pink dress with polka dots, also put my hair up in little barrettes. When my mother unwrapped the silver paper from the box, she found a locket with a picture of the three of us inside. My mother gasped at it, starting to cry.

"I was young and didn't know that the tears were happy ones. I told my dad, 'I don't think Mom likes it, Daddy.' At that, they both laughed, hugging me, explaining that Mommy was indeed pleased. We enjoyed a picnic dinner of egg salad, chips, and cookies. My mother says that was her favorite birthday ever, right to this day. She always recalls fondly that my father was one of the good guys and that she's always felt blessed to have spent whatever time she's had with him. Every year on her birthday, we have egg salad, chips, and cookies to celebrate."

Jessica felt that the loss of her father put a burden on her striving for excellence.

She felt obligated to become the person her father would want and expect.

Ed too had been kind and helpful, always thinking it was his duty to help those around him. He would shovel elderly couples' driveways in the winter, helping the lady next door to carry in her packages as her young children caused chaos at their mother's feet.

His presence left a lasting impression on those he met. Jessica felt an obligation to live up to her father's legacy of doing good, being good, and making a difference in the world. Although she was proud of her father's reputation, she also yearned to escape the confines of the memories of him, as living in a small town and being known as the great Ed's daughter got tiresome.

Jessica said with a sigh, "No matter how much time has passed, I'll always be known as the little girl who lost her father. Even after all these years, I still get sympathetic looks at the local market. It was sometimes exhausting to keep up with the image, and I was ready for a change.

"As you can tell, I had no choice but to turn out great!" Jessica giggled. "My dad was larger than life, and it always felt like the whole town was watching to see if I could turn out just like him. I did everything I knew he would have encouraged me to do had he been alive. I was funny, sarcastic, always kind, almost morphing myself into the stories I heard about him and the expectations of others of who I should be. Don't get me wrong. My father was an absolute legend, but spending my entire childhood living up to a ghost was no easy feat."

"Wow, Jessica, I had no idea that Dave wasn't your biological father. You two are as thick as thieves. When did he come into your life?" Myra questioned.

"I met David when I was eight. Would you believe, I was responsible for introducing my mother to him," she said softly. "I must've been drawn to him at the grocery store on a Saturday evening. As children are often curious, I think I approached him, asking him to lift me.

"To my mother's surprise and embarrassment, she tried to apologize for my forward behavior, but David didn't seem bothered by it. In fact, he was delighted! He lifted me with my mom's permission, and I immediately started playing with his beard, or at least so I'm told.

"My mother told me her face turned beet red, but David was calm and comfortable. Innocently, I introduced myself as Princess Jasmine and started belting out the lyrics to a Disney princess movie, Aladdin! It was 'I can show you the world.'

"Before long, Marie and David were dating, and within two years, they were married! David swears that I was meant to find him that day, and the connection from the beginning was incredible. I felt this astonishing bond with David right from the start.

"I can't quite explain it, but I always felt like I knew David, and he was meant to be in my life in some way. But while I welcomed him into my life, I always feared that he, too, would leave us. Sometimes, I was too frightened to be happy, afraid that David would somehow be taken away as well. I guess that's just the consequence of losing your father at a young age."

Because of the unexpected death of Ed, Jessica soon came to fear being alone.

She became attached to her mother in such an unhealthy way that if her mother was running late from work, Jessica would immediately go into a panic.

Marie had to take Jessica to a therapist who helped manage some of these anxieties, but these symptoms continued for years. Eventually, Jessica outgrew her insecurities but always had a nagging feeling that something terrible would happen if she became too happy.

Over time, Jessica would venture out to sleepovers and become relaxed and secure.

"Although I may not have had a fairytale start to life because of my father's sudden death, l feel fortunate to have had a lot of love surrounding me. Mom had to beg me to go away to college and I'm glad that she did. I was so afraid to leave her that I almost rescinded my acceptance into college. Mom kept pictures of Ed and us throughout our home though, and that brought comfort to me, making me feel safe knowing my past wasn't erased because of grief.

"I was open to talking about him, laughing at stories of him, and loving him like any other kid loves their father. David never tried to erase the memory of my Ed either, but he simply stepped in and became a dad to me just the same. David would attend every art show, dance recital, and softball game. He used to call me 'my girl,' and I lovingly and proudly called him Dad.

"David knew he would never be my biological father, but he didn't care. He was proud to call me his daughter and wasn't concerned about biology. He loved me as his own, wholly and entirely. From riding bikes to camping to my first heartbreak and a first fender bender, David was always there for me, to share a sweet smile, a concerned look, or a sympathetic hug.

"While my mother was stricter, David was the one who gave me the leeway for many mistakes, late curfews, and excessive absences due to cutting school."

Lynnie took Jessica's hand. "Pain brings people together. There are different pain levels, and all of it is relevant. Empathy is what makes us human."

Jessica squeezed Lynnie's hand in return, resting her head on Lynnie's shoulder.

"During the summer of my teenage years, I went to Maplewood sleep-away camp. My favorite part was peering up into the black night, watching the stars beam down. Those were the times I missed my real dad most but thought I felt the glow of his love coming down from the stars, making me feel connected to him. I wondered what life would have been like, how it would've turned out if he'd still been here. And I used to shout 'Dad, where are you?' into the sky."

"Well, it's more than OK to miss your father," Amanda said. "It'd be weird if you didn't."

"I did and do miss him, so much. I occasionally ached for the loss of him in quiet moments, though I'd mostly feel gratitude that David was in every way trying to be a father to me. From the beginning, I felt that my bond with David was an intervention and blessing from Ed.

"No matter the circumstances, when you lose a parent at a young age, there's always a small hole inside. You wonder *what if* and fantasize about who you would have been had your parents lived, knowing that no matter who you meet throughout life, the gaping hole will never be completely filled. There's so much you've missed out on sharing with them.

"But it was just something I had reckoned with, knowing that this was a piece of my life I had to come to peace about. And I had to work really hard to get there, through a lot of pain."

Realizing that she must have sounded indulgent, she looked around, embarrassed. "I know my story is probably stupid to you guys, and you're probably thinking *poor Jessica, she was so loved as a child. What a trauma!* Believe me, I know I was so lucky to have my great support system."

Myra took Jessica's hand.

"Jessica, everyone has a story, and no story is better or worse. It just is. Never apologize for missing your father, and never feel like we judge you because you were loved."

Amanda chimed in, "Absolutely. A loss is a loss, and pain is pain ... Whether losing a parent or not getting to experience a family at all, your loss matters."

Lynnie nodded in agreement and brushed Jessica's hair from her face. "We are in this together, no matter how big or small the issue is, with no judgment."

⸎

JOURNAL

WOW, I'M SURPRISED BY THE PAIN JESSICA ENDURED. SHE CARRIES HERSELF WITH GRACE AND POISE AND I WOULD NEVER HAVE IMAGINED THAT SHE HAS SUFFERED FROM HARDSHIP.

SHE IS THE BEACON OF HOPE AND BEAUTY! I WISH I WERE MORE LIKE HER!

⸎

# Chapter Eight

*Lynnie: Family Fortunes.*

Lynnie looked around the room, not quite sure what to say. The girls knew the troubles between her and her mother. She had made no secret of their tumultuous relationship or the stress it had caused, and right now, she was wishing she hadn't shared quite so much, so soon.

But the truth was that Lynnie frequently complained about it and simply had little patience for her mother's narcissism, although it often left her in tears. Lynnie had grown tired of making excuses for her mother's behavior or trying to keep the image of their family up to par. She no longer needed to portray her life as picture-perfect in the way her mother had trained her to do. Leaving for college had allowed Lynnie to break free from her mother's social etiquette.

"Guys, you already know about my mother. She's always been abusive and unkind to me. Her resentment of my existence is hurtful and I have to say, it's always been the source of much pain. I've never felt loved, and the aching absence of my mother's approval is the source of many of my insecurities. If my hair looked out of place, she would beat me with a brush, and if I didn't finish my cereal in the morning, she would leave it all day on the counter for me to have when I got back home. She called me an *ingrate* and was usually nothing more than cruel.

"Her primary goal in life was to make me proper and perfect. She picked out my clothes every day until the day I left for college. I could never choose anything for myself, from my friends to the food I ate or the clothes I wore."

Lynnie's demeanor looked tormented at the myriad of agonizing memories. Living in the house with Marylou had been torture. The privilege Lynnie had enjoyed, for which so many must have envied her from a distance, was in no way worth the torture she had endured.

"I think it bothers me more that my father allowed it. You'll probably think it's weird that I blame him even more than my mother. He knew. He *saw* it, and still he did nothing.

"Occasionally, he would even squeeze my hand under the table until my mother would notice and scream, 'Ron, we don't want to raise some weak, pathetic girl.' My father would slowly release his hand and not make eye contact with me again for days."

No one would have suspected quite how lonely and beaten down mentally Lynnie was from living under the roof of a mentally ill perfectionist, one who had been narcissistic too.

"My mother loved things and appearances far more than she loved me. Once, on a courageous day, I challenged her on it. I screamed, 'Why do you care so much about my appearance? Can't you see how unhappy I am? Why can't you just love me for who I am?'

"For a brief moment, I'd thought I had gotten through to her. The room fell silent just momentarily, and my mother started to laugh uncontrollably. 'Oh, darling, you are so naive,' she sneered. 'Appearance is everything, and happiness is only for the poor slobs who believe in it.'

"Her voice was even and controlled, but her eyes were wild. She laughed, walking toward me and whispered, 'Ungrateful bitch! Your happiness and your life have cost me my sanity.'

"So, I now was supposed to believe that I was responsible for whatever unhappiness and ill health she had in her pathetic life. And when you're young, you just take it all on, don't you, believing every word of it. Anyway, she walked off and slammed the door behind her. The sound of her voice was frightening, but even worse, the look in her eyes made me know she wasn't well. Somehow, somewhere, something had become broken inside my mother—just like she said, really—and I was never quite sure what that was or how it had happened, although of course, it was what she was blaming me for. Her anger boiled into hatred.

"I spent lots of futile time wondering why she was angry at me. What was so awful and detestable about me that it sent my mother into a perpetual state of rage and blame?"

Lynnie desperately longed for the love of her mother and never received it.

And she was resentful toward and disappointed in her father.

"There was always an imaginary wall between my mother and father, which I couldn't quite put my finger on. As a child, it was confusing, but as I got older, I learned to accept how things were, understanding that this was unhealthy. I knew very little about my mother."

When Lynnie was fourteen, curiosity got the best of her.

She snooped around her mother's bedroom.

"If I could get a glimpse into her life, perhaps I would understand her and even try to empathize with her more. I uncovered a box hidden in her closet under her winter coats.

"From what I gathered; my mom had lived a very different life before she met my father. I knew her full name was Marylou Metton, and that she'd come from a small town in the Midwest. When she was young, I knew she'd been very much in love with a farmer who'd grown up down the road. They'd even planned to marry. I once overheard her say his name, which was Jim, but when I entered the room, she stopped talking to whomever she was talking to on the telephone.

"I also know that my father was a third generational banker and had met my mother when her father, Harry, was going into foreclosure on the farm. Harry would have stood to lose everything had it not been for my father's family. From what I gather, there was some kind of an agreement.

"In exchange for my mother's hand in marriage, my father's family would provide economic safety for the farm. Her father, my grandfather, of course chose the farm.

"I never met my grandfather, Harry. When I'd ask my mother about her family, she would just say something about them being dead to her. I knew not to ask many questions but always suspected this arranged marriage had something to do with it. I believe my grandfather loved his daughter and wanted a better life for her than Jim, the farmer down the road, could've provided.

"So, from being used as a pawn for financial security, my mother, a once vibrant woman, became dead inside. Oh, and while I was rummaging in her closet, guess what else I found?

"There was another box with a pink bow on the outside. Inside it was a photo album filled with pictures from her childhood. My mother, even now, is beautiful, and as a young woman, she had a bright smile and energy so intense that you immediately felt happy staring at the picture.

"My father didn't want this arranged marriage any more than my mother did. His father had convinced him it would be good for business to marry a local farmer's daughter; it would make the family fortune seem even more genuine, and drum up prospective regular customers.

"It would 'make the family seem more relatable to the common folk.' That was how he put it. I sometimes wonder who my mother would have been had she followed her heart and married Jim. I was sure she would have been happier, and perhaps her smile would have been kinder. Sometimes, I even wondered ... If she'd managed to wed the man of her dreams and had lived a more joyful life, would she have been a better mother to me? I'm sure the answer is yes."

After discovering Marylou's past, it astonished Lynnie how all the resemblance of a meager country beginning was now gone. Marylou showed no signs of ever being a farmer's daughter.

"Mother became a cold, bitter woman when she left the farm. After she had a few drinks one night, and I could tell she was in a good mood, I dared to ask her about her childhood. She revealed it had been magical. For a moment, I saw happiness in her eyes as she spoke about the fields of grass she would frolic in and the moonlit sky she would spend hours looking up at.

"When I pressed her for more details, she immediately shut down. Her expression changed from warm to cold, and she had to say something mean about how I was dressed—straight back to her old self, in other words—insisting that I changed into something more appealing. That was the first and last time she mentioned her childhood to me, and I never bothered asking again.

"The arranged marriage made both of them miserable, neither one in love with the other. I never could understand why they never divorced after the passing of their parents! Can you believe that? It doesn't make sense at all because all they'd ever done was tolerate each other.

"They could have just moved on with their lives, and perhaps my mother could have found her lovely Jim again and had a second try at an amazing love. There was no passion in their marriage, no love, no desire, no way of hiding the fact that neither wanted to be in this situation.

"My parents obeyed their families' deals but were completely and utterly miserable in the meantime, the depth of misery that no amount of money or recognition would ever be worth.

"From the very start, I knew I was as unwanted as their marriage, just a reminder of the never-ending situation they had found themselves in. My mother's only way to deal with me was to control me and simultaneously make sure I had the best of everything, perhaps to give me the life she never had and make this all worthwhile. In any event, I assure you, this sad beginning for my folks didn't make for a very happy childhood for me."

Lynnie kept her head down to keep the girls from seeing the tears streaming down her cheeks.

She looked out the window, seeing the nighttime turning slowly into day, not really knowing what to say to the others.

The sun's warmth in February eased the chill from the old windows, and the birds chirped, and proof of another day began, despite all that had transpired the night before.

By the time the girls finished talking, the sun had risen, and they were understandably emotionally and physically exhausted yet no one was even yawning, all held captive and spellbound by all the discussion and revelation. There was nothing to say to one another, and much more to discuss. They had uncovered their unbound souls while releasing their trauma.

Despite the emotional running, they learned you never really forget the past.

Jessica said it best, "In a way, we all carry a part of it within us. It is the silent voice that pushes us to be better, as well as the tortuous echo that holds us back. Without releasing the pain, we could never really be free; perhaps that is how we evolve. Our tribulations remind us how far we have come and how things can go wrong if we are not careful of our decisions."

Perhaps that was why they became such fast friends, or maybe subconsciously, they all longed to belong somewhere that was their own. Reality, fear, and perseverance showed them that they must try, forge forward to the next day, and stand up every time life knocked them down.

They clung to the wounds of the past, wounds that may never be truly healed, and the aftereffects of what they had been through would forever be a piece of them.

Deep scars behind joyful eyes and sweet smiles could never be really erased. Those experiences were the ones that shaped decisions later, despite best efforts.

Myra said quietly, "The reality is that no matter where we go, our past finds a way to be there, constantly reminding us of the evil in the world, from addiction, neglect, and the devastation of loneliness. The only thing we cannot run from is the past."

# Chapter Nine

*Lynnie: South Oaks Nursing Home.*

Lynnie puts down the journal as her wrinkled hands tremble, a pit in her stomach making her hesitate to continue reading. She rubs her chin, thinking how oddly familiar these stories seem.

How can all these young girls have had such similar tales to tell, too?

Not similar in content but all so brutal, emotionally devastating.

Helen appears again with soup, quietly entering, setting it on the small table by Lynnie's chair.

"Reading anything good, baby?" she asks as she puts down the steaming hot bowl beside the pile of journals. "Look at all those journals! You will be here for days, reading. Don't forget to eat now, you hear me? I know what you're like when you get immersed in a good story."

Lynnie takes a sip of soup, opening the book again, beginning to read ...

Whether the contents will constitute 'a good story' remains to be seen.

Journal

I know this is a strange way to describe things but somehow, it feels as if last night was the most authentic night of my life. By 'authentic' I mean we bared our real selves to one another, holding nothing back. At least I believe so.

Vulnerability is hard, but hasn't accepting the truth always been the best way to learn?

Until now, we never realized the incredible gift of friendship we had gained through pain.

Although each of us had cause for fear that our lives were now becoming exposed, we knew this kinship was needed if we were to heal. The ironic part of the evening was that all of us had been attempting to run from our past, careful to create a new life at college and swearing never to look back. But despite all of our best efforts, it's turned out to be just the way Myra described

THINGS AFTER ALL: THAT WE CAN RUN FROM EVERYTHING BUT OUR PAST HISTORIES.

THERE WAS NO POINT IN RUNNING AT ALL.

THE PAIN AND HURT WE'VE ENDURED IN OUR PAST ARE NO LONGER SECRETS WE KEEP. WE HAVE EXPOSED OUR TRUTHS IN A WAY THAT FEELS RIGHT, THOUGH WE WERE PETRIFIED OF THE VULNERABILITY IT ENTAILED.

TODAY, AS I WALKED BACK TO MY DORM ROOM, I HAD AN ACUTE SENSE THAT THE WORLD AROUND ME HAD CHANGED. THE BIRDS WERE CHIRPING LOUDER, THE WIND SEEMED MORE ROBUST, AND THE AIR CRISPER. I GOT BACK TO MY ROOM AND DECIDED ON A HOT SHOWER. 'I NEED TO WASH THIS EVENING AWAY,' I THOUGHT. THE HOT WATER DRIPPED DOWN MY BODY, RELEASING THE TENSION OF THE EVENING.

THE HURT AND ANGUISH OF ALL OF US WAS A LOT TO PROCESS. BEFORE I KNEW IT, TEARS STARTED TO FLOW.

THOSE TEARS BECAME SOBS, AND I FOUND MYSELF CRYING YEARS OF ANGER, RAGE, DISAPPOINTMENT, AND FEAR. I CRIED FOR MYSELF, FOR MY FRIENDS, FOR ALL THE CRUELTY IN THE WORLD. WHEN I WAS DONE, IT LEFT ME FEELING EMPTY INSIDE, PHYSICALLY TIRED AND MENTALLY

EXHAUSTED FROM THE DAY. I DRIED MY BODY OFF, APPLIED LOTION THAT SMELLED OF FRESH LAVENDER, AND WAS READY TO SLEEP SOUNDLY. I WAS SURE TO PUT ON MY FAVORITE PAJAMAS, AND AS I SNUGGLED INTO BED, FELT A GREAT SENSE OF RELIEF.

I AWOKE TWELVE HOURS LATER AND STARED AT THE BEDSIDE CLOCK, THEN STARED AGAIN, RUBBING AT MY EYES THAT DIDN'T BELIEVE WHAT THEY WERE WITNESSING! I COULDN'T BELIEVE THE TIME! THERE HAD TO BE SOME MISTAKE, PERHAPS THAT MY CLOCK HAD MALFUNCTIONED IN THE NIGHT. NO WAY—NO WAY ON THIS EARTH—COULD I HAVE SLEPT TWELVE HOURS STRAIGHT AND MISSED MY DEAFENING ALARM.

BUT THE REALITY WAS THAT I HAD.

I HAD MISSED MY MORNING CLASSES AND WOULD HAVE A LOT OF UNEASY EXPLAINING TO DO. BUT IT DIDN'T EVEN SEEM TO MATTER. NOTHING WAS A WEIGHT ON ME NOW, NO MORE BURDENS; I FELT RENEWED.

UNLOADING THIS BURDEN MADE TIME IN DELAWARE MORE RELAXED.

## JOURNAL

I KNOW I HAVEN'T WRITTEN IN A BIT. LIFE HERE AT COLLEGE IS HECTIC, AND GRADUATION IS QUICKLY APPROACHING. I'M WORRIED ABOUT WHAT LIFE AFTER COLLEGE WILL BE LIKE, BUT ONE THING I KNOW FOR SURE, IS THAT I DON'T WANT TO LIVE WITHOUT THESE AMAZING WOMEN I CONSIDER SISTERS.

# Chapter Ten



*Life After Graduation, Main Street, Delaware.*

By the time it was graduation, the women were ready to start their careers and celebrate all turning twenty-one together. Their birthdays had always been special because they spanned within six weeks of each other. They celebrated every year, even when they'd left college and ventured out into the wider world and got jobs. Nothing would stop their frequent reunions.

The women had, unsurprisingly, chosen to live in apartments not too far from one another; in fact at first, they had all lived together as roommates in small but more affordable quarters. As the years had passed and their salaries increased, they were able to venture out independently to bigger apartments, though even then, they were always walking distance from one another.

Now, the girls gathered at Lynnie's for their weekly taco night and catch-up, looking forward to margaritas and gossip; this time, they were even going to enjoy a sumptuous rich chocolate cake that Jessica had made in celebration of them all turning twenty-one.

Myra, who had doubled up on her law classes and graduated early, was focused on her career. She worked long hours but always made time to join in weekly for a drink and a taco.

After a couple of cocktails, Lynnie took out her journal to read a little back to the girls, something she planned to do each time they got together like this.

On this occasion, the part she had marked to read was about when they had first met back in college, the time when she'd joined the swim team.

"Lynnie, wow! You've kept your journal all this time?" Myra asked. "And you wrote it right the way through college?"

"Yes, I've documented our friendship from the start," said Lynnie proudly. "And not only did I write it at the time, but I still do now! I haven't missed a day. It's amazing to be able to look back and when things get a bit faint and fuzzy in my mind, all I have to do is rummage out my journals and it all comes back as if it were only yesterday. It'll be incredible when I'm old ... Imagine that, girls, looking back at every single day since we all met the first time."

"This is wild," Amanda mused. "You have literally documented our entire friendship."

"It is both weird and sweet," laughed Myra. "Kind of nerdy!"

Everyone laughed.

"Nerdy, yeah," agreed Amanda. "Only Lynnie would do such a thing."

Lynnie wasn't even sure what that was supposed to mean, and for the briefest of moments, she almost forgot that they were her best friends and not attacking her. For a fleeting second, the old feelings of self-doubt and insecurity came flooding back. Her skin bristled, cheeks flushing red.

"I don't know. I figured we have a lot of history, and one day, we can reminisce when we're all in a nursing home together," Lynnie said, trying not to sound defensive. Then she relaxed.

These girls would never say anything to deliberately hurt her.

"I'll drink to that," Jessica said cheerfully.

The night ended, and as Lynnie crawled into bed, she thought of her friends and how much they meant. Together, they were navigating through adulthood and finding their way through life. Finally, it seemed they had also found something they had longed for, security. There was no price she could put on that. No value; to feel secure was beyond all treasure imaginable.

Lynnie would joke about their new-found confidence, saying, "We're all just securely insecure. Aren't we?"

*Securely insecure* soon became their mantra, something they wore as a badge of honor. Those two simple words carried a deep meaning, though they meant something a little different to each. But overall, it meant accepting the fact they had insecurities, learning to anchor themselves on solid ground regardless, having fought their way through and emerged as better—stronger—women on the other side. It was undoubtedly a feat of achievement; most people were insecure at least a little bit, but theirs came from trauma, something they hadn't had the ability to control.

Like any friendship, theirs had its ups and downs, and they worked together to help navigate those issues, too, nothing being insurmountable. They were friends and family by choice, and their organic family could never be more important than their chosen one.

Perhaps because they had all come from a place of desperately seeking connections, the resultant bonds were powerful, and loyalty to each other was unshakable.

Having a frantic and unreliable childhood also made it impossible to maintain solid relationships with their organic families, although deep down, they each longed for the traditional family structures that society had always told them was 'normal'. Life had denied them the luxury of a stable upbringing but, in the end, it had gifted them something even worthier in the form of lifelong close friendships, ones that ran deep within the soul. Far thicker than blood, more profound than family lineage, and more forgiving than any namesake.

This type of friendship was safe, secure, and would always be hard to sway.

Like all relationships, the women had plenty of screaming matches through the years; no one would pretend it had always been plain sailing. But wasn't that also a testimony to how secure their friendships had grown, that they were able to be brutally honest and open with one another, to cause offense and to form rifts, only to find themselves reunited before too long?

They could barely stand to be separated for a couple of days, even after some blazing fights!

Once, Myra had been so angry at Amanda for leaving clumps of hair in the drain, she had hurled a plate at her head, lucky that it didn't hit or it could have sliced her friend's scalp off!

Another time, Lynnie quarreled fiercely with Jessica over a misunderstanding of an unpaid bill, which turned out to be an error by the electric company. Both girls had been mortified, nearly throwing away their friendship over something so small and stupid. But it was nothing that a huge hug could not resolve, and this was the way in which they all sorted their differences.

Even in the midst of the most appalling arguments, Lynnie would marvel at how secure the women made her feel; it certainly was something special to know that despite any harsh words exchanged, there would be no residual animosity, nothing they could not overcome together. They each felt secure enough in their friendships to say whatever was on their minds.

This was good because one thing was a constant source of contention between the four. One of the biggest obstacles had always been with blossoming romantic relationships.

Because of their protective natures, at least one of the women would find fault in anyone else who dared to try and enter their lives. It was a strange dichotomy because they were independent, strong women, yet their opinions of each other's love lives were always a major issue.

In particular, when Lynnie met Luke, it was Amanda who took great exception to the relationship. It puzzled both Myra and Jessica.

Luke was a generous, fun man who adored Lynnie, so what was there to dislike?

Frustratingly for Lynnie, Amanda would never say exactly what it was about Luke that bothered her, so the others all speculated that it was jealousy.

"Amanda, there's a Luke for you out there somewhere too," quipped Myra, knowing it would rub up her friend the wrong way, certain to only annoy her. Sure enough, it worked.

"I wouldn't date anyone like Luke if we were the last two people on the planet!" she retorted.

"And if you carry on in such a foul mood, you *will* be the only woman on the planet because everyone else will get the hell out, just to be away from you," Myra joked back.

Amanda's face had turned as dark as a thundercloud, glowering. But only ten minutes later, they were giggling about it, Amanda laughing louder than anyone. Still, it was odd how she loathed Luke. It would continue to be perplexing for everyone and irritating for poor Lynnie.

Lynnie had met Luke at the local market. It was a day on which she had forgotten her wallet, having run out to grab avocados for a recipe. Her purse was still languishing on the kitchen counter. Embarrassed, Lynnie explained her error to the cashier.

"Please let me just put everything back where I picked it up," she requested, embarrassed.

But there Luke was, patiently waiting behind her.

"Hey, I got you," he casually said, offering over his money and pushing away Lynnie's hand as she tried to prevent him from paying. "The lady has to have her salad."

"Oh no, no, I'm so embarrassed!" she'd cried. "Please, you mustn't do that."

But the cashier had taken the dollar bills and produced a receipt for him.

"I already did do it, ma'am," he said, feigning a bow as if he revered her.

"Then I will have to pay you back. No, not *have to*. I want to, need to. I ran out to grab avocados for my recipe and stupidly forgot to grab my wallet. How dumb is that? I was so excited to try this new vegan dish ... I'd forget my own head if it wasn't attached to my shoulders," Lynnie said, her face burning hot and bright.

"Ahh, a vegan?" Luke inquired.

Flushed, she said, "Well, not exactly. I wouldn't say I'm a vegan, more like an aspiring one."

"Well, kudos to you for trying," Luke said admiringly. "I have great respect for that."

"Wow, well, thank you for the avocados. You saved me from veering off my diet plan."

And that was that.

The two were immediately attracted to one another, and before long, they were spending nearly all of their time together. Luke would come around often, bringing treats from the restaurant at which he worked as a pastry chef.

The cream-filled pastries were French inspired and were rightfully called artwork.

Luke had trained in France and would travel there often at the request of the famous bakery La' Pate. There, he would learn the newest techniques, indulge in the finest food, and enjoy the scenery of the beautiful landscape in the South of France.

After a couple of months of dating, Luke again had to travel overseas, but this time to Paris.

"Lynnie, come with me," he said one day as he chopped scallions in her kitchen.

"Go where?"

"Come to Paris with me to attend my conference. Of course, I'll be working a lot but I'll have free time in the evenings. While I'm working, you can explore the city and enjoy the sights."

It sounded like a dream come true to Lynnie.

"I will introduce you to the finest food, wine, and of course, the best desserts the country offers," he added. "In fact, I will endeavor to make them for you myself."

"I've never traveled abroad," said Lynnie automatically, though it felt like another fairly embarrassing revelation. What woman her age had never left the United States?

Lynnie had just gotten a passport because the girls were planning a trip to Mexico next spring.

Luke smiled as if he had a plan in mind. "It's always good to start something new," he suggested. "Just like we were saying when you told me about being an aspiring vegan."

"Hmm," Lynnie said, pondering on his words and smiling broadly. "Just let me think about it, will you? Just give me a day or two to see if I can take time off work."

Because of her insecurities, a tiny part of her was questioning his possible motives, resulting in Lynnie saying she needed to consider it. Time out of work would not be a problem, but she had to run this suggestion by her friends to see if it seemed to be a good idea or something nefarious.

Luke admitted to being hurt. "Fine. I know how careful you are with your decisions. Take all the time you need but just bear in mind that if you're coming, I need to buy you a flight and if we wait too long, we won't be able to sit together."

Lynnie made a joke to hide the real reason for delaying. "You are a big boy now, Luke. I'm sure you're capable of traveling alone."

"That's mean," he said, grinning at the quip.

Then Lynnie replied, "Just let me discuss it with the girls tonight. It won't be long."

Luke rolled his eyes. "The girls, the girls, the girls ... You do know you are a grown woman, correct, Lynnie? You are allowed to make decisions all by yourself."

That was a fair comment, considering. Now, they were even.

JOURNAL

THE GIRLS CAME OVER FOR DINNER TO CELEBRATE OUR BIRTHDAYS TONIGHT. JESSICA MAKES THE MOST AMAZING CHOCOLATE CAKE AND FINALLY, WE ARE OFFICIALLY LEGAL TO DRINK! EVEN THOUGH WE'VE BEEN DRINKING FOR AGES ALREADY...

ANYWAY, I TOLD THEM ALL ABOUT LUKE'S INVITATION TO PARIS. MYRA IMMEDIATELY STARTED LOOKING FOR A SUITCASE, MAKING ME PROMISE I WOULD BRING HOME SOUVENIRS. AND JESSICA JUST KEPT HUGGING ME AND SMILING, REMINDING ME HOW PERFECT LUKE WAS. 'IF YOU DON'T WANT HIM, FEEL FREE TO LEAVE HIM FOR ME,' SHE SAID!

ON THE OTHER HAND, AMANDA SAT QUIETLY, STARING AT HER PHONE. IT WAS KIND OF PREDICTABLE BECAUSE EVERYONE KNOWS SHE HAS THIS THING AGAINST LUKE.

I COULD TELL AMANDA WAS FUMING. SHE'S NEVER MADE ANY SECRET OF HOW SHE DOESN'T LIKE LUKE BUT I REALLY CAN'T FATHOM WHY, OTHER THAN SHE MUST BE CRAZY. ONE TIME, SHE ACCUSED LUKE OF BEING DOMINANT AND said he was trying to drive a wedge between us. And what's weird is, she was basing this on just one tiny conversation she heard between me and him, when he suggested I change my sweater for one that wasn't as tight! And even that was only after I'd asked him what he thought of it.

'Controlling, just like your mother!' she said, and it was uncalled for. What did she know about him—or about my mom for that matter? Sure, I'd spoken about her in not-so-glowing terms but it was nowhere near enough to draw a comparison like that. And Luke is nothing like my mother, not in any way, shape, or form!

I found it upsetting but said nothing because I just knew there was something else going on for her. She's not a nasty person.

Even so, I was so angry I didn't speak to her for three days. He was right after all, the sweater made me look frumpy, and he was just being honest. I know Jessica intervened and insisted that Amanda call me and make up. I thought it was all over until now.

BUT THEN AGAIN, I HAVE TO REMEMBER I DID ALSO ASK AMANDA FOR HER OPINION ON LUKE'S INVITATION AND I WASN'T EVEN SURE ABOUT IT MYSELF, WAS I?

---

The following day, the friends gathered at the park to burn off some of the cake and booze they had consumed the night before.

It was a breezy day, but the exercise and the wind in their hair felt invigorating.

"Don't you think Luke's a bit too much?" Amanda suggested, again on her *get rid of Luke* campaign which she never hesitated to engage in whenever we had a second together.

Lynnie was surprised. "I don't get what you mean. You hardly even see the guy."

"He's bossy and controlling, Lynnie. C'mon guys, I can't be the only one to notice this."

Jessica spoke up. "I think he's romantic," Jessica said. "He just likes to look out for her."

"By telling her that her clothes look frumpy ... that's protective, is it? Very considerate...not." Amanda's eyebrows were raised.

It was clear she couldn't believe that anyone would want to defend that awful man.

Lynnie quickly became defensive. "Well, anyway, whatever *you* think of him, Amanda, Luke wants us to get married. So, now you've got more to protest against than a trip away."

Myra interrupted, "Lynnie, for goodness' sake, slow down. Do you *want* to get married?"

"I told Luke I needed time to establish myself. He's older than me, and better equipped to settle down. It honestly hadn't crossed my mind that it might happen sometime soon, with him or anyone else. But you know Luke; he is so spontaneous. I mean it's great and all, but I'd love the opportunity to not always be the one who's planned and rational. I'm dazzled by his spontaneity, but it's not fun always being the responsible one. The boring one in other words!"

Suddenly, Lynnie felt embarrassed. She didn't want the girls to get the wrong idea about Luke or to think she was having second thoughts about the relationship itself.

"Luke's great, though, I just need to woman up."

"You don't need a man in order to woman up, Lynnie," Myra said.

"It's still romantic. It reminds me of my parents' love story," said Jessica.

Lynnie felt Amanda glaring at her with a slight smirk. "When it all goes wrong, I'll try not to say I told you so."

---

## JOURNAL

I LEFT FOR PARIS TWO DAYS AFTER BEING INVITED TO GO. I'M JUST NEVER SPONTANEOUS LIKE THIS AND STILL FEEL A BIT HESITANT BUT I'M EXCITED FOR THE ADVENTURE. THIS IS GOING TO BE MAGICAL.

## SOMETIMES, I CAN'T EVEN BELIEVE THIS IS MY LIFE!

---

Two weeks later, Lynnie returned home. It had all gone terribly wrong. She immediately called the girls. "Please could we all get together at my place? There's something I need your opinions on." They got there before Lynnie, waiting anxiously to hear about her trip.

She saw their smiles fade as they noticed her red-rimmed eyes. She had been crying.

"Oh honey, what happened?" Jessica asked.

"Luke showed his true colors. After a night of drinking, he accused me of flirting with the waiter. I admit I'd had a couple of glasses of Champagne and was giggly, but I wasn't flirting.

"Anyway, he was adamant—rude and obstinate—and he said I'd embarrassed him. He called me a slut, shouting at me. He even pushed me and at one point, had hold of my wrist. I mean really aggressively. Look."

She pulled up the sleeve of her sweater, revealing a dark purple and green bruise.

Amanda's head was in her hands. She looked incredulous, only whispering, "God almighty."

Lynnie could see Myra getting quickly agitated.

"What the fuck, Lynnie! What did you do?"

"He left right after and didn't come back the next day. He, of course, apologized, promising it would never happen again. And I know, I know ... All abusers do that. But there was no choice but to forgive him because we were leaving the next day, and I just wanted to get home.

"Later, at the airport, I looked at Luke and said, 'It's over. I'm done. Do not ever call me again.' I hailed a cab and came straight here."

Lynnie's heart was broken, and she was devastated, questioning her judgment. *How did I not see this coming with all his love bombing?* she wondered. *It was all a part of his control. And Amanda warned me over and over. I was too stubborn to listen.*

She exhaled deeply, exasperated by her own stupidity.

*At least I have the girls. They've been great all the time, and still are. Look at them, all and huddled around me, reminding me they're by my side through this breakup,* thought Lynnie.

Jessica was the most sympathetic. "Honey, we learn, we grow, we move on," she said.

She always had a way of wiping the tears, filling the void, encouraging.

Her often quirky quotes of 'Just hang in there' and 'Breathe and believe' made everyone cringe but in the most delightful way. During this time, as in so many other challenging times, Jessica was there. She just knew how to give the women hope.

Myra and Jessica handled despair differently.

Myra was more of a 'one less piece of garbage for you to dispose of' attitude, but still, in her way, she was there for Lynnie.

Jessica and Myra were supportive.

Amanda, on the other hand, grew very quickly cold and dismissive, distancing herself from this whole mess-up. It was hardly surprising since even now, it was clear she was waiting for Lynnie to say, 'If only I'd listened to you. I'm really sorry'.

At one pity party Lynnie was having, Amanda glared, not saying a word.

Lynnie noticed her lack of empathy, eventually screaming, "Do you have something to say, Amanda? Just say it! *I told you so!* Say it, say it, damn it! Your ignorance of me is disgusting! And this is all because you just have to be right all the time, isn't it?"

Lynnie was on the edge of tears. She needed all of her friends' support, and when there was one missing, it was just too painful. She craved Amanda right now.

Amanda calmly walked over to Lynnie and gave an insincere hug, embracing Lynnie a bit too tightly, saying, "All right. I'm sorry, honey, I am, but I did tell you so."

JOURNAL

FUCKING AMANDA! SHE'S ALWAYS SO JEALOUS AND NASTY!
IT'S REALLY PETTY HOW SHE BEHAVED TODAY.

I'M HURTING ENOUGH AND DON'T NEED TO FEEL ANY MORE
FOOLISH THAN I ALREADY DO!

IF SHE WAS EVER IN A BAD SITUATION, WHAT WOULD I DO?
I'D SUPPORT HER, NOT MAKE HER FEEL LIKE SHIT. WHAT
IS WRONG WITH HER? I'M GLAD THAT MYRA AND JESSICA
HAVE MY BACK THOUGH.

I NEVER WANT TO SEE LUKE AGAIN AND CAN'T BELIEVE HE
TREATED ME LIKE THIS. WHY DOES EVERYONE I CARE ABOUT
TREAT ME LIKE SHIT?

AND MORE TO THE POINT, WHY DO I KEEP ON LETTING
THEM?

# PART 2

# CHAPTER ELEVEN

*Myra: A Mother's Love.*

Myra grew up like many women, with the need to please. She wanted to be liked, seeking constant approval from those around her, and quite often at her own expense.

No one could help noticing she was always the first to step up and help when anyone needed a ride, money, or a listening ear. It seemed to make her feel worthy when she could help someone practically, always wanting to be the one to give aid. She was diligent as a friend.

Blessed with an outstanding intellect and work ethic, it was no surprise that Myra became the top lawyer at her prestigious law firm, taking on the most challenging cases and willingly taking on the most difficult caseload of the firm. She would work all hours of the night, barely having time to go home, shower and change before heading back to the office or to court.

Private by nature, she was also extremely cautious not to allow people to cross her boundaries of autonomy. Although society had come a long way, corporate work still had its hang-ups.

Most people would view Myra as a tough woman with a rugged exterior and a no-nonsense attitude, and she was all of these things; while she kept to herself, she was never shy about talking back to her superiors when necessary. No one would dare treat Myra as a doormat or fail to seek her point of view because if they did, there'd be hell to pay.

She was the firm's token bitch, and her sexuality had nothing to do with the unfair label. Myra said what she meant, meant what she said, and made no apologies for voicing any of these opinions, even if they were to prove unpopular, as they mostly were.

Work consumed Myra, and Myra thrived on winning cases, kicking ass, and taking names.

For Myra, the more challenging the case, the more rewarding the verdict.

She was well known for taking a special interest in sexual abuse cases, deliberately requesting the harshest sentence under the specific state's law. The public loved her tenacity, forever grateful and indebted when she would put the world's worst humans away for eternity. Or at least when she again attempted to. And on the rare occasions on which a judge meted out a lesser punishment than the maximum prison term, she was a loud voice of protest, never quieting.

A twenty-three-year-old woman named Melissa, one of her clients, had been brutally attacked and raped while running in the park. When interviewing Melissa, Myra had to resist showing the rage living inside her as she listened to the victim's statement.

Melissa had simply been an innocent young woman out for a run in tight black spandex and a pink short-sleeved shirt, with a light beige gloss protecting her lips during the summer sun.

Myra already knew how the defense would play the scenario.

Women everywhere would be ruthlessly scrutinized in such an indecent, callous way, asking them about the time of day they exercised, what they had worn, how much of their body their attire revealed, and the choice of location. In short, the defense would assert that the victims had been careless and thoughtless, donning clothing guaranteed to incite any male's urges.

More than that, they would state, their defendant, the alleged perpetrator—of course, always innocent until proven guilty beyond all reasonable doubt—was powerless to fight because of his poor mental health which had never been helped!

Then there'd be his appalling background of neglect or abuse from which he'd been unable to break free, usually due to a lack of support and resources. Time and again, cases went like this.

Now, in Melissa's case too, the defense team tried their utmost to victimize the victim, making all the above a factor in the case. During the trial, Myra went out on an act of vengeance, delivering a moving closing statement that even had the judge emotional.

"Ladies and gentlemen of the court, Ms. Melissa Knipp should be free to take her afternoon run without fearing any form of assault. The defendant, Mr. Keen, has altered the victim's life forever by taking away the security and enjoyment of everyday activities.

"In his grievous acts of brutalization, Mr. Keen has rendered Miss Knipp a young woman who now mostly keeps to her home for fear of such brutality. She is afraid to walk outside of her own front door. The defendant is guilty of inflicting this life of misery upon her via his acts of callous rape and assault. On April 22nd at 1:30 p.m., Melissa Knipp put on her running attire, laced up her sneakers, filled her water bottles, and went out for a run in the warm air, an activity many of us do without thinking we may never be the same again afterwards. This was a beautiful day, the sun was shining, and the flowers were beginning to bloom. Little did my client know that this day would forever alter her life. From that day forward, she would be permanently changed.

"Whereas Melissa Knipp set out with the sole intention of getting exercise and breathing in the fresh air, Mr. Keen went out that day with the purposeful intent to harm a woman.

"He brutally held down Miss Knipp, forcing himself inside her without consent, making her fear for her life. He showed no mercy or remorse as he grabbed the victim from behind, dragged her into the woods, and held her down, beating her to keep her submissive and quiet.

"He felt no concern, not even as he put a sharp hunting knife to her throat to quiet the terrified screams of my client. He didn't care about violating the victim's mind, body, or soul as he raped her in the woods and left her bloodied body there, only frightened off by a passing car.

"Had a further passerby not heard the moans of the victim in agony, she would have been left there for God knows how much longer. A run, I say to you. My client went on a run on a glorious spring day, only to forever be traumatized by the defendant.

"He hunted the victim, attacked her, and then left her for dead like an animal. No concern. No remorse. A despicable specimen of a human took something that my client can never replace.

"At night, she replays the day repeatedly, the fear, the terror, and the assault. Every day, she is terrified. My client lives with the unimaginable. Every. Single. Day. Every. Single. Night.

"I put it to you that my client or indeed any woman should be able to run, walk, dance or stand outside any time of the day without fearing being raped or otherwise attacked. Yet the defense dares to suggest that Miss Knipp brought all this upon herself, and they will tell you how she made, in their words, 'a series of unwise choices'. How despicable, and how unconscionable to even discuss what running clothes the defendant wore, how she wore her hair that day, or the time of day the victim was running—which, may I remind you again, was not long past midday!

"Let me ask you, ladies and gentlemen of the jury, to take one moment and imagine if your mother, sister, daughter, or a dear friend went innocently for a run and was victimized in the most horrid form, would you ever ask what time she went for a run or what she had been wearing? Only a weak, desperate individual would question those things. Perhaps a guilty person will try anything to get off by victimizing his victim. Disgraceful! Just disgraceful."

At that point, Myra noticed she had been shouting and showing more emotion than intended, the passion in her voice borderline inappropriately intimidating.

The courthouse was quiet. All eyes stared straight ahead. Some women wiped their tears, while most men looked down in embarrassment. Myra was so enraged that she felt ill.

Victim shaming was the lowest form of manipulation in Myra's mind.

Yet it seemed to be news to some factions of society, the media and courts, as well as criminal defense teams, having historically and systematically victim-shamed sexually assaulted women.

Myra would see red when this would happen, lashing out at the prosecution.

Her interviews with local news channels were brief whenever she found herself being questioned about a woman's outfit or the time of her assault, or whether she had been drinking.

She would look straight at the camera and ask coldly, "I trust you are not blaming the victim, are you? Would you be asking these questions in any other crime other than a sexual assault?"

She would keep the gaze of her interviewer, delivering a steely, resolute glare and leaving an uncomfortable, embarrassed silence. Then she would stand up and say, "I think I have had enough. I absolutely will not participate in this misogyny. You should be ashamed." She would walk off with an air of confidence and defiance, calling out the interviewer any chance she got.

During the interrogation, Myra would outwardly stay composed, but the bottled-up rage would bubble up until she needed to take a breath to compose herself. It felt as if every case associated with sexual assault brought her back to her childhood and the cold, scary nights when men would enter her room, climb onto her petite body, spread her legs, and have their way with her.

The sensation of pain ravishing her body, the smell of bourbon on the stranger's breath, and the pounding of his fat groin against her slight belly would overwhelm her every emotion.

As much as she tried forgetting, she could still see the look on their faces when they finished violating her. It was half sorrowful, half frightening.

They would leave just as quickly as they came in, leaving her alone in a dirty bed and scared in a stranger's house, confused about what it all meant.

Myra worked hard to repair her childhood's residual damage, but she could never be truly healed. The anguish and anxiety were something she lived with every day, numbing her pain with alcohol and excessive over-the-counter medication. She never wanted to be like her mother, but now, she had a better understanding and compassion toward her as an adult.

Sometimes at night, she would be the scared little girl in bed, screaming in terror.

Only with a couple of shots of whisky and some Xanax would her nerves calm so she could drift off to an unsettling sleep again. As time passed, she became more reliant on the soothing numbness and started drinking more often. Like most drinkers, she had convinced herself she could quit at any point and often did stop drinking for months, also staying focused on her meticulous and scheduled lifestyle; it helped her feel as if she were still in control.

Clutter and chaos only frayed her nerves more, so she was careful to wake up early and organize her day efficiently. Myra was diligent in her wardrobe, wearing black, gray, or navy-blue power suits and smart black shoes which bore a small heel, professional.

She managed her wardrobe like much of life, orderly and neatly, with a purpose.

She had no time for fashionable outfits and for figuring out matching patterns and colors, so she wore a uniform to protect her time and brainpower from such frivolous decision-making.

Although she had alluded to being a lesbian, Myra certainly didn't talk about it, her sexuality a bit of a mystery to her friends. She had never mentioned a relationship to anyone, also never admitting to one when questioned. However, a couple of casual relationships had come and gone through the years. Once the women started to get close, she would retreat, sabotaging any chance for a future with anyone. She dated a woman named Gail, for whom she had strong feelings.

They enjoyed each other's company, spending much time hiking and biking in the mountains.

As their relationship grew closer, the usual path opened up; Myra started to feel trapped, and like any caged animal, she clawed her way out. Gail couldn't handle the constant mood swings and sometimes abusive language Myra would use, or the way she would go into periods of silent refusal to engage, locking herself in her study.

One day, she had had enough.

As terrible as this may sound, she abandoned Myra in a dangerous predicament, leaving her behind on one of the trails they had been hiking, and driving off.

Myra tried to get in touch with her, but would Gail ever answer her calls? No. She had already blocked all means of communication, making it abundantly clear that she did not care if Myra died out there on that lonely gravel path, flanked by tall pines, in the bitter wilderness.

For some reason unlike her, Myra never pursued it further. She simply let it go.

For the past three years, no special someone had been in her life, which was also fine with Myra. She had dated several women after college, but the relationships had usually gone south within six months because of her demanding career. By nature, she was closed off and had difficulty having intimate relationships. Her friendship with the girls was an anomaly, one that Myra chalked up to one of her most mysterious blessings.

She knew she had trust issues and affording that gift to anyone seemed out of the question. It was easier to stay cynical and skeptical, doubting everyone and hiding behind her tough-girl façade. She had spent so much of her life shutting out much of the world that a committed relationship with a stranger seemed unfathomable by now.

But she had tried, especially with Gail, still determining she was incapable of that kind of intimacy and reliance upon another person. People were fallible, flawed, and therein lay the whole problem. God knew, she had enough flaws of her own, so the last thing she needed was to bring even more issues into an already troubled mind. Plus, what could she offer to a partner?

So, she knew it was kinder to let Gail go than to string her along.

As far as Myra was concerned, she was married to her work as a lawyer, which fulfilled her in ways that no relationship ever could. That was what she told herself anyway.

She spent many nights alone, wondering ... If her childhood had been different, would her desire for a family have been greater? It seemed almost certain.

From a young age, she had known that she probably would never have children. Her childhood had caused so much damage, and she was petrified to inflict that kind of pain on another human.

The confusing emotion for Myra was her love for her mother.

She felt a deep sadness for not having her mother in her life; despite all the trauma at her mother's hands, she loved and missed her contagious laugh and gentle touch.

The pain of her absence was immeasurable, the anger equally so.

Her mother had caused so much chaos and hurt to her only child, but malice had never been in Karen's nature so how could Myra feel angry about it? Karen was lost, that was all.

There was no law against—nor any simple remedy for—the afflictions of stupidity, selfishness, addiction, and self-loathing, all these the leading causes of Karen's many problems.

Inside, however, Karen was good, kind, and loving.

But she was broken. Broken beyond repair. Broken to the point that she allowed someone to break the one person she loved most, her daughter. She had hated herself for it but was helpless to rectify matters since her alcoholism had grown far beyond her control.

Myra longed to help her mother, but she was only a child.

She didn't have the tools to aid her mother toward sobriety, and that wasn't a child's responsibility either. Still, the immense guilt submerged her. Guilt that didn't belong to her, yet she carried it anyway as the weight of the blame was too heavy and burdensome for anyone else to take. It was the anchor that would drown her daily, the constant reminder of how much she had endured, and still her mother had died.

Myra hoped she would find happiness on her terms, but she was content, unaware that she was working herself to death. Her incredibly petite frame made her look skeleton-like and finding work suits that fit her was challenging because she was so tiny. Stress and anxiety caused her very little desire to nourish her body or soul. Myra had been accustomed to living like this, so her lifestyle of high pressure, stress, and being a workaholic became her norm.

She was sure to always fake a smile to everyone she met, greet the partners at the firm with respect and warmth, and from the outside, was a top-notch employee. Inside, Myra was filled with rage, regret, and sadness. She was always careful to keep those feelings deep, hidden within.

She could live this double life without anyone harboring suspicion; to them, she was just a woman with a passion for practicing law, desiring continued success through her diligence.

Myra would work herself to exhaustion so that by the time she got home from the office, she would be so tired that she would have only enough energy to wash up, falling into her unmade bed. When she couldn't fall asleep, she would lie awake, paranoid, thinking someone was outside her bedroom waiting to walk in to attack her. She kept a bat under her bed and a .45mm gun inside the drawer of her nightstand for protection.

She vowed never to be hurt again without a fight. She was no longer a child, now hyperaware of the reality of her childhood's deception and true tragedy.

She remembered the lonely nights in strangers' homes, acting as delicate prey to their deranged agendas. She understood she was at the mercy of their sick sexual desire and had no power to prevent it. To maintain some level of sanity, her purchase of the firearm gave her confidence that she could, finally, protect herself. The gun, fully loaded and close, comforted her with thinking that she could and would shoot any intruder without a second thought.

It was easier for Myra to be immersed in her career than to be tortured by memories alone in her bed at night, which was why she would work herself to utter exhaustion. Focusing on other people's problems and being the voice for her clients gave her the satisfaction of being heard.

Although her demeanor was stoic, she was compassionate, sincerely caring for her clients.

In the courtroom, Myra was known for being nothing short of aggressive and combative, and prosecuting criminals and ensuring they would be locked up for as long as possible was the revenge she sought for all those years ago. She was content to manipulate the justice system to avenge all the heinous crimes once done to her, although never openly admitting it.

Myra was reputed to be one of the country's toughest prosecutors, granting little leeway for negotiations or plea deals. You deserved every miserable sentence coming your way if you committed the crime, she insisted. The law was black and white, offering no gray areas, and although even the judges and some of her fellow law partners would try to get her to back off, Myra wouldn't, only ever pushing harder for a harsher sentence.

Sometimes, she regretted telling her friends about her past. It made her feel vulnerable.

Couldn't the day come when it could be used against her?

After that evening, she never spoke of those past traumas again, and when the others would try and press her into releasing more details, she quickly clammed up, changing the subject.

"I've said what I have to say on the topic," she would insist. "You girls talk all you like about all your past woes. But for me, life moves forward, not back.

There's nothing to be gained from always looking over your shoulder at what's gone. It is as it is. Can't change it."

As she had grown older, she'd become more guarded, and the wall she had carefully built to protect herself was solid. Quick to make a joke or be distracted by something, the only way to emotionally survive was to bury her past so far down that it could never hurt her again. The mere suggestion from Lynnie that she should 'see someone' was laughable. She didn't have the time or patience to feel sorry for herself, and no amount of talking would change a thing.

Myra's hard stance against therapy was infuriating to the others, especially to Amanda who believed everyone could benefit from it. "Every traumatized child should get counseling, if not at the time, then as an adult," she often said. "You girls can call and talk to me anytime in confidence if it would help." And the women would nod, except for Myra.

"It isn't right to mix friendship and therapy."

Amanda tried to sway her to talk to a colleague instead in that case.

"Listen, I know you wouldn't feel comfortable talking with me, Myra, but Kevin is one of the best psychologists I know," Amanda pleaded.

"Thank you, Amanda. Listen, I'm not judging your profession, but I honestly don't need a shrink. What I need is to win this case, so if you don't mind, please excuse me," Myra quipped.

Myra feared therapy would soften her, making her fury in the courtroom suffer. Her anger motivated her to do her job well, this rage being what put the bad guys in prison, the best way she could contribute to society. What she failed to realize was that her anger was eating her alive.

Myra's aggression toward criminals was emotionally drowning her, although she reasoned it was for the good of society. And all these mental tribulations were apparent to everyone but Myra. Even the partners at the law firm saw it, but they never questioned her.

Whatever she was doing benefited the prosecutor's reputation.

"OK, but the offer stands anytime."

On one such day, having had this conversation on the phone yet again with Myra, Amanda walked out of her office feeling defeated.

Waiting by the elevator, the stress of it somehow consumed her.

"I'm supposed to be better than this at getting hurt people to open up," she said to herself, then sighed as if the weight of the world rested upon her because of that one conversation. "She's just one person but happens to be one of the very few I care about. I feel so goddamn inept."

She thought about stopping at the liquor store on the way home that evening, quickly deciding against it because it turned out there was no need. Walking outside, the cool air hit. Snuggling her hands deeper into her pockets, she discovered a small bottle of something nestling there; it turned out to be the tiny flask of vodka from the other night. She quickly took the last couple of swigs, feeling relaxed the rest of the fifteen-block walk home.

A few days later, Jessica visited with Myra. Could *she* get through to her friend?

She tried to act casually, but Jessica had a terrible poker face, a hint of what was on her mind. Myra was immediately irritated by her visit.

"Good intentions are swell but awfully annoying to the person getting lectured," Myra said.

"Yes, but you don't have to put on this facade with me or us," Jessica pleaded.

"Who says it's a facade?" quipped Myra.

"C'mon, Myra, why are you like this? What happened to the fun-loving girl from college?"

"Now *that* was a facade," Myra admitted. "You never knew the real me."

Jessica sighed. "Myra, please ..."

"Listen, Jessica. I love you; I really do. But I've been through a lot, and life has taught me to be guarded. It's not a big deal, so don't take it so personally," explained Myra. "I don't know why you're all on some do-gooder's mission to fix poor Myra all of a sudden."

"We are not, and I also don't take it personally. I just want you to be happy," Jessica said warmly. Jessica always had a way of making Myra feel heard and important. She was kind by nature, and Myra held a loving admiration for her warmth. Jessica reminded her of Ms. Nali, her warm eyes and soft smile so welcoming despite how Myra felt about herself.

"This is my happiness, and only I know how I feel. Trust me, I *am* happy. I just need to live life on my terms and in my own way. I spent so much of my childhood hiding who and what my reality was. I decided that I didn't want to do that ever again," Myra said.

"Happy?" Jessica argued. "This is your happiness. Really, Myra? When was the last time you could say you felt true peace?" Jessica stood silent and stared, waiting for a reply.

"Jessica, stop," Myra said sternly. "Please."

"OK," Jessica surrendered. "You know I love you just as you are, right?"

"Yeah, I'm a cranky old bat and happy to be one," Myra said, then laughed.

They both chuckled at that cheerfully.

Myra waving her arms and making bat motions gave them both relentless giggles.

Later that night, Myra thought again of her conversation with Jessica. Perhaps she did have a problem with anxiety. Truthfully, she hated being left with her thoughts and memories.

As she got older, her past was returning to haunt her, leaving her emptier inside than ever before. Fragments of her life would appear in the silence of her small apartment, and on most days, it was just too much for her to handle. Myra had been disenchanted with her own life for a long time without any energy to change it. Practicing law was all she had known, and she was good at it, getting enormous satisfaction from putting criminals behind bars. Each time the jury said 'guilty,' pride swelled, healing her heart from its past trauma just a little more.

Her intentions were good and in the interests of society, but she also took personal satisfaction in being self-righteous and having the power to protect victims from being victimized.

Law fulfilled Myra in a way that she couldn't quite explain, but still, she also had a void inside that no career would ever fill. In her dark moments, Myra wondered what life would be like without her in it, and once, in a desperate moment, she had contemplated suicide.

One cold winter night, she went to her car drunk with a bottle of pain medicine she had kept from a tooth infection. She hobbled down the stairs and took the pills, hoping to subdue her emotional suffering. Becoming sleepy, her cell phone rang. She looked down, seeing it was Jessica calling. She let the call go to voicemail. Jessica called again.

Half annoyed and half relieved, Myra answered, sleepy, dizzy, a little drunk from the glasses of wine consumed with dinner.

Myra was going in and out of consciousness until Jessica, alarmed, demanded she stay on the phone. She frantically called 911, dispatchers finding their way to Myra's apartment. Perhaps this was why Jessica had been so demanding lately, so insistent that even Myra clearly had hidden pools of agony inside of her, a deep well of torment that would have to be healed if she wasn't going to allow herself to one day be submerged, drowning in those murky waters.

Once sober, Myra told the doctors she had accidentally overdosed. It was all an accident, a misunderstanding. As a criminal lawyer, she could be very persuasive.

Also, Myra was well known for her volunteer work and extensive career in the community, something of a minor local celebrity. With a stern warning from her doctors not to mix pain medicine and alcohol, she was released the next day. Soon enough, Jessica showed up at the hospital, challenging them about the quick and misguided release of her friend.

Myra needed a psychologist, she said. Could they not see this was more than an accidental overdose? Just because Myra was a professional and good at weaving arguments, it didn't mean she would never be at risk of taking her own life. Anyone could fall prey to darkness in that way.

Unfortunately, Myra's career and prestige granted her the gift of persuasion and dismissal of any wrongdoing. Ultimately, the staff believed the story Myra had handed them.

Jessica wasn't convinced of the accidental overdose story. Later that evening, at Myra's apartment, she stared at Myra as she made herbal tea, their silence awkward and unusual. Finally, after some time, Jessica stood and faced Myra, only inches away from her.

"Myra, I'll be honest. I don't believe this was an accident," Jessica said softly.

"Oh, I'm so sorry I worried you, Jess. I just had a terrible migraine and had some leftover painkillers. My head was hurting so much that I just couldn't remember if I'd taken any or not. I think the pain made me take them a few times, but no way did I know; I was beside myself with the most appalling headache. I'm so sorry, and terribly embarrassed. It will never happen again."

Jessica just stared as if trying to bore into her friend's soul, reading her mind.

"Maybe you're right," added Myra. "I should take a couple of days off to relax. I've been working a lot, and it's just exhausting."

For a moment, Jessica believed her, but a nagging feeling was deep inside of her, and she just couldn't shake it. This didn't make sense.

Myra was too meticulous to have an accidental overdose. Even with a migraine, she wouldn't have pills hanging around like that anyway. And she wouldn't take old medications. Jessica was sure Myra was deflecting and offering a fake surrender, with no intentions of taking any time off.

She knew Myra as well as she knew herself, and one thing Myra wasn't was stupid.

No, overdosing due to a migraine would not be something Myra could possibly do.

"You know, Myra, if you ever want to talk or need help, I'm here for you. Always will be."

Myra scoffed at Jessica's concern. "Jessica, I have a stressful job, and sometimes drink too much and too often, but I'm fine. I'll be much more aware and responsible. You have my word."

Jessica hesitated for a moment, looking deep into Myra's eyes.

"Myra, you are loved. You are adored and you are valued. Please think about slowing your drinking and taking care of your mental health," she said. "If not for you, do it for your friends."

Her voice was shaky, laden with emotion.

With that, the two embraced, leaving one of them with questions but no answers. An unsettled feeling of confusion pervaded the air.

Myra felt a pang of incredible guilt but masked it with avoidance.

Defensiveness and avoidance had become Myra's mask in uncomfortable situations. She could feel her heart rate speed up at even a hint of being questioned about her drinking habits.

The alcohol was just the consequence of depression and anxiety since Myra didn't even enjoy drinking. She loathed it. Drinking had stolen her mother, and it was not her friend. She wanted the pain to stop and the thoughts whirling around her mind to calm. She had thought about seeing a doctor for antidepressants but worried that it would change her work focus.

Had she sought professional help, she would have known that was entirely untrue.

Instead, Myra chose to wear a mask, keeping up the charade of being an overworked attorney just doing her job. A pro at wearing a mask by now, it was second nature.

Only when alone could she remove the mask, being left with her truth.

The memories that haunted her and ate at her soul would creep into every cell of her body.

The only way to avoid that was to keep her mask on tight, soldiering on.

It was a challenging task. She was human, after all.

Sometimes, the most stoic people were also the most vulnerable, their layers of armor only for protection from the world. They didn't want to be visible, and the only way to ensure that was to wear the armor and ensure there was never a crack in the shield.

It was an exhausting way to live, but also a necessary way for people who had been abused.

As much as she tried suppressing the many memories of dark rooms, creaky doors, and hushed footsteps, they all had a way of rushing back.

Her tears and gasps were quelled by a strong hand against her mouth as the stranger thrust his body inside her, violating her in the vilest way.

Myra would always find a crack in the ceiling to focus on, imagining it to be an escape to another dimension, knowing that within moments, there would be one hard thrust, a heavy breath, and it would all be over. She would be left alone, confused, and alone to gather her underwear and will her way to sleep. Of course, that would never happen.

She would never sleep on those nights in fear that he would return.

On those nights, the best she could do was plan her escape, think about her mother, and hope to someday be saved from this life. She knew better not to expect too much.

Hope was for people who had something to lose.

Myra had lost herself long ago, and the last thing she had was the hope that her mother would get sober and the two of them would move far away and start a new life together.

Anyway, she knew her friends didn't believe her story of the accidental overdose. The girls knew her too well, and she wasn't in a courtroom filled with strangers.

Though it felt terrible to be lying to her friends, Myra just wanted a way out of all the chaos.

⸻ ❧ ⸻

Jessica drove home that night in silence.

Had her dear friend truthfully made one unbelievably reckless mistake, or had she tried to commit suicide? The thought haunted Jessica for the thirty-minute drive, playing out every scenario. Eventually, she convinced herself that she had been overreacting, on high alert with the suicide awareness talks lately. Her head was throbbing, and she finally surrendered to the idea.

This entire situation had been just a random accident after all, one that she needed to let go.

JOURNAL

JUST FOUND OUT SOMETHING REALLY TERRIBLE.

THIS WEEKEND, I WENT TO VISIT MY PARENTS AND POOR MYRA MUST HAVE ACCIDENTALLY OVERDOSED OR SOMETHING. LUCKILY, JESSICA WAS THERE TO TAKE CARE OF HER, I MUST FIND OUT THE DETAILS LATER.

I'VE BEEN DISTRACTED, TRYING TO RECONCILE WITH MY PARENTS. AS MUCH AS I HATE TO ADMIT IT, I HAVEN'T LET GO OF MY CHILDHOOD EITHER AND STILL STRIVE TO MAKE THEM PROUD, EVEN THOUGH I'M NOT EVEN SURE IT'S POSSIBLE. FINALLY, I FINISHED MY INTERNSHIP AND WAS OFFERED A JOB ONLY TWO MILES AWAY AT A LOCAL SCHOOL. BEING A TEACHER SURROUNDED BY NOISE AND CHAOS

SEEMS TO BE MY CALLING, AND I'M EXCITED TO FILL MY DAYS WITH THE ENDLESS CHATTER OF CHILDREN.

BEING AN ONLY CHILD, I HAVE NEVER WANTED THE DEAFENING SILENCE OF MY CHILDHOOD TO BE PART OF MY PROFESSIONAL LIFE.

SURELY, THE BEST PART OF TEACHING IS MEETING WITH DOTING PARENTS ABOUT THEIR CHILDREN'S PROGRESS. IT WAS WHAT I ALWAYS WANTED AS A CHILD. SO, I'M REALLY SENSITIVE TO CHILDREN WHO SIT ALONE AT LUNCH. NO ONE SHOULD BE LONELY.

IT'S MY MISSION TO MAKE SURE THAT EVERYONE HAS A FRIEND.

I WANT TO MAKE A DIFFERENCE IN THEIR LIVES AND GET TO EXPERIENCE CHILDHOOD ALL OVER AGAIN, THIS TIME WITH THE JOY IT SUPPLIES. WEIRDLY, TOO, BEING SURROUNDED BY CHILDREN MAKES ME WANT TO VISIT WITH MY PARENTS. THAT IS SOMETHING I NEVER THOUGHT I'D WRITE! SO, I DECIDED TO GO.

I ARRIVED AT MY CHILDHOOD HOME WITH A NEW PERSPECTIVE.

Driving down the street, I was anxious and excited. The trees I had loved many years ago were still there, which was a strange feeling as for some reason, I had expected the urbanization, decay and dilapidations over time would have seen the trees dead or removed.

Of course, they were bigger than I remembered. And now, suddenly, something else was bigger too—the sense of apprehension at seeing my parents' home.

Even from the street, the house's silence was daunting, but now, it didn't seem so intimidating as I took in some deep breaths and reassured myself. 'It will be fine, Lynnie. Just deal with it.' That was the inner message I was giving myself.

I kept telling myself that I was grown now, an adult with a career and living my own life.

There was nothing to fear, nothing they could do to hurt me anymore.

I didn't—wouldn't—let my childhood bleed into my soul the way it once had. My parents' lives were

THEIR OWN, AND THEY DIDN'T LOVE ME OR EACH OTHER THE WAY I HAD NEEDED—AND DIDN'T EVEN LOVE THEMSELVES FOR THAT MATTER.

I ACCEPTED IT AND WAS READY TO REDEFINE MY RELATIONSHIP WITH THEM AS AN ADULT. I HAD SPENT MANY YEARS AWAY FROM THEM, AND THIS VISIT AND THE CORRESPONDING LURCHING OF MY STOMACH WERE REMINDERS OF WHY.

WHEN I KNOCKED ON THE DOOR, THERE THEY WERE. 'WHEN WAS THE LAST TIME I WAS HERE?' I WONDERED. IT HAD BEEN A LONG TIME. SO MUCH HAD CHANGED, AND YET AT THE SAME TIME, SO LITTLE.

I NOTICED MY MOTHER FIRST, REACHING OUT AND TOUCHING HER HAND; HER WRINKLED AND BONY FINGERS GREETED ME, BUT HER COLD EYES WERE NOT WELCOMING. WOULD I HAVE EXPECTED THEM TO BE?

'HELLO LYNNIE,' SHE SAID COLDLY, HER FOOT SCUFFING AT THE STEP AS IF KICKING SOMETHING INVISIBLE. IT WAS CLEARLY SOME NERVOUS TIC, SHOWING SHE COULDN'T WAIT TO BE RID OF THE SCOURGE THAT HAD DARED PRESENT ITSELF AT HER OWN FRONT DOOR. I DIDN'T CARE. IT MADE NO IMPACT ON ME.

My father's appearance, however, made me disappointed and sad. He seemed even more aloof and defeated, standing there at the door with a yellowed, parchment-like look to his sagging and wrinkled skin. He appeared at death's door, looking as light as a feather, frail and gaunt.

Besides that, any light in his eyes, the spark that had always been there whenever just the two of us had been alone together, had gone, flitted as if there was no point in continuing.

He looked out dully on the world now, and was saddened and defeated, palpably absent.

He spoke with me casually and without any genuine interest in my life. I kept trying to make a connection with them until they, both of them, exchanged looks and accused me.

'Well, I suppose you want the big welcome, do you, Lynnie? You want me and your father to say we're so happy to see you? Well, we're not. I don't know what you expected by coming here, but this is as good as it gets. You can go back to where you emerged

FROM. YOU ABANDONED US, SO WE CAN ABANDON YOU AS WELL. IT WORKS TWO WAYS, LYNNIE.'

AS MY MOTHER SAID IT, SHE LOOKED AWAY, DISTANT, AS IF LOOKING FORWARD TO A TIME WHEN I WOULD BE AWAY AGAIN. THEN, SILENCE, STONY FACES, HARSH GLARES.

MOTHER, AS USUAL, WAS DRIVING IT ALL. FATHER WAS YIELDING, ACQUIESCING, BUT NOW HE ALSO HAD NO INTEREST IN ME AND HAD SOMEHOW GROWN TO BE AS UNCARING AND COLD AS SHE WAS. IT SHOULDN'T HAVE BEEN A SURPRISE OR A SHOCK, SHOULD IT? BECAUSE IT WAS TRUE THAT TO ALL INTENTS AND PURPOSES, I HAD ABANDONED HIM, LEAVING HIM WITH HER FOR ALL THESE YEARS. SO, WHY SHOULD HE CARE ABOUT ME?

BUT STILL, IT HURT IN A WAY I HAD NOT EXPECTED, SOMETHING DEEP AND VISCERAL BITING AT MY PSYCHE AND SENSE OF SELF-WORTH. I WANTED TO HUG HIM AND SEE IF THE DAD I HAD KNOWN WAS STILL IN THERE SOMEPLACE. BUT I DOUBTED THAT HE COULD BE, AND JUST DIDN'T DARE TO APPROACH HIM.

WE WERE IN A STAND-OFF.

It was clear they found me disloyal and unappreciative.

The reality, though, had been that I'd needed to protect myself from the toxicity dwelling inside that house. I had worked hard to overcome my childhood trauma and couldn't risk them compromising my mental health anew, couldn't risk that I would get unwittingly dragged back into that terrible abyss.

I made my visit short and sweet, assuring them both that I loved them no matter what, and it hurt in my throat, creating a strange bolus of unspent tears that had to be swallowed down as I passed along all the old familiar roads, ones that had also changed so much.

As I drove away, it made me even more appreciative of the career I pursued, and that I had the opportunity to change how young people viewed the world. I was more eager than ever to start a new life without the confines of my parents' poisonous ways.

# CHAPTER TWELVE

*Amanda: Love and Consequence.*

Browsing the bookstore, Amanda met Paul while looking for an 'Ethics in America' textbook.

"Ethics in America," Paul snarled. "That's a funny one. I dare say there aren't any."

Amanda was taken aback by his comment, laughing at his skepticism.

She couldn't blame him.

The country was a mess; money and power had taken over common sense and humanity.

"Wouldn't it be great if that title were The Reality in America?" Amanda said with a giggle.

Paul stared at her for a moment. "Would you like to grab a coffee at the café across the street and chat about politics?"

Amanda cheerfully agreed, curious about this new stranger.

Over three hours, the two spoke nonstop about the political divide, the environment, and how quickly the world continued to change, usually not for the better.

He was exciting and adventurous, and from their initial meeting, they spent most weekends together hiking, camping, and in nature.

Paul dreamed of living off the grid, and while Amanda didn't share the same enthusiasm about his future goals, she enjoyed his love for nature and his appreciation for simplicity.

She had always had a passion for the unknown, naturally curious. She never minded not being in control either, allowing Paul to make many of the decisions in their relationship.

Her laid-back manner made it easy for Paul to sometimes manipulate Amanda into things she wasn't entirely comfortable with, shamelessly pushing and persuading her until she conceded.

Amanda soon discovered she had fallen for his dimples, wide smile, and ability to sweet-talk her into all sorts of situations. But as the months passed, he became bolder with his requests for her money and time, demanding and expecting them as if he held ownership of her.

She hadn't mentioned to her friends the money she would loan Paul for his 'grassroots' investments to which he subscribed or how he was sometimes controlling.

She also knew not to mention that Paul had once followed Amanda and her girlfriends to dinner, later berating her for how long she'd stayed out with them.

At first, she thought his jealousy was protective and romantic, but as time passed, he began commenting on how she looked and dressed, making her start feeling uneasy and insecure.

Amanda spoke less to the girls out of fear of Paul's reaction, even canceling two coffee dates with the girls, blaming an emergency at work for her absence.

She wanted a relationship with Paul to validate her insecurities, ignoring the gnawing feeling of doom inside.

---

JOURNAL

AMANDA KEEPS CANCELING ON US WHEN WE SAY WE'RE GOING TO MEET FOR COFFEE.

LOOKS LIKE SHE'S CONSUMED IN HER RELATIONSHIP—OR CONSUMED 'BY' IT, ONE OR THE OTHER. IT'S LIKE SHE'S ALLOWING IT TO TAKE OVER HER LIFE THESE DAYS, TO DEVOUR HER! EVERYTHING SHE SAYS AND DOES IS ALL ABOUT PAUL AND I'M WORRIED.

I'VE REACHED OUT TO. HER, BUT SHE DOESN'T RETURN MY CALLS. IT'S SO FRUSTRATING!

I WANT TO CONFRONT HER ABOUT THIS RELATIONSHIP, BUT I'M SCARED OF HER REACTION. AND I HAVE A REALLY BAD FEELING ABOUT IT.

---

Paul was intense by nature, so Amanda knew how to keep the peace, trying not to do all the things that she knew would irritate him. And there seemed to be so many of them. Paul had a quick temper, often showing signs of aggression toward the world's injustices, though, at the time, Amanda chalked it up to passion. He revealed that once, he'd got arrested for standing outside a slaughterhouse screaming profanities at the owner for killing its livestock for food.

The police stand-off came to a head, of course.

Paul threw human feces and fake blood at the officers trying to minimize the disruption.

He was outraged, righteous, and indignant.

Amanda admired these qualities about Paul but would often become tense when he'd

'discuss'—or go on about, whether she cared to listen or not—the world's injustices.

It was a side to Paul that often left Amanda feeling insecure about his mental state and her

safety. Still, she hushed the quiet voice inside her, assumed she was being dramatic, trying to

defuse the situation whenever Paul became outraged.

The relationship finally reached its expiry date when Paul found an empty shopping bag with a receipt from a local shopping mall. Whoever would have known that a five-inch slip of paper could have caused such chaos between the couple? But it did, explosively so.

Amanda had been in the bathroom, finishing preparing for a night out with him.

They had decided to check out a new local vegan restaurant that contributed ten percent of its profits to sustainable farming, something Amanda had suggested when they were at the farmers' market, and a tall thin man had been handing out flyers about the restaurant's grand opening.

Both she and Paul celebrated small businesses, and Amanda had been trying to get a handle on her health. She had gained a lot of weight and was trying to return to a healthy lifestyle.

It was exciting to show Paul that she equally cared about the environment, valuing his passion for sustainable living. Paul had complained many times that he felt Amanda didn't understand what was happening to the planet; she was sometimes just as irresponsible as the rest of the world, he'd claim. While Amanda tried to defend herself, she knew it would be useless.

Paul thought in black and white, having zero tolerance for small changes. He was an extremist who couldn't fathom any other way of life. But he'd seemed excited about the upcoming date night at Vegans Unite, appreciative of the gesture of Amanda's suggestion.

That day's mood was light, Paul seeming in good spirits. He had a habit of being dark and agitated, often a bit forceful with Amanda. But today, for what it was worth, he appeared joyful.

So, when he stormed into the bathroom, pushing the door harshly to make his way in to confront Amanda, she was taken by surprise. He began screaming at her in a rage so immediately terrifying that she wet herself. She didn't understand; what could have triggered Paul to this extent? She whimpered, trying to secure the door, but as the struggle escalated, it slammed into her head, hurling her forcefully to the ground.

As Paul lay on her, calling her a fraud, he shoved the receipt in her face.

"So! You went out for a steak dinner with your friends, did you?" he spewed. "Made you feel good, did it? Vegan, my ass. You're a bloody liar. I should've known."

"Paul, we were celebrating Myra's birthday. Where did you find that?" Amanda pleaded.

"So, you tried hiding it from me in a shopping bag, hoping I wouldn't find it. You are a snake and a lying bitch," he shouted.

"Paul, please calm down," Amanda quietly begged, trying to defuse the situation but there was little she could do to reason with him in this mood. As he was screaming about the environment and how Amanda was just like the rest of them—or worse because of the lies and all the pretense—she saw in his eyes what she had never seen before, a possessed look.

He was dangerous, and she was frightened; he was ready to explode.

She tried to get out of the bathroom to run from the house, but as she tried, Paul pinned her to the floor, putting his hands around her neck, squeezing.

Amanda couldn't breathe and wanted to fight him off her. At that moment, she heard her phone ring, startling him. He kicked her in the stomach before running out of the house.

Amanda gasped in disbelief, sure she would have died if her phone hadn't jolted Paul out of his murderous rage. Afraid of his return, she quickly gathered her things, packing her car with only essentials, hurriedly heading from the house. There was no time to gather up anything other than clothes and jewelry. Once down the block and away from harm, she pulled over.

Now, in a layby, she sobbed and sobbed, shaking so much she could barely drive. Her vision was blurred from the temporary loss of oxygen, and she was in shock. Everything happened so quickly that she couldn't wrap her mind around it. She knew one thing for sure, though, which was that Paul was too dangerous to be with now, that he had reached such a level that her instincts told her he'd eventually kill her if she didn't leave this toxic relationship right now.

She had to take control and escape his abuse.

The warning signs she had been ignoring for the past six months could no longer be avoided.

How had she even gotten herself into this dead-end relationship?

She was a therapist, for goodness' sake! She should have been far savvier regarding her relationships. She had even identified such tendencies when Lynnie had been dating Luke and still when it came to her own life, she'd ignored all the signs.

Once Amanda gathered her thoughts, caught her breath, and stopped shaking, she made her way to the local police station to file a report. When she walked in, the lights were bright, and she could hear a man yelling that he was innocent from across the way.

A woman was hanging around the booking-in area, clearly intoxicated, swearing she was sober and asking where her children were.

Then Amanda saw another tall, broad man in handcuffs just staring off in the distance. As Amanda was approaching the desk, a female officer looked up at her with concern.

"What can I do for you?" the short, plump woman asked.

"Please help me. My boyfriend, Paul Rogers, just assaulted me, and I'm afraid to go home."

She was led into a small room, where two female officers sat across from her. They sympathetically but professionally asked her to tell the details of the attack.

"Now, you're sure you're all right, Amanda?" one asked. "We can call a doctor if you think you may have some injuries. Even if it's just bruises, we may need to photograph it."

They did that first, Amanda stripping to the waist to show where Paul had held her against her will down on the ground, his hands clamping her upper arms, elbows once in her ribs, and she also wanted to mention his hold on her neck. "And at one stage, he had me here and—"

The single lens reflex camera, old-school style, snapped image after image with a heavy *thunk*.

"Amanda," said one officer. "We can see the marks on your throat. It's probably worse than you even imagined. We'll take pictures from every angle, Amanda, so just bear with us."

The session went on and on, the upper part of her body bare and chilled, and it ought to have been embarrassing, mortifying. For a brief surreal moment, Amanda tried imagining she was a supermodel, creating stunning art images for some glossy magazine. It helped her through it.

Amanda recounted the events, composing herself and taking moments to gather her thoughts. The recollection had caused so much pain and anxiety that suddenly, in an unexpected outburst, she started shaking and crying. Through heavy sobs, she was able to tell the officers everything.

In due course, though painstakingly slowly, they fill out the police report before sending an all-points bulletin out on Paul. Amanda was relieved but worried that Paul would retaliate.

The officers told her she should not return to the apartment and to find a place to stay until this was sorted out. She left the police station, immediately wondering how to retract her report.

Perhaps she had been to blame for Paul's outburst after all.

*Why did I order steak? How careless. God, I'm so selfish, and no wonder he got mad. I say I'm all for the animals and then I go do this!*

Amanda turned around and went back into the police station.

"I ... I just made charges against my partner," she said. "And I've been thinking it wasn't as bad as I said. It was a mistake; I was shaken up by an argument and just reacted badly. I'd like to drop the charges, please. So sorry for wasting police time."

The officers—who had seen this pattern before in domestic violence cases—pleaded with her to follow through. "I—I'm sorry," she said again. "I just made up the story. I've been drinking, you see, and don't normally drink at all so it went to my head."

Little did Amanda know that her decision not to press charges would later return to haunt her.

Amanda didn't see Paul for three days after that, but eventually, he showed up with flowers and a tearful apology. She was hesitant but had, in some peculiar way, missed him.

She had missed his insults and his slights, and his bad moods. Somehow, they meant familiarity, and that was better than having to begin again, to be out on her own with no one.

"I think Paul really meant it," she said to herself. "And I know he'll never touch me again because he came so near to losing me; I know he wouldn't want that because for one thing, he'd be constantly imagining me with someone else. And I honestly think he's beyond impressed I didn't call the police to come and arrest him for that assault."

"Babe, I can't believe you didn't get me in trouble," he voiced to her. "I love ya."

Yes, he was impressed by it. But would it keep him on his best behavior?

Sure enough, the next three months were great between them, their relationship obviously on the mend. Or possibly not, but Amanda was unwilling to take off her emotional blindfold.

He suggested a camping trip, out of the blue.

The mere thought of it made Amanda's eyes sparkle and her heart beat fast. Small gestures—romantic ones like this—were exciting, even now. She was eager for some well-needed time away, a chance to reconnect. Plus, there had to be some reason behind his gesture because he wasn't one for spontaneity. Maybe Paul would propose to her, but she kept her wishful thinking to herself. It would ruin his surprise if she showed she had him all worked out.

And she also wouldn't mention a word to the girls.

For one thing, Myra would object to her going away with Paul, and there was no way the others could keep her secret from Myra. So, she had to think up a story.

"I'm going away for a few days to see Tommy," she said, looking away as she did so. Jessica eyed her, askance as if reading her mind to see if this was a fabrication.

But why wouldn't she want to see Tommy? She hardly ever did get the time these days.

Amanda was initially apprehensive, however; how would it be to go off camping, hiking, and exploring with Paul with no reprieve of a warm bed and quiet?

What if they argued and he went into one of his moods?

But life was for living and she would take the plunge and join Paul in his adventures, hoping this would bring them closer. If nothing else, it would be a once-in-a-lifetime experience. For most people, a camping trip was nothing.

But for Amanda, who never got the freedom to do anything different these days because of how Pual ruled over everything, it really was an adventure. It was odd, though, to see Paul becoming increasingly manic about the details.

She tried to tell herself it was endearing, that if he was going to propose, everything just had to be exact and meticulous. Before too long, what had started as a fun trip away was becoming incredibly detailed and treated more like a mission than a vacation. But she would not mention it or protest for fear of upsetting him when he was doing his best to make this perfect and special.

Paul was also packing as if going off on a combat mission, becoming easily agitated by the slightest inconvenience. Amanda caught him on several occasions mumbling under his breath, agitated. Confronted, he would be in a profound daze, quickly retorting that he was fine, just very excited for the trip, wanting to ensure they were adequately prepared just as she'd thought.

She brushed off his concerns as stress, especially as this would be their longest time together.

The trip started as fun and romantic, holding hands and singing to the music on the radio. They sat by their campfires at night, snuggling up warm, talking about the day's adventures.

The next morning, they were averaging twenty-mile walks a day, much of it uphill terrain.

Amanda would ask for small breaks for water, and Paul would impatiently wait.

"You ... you'll never survive an apocalypse. Not much of a prepper, are you?"

*And I never pretended to be a prepper either,* her mind said to her. She dared not voice it, instead answering, "No, I have a long way to go to be like you."

He eyed her skeptically. Was she being sarcastic?

But she wasn't, only seeking to keep the peace.

Although sore and tired, Amanda was amazed by the landscape. The never-ending greenery, the fresh air, and the peacefulness were blissful and the blisters on her feet and her aching bones were far worth it, to see the sights of the mountains. She encountered bears and even caught a glimpse of a cub nestled against the mama bear. Amanda was sure not to disturb the wildlife—Paul would go mad if she did—instead capturing photos and writing journal entries.

Later, she could show her friends back home her adventures.

As the days passed, Paul's mood became predictably more somber and more agitated; by the eleventh day of their trip, he was moody and dark, leaving Amanda to find her way to the next campground alone. Once there, he ignored her and become verbally aggressive.

"Paul, are you OK?" she innocently inquired, not knowing this question would be like detonating an incendiary device. "Have I done anything to upset you? You seem subdued."

By *subdued* she meant mean, morose, icy.

"No, you haven't done anything to upset me but the whole world is a disaster in case you haven't noticed. And another thing: it also does not revolve around you, Amanda. Or them."

She reeled. "I ... I don't know what you mean." And she really didn't. She hadn't said or done a thing to imply the world revolved around her. And who were *they* supposed to be?

"It's all those watchers. They're everywhere. Following me. Nosy little shits. They'll get what's coming to them. Just watch and wait, Amanda, watch and wait."

He was on medication for anxiety but was that all? Was there some other condition she didn't know about? *Watchers* sounded too ominous. But she never further questioned his mental state. After all, anxiety wasn't an uncommon condition, and he was clearly having an off day.

It wasn't until about two weeks in that Amanda realized that Paul had stopped taking his medication altogether. He was on the verge of a mental breakdown.

She tried reasoning with Paul, using the tools she had learned in her clinic class about mental illness. Although she'd become a therapist, she hadn't had hands-on experience with violent outbursts. She had spent most of her time helping teenagers with self-esteem trouble. Men like Paul were not within her area of expertise, but it left her with a great vulnerability.

With Paul's behavior becoming so erratic, Amanda was frightened, both for him and for herself. One thing her training had certainly taught her was that if someone was speaking aggressively, it was the beginning of a condition that would likely only worsen unless the person sought specific help. It could mean that before too long, physical violence would ensue.

Amanda put her hand on his back, begging Paul to eat something.

He eyed her suspiciously. "What have you been doing to my food? You're putting something in it, I know you are. From now on, you also eat everything you give me. You're not going to kill me so you best get used to me, right?"

"Right."

She had long since learned not to argue, not to deny, not to … anything. If he was acting paranoid, denial was the worst thing she could show him.

He threw her to the ground, putting his hands around her neck, expecting her to try to convince him otherwise regardless. "You deny it, don't you? You bitch? I'll show you what happens to clever little bitches who think they've got one over on me."

In his eyes, she saw blankness, the mild man she had once met suddenly transforming into a wild beast she could not control. Just as she was about to pass out, Paul stopped himself and started to cry. Through tears and shame, he made an admission.

"I never told you this, babe. I was released from a mental facility about two years ago."

"A … a what? What do you mean?"

Had he been in residential treatment for his depression?

"Everyone gets depressed, love, to some degree. You could have just told me."

"Depression? Hah. Wait till you hear. I have bipolar, like *massive* mood swings. You get high as a fucking kite, then low as a worm on the ground, slithering." He made the motion of a worm with his hand. "And if that's not enough, I've got schizophrenia as well. That's when you—"

He didn't need to finish; she knew all about these conditions.

"Paul, I know. But you take *loads* of medications. You're all right."

She turned and stared, and he stared back, saying not a word.

"Not anymore, I don't."

And that was that.

He had stopped taking his medicine about three months ago, which explained why there had been such a sudden change in his behavior; he believed that the FBI was out to kill him.

Amanda knew she needed to get Paul some medical attention but needed to tread lightly, so as not to cause him more agitation. Paul was already distressed and hyper, and Amanda was concerned about her safety. Because she was off the grid, she couldn't contact anyone for help.

She waited outside the tent while Paul tossed and turned inside, grumbling and mumbling to himself about the people who were always watching him. He cursed a lot too.

Later, she dared to venture into the tent's warmth. After all, she could hardly sleep outside all night, could she? Anything could happen.

Amanda had started to doze off when she felt the presence of someone watching her. She sat bolt upright. The door to the tent was wide, flapping around.

By the firelight, she could see Paul was in the bushes, naked, fire in his eyes and arms flailing.

"Amanda, they're here. They're coming for me. I will have to kill them all before they retake me," Paul said in desperation. "You know that, right? We're a team, right?"

For a moment, Amanda looked around, convinced that people were everywhere, and soon realized that Paul was hallucinating again. She said nothing, not knowing what the right answer was supposed to be. He charged at Amanda.

"You're in on that fucking sting!"

As he came closer, Amanda knew.

He would kill her this time. She was either with him or against him, and in her hesitation to answer, he had decided: she was against. The enemy.

He had to get rid of her. Slaughter her. Bury her in a place where no one would find her.

She felt it in her bones, every part of her soul screaming to get out of there as soon as possible. Suddenly, and with no other option, Amanda started to run, with Paul behind her screaming, "I will kill you, Amanda, you fucking bitch. I will cut your fucking throat and drink your blood! That will get all the demons gone!"

Amanda found strength from somewhere and, at full speed, she continued running, chasing through the fields, through the long grasses and the brambles, leaping the fences.

Her time in college had been spent on the swim team, and she had both the endurance and speed to escape Paul.

Amanda kept running for over an hour, not once looking back.

She was visibly shaken, dehydrated, and exhausted when she reached a campsite and came upon a family gathered, roasting marshmallows, and singing campfire songs. It was a middle-aged woman, three children who all looked to be in their mid-to late teens, and a slim man.

With a look of shock, they all stopped and stared at her.

The woman, who saw the terror in the newcomer's eyes, jolted up from her seat.

"Are you OK?" the woman asked, and slowly approached Amanda. "Do you need help?"

Her soft gray hair looked somehow motherly, the stranger's eyes showing concern and compassion. Amanda was numb and couldn't say a word, just standing wide-eyed and tearful.

The plump woman carefully walked a bit closer to Amanda without losing eye contact.

Amanda could hear the crackle of leaves under her feet, backing away step by step. "Sweetheart, you're completely safe. It's OK, honey. Just stay still. We won't hurt you."

There was so much concern and softness in the stranger's voice but she was shocked, unable to find words to speak back to the family.

"You are at a campsite, love. Just breathe," the woman continued slowly.

She must have looked ghastly from running for so long, also soon realizing that her neck was still filled with bruises from Paul's most recent attack. For the first time, Amanda felt blood dripping down her lip again from when he had pushed her to the ground just that morning, when he'd accused her of calling the police and giving his social security card to the authorities.

Amanda's mind raced, unable to quite articulate the horror she had been experiencing.

While she was still worried for Paul, she couldn't help but fear that he would, in fact, kill her this time. Trembling, she allowed the kind woman to walk her to a bench nearby.

Her children followed their father off to the side, to a spot from which he watched intently to ensure his wife wasn't in any kind of danger. She heard him quietly say to the kids, "Don't stare. There's something wrong with the lady, and your mom's going to try to help."

The woman said to Amanda, "Honey, we see this type of thing all the time. Men go crazy out here. But let me assure you that with me—with us—you are safe. I have a walkie-talkie to reach the nearest park rangers. My daughter has type one diabetes, and the folks here were kind enough to accommodate us. I need you to breathe, and when you're ready, I'll call to get you to safety."

Amanda's shock started to wear off and she was able to tell the kind stranger her name.

She began explaining what had happened too, but suddenly stopped. It was too much to recount in this state of mind. From the look of Amanda, the woman—who'd told her earlier that her name was Denise—was able to splice all the pieces together on her own.

"Right. Well, we're going to get you safe, dear. You are OK; he won't come after you here, and if he does, I have a gun that I'm not afraid to use," Denise said with a chuckle.

Amanda started to nod slowly. "Thank you. Thank you. You're a godsend to me."

"He doesn't have a firearm does he?" Denise wanted to know.

Amanda shook her head. "He doesn't believe in guns. He's a pacifist."

It sounded laughable, the most stupid, ridiculous, silly thing she could ever have said.

*My partner has beaten me black and blue and chased me for miles, threatening to cut off my head. But he's a pacifist and he wouldn't dream of killing a fly or an animal. Only me.*

"Let's clean you up and get a drink and a hotdog," Denise said, cutting into her thoughts, something for which Amanda was truly thankful.

All Amanda could think now though, was, *a hotdog. A hotdog ... If Paul comes ... If he sees I've been eating meat, then I'm dead for sure. Never, ever, can I risk that mistake again.*

She just couldn't imagine that he would not find her now, not even when so far away. Fitness was not his thing though, and anyway, he didn't feed himself well enough to have the energy to run for an hour the way that she had done to escape him. She really was safe. But even so, she jumped at every small sound, every twig cracking, every squirrel landing out of a tree.

Sensing the tension had eased slightly, the teenage children came up to their mother.

"Mom, when are we having the hotdogs? Is the lady having some as well?"

They smiled at Amanda shyly.

"We have loads of food. Mom always brings too much," said the girl, tall and pretty, with straight dark hair pushed across one eye in a fashion that was all the rage among girls just now.

Soon, they were all sitting by the campfire as if it was normal to have a bloodied stranger sitting in on their family time. One of the woman's cheeky older boys sidled up to her and asked, "Why are you in such a mess? Even I don't get myself in such a mess in the countryside."

Amanda giggled, feeling glad and blessed to be in good company. Of course, she was not about to reveal the awful truth to a kid who didn't look as if he was older than fourteen.

Amanda sent a strange text to the girls once she was safe. It simply said, 'I need you.'

The first call she made back at the police station was to Lynnie.

Her voice was soft and hoarse, and all she could mutter was, "Why am I such an idiot?"

Before hanging up, Lynnie offered, "You're safe, I will be there soon."

Lynnie arrived at the police station to gather Amanda and took her immediately into her arms. Once safe and warm, Amanda began confessing to Lynnie all she had endured in her relationship with Paul. They cried and laughed together, but mostly, Lynnie repeatedly assured her that she was safe now, away from harm.

But it took a very long time for Amanda to feel normal again.

She had become skeptical and fearful of crowds, also no longer interested in romantic relationships with men. Her experience had jaded her, making her suspicious and distrustful.

Home from the camping trip, she slept with the light on, fearing the dark, and installed an alarm system in her apartment. The mace at her end table gave some solace, but even so, she often awoke due to nightmares of running through the wood and being chased.

She had gained about fifty pounds in the last year, too. Being heavier made her feel stronger and more protected, but also less desirable, for which she was thankful since it kept the men at bay, and men were bad and untrustworthy. Lynnie had suggested she get some therapy, but instead, Amanda had made a decision.

"I'm going to go for my master's degree in psychology," she said as if that resolved everything. "And before you say anything, I know it won't help the actual problem but it will keep me busy. The less I think about things the better."

As a distraction, she submerged herself in psychology research, passionate about learning to understand every facet of mental health.

Jessica was Amanda's biggest cheerleader.

"I just stopped by to bring you some lunch. You need to keep your strength up," she'd say.

"Ahh, my favorite, a turkey club. Thank you so much!"

"Extra mayo, just the way you like it," Jessica offered. Then, after a brief pause, "OK, Amanda, I'll leave you to your studies. I'm proud of you, my friend."

Amanda gave a slow smile and finished eating her lunch, more determined to make a difference in the field of psychology. Studying this major in grad school was difficult, and it took a lot of discipline to stay focused. What she had been through was still playing on her mind.

Amanda's past had caused a lot of traumas, and she still had difficulty dealing with it.

Somehow, she reasoned that majoring in mental health would benefit both her and the eventual patients, but there were so many times when it all seemed too difficult.

Still, she was determined to finish her studies and get her degree, continuing to help people who were struggling with mental illness. She learned genuine compassion for all those who suffered from depression, addiction, and other brain health issues.

Although behaviors from some of her clients triggered her, she knew how to compartmentalize those feelings, focusing on helping her patients deal with their own issues.

She needed to help remove the stigma of brain health problems, being an advocate for those who much needed it. "I like to think of myself as a brain doctor," she'd say. "I treat brains, just like people with a bad heart go to a cardiologist."

Why were heart issues never stigmatized, while matters of the mind were?

Brain and heart health should no longer be so differentiated, she believed, so being on the frontline could impact how people viewed the issue.

She learned to suppress her fears and prejudices about mental health, putting more effort into eliminating the stigma to justify all she had experienced.

If a slight bit of hostility was still embedded in her, she fiercely tried to tame it. Her intentions were noble, but there were times that the stress of the job had her gasping for breath.

During her internship at Delaware General Hospital, she encountered many people from all walks of life, from a man suffering lifelong brain health problems to a young woman experiencing a mental breakdown; many stories were heartbreaking, but some were inspirational.

A young mother suffering from postpartum depression had become so scared of herself and of the harm she wanted to do to her baby that she'd voluntarily checked herself into the hospital.

Once so excited about the birth of her baby girl, after the child was born, she became overwhelmed, depressed, violent, and suicidal. Her brain knew her mind wasn't well, and she sought help, knowing that the feelings inside were more than just the blues. Once she got the medication and help she needed, she was able to help other young women do the same.

The most exciting part of this field for Amanda was so much of the unknown.

The workings of the brain weren't studied as intensively as many other human body organs, though mental wellness was so vital. What had made Paul snap years ago? If he'd had more support, could this entire nasty and terrifying situation have been avoided?

There was a deep sense of both remorse and guilt for not being able to identify Paul's mental illness and help him get the support he needed before his mental breakdown.

She simply hadn't known the signs, hadn't understood it as she did now. For Amanda, this was her way to give back, to make amends and feel as though her experience wasn't for nothing.

As much as Amanda had wanted to be a researcher, she'd followed her passion as a therapist, enjoying interacting with her patients. By making eye contact with them and giving them a sense of love and security, she could reach not all but some of her patients in some form.

Often, she would lie in bed at night and replay some of her sessions, worrying if she had made the impact she had set out as her goal for the day.

Many times, the troubles of her patients became her own, taking a toll on her. White wine had become Amanda's all-too-familiar friend after a long day of patients.

At times, she promised herself that she would focus on her own health and get to the gym, but usually, she was far too exhausted, finding herself sitting on her couch, replaying her day.

By 9:00 p.m., and after finishing two bottles of rosé, she would pass out.

The prolonged lonely night drinking and morning fogginess were getting gradually worse. Although, in the evenings, she always meant to have only one glass of wine, lately, she would awake to three empty bottles sitting on the kitchen counter, often alongside a half-eaten rice cake or something similar that she must have devoured as a late-night snack.

As much as she desperately tried drinking less, she always ended up with an empty bottle. Her weight and drinking had become a detriment to getting healthy, and Amanda noticed that her once slim body was becoming plumper and far less defined.

Every Monday, the intentions were always good, promising herself that she would hit the gym, make a salad, and drink plenty of water. Unfortunately, like clockwork, Monday would come around, and again Amanda would find herself with a slight headache and gurgle in her stomach.

Amanda had been burying her relationship with food all the way back from her youth but had no issues living a healthy lifestyle for many years. As the stress and anxiety of her work became more intense, however, her will to monitor her behavior suffered, and she lost control of her weight. Although no longer binging, she would overeat and drink too much alcohol.

It was a way to comfort herself from her own life.

Sometimes, she would wonder how she could possibly be in the same dark place she had occupied since being a teenager, eventually convincing herself she was no longer the same.

*I have complete control of what I eat and drink these days*, she said to herself. *It's not as if I have a 'need' to drink, is it? I just enjoy it, that's all, now and again.*

*I can go without a drink anytime. Besides, having wine after a long day's work is customary!*

At the time, she truly didn't understand the impact of her drinking on her own life or the drastic consequences it would later play. She had no way of knowing that it would eventually shatter lives, incomprehensibly changing her too. Although spending countless hours helping those around her, she needed to help herself most of all, but did not see it. The time she was happiest was still when talking with her most treasured friends; at such times, it was easy to feel relatively happy and whole. They had no way of knowing their dear friend was heading for disaster.

———— ⋅⊰⊱⋅ ————

*Lynnie: Worried for a Friend.*

Something Amanda did not know was that her dear friend Lynnie was writing notes about her in her journal:

———— ⋅⊰⊱⋅ ————

JOURNAL

TODAY, I REACHED OUT TO AMANDA. ALL I CAN SAY IS THAT I'M WORRIED ABOUT HER; SOMETHING SEEMS LIGHTLY OFF. I CAN'T PUT MY FINGER ON IT, BUT IT'S A SENSE I'M GETTING.

ANYWAY, AMANDA ASSURED ME SHE WAS FINE, BUT THE CONVERSATION WAS TENSE AND SHE SNAPPED AT MY QUESTIONS. I CALLED JESSICA FOR GUIDANCE AND TO HEAR HER THOUGHTS. SHE, TOO, WAS CONCERNED WITH AMANDA'S WAY TOO QUICK ANSWER OF "FINE."

I JUST HAVE AN ODD FEELING THAT SOMETHING ISN'T RIGHT. BUT WHAT CAN I DO?

———— ⋅⊰⊱⋅ ————

"Amanda doesn't answer our calls or texts these days," Jessica said.

"Well, she's been through a lot. Maybe she just needs some time," Lynnie suggested.

"She's so fucking stubborn. Why is she just shutting us out? We've been through so much together. I call bullshit," Jessica said, exasperated.

"Didn't she say anything else?" scoffed Jessica.

"I thought we were beyond this with one another. We can't guess what's happening with Amanda, can we? How are we supposed to help her like friends do if she won't share? She needs to use her words. After all, she is a fucking therapist! Or has she been making it all up?"

They sat silent for a while, lost in thoughts.

Amanda's behavior had changed so drastically from confident and happy to sullen and dark, barely even making eye contact whenever they saw her anymore, as if she was hiding something.

"Do you think she's reverted back to her old addictions?" Jessica pondered.

"Maybe," Lynnie said quietly. "I just feel so helpless. How can she let this happen, especially since the past addiction issues her brother experienced?"

"I'm so over this. Let's call her and drag her ass to rehab if need be," Jessica snapped.

Lynnie chuckled. then saw the determined look on Jessica's face. "Wait, you're serious?"

"Fuck yeah, I am. This is what friends do. Real friends make each other accountable for themselves and tell them the truth even when they don't want to hear it."

"Should we call Myra?" Lynnie inquired.

"Yes, of course, I know she's been super busy at the firm, putting away every jaywalker throughout the city, but I think we should tell her. Grab me my phone," Jessica said.

In no time, the girls had Myra on speakerphone, explaining the situation. Myra seemed distracted but concerned.

"Well, have you reached out to her yet?" Myra asked. "It's her life, isn't it? It's not for us to say what she has to do. We are not her keepers as the saying goes. I care but there are limits."

"Yes, of course, we have reached out," said Lynnie. "Several times, in fact, and she isn't taking our calls. I even called her office, and she hadn't been at work for three days, saying she had a family emergency."

"Now that doesn't sound like Amanda at all. Do you think she's OK?" Myra said, half listening.

"Jesus Christ!" Jessica interrupted. "If we thought she was all right, would we be on the phone with you to discuss this?"

"OK, let's calm down," Lynnie reasoned. "Let's give her the benefit of the doubt. I know her Aunt Erica was ill, and maybe something did happen. Perhaps she had a family emergency and had to leave town in a hurry."

"Doubt it," Jessica sarcastically cut in.

She was unusually curt today, which puzzled Lynnie.

"Guys, we all know that Amanda has a history of addiction. What are we waiting for before intervening?" Jessica pleaded.

For a moment, the girls went silent. This indicated that they knew what they had to do and had to wrap their minds around Amanda being in trouble.

"Let's meet tomorrow after work. I have to wrap up a couple of things here, then I'll be able to head out of the city to meet you guys. We'll drop in on her and see what's up," Myra suggested.

"Don't you think that is kind of intrusive?" Lynnie said.

"Intrusive? What do you expect us to do, send smoke signals? She isn't answering our calls, texts, or emails. She has left us no choice," Jessica impatiently shouted.

They met at a small coffee shop, grabbed a bite to eat, discussing the situation further.

"Still, no word from her, right?" asked Jess.

"No, nothing," Lynnie confirmed.

"OK, so we drive to her house and talk to her. Maybe she's depressed, perhaps she's sick, or she just wants to be alone. Any which way, we'll find out," said Myra.

The twenty-five-minute ride to Amanda's house seemed longer, the car quiet through most of it. It was known that Amanda had a dark side, one that she'd tried to keep secret.

It was evident that her life was beginning to spiral, but when they got to her house, they were unprepared for the scene. Broken glasses, scattered garbage, and the smell of rotting food hit them like a ton of bricks. Dishes had been piling up in the sink for weeks and overflowing garbage had attracted bugs. Among all the muck lay Amanda, hair matted against her scalp, clothes looking as though they hadn't been washed in ages.

The smell of alcohol was so strong it was hard to get too close to her.

Lynnie gasped in horror, Myra stood speechless and shocked, and Jess got angry.

"Amanda!" she shouted. "What in the actual fuck are you doing?"

Amanda didn't move.

She was passed out so profoundly that she hadn't even heard them come in.

"Amanda!" shouted Jessica. "Get the fuck up. Myra, call your friend James at Surrender Rehabilitation and see if they have room for her. Call in a favor and do whatever you need to do. We're admitting her to rehab today. We just cannot leave her here like this."

This explosion was so unlike the usual calm, nurturing Jessica.

She was visibly shaken and, in her typical mannerism, tried to make things right. This time though, Jessica was far more aggressive than usual.

"Jess, wait, this is her choice. Let's talk with her."

Lynnie was trying to make sense of what they were witnessing.

"Talk with her? Are you out of your fucking mind? Look around. Look at her. Does this look like someone who could be reasoned with?" Jessica shouted.

With all the commotion, Amanda started to stir a bit. When she slowly opened her eyes, it was hard to focus. At first, she didn't say a word but lay there confused and stunned.

"Guys? What are you doing here?" Amanda slurred.

"Get up," Jess demanded.

Slowly, Amanda began to understand the situation, immediately becoming embarrassed and defensive. "Why are you even here, and what right do you have to barge into my apartment?"

"What right do we have? We drove out here because we're your friends. We knew you were in trouble and needed us," Myra said.

"I don't need anyone now. Get the fuck out," said Amanda.

It was too much for Lynnie to handle, and she found herself pleading, "No! No, stop! Amanda, please, we're here to help. Please let us help; we love you, and you need some sort of assistance. You can't go on like this." Lynnie's voice was shaking.

She tried to keep her eye contact steady to allow Amanda to feel safe.

"I pulled some strings, and they could admit her within the hour," Myra announced.

"Admit me? Admit me where? I'm not going anywhere. Now get out," said Amanda.

Myra took over. "Amanda, I just spent the past fifteen minutes pleading with a contact of mine to make room for you at a rehabilitation center. You can rest there and get the help you need."

She reached for Amanda's hand. "We know we can't force you, but I'm asking you—no, I'm begging you—to please come with us and let us help you."

Tears rolled down Amanda's face in defeat.

She knew she needed help and that this intrusion was a gift of love.

"OK," Amanda whispered, "I'll go."

Amanda surrendered to the wisdom of her friends, faced with no choice but to trust them to help her get sober. Her only other option was destruction, and she wasn't so self-loathing as to completely give up on herself. Embarrassed, disheveled, and broken, she put a couple of things into an overnight bag and followed her friends out of the door.

The mood was somber, and Lynnie desperately tried to do what she did best, fix the situation. "Listen, Amanda, we love you; we all love you. We want to see you whole again, and we'll be here when you're ready for us."

Amanda didn't move, simply staring out the window.

# CHAPTER THIRTEEN

*Amanda: Rehabilitation.*

Being in the facility was dreadful, the first couple of days utterly brutal. Amanda would shake, sweat, and wish for death. At night, she would curse at her friends for taking her to the facility, and almost every moment was considering signing herself out. Had she not met a fellow patient, Carissa, who was feeling the effects of withdrawal, she wouldn't have lasted.

Together, the two would talk, pace, and chain smoke in the common areas. Amanda couldn't imagine a worse place to be mentally or physically, yet eventually, against all expectation, the darkness grew a little lighter, Amanda feeling a slight twinge of hope every day.

By the eleventh day, her shakes had stopped, and she was able to eat and socialize with the other patients. She would especially sympathize with the small-framed woman in the corner, scared and in physical pain from withdrawal. Just days before, Amanda too would most likely have looked just as helpless. When she approached the woman, she noticed marks on her arms, indicating that her withdrawals were from more than alcohol. Amanda looked kindly at the stranger, hoping to meet her gaze, but the woman was gone and hadn't even seen her. Amanda could relate to and understand this behavior, hoping she would never be in that same situation.

She attended every meeting, speaking with her sponsor, closely interacting with Carissa.

The woman was tall and lanky, her gray hair straggly, the dark circles under her eyes making her look far older than her age. Carissa was soft-spoken and apologetic for her current state.

She was an artist, and the long, lonely nights up creating paintings were accompanied by vodka with lime. "The lime makes me feel sophisticated," she claimed.

There was a slight twinkle in her eye when she said it.

Clarissa and Amanda leaned on one another during the long nights and grueling days, and once they reached their seventeenth day, they were both granted permission to walk the grounds.

Amanda, still struggling with her weight, began walking daily, allowing her to change her behavior while working on her bodyweight goals. By the twelfth week, she was down over ten pounds and considering returning to her life. Her insurance was about to run out, and she knew that if she kept up with her sponsor and stayed in close contact with Carissa, she would be ready to get back to her life. She called her old boss, convincing her to let her see patients again.

It took some persuading; while Elizabeth was fond of Amanda, she knew that she had some personal issues to figure out. "Amanda, I will let you take on two patients a week. If you can prove yourself to me and, more importantly, to your clients, I will consider putting you back on the schedule on a more permanent basis," Elizabeth explained.

"Great," Amanda said. "That suits me. I'm looking forward to helping patients again. These last three months have taught me a lot, and I'm ready to use my new skills to help others."

Amanda filled out the paperwork three days later, being released the following afternoon; walking out of the facility, she was greeted by Lynnie, Jessica, and

Myra, all eager to hug her lovingly. But how would they react to seeing her after everything that had transpired?

They embraced her instantaneously.

If there was any hesitation or ill feelings, it was all swept away as they hugged.

"We've really missed you, Amanda," Lynnie said joyfully.

"So proud of you," Jessica chimed in. "All good things ahead for you, Amanda!"

"I knew you'd be OK," Myra said confidently. "You're a survivor."

They drove to their favorite Mexican restaurant, enjoyed a meal, and caught up on live happenings. Amanda was particularly excited to eat the chicken fajitas, devouring the entire plate. "I haven't eaten real food for months," she said as cheese dripped down her chin. They sipped on their soda waters, even though Amanda assured them it would be fine to enjoy a drink.

"Guys, please; I don't want it to be awkward each time we go out to eat," she pleaded.

"Amanda, we want to support you, and anyway, we're just so glad to be together. I'm drunk on happiness," Jessica said. And sure enough, they giggled as if they'd drunk their fill of alcohol.

They enjoyed their meal, laughing.

Finally, the waiter politely came along, saying, "Ladies, so sorry to spoil your night and cut it off early, but we'll be closing shortly."

After a lovely evening, an odd thing occurred as the women were saying their final goodbyes.

Jessica screeched in pain, clutching her head.

"Jessica, what's happened?" Amanda asked, happy the spotlight was no longer on her new-found sobriety.

"I don't know. I keep getting these weird pains in my head. I need to drink more water."

Myra chimed in, "Well, since that's all we're going to be drinking for a while, that won't be much of a problem." The laughter consumed the air as the ladies departed.

⸻ ❦ ⸻

JOURNAL

AMANDA'S FINALLY HOME. IT'S SO WONDERFUL TO SEE HER HEALTHY AND SOBER AGAIN, AND I PRAY THIS IS THE LAST OF OUR TROUBLES—WELL, HERS AT LEAST. I'M GOING TO BED, GRATEFUL TO HAVE MY FRIEND BACK, AND I'M LOOKING FORWARD TO SOBRIETY AND GOOD HEALTH FOR ALL OF US.


I'VE BEEN SO PREOCCUPIED WITH AMANDA THAT I HAVEN'T EVEN WRITTEN MUCH ABOUT THE AMAZING MAN I MET. I'M SO EXCITED BUT I'LL WRITE MORE ABOUT IT LATER!

⸻ ❦ ⸻

Now that things had calmed down with Amanda, Lynnie needed to focus on her career; she'd decided to take a weekend seminar trip to Miami, and she'd met Marc on the way.

She was immediately lovestruck, and even though Lynnie didn't believe in love at first sight and scoffed at the irony, she uncharacteristically took a chance.

Lynnie approached him first to say hello, pretending to show an interest in some items in an airport store. Marc was nearby, browsing too. He stood with confidence and warmth, and before she knew it, she was introducing herself. "Hi! Hi, I'm Lynnie."

"Well, hello there, Lynnie, I'm Marc with a c not a k at the end," he said with a chuckle.

"OK, Marc, with a c, glad you cleared up that mystery," she said sarcastically.

Marc was clearly receptive.

"You're buying a magazine? Is it too intrusive to ask what it's about?"

She stared, clueless for a moment.

Then she realized what he meant, looking down at the item in her hand.

"Oh, this!" she said. "If I'm being honest, I'm not in the market for this magazine. I was just trying to get your attention."

"Is that so?" replied Marc. "Well, now you have it. So, now what?"

Lynnie blushed at her unusual boldness, but before she could retreat, Marc quickly asked her to grab a drink at the bar across the way.

She happily said yes.

They hit it off immediately, as if they'd known each other for years. They had the same interests, values, and, most importantly, humor. Both were quick-witted and kind and although neither believed in love at first sight, they certainly had a unique connection.

They were both headed to Miami, though Marc was visiting a client for a business meeting. He upgraded their seats to sit together in first class. Lynnie had never sat in first class and was impressed by how unpretentious Marc behaved for a businessman.

He was casual and smooth, hating formalities as much as she did.

Marc invited Lynnie to a cocktail party he was attending later that evening. These kinds of events weren't really her thing but how could she decline? She was so interested in him! If she said no to the first thing he invited her to, maybe he would never invite her again.

Lynnie blew off part of the seminar, joining Marc at his events.

She knew it was irresponsible, but for once, she just wanted to be spontaneous.

The pair drank, danced, and enjoyed the evening.

Lynnie watched as Marc worked the room, though never taking his eyes off her, returning to her now and then to check that she was OK. The energy between them was magnetic, and when the evening ended, Lynnie accepted the invitation back to Marc's hotel room. Once inside, their lips met with a slow rhythmic pace as they looked deep into each other's eyes.

Slowly, Marc unzipped her dress, watching as the yellow material fell to the ground.

He began kissing her neck as she absorbed his touch, unbuttoning his shirt slowly, never leaving his gaze as her heart beat faster. She felt the hair of his chest brush up against her breast, and she began unzipping his pants urgently. The two fell onto the bed, the urge to unite inevitable. For hours, the pair devoured each other, unable to release from their embrace, and after a long while, their bodies went limp, falling into a deep sleep.

During the night, Marc awoke to find Lynnie staring up at him with a look of pure satisfaction.

"Well, hello there beautiful," he said sleepily.

"I know this is crazy, and I probably sound insane, but there's just something … Sorry, forget I said it. You must think I'm mad."

"No," he said, grabbing hold of her hand. "I feel the same too. There's this energy that I've never felt. An attraction I didn't even know I was capable of feeling."

"Yes, and I'm so glad this is mutual. I knew you were out there, and one day, I'd find the missing piece to my puzzle," Lynnie said.

The two spent the entire day in bed, laughing, talking, and making love.

When it was time to depart from the seminar that Lynnie had never actually attended, she was sad to leave Marc.

"So now what?" asked Lynnie.

"We find a way, and make it work. I finally found you, and I'm not going to let a little distance come between us. Frankly, I always wanted to live on the East Coast, so who knows what will happen?" Marc said.

The two bid farewell, but by the next week, Lynnie was on a plane to visit with Marc. Although the travel was brutal, it was worth it, Marc paying for all her flights, knowing she was unable to afford the expense.

JOURNAL

I'M SCARED TO WRITE THIS. I SWORE THAT AFTER LUKE, I WOULD NEVER ALLOW MYSELF TO BE IN ANOTHER RELATIONSHIP. THE TRAUMA WAS TOO MUCH.

BUT NOW, I'VE MET MY SOULMATE. I KNOW HE'S IT! I FEEL IT IN THE CORE OF MY BEING THAT THIS MAN IS THE BEST THING TO HAPPEN TO ME, AND IT LEAVES ME FEELING SCARED AND EXCITED ALL AT ONCE.

I CAN HARDLY BELIEVE I ACTUALLY BLEW OFF MY SEMINAR TO GO TO HIS BUSINESS FUNCTION; HOW CRAZY IS THAT? BUT MAYBE THIS IS THE NEW ME, LESS UPTIGHT, MORE CAREFREE—AND IT'S ALL DOWN TO MARC AND HOW GIDDY AND UNINHIBITED HE MAKES ME FEEL.

Anyway, while we were at his 'cocktail party,' I enjoyed watching him work and move around the room with ease. While I'm so awkward with strangers, he has a knack for captivating the room. So, I sat by the window, watching him, so amazed at how he interacts with potential clients; I kept catching his gaze as he was mingling with strangers.

I gave him a soft smile, and he returned a quick wink with a contagious smile back. And I swear that without missing a beat, he maintained his conversation, not ever taking his attention off me. I could feel the attraction from across the room. The energy between us is magical.

His calm demeanor and focused attention on me are erotic, overwhelming me with emotion.

When I left the event slightly tipsy from the champagne, I knew I had to have this man. At his hotel room, he devoured me, making me want him even more.

This man has unexpectedly set my world on fire.

Sadly, there is just one major glitch in all of this. He lives in California.


Why does life have to make this so difficult for us?

---

*Lynnie: South Oaks Nursing Home.*

"That is some love story," says Helen, glancing back. "Well, what happened next?"

She seats herself next to Lynnie.

"I'm not sure; there seems to be a gap in time. The date appears to be a year later."

"Well, read it," Helen demands. "I'm invested in this story now."

Lynnie begins reading some more ...

---

Later that night, when Lynnie crawled into bed, she cried, but this time, happy tears.

Marc opened her mind to enjoying life without boundaries or fear, easing her mind and delighting her body. He was kind by nature, curious by design, witty in all circumstances, and full of love for Lynnie.

She had finally felt loved unconditionally, understanding now more than ever her value as a person, not a pawn, in her mother's demented games.

With Marc, this was genuine love, not feigned, not thrown away if she didn't follow some silly set of 'rules' he imposed on her. She didn't have to earn his love or prove it the way she had with her mother. For sure, her mother would disapprove of this relationship with Marc.

She would have been disappointed with the patriarchal rules that Lynnie broke, ones she'd embedded in her at a young age. Lynnie explained her relationship with her mother to Marc.

"She would tell me not to act too bright, or I would never land a man."

Marc was astonished, visibly reeling.

"What kind of mother would give their impressionable young daughter that advice?"

Lynnie replied, "A dangerous one. Anyway, let's not talk about my mother. It's my fault; I should never have brought her into our conversation."

They strolled the streets, the night chill unusual for California, the wind causing it to feel cooler. Lynnie's floral dress didn't protect her from the elements, and she felt Marc's warm body against her shaking skin, his touch electrifying.

He hesitated and kissed her, thrusting her body into his arms. He stumbled two steps and recovered, holding her tight to balance the fall. They found themselves in a vacant park under the moonlight, the night's cold edge becoming a magnificent blur filled with passion.

Pensively, she looked deep into his eyes as he slowly removed her clothes.

She unbuttoned his shirt, hands trembling with anticipation and nervousness. They lay on the soft grass, giggling at the gracelessness and boldness of their risky indiscretion.

He smirked at her slowly as he climbed on top of her body, caressing her face while never taking his eyes off her. She had his full attention, and there was magic all around.

His energy consumed her, a feeling of complete euphoria. Peace and clarity spiritually washed over her, and she was in a dream-like state.

Almost at a loss for words, they spoke a silent language both easily understood.

Lynnie's hands went through his chest hair, pulling him even closer, feeling him slowly enter her with gentleness. Their eyes remained locked as their bodies thrust together, their breathing becoming heavier. She gasped, feeling his body collapse with satisfaction.

Marc kissed her softly, his breath whispering, "Wow."

They lay together, holding one another, talking, laughing, sharing secrets.

That was the moment she knew she was in love.

She wanted to spend the rest of her life with Marc, and there would never be another man who could ever capture her heart the same way.

*Lynnie: South Oaks Nursing Home.*

*There are so many books that feel familiar,* Lynnie thinks. She keeps reading but worries for these young people, wondering what's happened to them.

Lynnie takes another sip of tea that Helen has brought in earlier and continues to read ...

## JOURNAL

THE DISTANCE SUCKS. I LEAVE DELAWARE EVERY FRIDAY AND COME HOME EVERY SUNDAY NIGHT. THE TIME CHANGE IS ALWAYS A HASSLE, LEAVING ME PERPETUALLY EXHAUSTED. IF I'M BEING HONEST, I DON'T CARE BECAUSE THIS MAN IS WORTH EVERY JET-LAG NIGHT I SPEND AND EVERY LONG MONDAY MORNING AFTER BEING AWAY ALL WEEKEND. HE TAKES ME TO ALL THE BEST RESTAURANTS, BUT OUR MOST SPECIAL TIME IS WHEN WE SPEND HOURS IN BED TOGETHER, JUST LAUGHING.

He makes me giggle as if I had never known laughter before. Our banter and compatibility are pure and natural, and it doesn't hurt either that the sex is off the charts. The passion we have makes the experience even more intense. I long for each moment to be in his arms, losing myself between the sheets as we intensely ravage one another.

The sexual chemistry is so strong that it is often challenging to sit in a public restaurant without rushing to get back to his apartment. We mostly get takeout anyway since our time together is precious and limited.

The pause between the work weeks makes our passion powerful, counting down the moments until I'm boarding a flight, filled with anticipation until we're together. I love how Marc makes me view life too, feeling that every day is an adventure, and all situations are humorous. This is the happiest, most fun time of my life.

I see a future with him, and it's time for me to finally tell the others.

◆─◆◇◆◇◆─◆

Lynnie met the girls at a pub across town to tell them her news, and before anyone could even say hello, she blurted out, "I found the love of my life! From the moment I saw Marc, I just knew. He felt like home." She was rambling now. "He's like a quiet resting place, the comfort of being my authentic self. It's refreshing and exciting to be around him, and our conversations never end. In the simplicity of his company, I found a space entirely our own."

Lynnie was talking fast with excitement, beaming with joy.

Before she could continue, Jessica interrupted, "Wow! Lynnie, I've never seen you so happy."

"I'm proud of you, Lynnie," Myra said earnestly.

Lynnie looked over at Amanda, curious as to her reaction. To her surprise, she smiled and said, "Good for you. You deserve love."

The ladies sipped beer and caught up on life, and for a moment, things appeared to make sense again.

JOURNAL

CALM IS GOOD! EVERYTHING SEEMS TO BE FALLING INTO PLACE FOR ONCE!

For two years, Marc and Lynnie commuted to visit one another as often as possible. They were deeply in love and for once, Lynnie felt that life would work out better than she had imagined.

Marc was hoping for a transfer to the East Coast so that they could finally live together.

They talked about this a lot, also about getting a bigger apartment once he was able to move there permanently. The distance lately had been getting to Lynnie, making her decide that on the weekend when she went to visit, she would discuss his transfer, urging him to make it happen sooner rather than later.

Lynnie arrived in Los Angeles later than expected due to flight delays. The weather had been wicked, the airlines backed up.

When she got off the plane, Marc was waiting for her looking a bit distressed.

"Gosh, I missed you," Lynnie gushed.

Marc didn't say anything for a moment.

"Can we take a ride out of the city this weekend? I want to go hiking," said Lynnie.

"Umm, Lynnie, we need to talk, so let's go grab a drink," said Marc.

Lynnie's heart fell to her stomach; her hands were sweaty. She followed Marc, not making eye contact as she tried getting her thoughts in order.

She had never seen Marc like this and was worried about the news he wanted to share.

As they sat, Marc took Lynnie's hand.

"Lynnie, you know I love you," he said tearfully. "And it's difficult for me to say this, but I need to move to Australia for nine months to help a start-up company.

"I'm not saying it will be easy, but once we get through the next nine months, I promise I'll move in with you, and we'll get married."

Lynnie wasn't sure how to react. She was excited by the thought of marrying Marc but devastated at his news of leaving the country.

"Why can't they send someone else?" said Lynnie.

"Lynnie, you know why, and I wish I didn't have to go, but I'm the only one on our team with the expertise. I promise, Lynnie, it will all work out."

## JOURNAL

I'VE BEEN SPENDING SO MANY HOURS TRAVELING TO MARC THAT THERE SEEMS TO NEVER BE ENOUGH TIME.

SO OF COURSE, I'M DISAPPOINTED THAT HE'S CHOSEN TO TRANSFER TO AUSTRALIA. I WAS HOPING HE WOULDN'T TAKE IT AND CHOOSE TO STAY HERE INSTEAD, BUT THIS CAN REALLY PROGRESS HIS CAREER.

THE THING IS TOO, BEING A COUPLE MEANS SUPPORTING ONE ANOTHER'S DREAMS AND I CAN'T HOLD HIM BACK. IT'S ALSO ONLY FOR NINE MONTHS, SO IT'S HARDLY THE END OF THE WORLD, IS IT?

STILL, THOUGH, IT LEAVES ME FEELING SAD AND DISAPPOINTED ALTHOUGH HE PROMISES HE'LL BE BACK STATESIDE AFTER HE GETS THE NEW VENTURE RUNNING. HE'LL RELOCATE TO DELAWARE FOR GOOD THEN.

THE THOUGHT OF BEING AWAY FROM MARC MAKES ME HEARTBROKEN. HE'S EQUALLY TORN BY THIS DECISION BUT CONFIDENT OUR LOVE WON'T FALTER. BEING THE MORE LEVEL-HEADED OF US, HE KNOWS THAT LIFE BRINGS

UNEXPECTED CIRCUMSTANCES. BUT WITH DILIGENCE AND FAITH, IT WILL WORK OUT FOR THE BEST. I HAVE TO BELIEVE IT'S TRUE.

—◦◦◦◦◦—

Lynnie flew to Los Angeles to surprise Marc on the last weekend before he was due to leave for Australia. When she arrived, she was excited to see him, but dreading the thought that this would be their final goodbye for some time. They pulled out all romantic stops to celebrate their time together in nature walks, romantic dinners, and endless hours in bed. No one could deny they were soul mates, and it felt as if their souls were being ripped apart, even if just temporarily.

As the weekend was ending, Marc's belongings were boxed up, lying scattered around his apartment. It would soon be time to head to the airport and say their dreaded farewells.

Lynnie tearfully said, "Marc, I'm going to miss you so much."

"Lynnie, don't cry!" he said with his usual bright, warm smile. "Summer break starts soon, and I'll fly you out for the summer in three months' time. And when this is all over, we'll begin our lives together in Delaware." It was just so typical of him to always see the bright side.

They embraced with tearful eyes as it was time to let go, at least for now. This seemingly impossible situation would have to somehow become tolerable until they reunited. Nonetheless, the last goodbye was painful. Lynnie sobbed into his shirt, and he held her tight, promising to keep in touch and insisting they would find a way to make it work.

With a crackle in his voice, Marc said, "I will love you forever. I'll be back soon and marry you. It will all work out. It always does."

She watched him walk through security, glancing back only once with a wink and a smile.

182

Her heart broke a little more, sobbing under her breath. Watching him walk away, his body becoming smaller as the distance grew, she decided right then and there to take a leave of absence from work and move to Australia.

*Why didn't I think to offer that before?* she wondered.

By the time she reached the steps to her apartment, she had already made her decision. She was moving to Australia to be with Marc and would figure out the job situation once she settled in, even if it meant taking some sort of odd job in the meantime.

Breathless, she turned on the computer to research flights.

She was sure that when she told the girls, they would try and talk her out of it so she needed to have everything firm and in place before they even got a whisper of the news.

In her mind, she could already hear Myra warning her not to chase a man around the world, and Amanda would no doubt be passive aggressive, making some sort of cynical comments about how pathetic it was in this day and age for a woman to be unable to stand on her own two feet for a mere nine months of a man's absence.

But Lynnie didn't care. It was the right decision, and before anyone could talk her out of it, she booked her flight to Australia. She would be leaving in nine days' time.

*Once Marc lands, I'll tell him my plans,* thought Lynnie.

But the landing time came and went, with no news from him.

The next day, Lynnie found herself staring endlessly at her phone, willing it to ring or for a text message to come, saying he had arrived safely and was at his hotel. But still, there were no incoming calls or messages. Lynnie's heart lurched. Something was feeling really off by now.

She had waited three days for Marc to call and had seriously begun to worry. She'd tried his cell phone numerous times, and it kept going straight to voicemail.

Finally, on the fourth day, she received a call, bringing a necessary update.

"Hi, is this Lynnie?"

"Yes, it is."

"Hi Lynnie, this is Marc's boss, Jacob Southeber."

"Oh, hi. I've been trying to reach Marc for days. Is he all right? Has something happened?" Lynnie asked, but there was a long sigh on the other end. "Hello! Are you still there?"

"Yes, Lynnie, I'm still here. Lynnie, I'm so sorry, but there's no easy way to say this—"

"What is it?" Lynnie interrupted. "Please tell me Marc is OK."

"Lynnie, Marc was involved in a fatal accident. He was killed on the way to his flat for the very first time when an eighteen-year-old inexperienced girl lost control of her car and crashed head-on into Marc's Uber. This is horrific, I know, but neither he nor the driver made it through. He wouldn't have known a thing about it, Lynnie; I'm told he died right there, instantly."

"B-but it can't be ..." Lynnie stuttered, then dropped the phone and began hyperventilating.

"Lynnie, I'm so sorry ... Lynnie?" Jacob said, but all he heard were Lynnie's screams.

⸻ ❦ ⸻

JOURNAL

I CAN'T WRITE ALL THE DETAILS OF THIS. I'M STILL SO DISTRAUGHT. THIS NEWS HAS ABSOLUTELY DEVASTATED ME, AND MY LIFE WILL NEVER BE THE SAME. HOW COULD THIS HAPPEN? WE WERE PLANNING OUR LIFE TOGETHER. THE AGONY OF LOSING MARC IS JUST TOO MUCH, SO BAD

THAT I CAN BARELY FUNCTION. I CAN'T STOP SOBBING, NO MATTER HOW HARD I TRY.

MY WORLD HAS FALLEN APART. I'M SICKENED AT THE THOUGHT OF FOOD, BARELY MANAGING TO LIFT MY HEAD TO DRINK WATER. THE FATIGUE'S WORSENING, AND I CAN'T SHAKE THE UNRELENTING TIREDNESS OF MY BODY AND SOUL. MAYBE IT'S MY BODY'S WAY OF SAYING IT JUST WANTS TO GO WHEREVER MARC IS.

THE GIRLS HAVE BEEN SO SUPPORTIVE OF ME. THEY CHECK ON ME DAILY AND KNOW I NEED A LITTLE TIME TO GRIEVE. THEY STOP BY, BRINGING FOOD, TRYING TO GET ME DRESSED. BUT I'M NOT READY YET.

WILL I EVER BE?

*Lynnie: New Life.*

On a spring day, Lynnie crawled out of bed, opened the window and made herself oatmeal. The smell of the cinnamon sugar permeated her senses, sending her directly to the bathroom to vomit. Her head was spinning, and her stomach lurching. *Could it be? Have I missed my period without even realizing it?* thought Lynnie. She ran down the stairs of her apartment block, heading to the nearest drugstore. Scouring the aisles for a pregnancy test, she could barely make sense of her emotions. She shakingly handed the cashier a twenty-dollar bill, running back out, not waiting for change. The cashier tilted her head, shrugging and smiling.

Lynnie rushed home as fast as she could, anxiously ripping open the package even before opening the apartment door. The excitement overcame her as she sobbed quietly.

"Oh, Marc, please, please let this be real ..."

And so, it was, two clear lines on the pregnancy test.

Lynnie was pregnant with Marc's baby.

She fell to the floor and sobbed, some tears of happiness, others of sadness. Sadness that Marc was not there to experience this joy, disappointed that their child would never get to know their father, and fearful of what the future held.

"I believe this is a sign from Marc, assuring me that he's always with me, entrusting me with his child, and knowing our love will carry on forever," she said between sobs.

Lynnie tried to navigate the conception and due dates, but it all seemed jumbled up.

She called the gynecologist to make an appointment. When the receptionist, Holly, answered, she immediately recognized Lynnie's voice.

"Hi there, Lynnie. You already have an appointment for your annual next month," she announced.

"Umm, no, Holly, I seem to be pregnant! I need an appointment as soon as possible."

"Oh, OK, wow, that's something I wasn't expecting to hear! That's amazing! Congratulations," Holly said, hearing the urgency in Lynnie's voice.

After placing Lynnie on hold, Jenny returned.

"OK, I have one urgent appointment in a week exactly, next Thursday at 3:00 p.m."

Lynnie hung up in wonderment, subconsciously patting her tiny belly. After Marc's death, she had already taken leave from work, using up vacation and bereavement time.

To keep her mind busy, and because there would be a ton of stuff to organize—Lynnie had the urge to sort her finances and get to the mail that had been lying around for the last six weeks.

Rummaging through the stack of junk mail and bills, she noticed a plain white envelope beneath the pile, addressed to her.

Her heart skipped; it was in Marc's handwriting.

She froze for a moment, glanced at his block letters with her name, and gingerly opened the envelope using a sharp knife. Inside was a handwritten letter.

---

*Dear Lynnie,*

*I am by now on my way to Australia. I want you to know how much I love you and will forever be in love with you.*

*And as crazy as this sounds, I've had a thought. I know you have a life and career here, but please leave it all and come live with me in Australia once I get settled!*

*Could you?*

*Would you?*

*We will be happy together, the beginning of spending the rest of our lives as a couple.*

*Love, Marc*

⸻ ⬥ ⸻

A one-way ticket to Sydney, Australia, lay folded neatly beside the letter. Lynnie gasped at the romance, at the *what-if* possibilities, and then the reality of the gesture made her sob.

She cried in self-pity, and for his lost life, but mainly for a robbed future. It was all tragic. Holding the ticket, she knew the last gift he had left was the tiny being growing inside her.

How would she manage and what would become of her career?

She had more questions than answers, but all that mattered was that she had Marc's baby growing inside her body.

She was elated at the thought that a part of him would always be connected to her.

Lynnie insisted the girls meet her out for dinner. To their surprise, she was finally excited to leave her apartment, and the girls took that as a good sign.

"We are thrilled to see you out, honey," said Jessica.

"How are you doing?" inquired Myra.

"How are you feeling?" asked Amanda.

Before she could answer either question, Lynnie said loudly, "I'm going to burst with joy."

Myra was looking at the specials, and Jessica had been waiting for Lynnie to say something, just staring patiently.

"Wait for it … I'm pregnant, I'm pregnant, I'm pregnant! And before you ask, of course, it's Marc's! I found out today, and I'm super scared but also super excited, and ahhhhh!"

Without hesitation, Lynnie was received with hugs and love. It had been so long since she'd felt alive, and the prospect of the baby had made her ecstatic and scared too.

"We got you," said Myra.

The others nodded in agreement.

Lynnie held up her seltzer, tearfully making a toast to Marc.

"To the love of my life, Marc, we will always protect this baby. And I know you are up there, looking down on me—on us. Me and your girl. Or me and your boy!"

She giggled, wiped her eyes, patted her belly, and knew that with the help of her soul sisters, all would be OK.

As the months went by, the little life inside Lynnie grew, tiny flutters presenting themselves and then small movements. By the end of summer, full-on strong kicks had invaded her insides, often making her wince in pain.

"OK, baby, I know you're in there," said Lynnie.

Being pregnant alone posed challenges, making her miss the support of Marc.

She never went to any checkups alone, one of the girls always sure to be at her appointment, even if it meant rearranging their schedules. Lynnie was grateful to have her friends, but listening to the tiny little heartbeats, *thump, thump, thump* ... she wished Marc were sitting next to her to experience this miracle.

When she was sick, uncomfortable, or grouchy, she wished he were there to hold her hand, assuring her that she was still pretty, and rubbing her belly as the baby kicked.

Lynnie felt robbed of the joys of pregnancy and was mostly sad that Marc wasn't with her throughout the journey.

At night, she would cry for him, wondering if it was his breath she felt in her ear or was it only her imagination? Sometimes, she would swear she would see him in a crowded street, then rush through the crowds, dodging her way around everyone to get a closer look, only to be disappointed. She never wanted to let go of him but knew her focus and love needed to go toward their baby. Marc would have liked that, and to honor him, she had to be strong for their little miracle growing inside. She had been reading every book and article to prepare for the upcoming challenges of motherhood. *Me, a mother,* she thought in wonderment.

By fall, Lynnie's ever-growing belly left her uncomfortable and shuffling about the apartment. Her shoes barely fit and tying the laces had been so tricky, she had finally invested in slip-on sneakers. Looking around the small office, she knew it was time to decorate it as a nursery.

Myra showed up first with a crib. "We need tools, so I bought a small toolbox."

Amanda showed up next with diapers and baby bottles, her arms filled with loads of supplies. "We're going to need to clean out one of your cupboards to fit all of this."

"I hadn't even thought of any of this, thank you. What would I do without you?"

"Starve and die," said Jessica, walking into the apartment with two cheese pizzas.

Lynnie snickered. It was still strange, too, to feel positive again, to have something to laugh and smile about. Even to want to smile was still relatively new, but every time she felt the baby kick or turn, there was that—slightly agonized—grin again. Agonized because there was sometimes a little discomfort when the baby turned but it was always, always, worth smiling!

And the weird thing was that after Marc had first died, she had felt so much guilt each time she laughed, knowing this was something he would never have the chance to do again. Now, since the pregnancy had begun, she knew she had, in some strange way, his permission.

Marc was telling Lynnie, *go on and live your best life, you and my child.*

"I already know I'm going to be the favorite auntie," Amanda announced.

"There is no way," Jessica said. "Babies love me."

"Listen, I don't care if I'm the favorite but know this, he or she will always be able to rely on me," said Myra.

After hours of painting the small but cozy room a warm yellow, with an adorable theme of giraffes, Lynnie was hungry again, insisting they order from a taco shack down the road.

They indulged in nachos and burritos, and while the girls enjoyed a cold beer, Lynnie savored a cold lemonade.

"Dear Lord, Lynnie, we aren't all pregnant. We aren't eating for eight! I'm going to have the worst heartburn if I keep eating like this," Myra said. "Plus, my pants don't fit anymore."

"I've just ordered some with elasticated waists!" said Jessica.

Everyone stared, aghast; while the foursome never tried to dress like glamor models, it was going a bit too far to buy frumpy outfits!

"Tell me you didn't," said Myra.

"OK, I didn't!" Jessica agreed, bursting into laughter.

The day was productive and magical, and as they hugged goodbye, they reviewed the birthing plan one last time.

They embraced, Amanda squeezing Lynnie's hand, looking into her eyes, assuring her she would never be alone.

When they left, Lynnie cleaned up the remaining dishes, and munching on the last of a taco, she walked into her baby's new nursery, sobbing, barely able to believe her eyes though she had been looking at it for hours by now. It was so beautiful, and this miracle was coming.

While she missed Marc tremendously, she had the confidence to live a life wholly, to provide a life for her child to be proud of. She glanced one more time at the small crib that would soon hold her baby, folded a blanket neatly, and shut the door to the nursery.

⸺◦⟨◦⟩◦⸺

## JOURNAL

TODAY, THE GIRLS CAME OVER TO HELP ME SET UP THE CRIB, SHOP FOR DIAPERS, AND THROW ME A VERY INTIMATE BABY SHOWER. WE ATE PIZZA, LAUGHED AND CRIED, DREAMING ABOUT HOW THIS CHILD WILL HAVE ALL THE SUPPORT AND LOVE IT WILL EVER NEED.

THEY VOWED TO BE BY MY SIDE AND PLAY THE ROLE OF AUNTIES, AND I KNOW IT TO BE TRUE.

⸺◦⟨◦⟩◦⸺

The weeks went by slowly, Lynnie beginning to walk with an ache as her swollen ankles made it difficult to take every step. Everything hurt. Her loins were stretched, her back ached, and she couldn't get comfortable no matter what position she tried to sleep in. It was a grueling couple of days, and the doctor said she didn't think she would go into labor for at least another week.

For poor Lynnie, that day could not come soon enough!

"Be patient," the obstetrician reminded Lynnie with a smile. "Enjoy the calm, the peace and quiet. Believe me, when that little bundle arrives, you'll be getting eighteen years of noise and mayhem along with it."

Patience was undoubtedly not one of Lynnie's virtues, however.

It was a Saturday when Lynnie felt the first pang of pain as she was cleaning out the lint from the dryer. At first, she thought it was gas, but as the pain grew, she suspected she was in labor.

The contractions intensified more quickly and more frequently. Lynnie called Myra, whose job was to get her to the hospital, then she called Amanda, who had agreed to be in the room while the others waited to meet them. Jessica had volunteered to stay put, to be the one making calls, and getting ready for the big reveal of the baby's name.

Myra arrived almost immediately when she got the call, and Lynnie wondered what she had been doing that had brought her to her apartment so quickly. She worked on the opposite side of town; how could she have been at her doorstep within minutes?

Later, Lynnie found out that in Myra fashion, she had been renting a small office space two blocks away from her apartment for the past month so she wouldn't have to worry about getting to Lynnie on time; that was how seriously she took her 'auntie' duties!

That was the thing about Myra; she never mentioned that she had been inconvenienced for the last month. She just did it, and never would have breathed a word about it if Lynnie had not directly asked. Lynnie knew Myra would show up every single time, no matter what.

When Lynnie and Myra arrived at the hospital, Amanda was already waiting in the lobby with a huge grin and an adorable oversized stuffed giraffe for the baby.

"It's time," she squealed in delight. "Sorry the giraffe is yellow. If the baby's a boy, we'll have to paint this blue."

"Don't be insane," Myra scoffed with a wink. "Yellow is for either gender! Anyway, these days, anything goes. We have to drop those old stereotypes."

Lynnie said, "Yeah, Amanda ... you need to get with the times!" She gave a brave smile and then said, "Let's do this," punching the air slightly nervously.

Amanda had been so touched when Lynnie asked her to be her coach during delivery; she had sent a mass email to everyone they knew, letting them know her role in the birthing process.

Lynnie noticed Amanda was wearing a white V-neck t-shirt with the words in hot pink, 'I am the Birthing Coach.' She laughed at the ridiculousness until Amanda pulled out a hat from her bag, with 'Coochy-Coo Helper,' embroidered on the front.

"Promise me you will not wear that hat. Please promise me. There is no way I will give birth if I look at you, and you are wearing that insanity!"

"OK! OK!" Amanda promised. "Maybe the hat is a lot, but the shirt is staying on."

Another labor pain barreled in, and Lynnie screamed so loud it echoed through the halls.

"OK, let's get you checked in and into bed," the nurse said sternly.

Amanda said, "We are ready to have the baby!"

"We?" Lynnie said dryly.

Soon, Lynnie was taken into a sizable cheerful room and hooked up to machines. Nurses kept coming in to check the machines and her vitals, scribbling something on her chart and saying happily, "Baby is on the way. All is well."

It seemed to take forever, the pain intensifying so much that Lynnie was begging for an epidural. Myra reminded her that she had planned on not receiving pain medicine, encouraging her to soldier on through the pain.

"Fuck off, Myra!" Lynnie screamed. "I never said that. And if I did, I was lying! I want it!"

Myra giggled, calling the nurse over to instruct her there would be a change of plans. Once the epidural kicked in, Lynnie relaxed, ready to give birth.

At the urge to start pushing, she held onto Amanda's hand and squeezed tightly, the doctors assuring them everything was going well and not to worry.

"Lynnie, you are doing great. You just have to push when we tell you."

When the doctor said, "I see the head. You're doing great," relief overcame Lynnie, giving her the extra energy for one more push.

Lynnie screamed, cried, and was beyond exhausted as she pushed.

Soon, there came the wailing of a new life and she sighed a deep breath of relief.

"Oh, my goodness, let me have my baby," said Lynnie.

Amanda screamed with delight, "It's a girl!"

Lynnie was tearful but also ready to sleep for a whole week if they let her.

---

JOURNAL

ELLIE LANNIE WAS BORN ON JANUARY 2ND. MY DAUGHTER IS NAMED AFTER MARC'S BELOVED GRANDMOTHER, OF WHOM HE SPOKE FONDLY SO OFTEN. HE WOULD TELL ME STORIES OF SPENDING SUMMERS WITH HER IN VIRGINIA AND THE MANY LESSONS SHE TAUGHT HIM ABOUT LIFE AND LOVE.

MARC WOULD BE THRILLED THAT HIS DAUGHTER CARRIED THE SAME NAME AS THE WOMAN WHO RAISED HIM AS A CHILD.

THE DAY Ellie WAS BORN, THE ROOM FELT FILLED WITH LOVE, AND I DIDN'T DOUBT THAT MARC WAS THERE WITH US.

# Chapter Fourteen



*Jessica: No False Hope.*

Shortly after Ellie's birth, Jessica started to feel that terrible pain in her head more frequently. It went down through her eyes, making her see black spots that would last for hours. At first, she thought that she was dehydrated. The next time it happened, she assumed she was tired and stressed, and then the excuses kept coming up for her strange symptoms which, many times, she dismissed as being hormonal. The headaches came and went, the pain slightly more severe each time. Jessica chalked them up to a phase, not worrying.

During a visit to see her folks, Jessica offered to run some errands for her mother, who was busy making Jessica's favorite meal, chicken with rice. The plan was to have a lovely evening catching up on life before Jessica had to head back to Delaware. Jessica adored her time with her mom and stepfather, looking forward to every visit and their nightly chats together.

She couldn't have felt more loved and cherished, and when life started getting complicated, there was no other place she would rather be than at her childhood home.

Jessica made every effort to have a close relationship with her parents, admiring their marriage and the support they had always provided.

However, on the short trip to the market to pick up some fresh ginger, she had yet another headache episode. It seemed to come on suddenly; lately, they'd been becoming even more frequent and more severe each time. She pulled into the market's parking lot; thinking she needed air, she hoped the pain would subside. The throbbing pain radiated through her head as Jessica's body fell to the ground, trembling as her head crashed on the concrete floor.

She awoke in an ambulance, surrounded by strangers, and after being admitted to hospital, she was asked a series of questions, answering the best she could. Her memory was a bit foggy, leaving her confused about the chain of events leading her to this hospital bed.

Jessica spent the day at the hospital, regretful that she couldn't enjoy her parents and the meal they had planned to eat together. Aggravated by the inconvenience, Jessica was becoming impatient with the wait time. Her parents arrived at the hospital hours after Jessica's admission, doing all they could to keep her spirits up.

"Jess," said her mother. "We'll still have time to have dinner together. This is just a tiny inconvenience to ensure that nothing else is going on to cause the headaches. It's necessary, just something you have to go through, honey."

Jessica sent her parents home, knowing she would be waiting a couple more hours.

"I'll call soon when the doctors come to discuss the results. So, Mom, go! I'm looking forward to that meal so the sooner you get home to finish it, the better."

"I'll be back in a couple of hours, but I'll run home and grab you some clean clothes," her mother said. After hours of testing, the doctors came in. They looked so oddly somber, and Jessica could tell the news was not good.

Dr. Richardson sat quietly next to her, staring at her momentarily.

Jessica had known Dr. Richardson since her childhood.

When Jessica had fallen off her bike in the sixth grade, Dr. Richardson was the one who had given her the eight stitches on her arm. She looked down at the small scar, glancing back at the doctor. His big brown eyes were glassy, the wrinkles on his forehead contorting his otherwise handsome face. Seemingly, he was lost in his thoughts.

His mannerisms were odd, and Jessica felt the mood changing in the room. Since she'd been a kid, Jessica had felt comfortable around her doctor, but she was feeling unusually ill at ease now.

The doctor's eyes were distant with concern and worry.

"Hey, Dr. Richardson, I'm OK. I must have just gotten a little dizzy. Sorry to worry you, but I'm already feeling better now," said Jessica.

Dr. Richardson briefly looked away before he spoke.

"Jessica. I have unfortunate news for you," he said slowly. "And I have known you such a long time that this is very painful for me to say it but sometimes, hard things need saying."

"Oh jeez, I'm sorry I've been burning the candle at both ends and overdone it. I promise to take better care of myself. When can I get out of here?" Jessica interrupted. "I promise, I'll slow down and do everything I should be doing ... and refrain from doing what I shouldn't be doing."

She giggled at her own quip.

Jessica could have sworn she saw tears forming in Dr. Richardson's eyes. But was it just the glare of the sun shining through the drab hospital room's dirty windows?

"Jessica, please listen carefully to what I'm about to tell you," Dr. Richardson said sternly.

Jessica knew this was far worse than she had imagined and took a deep breath.

"Jessica, honey, you have a brain tumor. A big one. And sometimes, these things are operable because we've caught them at the right time, and they happen to be low-grade tumors and they are in the right place to be accessible. But at other times, we find inoperable ones. Too fast growing, in too dangerous a location to reach and excise, or some have progressed just too far."

She waited, her eyes glazed. So, which type of tumor was he saying she had?

"I'm sorry," Dr. Richardson said, choking up. He never even needed to fill in the rest.

"But I'm only in my twenties. How is that even possible?"

Her demeanor was saying, *young people don't get brain tumors!*

"It happens more than you realize. Even children get certain brain tumors. It's cancer, and the prognosis is not good. I suggest you spend lots of time with your family and friends, have the time of your life, but at the same time, take this seriously and get your affairs in order."

"Affairs? In my twenties?" Jessica reminded him again. "What do you mean? I don't even have any affairs to get in order! You mean like—"

The heaviness of the implications hit her.

Now Jessica's breathing became heavier, and the room started spinning.

Jessica was trying to follow her doctor's words, but all she kept hearing was *cancer, inoperable, terminal, affairs in order.*

Jessica was so overwhelmed and stunned by this news that she became instantly physically ill. Before she knew it, she vomited in the garbage in the corner of the room.

What could she do next?

The doctor rang for a nurse to come in and assist his patient, and a young, blue-coated Asian girl dashed in, saying, "Oh, honey, let me help you."

She grabbed a wad of paper tissues from a dispenser mounted on the wall.

Lifting her head from the tiny trash can, Amanda just wiped her mouth with her hand and asked, "How much time?"

"Not long, Jessica. The cancer has already progressed," Dr. Richardson said sympathetically.

"What does that mean?" Jessica said, sobbing.

"Weeks, maybe. If you are lucky, a month or so. Let me clarify that with this kind of tumor, even when we are able to treat it, the best we can often achieve is a month more life, something of that ilk." He rested his hand on her forearm, the warmth permeating through her shirt.

"I know many good hospice facilities and can make some phone calls," Dr. Richardson said, his voice trailing off. "But it's *glioblastoma multiforme,* no doubt about it. Untreatable. It grows incredibly fast, even with radiation, and is widely considered the deadliest brain cancer. No matter how young and otherwise fit the patient is, glioblastoma kills within five years, latest."

Choosing to ignore what he had said about hospice, at first, Jessica took it as a sign that she could be part of that five-year survival rate.

"No, Jess," he said in a soft tone. "This tumor's very advanced now, very large, right by the brainstem and you are already at what we call the end-of-life stage."

The doctor's words kept swirling around in Jessica's head.

She felt light-headed, terrified, unsure of what to do with this information.

She wanted to scream, cry, and run away from this truth. She felt angry and out of control but couldn't articulate these feelings in words.

So, she just stayed silent, unsure of her next move.

"End-of-life hospice then?" Jessica said, not really expecting an answer. "I've heard they're nice places." It sounded bizarre and surreal as if she was suggesting a vacation in a sunny place.

Finally, Dr. Richardson broke the awkward silence with a simple and soft, "I'm sorry."

The words seemed shallow and empty, ringing in her ears.

Jessica wasn't sure what, if any, words would have been appropriate, but a simple 'I'm sorry' was definitely not it. She became hysterical.

"Please, Doctor Richardson, just be kind enough to give me some hope! I have known you a literal lifetime!"

But it was clear he had nothing of substance.

"Now, Jessica. You know it doesn't work like that. You know I'm just a medic and these things are way bigger than me too. I can't have any influence on who lives and whose case is beyond surgical or medical management, as sorry as I am to say it. Please, let me know if I can be of any other assistance," Dr. Richardson announced before patting her head and gently rubbing the side of her cheek. "You know I am always here for you. Just ask a nurse to let me know, and I'll come and see you while you're in here. But I expect you can go home tomorrow."

The words *go home* now carried a most ominous meaning, appearing thoughtless.

The doctor rose and waved a hand. "Bye for now, Jessica."

*A pat on the cheek and a death sentence,* Jessica thought. *In a few weeks, I will be in the cold earth.* "No options. How can that be?"

It was too late; the doctor had departed the room, leaving her to her thoughts. The door through which he had disappeared was swinging shut.

Gasping for air, Jessica's lungs hurt from the cold while her head filled with unthinkable thoughts. *I'm going to die. No, I'm already dying, in the actual process of it.*

*How can this be? I just ran a half marathon for God's sake! To raise funds for cancer care!*

Her thoughts were scattered, her heart beating fast and her hands shaking. Jessica wasn't sure what to do with these emotions or this information.

⸺⸺◈⸺⸺

Jessica walked along the river right by the hospital, trying to calm her mind with the pace of her gait. She looked down at her legs, seeing how toned they were from running.

It was nigh impossible to imagine that her body was dying.

She didn't look or feel like someone with only a few months to live.

The sky was blue, and the air was cold, and Jessica was trying to grapple with the idea that she would likely not be around for another year. Death suddenly petrified her. She hadn't thought much of dying, and now the thought was consuming her. She watched people around her go on throughout their day, laughing, chatting on the phone, busy with their lives.

While the world was still living, Jessica was reconciling with the fact that her life was ending.

She didn't have much time and couldn't spend the rest of it mourning her death way too soon.

She needed to accept her diagnosis and find a way to secure some peace before she would be able to face her reality. But how would her friends react?

She cried for her family's pain in the coming days. It pained her to think of the tears her loved ones would weep and the devastation they would feel in her absence. The thought of the hurt and despair this would cause to those she loved most was more than she could bear.

As tears flooded her cold cheeks, she noticed the birds chirping in a big oak tree. She stopped momentarily, observing their chatter and the freedom they had to fly aimlessly.

She envied the way their wings were in sync with the wind; were they worrying about the next moment or enjoying the present? She took this as a sign to take in the present time instead of dreading what was coming. For an hour, she sat and watched those birds, determined to spend the rest of her time enjoying each moment as it came.

An overwhelming emotion of anger overtook Jessica. "How can I fucking be dying? How can this be happening?" She screamed it to no one in particular.

Jessica paced around as the birds in the distance chirped around her head.

For a moment, all the hurt and pain she had spent years covering up with her bright smile was causing her a feeling of resentment. "Was it not enough that I lost my father as a child, and now my mother has to lose me too? I've spent a lifetime making everyone comfortable with difficult emotions, always putting on a brave face."

Jessica came to the realization that despite the feeling of despair, she would honor herself and her friends and keep up the facade of positivity.

It would be her parting gift to those she loved and to those who loved her.

She couldn't change the circumstances; fighting it would be futile, so wiping the last tear from her eye, she stood, and committed to die the way she had lived, with grace, dignity, and humor.

She would choose not to be a victim of circumstance but a pillar of gratitude.

Although she couldn't control her body failing or her health declining, she could choose to live out her days in peace and not to distress everyone by seeing her mental health falling apart alongside her physical health. The warm sun shone out of the cool clouds at that moment, and she knew she had to choose peace, not just for herself but for those around her.

It would be for all those who had loved and cared about Jessica throughout her life.

She would not allow anger or fear to swallow up the rest of her days. Once composed, she called her mother, telling her all was good. "Mom, you can come pick me up from the hospital now," she said. Telling her parents would be the most challenging thing she would have to do.

The drive to their house was filled with emotion and fear, her mother asking questions, and Jessica avoiding the conversation. "I just need a little nap on the way home."

As they traveled along the long road, she noticed the tall trees that seemed more prominent than she had remembered, so lush, the gangly limbs reaching to the sky, growing each year.

She sat in the passenger seat as her mother drove with the windows down, enjoying the fresh air, giving her time to process what she would say. There would be no easy way to tell them, but she had to be direct while holding back her fear. Her parents would need time to process this information and she had not planned on staying long at their home.

Upon arriving at the house, Jessica splashed cold water on her face. When she returned to the kitchen, her parents were staring at her, waiting for an explanation.

Jessica blurted out the information more abruptly than planned.

"Mom, Dad. I have an inoperable brain tumor. I'm dying."

Maria gasped. "Jessica, no, there has to be a mistake. You're kidding, right?"

"Mom, no, it's real. Can you give me a moment? I just need a breath," Jessica said.

When she left the room to get some water and give her parents a moment alone, she overheard her mother reason with her dumbfounded father.

"There must be some experimental drug to give her a fighting chance ... She is young, tenacious, and willing to try anything." Her mother's voice was strained.

With the sound of her mother's desperation embedded within her mind, Jessica set about researching the type of cancer the doctor had written on the paper.

Her head was spinning, and her mind was racing for some sort of hope.

She spent hours searching the internet for hope, for survivors, for something to grasp. Sadly, all her research highlighted the odds would have been set against her even if she had been ten years old and the tumor small. Hadn't the doctor said exactly that?

Now, she felt so bad for shouting at him, almost blaming him for his negativity.

But it had been better this way. No false hope. She sat silent for a moment, breathing deeply, trying to reconcile in her mind her fate, coming to terms with the evidence.

One slow tear dripped down her cheek as she sat for some time, trying to wrap her head around this unexpected news.

Time seemed to stand still, yet Jessica knew she had no time to spare. Despite all this, she would live and love the rest of her days as if they were her last. Because she knew they were.

Jessica told her parents that she just wanted to enjoy what little time she had left, wanting their last days together to be special.

"You will have plenty of time to grieve when I'm gone. I'm here today. Please, let's make happy memories," Jessica begged.

Her mother just nodded, not able to speak.

Jessica spent three weeks with her parents, going through old photo albums and watching as her mother wiped wet eyes. She tried earnestly to comply with her daughter's request to spend this time happily, but her emotions got the best of her as expected throughout the day.

The mother and daughter slept the nights together, holding one another as they had done when Jessica was a child. Hearing her mother sob in the late hours, muffled by the blankets, was heartbreaking, reminding Jessica of many years ago when her biological father had died.

Making Jessica think of her father, she wondered ... *Is there an afterlife? Will he be the one to greet me when I get there?*

For the most part, in front of Jessica, her mother fought to be strong and steady, making the most of their time together. After tears and tight hugs, she left her parents' home to do the next hardest thing she would have to endure.

Even though her parents were skeptical about her driving home, Jessica was adamant, not quite ready to give up her independence. She drove back to Delaware in silence and as the miles passed, she was lost in her thoughts, contemplating what she would say to the girls.

*Perhaps I won't tell them at all.* She knew, though, she had to speak the truth, as difficult as it was for her; they deserved to know. *How do I tell my friends that I'm dying?*

She had no idea and had little chance to dwell on it, the situation yielding no time to be in denial or angry. She would not allow sorrow or grief to infiltrate her last days spent with her beloved friends, also denying a chance for fear to be her last companion as her time neared.

She needed to be as direct as she had been with her parents on how she wanted to spend the rest of her days on this earth, bringing joy to one another as they had throughout their friendship.

Arriving home from the drive from her parents' house, she strolled from her car, fumbling with her phone, anxiously trying to type the name of their group text, 'Forever.'

She asked if they could meet her at their favorite Italian restaurant Vincenzo's that evening. "It's important you show up," she said. Confused by the urgency of the text, her friends began speculating what the impromptu dinner might all be about.

'Are you pregnant, or did you meet some hot guy?'

'What is the emergency?' All the messages were followed with laughing emojis.

Jessica responded with a simple smiley emoji.

She then typed, 'Meet me at 7 p.m., and don't be late. I love you all.'

Jessica sat for a moment in silence, thinking about the next right move. She slowly headed into the shower, letting the hot water wash away her worry. Rinsing her body, she took note of all her freckles and perfectly imperfect features, wondering how her body could fail her.

She cried in the shower, tears of fear, sadness, and self-pity. Watching the soap wash away down the drain, she vowed that this would be the only time she would allow herself pity.

She needed to come to terms with her destiny and not spend any more time being bitter.

She screamed into the hot water, "Why me?" There was no possible answer to this.

Her father's death had prepared her for how life could be unfair and that the unthinkable could happen to anyone at any time. She found solace in knowing that she would reunite with her father someday soon. She lamented about her dreams and the life she had hoped for, wondering what would become of those around her.

Her parents and friends would surely feel the void of her contagious smile and quick wit.

These next weeks or months would be harder for them than for her, which hurt her heart even more. She wanted to fill her last days on earth with joy and love.

Again, she reminded herself of what she had already vowed, that she would die the way she had lived, with grace and humor, and surrounded by those who meant the most to her.

After about thirty minutes, she shut off the water and wrapped the warm towel around her, feeling a sense of security and calmness. She browsed through her closet and decided upon a new dress with the tags still attached, keeping it for a special occasion.

She remembered just months before seeing the dress on the mannequin, knowing she had to purchase it, the bright yellow flowers and blue accents bringing out a cheer. It fitted as though it was meant specifically for her. There was no better day to wear that dress, knowing now that every day was a special occasion and beautiful things should be enjoyed.

Death being so near, she no longer had the privilege of special occasions or wasting any moments on trivial matters as she had in the past. She carefully dressed, put her hair in a meticulous bun showing her beautiful jawline, and smiled at the mirror.

She made sure she looked and felt beautiful, and before leaving, went back to her dresser to put on her favorite perfume; it smelled of flowers, reminding her of summer.

Arriving early, she ordered the best Champagne on the menu. Jessica decided this would not be a sad night, but an evening filled with friendship and love, a celebration of sorts, of her life and the love she had for her most beloved friends. As each woman hurried toward the table, Jessica stood beaming, the most beautiful woman and the one she adored.

They all greeted her cautiously, curious about this impromptu dinner.

Lynnie walked into the restaurant and saw Jessica beautifully dressed, looking radiant as she stood there, like a flower that had just blossomed, her hair flowing away from her face.

They hugged and chatted briefly, catching up on the week's gossip, when Lynnie finally inquired, "As much as I love seeing my most favorite ladies, what is this about?"

The women had no idea what was to come next.

Jessica poured Champagne and said, "Ladies, my love for you is eternal. You have made my life happy and whole, and I will forever be grateful to you. Sometimes, life doesn't turn out how we expect, but that will never take away from the memories of the laughter we shared." Jessica looked around the table at the puzzled looks and boldly announced, "I'm dying."

The room seemed to stand still.

She watched the horror on their faces, all unsure of what to say next.

"What, wait, what?" Amanda said.

"Jessica, are you being dramatic?" Myra inquired. "Or is this meant to be some sort of joke?"

Without any clarification, Lynnie knew Jessica wasn't joking.

She had never been overly dramatic or exaggerated. And she would never pull such a cruel stunt. Lynnie started sobbing without any other information provided, just that she'd heard the words come out of Jessica's mouth. What she had heard, she knew was the truth.

"Please, this is not how I want this evening to go. I have little control of my body or diagnosis, so please let me have control of my final days," Jessica pleaded. "Tears make me feel so bad. And God knows, I have been to hell and back over this already. Please, please smile for me."

Her voice was faltering but she refused to let it break.

Jessica explained the type of cancer and what the doctors and her research had found out.

"I don't understand. How can there be no hope?" Myra said. "It's only just been located so it's got to be early days, right?"

Jessica, who couldn't make eye contact, shook her head no, pained to see the girls fighting back tears. "No, Myra. Late days, not early. Too late. They found it too late. As the doctor explained, I'm in the end-of-life stage. And we will not cry, my friends. We will live."

This was Jessica telling what she commanded her friends.

Lynnie looked around the table, trying to make sense of it.

Myra sat dumbfounded and unable to move.

Amanda was quiet for a while and stared at Jessica before saying, "We love you, Jessica; you are one of us, and I think you can fight this. We can get a second opinion or go overseas. There is always hope, and we can try experimental drugs. And we can start a fund and send you to—"

"No, no. Please, guys, this is really happening, and I don't want to spend any time convincing myself there's hope. I've made peace with that fact and the last thing I want is to be traveling here and there on some pointless mission, racked with pain. I want to live while I still can, I want to laugh my way to death, and then I want to end my life in peace. Before I get any worse, I want one more adventure with you guys. Let's visit the mountains this week and spend time at my mom's lake house. From there, I'll be moving back home with my parents."

The girls wiped away their tears, and Amanda was the first to announce, "I'll start packing."

"We're all in this together. I'll be back soon," Lynnie agreed as she got up to leave, worried about who would watch Ellie. She called a babysitter, begging her to keep Ellie for the weekend.

Thankfully, she was available, and Lynnie promised to pay double for the short notice.

Her sad demeanor seemed to say, *this could be the last time we'll all be together.*

"Everybody meet at my house in an hour!" shouted Myra as she paid the check and the girls scurried out.

Driving to the lake house, the girls belted out the lyrics to their favorite songs from college. A passerby would never have guessed that despite the appearance, the car was filled with heavy hearts just trying to make sense out of the senselessness. "Hey, Lynnie, remember when you ran out of gas and had to push the car to the gas station, and when you got there, you realized you must have dropped your wallet somewhere along the way?" Jessica teased.

"That was a dreadfully long day," Lynnie said, rolling her eyes.

"I had to flirt with the fifteen-year-old cashier and promise to give him my number if he let me fill up my tank and repay him when I got back my wallet."

"Yeah, except you gave him *my* number instead," laughed Jessica.

"Oh, that was classic," chimed Myra.

"I still don't understand how I had to deal with a horny fifteen-year-old teenager for three weeks because you ran out of gas!"

"Well, I wasn't actually going to give him *my* number, and anyway, it was payback."

"Payback? For what?"

"At the bar, you'd offered for me to dance with that creepy fifty-year-old guy, telling him I liked older men! I'd just turned twenty-one, and he thought he'd won the night lottery!"

"Oh yeah, I did do that, didn't I? Sorry."

The girls burst out in laughter as they poked fun at one another. For a time, Jessica had forgotten that a tumor was inside her head, robbing her of her future. Anytime the thought crept into her mind, she quickly dismissed it, focusing on the present moment with her friends. It was as if they were back at college again when the days had seemed long and full of hope.

*The thought of Jessica's absence is unfathomable,* thought Lynnie.

The empty chair at Friendsgiving would be brutal. The women tried to keep it together, but they were struggling to process the news. There would be time for sorrow, grief, and anger, but for now, they just made their best effort to celebrate whatever time they had together.

Being in nature was a reminder that the earth had a beauty all around despite how cruel life could be. The smell and feel of the air, and the distant chatter of others helped them recognize that despite what was happening in their lives, life still did and should go on.

Every sunset had a sunrise, and the moon and ocean would still dance for one another. The warm air, blue skies, and pure love surrounding them was surreal.

Lynnie caught herself getting angry, however.

How could this be happening? *Why would Jessica, of all people, get sick? How can this be happening so soon?* she thought, but she quickly reminded herself of the promise they'd made before taking this trip. No tears, no talking about it, and no dwelling on the circumstances.

The weekend was filled with everything Jessica was; happy, soulful, pure, and fun.

Getting closer to the destination, the tall trees swayed lightly and the smell of the earth as the sunshine beamed its light on the greenery around them was proof there was life after death. The peacefulness made it impossible not to be grateful for all life had to offer, even the bad stuff.

The weekend trip was everything Jessica had wanted it to be and they made plans to visit her at her parents' house the following week. But as they kissed her before she departed, not knowing how long Jessica had left, it was clear that every goodbye was a final one.

That night, returning home, Lynnie tried processing her emotions. She knew she couldn't be the only one feeling the way she did, so she made a three-way call to Amanda and Myra.

"Hello," Amanda and Myra said in unison.

"How the fuck is this happening?" Lynnie said.

"It is so fucking unfair. If anyone does not deserve this, it's Jessica," Amanda continued.

Myra said nothing as the other two women carried on.

Lynnie thought Myra's silence was odd and said, "Myra, are you there?"

In a low voice, Myra answered with a somber, "Yes. I just don't have any words; I can't get myself to reconcile how this could happen to someone like Jessica."

The conversation went on for well over forty-five minutes. They'd held back sobs in front of Jessica, but now alone as a threesome, they were able to release their sorrow.

"Let's pray," Lynnie suggested.

Before ending the call, there were lots of mentions of 'I love you' and when it finally ended, Lynnie sobbed into her pillow, begging the universe for a miracle.

---

## JOURNAL

TODAY IS THE SECOND WORST DAY OF MY LIFE. THE FIRST WAS WHEN I FOUND OUT MARC HAD DIED, AND NOW THIS NEWS HAS ROCKED ME TO MY CORE. I'M TRYING TO GET MY THOUGHTS IN ORDER AS I WRITE THIS, BUT SOMEHOW, MY MIND JUST CAN'T PROCESS ANY OF THIS.

JESSICA DIED FIVE WEEKS AFTER THE TRIP TO THE LAKE HOUSE.

JESSICA'S STEPFATHER, DAVID, CALLED ME. AND ALTHOUGH THIS WAS EXPECTED, I COULD HEAR JESSICA'S MOTHER WAILING IN THE BACK, SCREAMING, "WHY, WHY?"

IT STARTLED ME A BIT, AND THE PHONE CALL ENDED QUICKLY. AFTER THAT, I CALLED EACH OF THE GIRLS, LETTING THEM KNOW OF JESSICA'S PASSING

IT'S SUCH A HORRIBLE AND SOMBER RAINY DAY, AND THIS HUGE LOSS HAS LEFT EVERYONE WHO KNEW JESSICA WITH A HOLE IN THEIR HEART, MINE ESPECIALLY.

---

Weeks after Jessica's death, Lynnie was putting away her suitcases from the lake house trip.

The weeks since then had been a whirlwind, and Lynnie saw the flowered suitcase tucked away in the corner, still not unpacked. Tears flowed as she found the strength to unload the memories, wondering how she would manage without Jessica.

"Jessica, sweetheart, please come to me and show me where you are," she begged. "Tell me that you are someplace safe, someplace happy, bathed in yellow and feeling so, so loved."

Perhaps she just needed a distraction from the loneliness of her thoughts, but something was nudging at Lynnie to unpack that suitcase. While tears started flooding, she picked up the case and began opening the zipper, which was broken and challenging to open. The colorful floral pattern seemed dim and fake, and she now hated her once-beloved travel bag. Slowly unzipping the suitcase, she mindlessly started unpacking clothes. Pulling out the last pullover sweater and feeling the warmth against her skin, an envelope dropped to the floor.

*That's odd. I don't remember putting any letter in here,* she thought.

Stunned, she looked down at the folded envelope, and noticing the handwriting, Lynnie became overwhelmed with emotion. "Jessica," she said. She was overcome with tears.

She carefully opened the letter and read it slowly.

*My Dearest Lynnie,*

*There is no way to know for sure when you will unpack but I suspect that I may be long gone if you read this, transcended into another dimension. You procrastinate in everything, and by the time you unpack this beaten-up old suitcase, years could have passed. Only kidding.*

*But if I'm right and I have left this plane, I didn't lose my battle with brain cancer. I didn't die. I simply went on my next journey to heaven. The details as to why or how I'm gone are not necessary. The fact that I lived is what matters most.*

I lived my life with love and happiness. I experienced friendship, heartbreak, success, and many failures. I lived a whole life, too, albeit not for as long as we all would have liked. But who is to say how short is too short anyway? I would rather have lived my short life filled with enormous joy and gratitude than to have lived a long but miserable one.

I was fortunate to have had friendships most never get to experience, laughing so much that I cried. I considered you a sister to wipe my tears when I cried, someone I looked forward to most to share in my successes. But we all must leave this earth at some point, and I refuse to be a victim of cancer. I'm not afraid. I'm excited to explore the next world now.

Life is a journey and does not end here on earth. We are eternal, our friendship is forever, and our souls live on, that I am sure of. When you miss me and feel sorry for yourself, remember how we each loved and laughed and how much living you still have to do.

Do not dwell on the past and what could have been. All we have is this moment, and do not squander it by wasting time.

Although I will miss you terribly, I will always be close by watching, cheering on your success, and loving you through your failures. When the time is right, I will await your arrival for our next journey together with an open heart.

Until then, my friend, thank you for walking me home.

The stroll together with you was magical, our friendship is endless, and you and my love will continue to spread your light across this world for many years to come.

With much love and gratitude,

Jessica.

# CHAPTER FIFTEEN

*Lynnie: The Aftermath.*

Feeling as if her heart had been ripped out of her chest, Lynnie walked around in a fog, incapable of coping with the loss. It was a painful reminder of losing Marc, and the immense feelings stunned her to the core, but Lynnie was grateful for the distraction of a toddler.

However, Jessica's death also forced Lynnie to consider her life.

*I want to start writing. It's always been my dream, but because of financial obligations and fear, I took the safer route of teaching. If Jessica's death has taught me anything, it is that life is short and precious, and now is the time to live.*

Ellie interrupted her thoughts and began fussing.

Lynnie looked at her beautiful daughter and smiled, seeing Marc's reflection staring back.

"Baby girl, Mama must make some changes. I have to be a good example for you. Your daddy would want that too," Lynnie said, smiling.

Lynnie yawned as Ellie squirmed to get down, wanting to explore her surroundings. She'd recently begun walking which left Lynnie little time to focus on herself. As much as she loved motherhood, Lynnie desired to write and pursue her career, and it pained her to think about letting down Ellie or herself. The time for change was now.

JOURNAL

I MADE A PRETTY BIG DECISION. I WANT TO PURSUE MY DREAM TO BE A FREELANCE WRITER. I NEED A CHANGE, A PURPOSE. IT FEELS LIKE I'M IN A WHIRLWIND BETWEEN MARC'S DEATH, THE BIRTH OF ELLIE, AND NOW JESSICA'S UNTIMELY DEATH AS WELL. A FEELING OF DOOM SURROUNDS ME, AND I FIND MYSELF FEELING SO PARANOID ABOUT HAVING ANY OTHER LOSSES, FEARING THEM ALL THE TIME.

I'M OFTEN OVERLY PROTECTIVE OF ELLIE, NEUROTIC, AND UNREASONABLE AT TIMES.

I HAVE VIVID DREAMS OF JESSICA AND MARC WAITING AT HEAVEN'S GATE. I'M TRYING TO MAKE OUT WHAT THEY SAY BUT ALWAYS WAKE BEFORE FIGURING IT OUT. I CAN'T SHAKE THIS NAGGING FEELING OF DOOM AND NEED TO LEARN TO QUIET THIS ANXIETY.

I HAVE TURNED TO GOD FOR SOLACE. ATTENDING CHURCH HAS BECOME ESSENTIAL, GIVING ME A SENSE OF FAITH AND

CALM. JESSICA'S DEATH HAS MADE ME REEVALUATE MY RELATIONSHIP WITH MY MOTHER AND REFLECT ON THE IMPORTANCE OF FORGIVENESS. DEATH HAS A WAY FOR PEOPLE TO TAKE STOCK OF THEIR LIVES AND THESE LAST COUPLE OF WEEKS HAVE ME THINKING ABOUT MINE, THAT'S FOR SURE.

❦



CALM. JESSICA'S DEATH HAS MADE ME REEVALUATE MY RELATIONSHIP WITH MY MOTHER AND REFLECT ON THE IMPORTANCE OF FORGIVENESS. DEATH HAS A WAY FOR PEOPLE TO TAKE STOCK OF THEIR LIVES AND THESE LAST COUPLE OF WEEKS HAVE ME THINKING ABOUT MINE, THAT'S

# CHAPTER SIXTEEN

*Amanda: In a Tailspin.*

Jessica's death threw Amanda into a tailspin too. She couldn't comprehend that her beloved friend was gone for good. It didn't seem real, and it certainly didn't seem fair. Amanda had given up on redemption and decided to treat life as temporary, just as Jessica's life had been. Unlike Lynnie, however, she had become bitter and skeptical, no longer trusting in the good of people, developing a hard outer shell. Amanda started pulling away from Lynnie and Myra.

At first, the distance had been gradual, but eventually, Amanda stopped returning calls altogether. Lynnie would regularly phone, only to be greeted by Amanda's voicemail.

She left message after message until eventually, the voicemail was completely filled, and she couldn't accept any further messages. In fact, Amanda would often be there, dreading the calls.

For some reason, answering them no longer seemed so enticing now Jessica had gone; something significant had changed, never to be the same again. Seeing the call come in, she'd quickly press the *send to voicemail* button, needing space from the suffocating friendships and no longer feeling the desire for codependency. Likewise, Amanda had retreated from many of her hobbies, letting her gym membership expire and no longer finding enjoyment in life, letting herself go by not getting her hair done or doing the laundry.

Gradually, her apartment became a dumping ground of dirty clothes and empty take-out containers. This triggered her to remember when her brother had been in the hospital and her home had become chaotic and unreliable. The revelation of her past only threw Amanda into a deeper depression. She became disenchanted, her depression consuming her everyday activities.

She started calling in sick to work and canceling appointments.

Eventually, her patients stopped rescheduling therapy sessions with her because she either never showed up for them or was dismissive of their issues, appearing disinterested and disengaged. After three months, the clinic relieved Amanda of her duties.

She survived on her savings, making minimal effort to find another job. She started rethinking her career, citing that she had her own problems and was tired of trying to fix other people.

It was clear that Amanda was headed into trouble when her drinking again became out of control. Her nightly binges and morning hangover were a regular occurrence and soon, she was compounding it by illegally buying prescription medicine on the streets.

OxyContin eased her stress, allowing her to drift off into another dimension, one in which she no longer felt the pain of loss.

# CHAPTER SEVENTEEN

*Myra: Avoidance Tactics.*

In typical Myra fashion, she became enthralled with her work, specifically to avoid her feelings about the loss of Jessica. Some nights on her way home, her mind wandered, thinking about Jessica, wondering how her life might have been had it not been for the cancer. Jessica was vibrant and beautiful, and Myra couldn't comprehend how life could possibly be so cruel.

Myra was obsessing over work, increased her billing hours, and spending late nights at the office to avoid being alone with her thoughts. She, too, had tried reaching out to Amanda, but when she didn't get a callback, had quickly dismissed it. If Amanda didn't want to talk, then why would she try to force her? She was not going to waste her time trying to chase Amanda who was a grown woman who had to take responsibility for her own choices, good or bad.

Myra would talk with Lynnie now and again, but Lynnie was busy writing and taking care of Ellie. Myra had promised to visit her and Ellie, but time passed, and Myra was in the middle of a big murder-for-hire case. It was shocking just how fast the time flitted by a week soon melding into a month, and a month into three months.

Cases like this consumed not only her time, but also her reputation if she did not win.

Therefore, she was spending her weekends either at the office or catching up on sleep.

Life seemed to pass Myra by. Soon, it had been months since she had heard from either Lynnie or Amanda. How would they be handling the death of Jessica? Surely, it was just as hard for them too, perhaps even more so if they did not have anything so intense to occupy them.

But somehow, she couldn't persuade herself to reach out. Instead, Myra continued to work extra hours until, eventually, she was rarely going home at all to sleep. She noticed her clothes becoming looser on her, forever reminding herself that she should eat more.

*When was the last time I had a meal?* Myra wondered.

She grabbed another protein shake from the fridge, promising herself that tonight, she would go home, eat a meal, and get a proper night's sleep. As the hours rolled by, she realized she had been working again till the early morning hours and the dark skies were giving way to the bright dawn sun. This avoidant and unhealthy cycle continued, leaving Myra devoid of any feelings or basic human needs until she was so accustomed to blocking out any emotions, she became a shell of herself. Myra's thoughts would sometimes turn dark, but she would dismiss the feelings.

She was becoming colder and more withdrawn, even from herself.

Myra had meant to reach out to her friends in the hope it would improve her mood, but instead, she slowly went deeper within herself. It all reminded her of the times she'd been in strangers' homes, trying to escape into her mind to flee from reality.

*Lynnie: Loneliness.*

Lynnie was missing not only dear Jessica, but also Amanda and Myra. They were oddly absent from her life these days, almost as if the death of poor Jessica had dissolved the bond of the three. Life was beginning to feel lonely and sad, despite little Ellie always doing her best to brighten it for her mommy. The fact was, Lynnie was craving adult company, but more than that, she desperately missed her best friends and was also worrying for them.

She had to immerse herself in other pastimes simply to make it through the lonely week.

In the late nights, she would put aside a little time after Ellie was asleep to sum up her abysmal sense of desolation, penning just a few lines in her journal. It felt wretched to do so.

The problem was, when life was this depressing, writing in the journal could exacerbate it.

She never completely missed a day of writing in it, but at low periods, the lines were fewer.

One such activity on which she relied to keep her busy was that on Wednesday nights, Lynnie and Ellie would do their food shopping together. Ellie was now six, an age at which she knew all her mother's moods and would do her best to pull Mommy out of her black state of mind.

They enjoyed their weekly trips together. Lynnie would allow Ellie to pick a sweet treat for them to share while watching a movie on grocery shopping night, something to which they both looked forward each week. As they were turning the corner toward the produce section, Lynnie found herself coming face to face with Luke for the first time in many years. Time stood still.

He still looked the same, perhaps a bit thinner, but his piercing blue eyes were unmistakable.

Their gazes met for a moment, both standing paralyzed with shock. Suddenly, the realization of the small child by Lynnie's side caught his attention. "Who is this cutie?" he asked.

Struggling to speak, Lynnie slowly muttered, "Hello, Luke; this is my daughter Ellie."

"Wow, she's a pretty one," he said slowly. "Your daddy must be very proud."

Luke was never taking his eyes off Lynnie.

In her sweet pink unicorn shorts, Ellie quickly corrected the stranger, saying, "My daddy died. I never met him, but he still loves me. Mommy tells me so."

"Is that so? Well, I'm so sorry to hear that, young lady. That must be very sad for you both," Luke said. "Let me help you ladies with your packages." Lynnie was stunned, unable to articulate words as she followed Luke who was now pushing the cart to the car.

Her heart was racing as she buckled Ellie into her car seat. She was nervous about being alone with Luke, but he seemed different than she remembered. Softer, kinder.

"Look, Lynnie, I'm sorry about how things ended between us. I'm a changed man, I promise. I always think about you and never stopped loving you."

There was silence for a moment, Lynnie saying nothing and staring at him blankly.

Finally, she began talking. "Luke, really, it's in the past. I'm not interested in rekindling a relationship with you if that's where you're leading to ... I have my plate filled with Ellie and my job. But it's good to see you and to hear that you're on the right track."

"Wait, please, Lynnie. I'm begging you. Hear me out. Let me take you for a coffee so that we can talk. I'll leave you alone if you still don't want anything to do with me after that, but just give me a chance. There's so much I've wanted to say to you and now is my chance."

Lynnie thought, *why is he so damn desperate to speak to me when we only happened—quite by chance—to run into one another in the store? That's bizarre.*

*You'd think he was about to declare undying love for me, but he's made no effort to find and contact me! Weird.*

*Talk about being an opportunist! But I suppose he sees me as weak, being a widow and a single mom! Well, he can think again.*

"I don't think that would be a good decision, Luke. It was nice seeing you."

As she turned to walk away, Luke pleaded again, "Lynnie, I'm nothing without you. I beg you, please give me another chance to prove that I'm a changed man. I owe it to you to show that I'm kind. Hell, I owe it to myself. You probably won't even believe me but I've spent years thinking about you, wishing I could change the past. I was young, stupid, immature. And I'm so sorry."

Lynnie tried to argue, but Luke interrupted.

"One coffee, one hour, one conversation. Lynnie, please."

Always mesmerized by his charm, she reluctantly surrendered with a half-smile. "Luke, meet me at Francine's at the corner of Bristol and Brook Farm Drive on Friday at seven."

Luke smiled widely. "I'll be there, Lynnie, and you won't be sorry."

She had always been a bit irritated—when dating—by men who said dumb things like 'you won't be sorry'. Talk about arrogance! How could they possibly know what was in her mind or that he had something to offer that could match what she needed? Hell, she wasn't even searching for a new partner, let alone one resurrected from the past. It was annoying.

"Right, well, one coffee," she muttered. "And one hour, and that's it."

As Lynnie approached Francine's, she could smell the fresh coffee and baked muffins from a block away, immediately taking her back to that time in Paris with Luke. Suddenly, she realized that this was a mistake and started retreating but before she could walk away, Luke sauntered up behind her. "Oh great, you came.

I was worried you were going to stand me up. Let's go in. I hear this place has great apple turnovers."

She hesitated for a moment but proceeded to follow behind Luke. It would be rude to cry off now and refuse to come inside. Besides, one hour was hardly going to hurt, was it?

They caught up, and she told Luke about Marc and how much she missed him. Luke was genuinely interested, sympathizing with her loss. It turned out that Luke was sweet and kind, far more than she remembered. And hadn't he already told her exactly that?

It was ever so slightly irritating that his self-proclamations about being nice these days were being proved true! It would have been easier, in a way, if she had disliked him.

The one-hour meeting turned into three, and by the end of their encounter, she had remembered why she had fallen in love with Luke so many years ago. He was charming and fun, he listened too, knowing exactly what to say to make someone feel special.

Lynnie hadn't realized quite how much she had been missing male companionship.

*In fact,* she recognized, *I've been missing having any kind of companionship these days because Amanda and Myra are hardly ever in touch or around. We're all so distant now.*

Luke was familiar, and in some ways, familiarity was warm and safe.

Lynnie took things extremely slow with him, but the fact they didn't have to start right at the beginning with one another was an easy place to land at the end of a long day.

The weekly dates also gave her something to look forward to, and Luke was always a complete gentleman, the ease between them making it easy to want to be together more often.

Lynnie wasn't ready to share that she had rekindled their relationship, though she did allow him to come over in the evenings for dinner, also spending time with Ellie.

It was a beautiful thing, wonderful for both Ellie and Lynnie. To see how great he was with the child was heartwarming since little Ellie had not had the joy of a father in her life. She would stare up into his big blue eyes, touching his face with a hand, almost wistfully.

It was clear that Ellie had immediately been drawn to him and Lynnie would watch from afar, amazed at how gentle he could be with her precious daughter. *Has he really changed?*

Luke was patient too, possessing no agenda. It took nine long months before Lynnie began to be brave enough to open her heart fully, starting to contemplate a complete reconciliation.

But how would Amanda and Myra react to this news? Did it even matter these days? It was a sorrowful thing that perhaps it was now of no consequence, and she would have given anything for Amanda to huff her cynicism or for the ever vigilant Myra to tell her to be careful.

But the truth was that they had grown apart since Jessica's death, rarely speaking nowadays.

Their lives had gone in different directions, and for the first time in a long while, Lynnie was not sad or wary despite having no allies to warn her of the new man in her life.

She was excited.

JOURNAL

LIFE HAS A WAY OF SURPRISING YOU IN THE MOST UNEXPECTED WAYS. I RAN INTO LUKE, I HAVEN'T SEEN OR SPOKEN TO HIM IN YEARS AND YET THERE HE WAS SUDDENLY SAYING HE LOVED ME AND HAD BEEN MISSING ME FOR ALL THAT TIME. IT WAS EASY TO BE SKEPTICAL, BUT HE WON ME OVER SO EASILY.

WE WENT FOR COFFEE, AND HAVE BEEN SPENDING A LOT OF TIME TOGETHER. I EVEN LET HIM SPEND TIME WITH ELLIE. THINGS ARE MOVING FAST, AND WE'VE REKINDLED OUR RELATIONSHIP. AFTER ALL OF THESE YEARS, I NEVER IMAGINED I COULD HAVE FEELINGS FOR HIM AGAIN. I'D BEEN LONELY FOR SO LONG, AND IT'S REALLY NICE TO HAVE COMPANIONSHIP.

THERE IS A PART OF ME THAT FEELS LIKE I'M BETRAYING MARC, BUT I NEED TO ACCEPT HE ISN'T EVER COMING BACK AND LET LOVE BACK INTO MY HEART.

Despite the rough start to their relationship, Luke started hinting about marriage a year after they reconnected. Lynnie initially ignored his suggestions, but the more Luke brought up the subject, the more enticing the idea felt. And it was clear he wasn't going to stop asking, no matter what.

"Lynnie, c'mon, let's get married," said Luke. "You know how I feel about you, and you have to admit it will be so much better for Ellie to have a dad."

*She already has a dad,* thought Lynnie. *A dad in heaven, looking down on her, protecting her.*

"It is just a piece of paper, things are fine the way they are," Lynnie protested.

"Don't you want to be a family?" Luke said. "Can't you see how good it is?"

"Luke, listen. My parents' marriage was awful, and I would never want to put Ellie through that," Lynnie said.

"Just think about it," Luke said. "I don't mean to in any way dismiss or seem to belittle what you are saying but your parents' marriage was their own relationship and was only one out of so many happy ones. We are not your parents, and we already know how good we are together."

"I'll think about it then," she replied begrudgingly. "And I promise to tell you if ever I feel ready for it. But it's such an enormous step."

Luke waited for Lynnie to bring up the discussion of marriage. She never did.

Finally, Luke couldn't wait anymore and six months later, he formally proposed to Lynnie at the park as Ellie watched with excitement. "Luke, I thought we were going to talk about this?" Lynnie said, stunned and giving him a hard time. From the corner of her eye, she watched Ellie smile broadly.

She would have preferred him to keep this between him and herself, not involving Ellie because if a child heard such a thing ... As predicted, the consequence soon became apparent.

"Say yes, Mommy," Ellie squealed, and the look on her face made it clear she would keep asking until her mother said yes to allowing herself a chance to be truly happy and settled.

Lynnie searched for words, but nothing came out.

So, she nodded agreeably as she and Luke embraced.

Later that night, as Lynnie was putting Ellie to bed, she watched her daughter snuggle up with her stuffed giraffe. Six now and in first grade, she already loved Luke like a father. Lynnie felt a pang of guilt, thinking of Marc and of all he'd already missed.

But in her heart, she dearly wanted to be settled just as Luke had said.

She yearned for the pain of losing Marc and Jessica to go away, believing this news would be a happy event and a distraction from all the sadness she had endured. As the days went by, she also found herself gradually losing the sense of guilt and shame at allowing a new man into her daughter's life, and for loving someone who was not Ellie's father.

------

JOURNAL

LUKE PROPOSED! PART OF MY HEART IS STILL HEALING FOR MARC AND JESSICA BUT THE PROSPECT OF GETTING MARRIED AND BEING A FAMILY IS ENTICING, LIKE AN ADVENTURE.

BESIDES, ELLIE AND I ARE ON OUR OWN NOW, AND LUKE IS SO GOOD TO US. HE IS SO EXCITED TO BE A FAMILY, EVEN TREATING MY DAUGHTER AS HE WOULD HIS OWN. SOMETIMES, I FEEL THAT HE SHOULDN'T DO IT, THAT IT'S DISRESPECTFUL TO MARC. THEN I THINK, WHAT WOULD MARC HAVE WANTED?

I KNOW HOW MUCH HE LOVED ME, AND IF HE WERE HERE FOR ME TO ASK, HE WOULD SAY THAT HE WANTED US TO BE HAPPY AND LOVED. THAT IS TRUE LOVE AFTER ALL, TO WANT THE PERSON'S HAPPINESS.

MAYBE SAYING YES IS NOT SUCH A TERRIBLE THING AFTER ALL.

---

Luke and Lynnie married in a quiet whimsical garden, only little Ellie and the pastor attending as their guests. The ceremony was short and sweet, and as time passed, things only got better and better. Lynnie was now finding an unexpected feeling of security with Luke.

She missed having Myra and Amanda there but wanted an intimate ceremony.

Their relationship had been strained and to make things easier, Lynnie thought it best keeping the nuptials as low-key as possible, and the security she had longed for since Marc's death, she was finally feeling by being married to Luke.

It still was not easy, however, to promise herself so steadfastly to any other man than Ellie's father; this was not because Luke was deficient in any way, but because she had never even begun her journey with Marc, the love of her life. It didn't seem fair to compare Luke to Marc in any way, but in thinking of Marc so fondly, it felt as though this was what she was doing.

Lynnie even thought about Marc on her wedding day, feeling a profound guilt about her sadness that it wasn't Marc standing up there. Luke deserved all Lynnie's focus now, but Marc would forever hold a piece of her heart, especially with his connection to Ellie.

*Marc would want me to find happiness, though, wouldn't he?* Lynnie reasoned. *And while I love Luke differently than the way I did Marc, he still gives me security and familiarity.*

Lynnie finally understood her mother's dilemma when she had decided to marry her father and it was strange how it took having a child to pull everything—the ghosts and many torments of the past—into perspective. It was only fair for Ellie to have a father figure too.

Marc was gone, and Luke was not only willing to step in, he was also deeply committed to doing so, promising to be the best husband he could be, also a father figure and role model for Ellie as she grew. And even if it wasn't the love she once shared with Marc, it was still *a* love. So many couples spent a lifetime in disharmonious relationships. If she had been so blessed as to have been delivered a second chance at love, why would she not grab it with both hands?

Now more than ever, Lynnie found herself wondering how her parents could exist in such a cold, loveless marriage but understood the sacrifices they had needed to make to survive. More than anything, she never wanted Ellie to bear witness to her relationship with her parents.

"I want more for Ellie, you know? I want her to see a happy marriage," Lynnie said. "A truly stable one, a relationship with firm foundations, a traditional-style love that lasts."

Luke studied her for a bit. "We will," he said. "Lynnie, let's have a baby! There is nothing more traditional or stable than that! And babies certainly last ... Well, they grow but ..."

He was serious about the suggestion, but there was a sparkle in his eye as he teased her too.

"A baby? Luke, I just started my freelance writing career full time, so I don't know what that would mean for my career opportunities. Let's discuss it more. I need time to think about it."

She turned to look at him, expecting to see a downcast look of dejection because she never seemed to meet any of his suggestions with the same level of enthusiasm he demonstrated.

But to her surprise, Luke was already singing, "We are going to have a baby ..."

# PART 3

# CHAPTER EIGHTEEN

*Lynnie: Life at Thirty.*

Years passed, and while the girls occasionally kept in touch, their friendship had irrevocably changed after Jessica had passed. It was almost as if Amanda and Myra had been triggered by it into accepting that their formerly cozy and cute 'foursome' had belonged to their youth rather than to the lives of the mature women they had become. Now, they would call one another about job promotions and humdrum happenings, keeping the details vague and conversations brief.

The three friends were all doing well in their own ways although an unexplained distance and sadness permeated their voices. It made little sense to Lynnie.

The loss of Jessica had been a terrible thing for everyone, but although their little group had altered, Lynnie would have expected them to hang onto their old ways.

Could they not be mature women but still be playful, still have fun, and still meet up to giggle the night away over bottles of wine? Were they willing to forgo all they had built up?

But it seemed she was the only one to see it that way, each contact leaving her empty.

After hanging up the phone with Myra, Lynnie felt especially regretful.

*Why have our friendships fallen apart?* she thought. *At least, we're nothing like we used to be.*

There really was no particular reason, but perhaps Jessica's death had caused such heartache the two had retreated into their own worlds, frightened to let anyone in, including one another.

Lynnie had also protected her heart from further damage, of course; she had focused on the transition of motherhood, pouring copious energy into being the mother she had never had.

But even so, being more aware of their mortality should surely have made the women enjoy the time they had with each other, nurturing what they had established, treating it as precious.

She couldn't let the feeling of tension go, picking up the phone again to call Myra.

"Hello," Myra replied slowly as if she almost resented another call so soon.

"No, I'm not losing my mind. I know we just hung up the phone moments ago." Lynnie hesitated, a slow crack in her voice starting, and she unexpectedly started to weep. "Myra, I miss you so much. I really miss Amanda, the real one I used to know. I miss our friendships and the bond that we swore would never change," Lynnie rambled. "We are losing it. I miss *us.*"

"Me too," Myra said softly.

There. The unspoken was now out in the open, suspended between the two women. It danced between them despite their considerable distance, a frisson of rare magic returned to the air.

"Let's call Amanda and get together for dinner to celebrate our thirtieth birthdays."

That was all it took to reunite the women. A friend in need, and the others would all come running. It had been that way their entire friendship, and Lynnie's boldness had fixed the rift.

The reunion was a tearful one, the three promising never to let time pass again without seeing each other. The women drank, singing and laughing as if no time had passed, but Lynnie was a little uncomfortable watching Amanda enjoying a martini.

She didn't want to pry, but when had Amanda started drinking again?

Amanda noticed Lynnie watching her curiously with her half-drunk martini. "Relax, Lynnie. I can handle one drink. You don't need to look so worried."

Myra glanced around nervously, saying over jubilantly, "Cheers, fuckers! I've missed your sorry asses. How the fuck are we all thirty already? We were just in college five minutes ago."

The women locked arms as they sat at the oval table of their favorite Italian restaurant, Vincenzo's, the same one Jessica had chosen when she'd told them about the cancer. Astonishingly, the sadness they had expected by booking to come here was no longer evident. It was as if the atmosphere sang for Jessica, unwilling to allow them their continued grief.

For the first time, Lynnie was noticing the warmth of the decor.

A large chandelier was hanging from the ceiling, soft ivory fabric laced around each clear crystal; they were dancing in the light, creating such a magical, warm ambiance.

Lynnie had selected this restaurant because it had been a special place for the friends, thinking familiarity would help ease any hesitation or anxieties about reconnecting after so much time. The choice of the restaurant wasn't lost on them as a pang of sadness filled the air.

Myra interrupted it immediately, raising her Champagne glass high.

"To Jessica, our beautiful soul sister who lives on in each of us."

The women cheered, drinking in honor of their lost friend.

Lynnie looked around the table, grateful to be reunited, swearing she would never allow distance between them again. Yet she couldn't help but notice how aged Amanda had become, the dark circles around her eyes and the distance in them so apparent. She dismissed that thought, realizing that the meeting could have been more difficult for Amanda and that she was emotional about the reconciliation. Not wanting to ruin the evening, guilt surged in her; why was she allowing negative thoughts about Amanda to infiltrate her mind like this?

*First her drinking and now her appearance,* thought Lynnie. *I'm being so judgmental; jeez, am I turning into my mother? Or is it too late for me and I've already become her? God help me.*

She quickly dismissed her destructive musings to focus on her friends.

The conversations flowed as they had in the past, the women laughing about old times, reminiscing about Jessica, and speaking about family and work, but they were always careful not to mention why they had grown apart. It was as though no one dared reopen that wound.

Time flew by as the women were the last to leave the restaurant.

It was time to part ways.

"Promise me we'll get together again for dinner soon," Amanda pleaded.

"Absolutely," Myra promised.

"Yes, please let me know. I can call in a babysitter or see if Luke can get home a little earlier," Lynnie ventured, looking around in anticipation of a reaction.

There it was, the mention of Luke.

Somehow, they'd avoided that topic throughout the night, and Amanda's eyes darted to Myra.

"How are things going with him then?" Amanda asked carefully.

Unlike Lynnie, Amanda hadn't completely forgotten what had transpired years ago.

"It's great," Lynnie said, too cheerfully for everyone else's comfort. "Honestly, he's a totally different person now. I promise. Come on, do you think I would allow Ellie around someone I didn't trust? If this had still been the old version of him, then no way ..."

Myra immediately jumped in with, "No, no, I know Amanda didn't mean anything by it, Lynnie. Honestly, we're so happy for you. We're just making sure you're happy."

"And I *am* happy," Lynnie voiced. "Happier than I've been for quite some time, actually. But I really do love the fact we all still look out for one another. Thank you."

Myra had always been the peacekeeper, and not wanting to ruin the evening, the subject was quickly changed, the girls continuing with their prolonged goodbyes.

As the women departed, blowing kisses and waving goodbye with the promise to see each other soon, Lynnie had a sinking feeling. *"We* are happy for you," Myra had said, as if they had been talking all along and Luke was the topic of conversation between the two of them.

Had Myra and Amanda been in touch this entire time, and Lynnie had been the one outed from the friendship? The nagging feeling made Lynnie wonder how little she might know about the last year in her friends' lives. And if they'd cast her aside because of Luke coming back on the scene, that was hardly fair, was it? Everyone deserved a second chance.

But now she considered it, it seemed certain they had been avoiding her for some reason. Perhaps it had little to do with her and Luke though; it could be something to do with Amanda.

Lynnie thought back, remembering when she had asked Amanda about work, and she'd brushed off the topic, requesting her to just pass the wine.

Myra seemed to have given Amanda a stern look, but at the time, she'd put it down to Myra being distracted by the waiter bringing their entrées to the table at the same time.

Lynnie scolded herself. *Why do I always have to think the worst of my friends? None of us is perfect, least of all me. Being so critical of people isn't a nice trait. Get rid of it, Lynnie.*

She tried to push the thoughts about Amanda out of her head. It didn't work at all because there was still *something,* a horribly nagging doubt. Sometimes, wasn't intuition right? And was it always a good thing to overlook the suspected problems of friends and loved ones?

Maybe someone might need help, and if everyone just said, *ah, well, let them get on with it ...*

For a moment, Lynnie thought back to how many times she'd had a feeling that she dismissed, only to find out later that her gut instinct had been right. She needed to trust herself more, but even all these years later, her mother's voice danced in her head about not being worthy, not making good decisions in life, and about Lynnie's mind being weak and unreliable.

❦

The following day when Ellie woke her up at 6 a.m., Lynnie's head was a little foggy, but her heart was full. She thought again about the evening and how wonderful the night had been although she still couldn't shake the sensation of not being privy to how Amanda was really doing. Lynnie brushed off her negative feelings, thinking she'd had too much to drink the night before. She started making Ellie breakfast.

Journal

It was so nice to celebrate turning thirty with Amanda and Myra.

I have missed them and am so glad we've reunited; it was the best possible birthday gift!

I know life and age changes everyone, but I can't help feeling Amanda's hiding something.

She's drinking again, for sure; I've seen it with my own eyes isn't an alcoholic supposed to stay completely dry after they've kicked the addiction?

Otherwise, it's a slippery slope and I'm so scared she may be back on it.

Why would she risk everything though? I can't say and anyway, it's none of my business.

# CHAPTER NINETEEN



*Lynnie: Reconciliation.*

The reunion with Myra and Amanda had made Lynnie nostalgic. She decided to pay a visit to her parents, bringing Ellie along. Her father's health was slowly declining, and she could see how her parents were aging. She had barely spoken to either of them or in the past, her marriage to Luke had all but destroyed any chance of building any relationship.

They looked down upon Luke; in their eyes, he was nothing more than a lowly 'kitchen help,' even though he was a renowned chef with impressive credentials.

But whoever she married, they would never approve. As it stood, they barely recognized Ellie because she had been born out of wedlock with a man they also knew nothing about.

Tolerance and understanding had never been her parents' forte and as they'd grown older, they had only become more bitter and even less tolerant. Lynnie had always hoped that age and time would reconcile the pair in a less judgmental way, but unfortunately, that hadn't been the case.

Still, Lynnie felt obligated to visit once a year and there was no better time than Thanksgiving.

Luke, of course, couldn't join her as he would be working throughout the holiday season, and it as a good thing anyway, since they would never make him feel welcome in their home.

This way, she didn't have to create an uncomfortable situation for anyone.

The visit would be awkward enough in any case; Lynnie suspected she might be pregnant but hadn't even taken a test to confirm it yet.

She vowed not to share the information with her parents as it would not be received well but at the same time, keeping such an important thing a secret also did not sit well.

Approaching their home, Lynnie looked carefully at Ellie.

She was protective of her daughter and was having second thoughts about the visit. Before she could reconsider, Ellie said, "Mommy, where are we?"

"This, my love, is where Mommy grew up. You are going to meet my parents." She stopped short of saying *your grandparents.* They were never going to deserve that title.

Confused, Ellie looked at the large house from the curb. "Mommy, *you* have a mommy?"

"Yes, Ellie. I do. We won't be staying long. And I need you to be on your best behavior."

It was a desperate plea, Lynnie already imagining her mother's disapproving looks if Ellie so much as raised her voice or asked for something.

Quietly, the pair made their way to the front door, holding hands. Lynnie hadn't noticed, but hers were shaking ever so slightly, her palms also growing clammy. She took a deep breath and rang the bell, hoping her father would answer the door.

But he did not.

"Hello dear," her mother said coolly.

"Mother. Hi, how are you?" Lynnie said with a bit of nervousness.

Her mother's eyes trailed to Ellie.

"And who do we have here?"

"Hi, I'm Ellie. Are you my mommy's mommy?" Ellie asked innocently, but before she could answer, Lynnie's father approached from the garage.

"Ah Lynnie, sweetie, how are you? I'm so glad you made the ride to visit. And who do we have here? Are you a beautiful princess from a faraway land?"

Ellie giggled. "No, I'm Ellie, silly!"

Lynnie exhaled just a little, knowing her only hope during this visit would be her father.

Yet despite everything, he was at just as much of a loss as she was. Maybe even more since he was the one who was stuck with her mother night and day, life offering no respite for him.

As an adult, Lynnie understood he had to escape her mother's viciousness any way he could.

The last time she'd come to visit her parents, it had erupted into a huge argument, one that Lynnie vowed would prevent her ever stepping foot in that home again.

Lynnie recalled the night, one on which she had reflected numerous times since.

⸻ ❦ ⸻

"You broke his heart, Lynnie. You did this to him, so please don't go around thinking you do not hold responsibility for your father's failing heart. We gave you every opportunity to succeed, from the best education to the most prestigious town, and it was all for nothing. I don't suppose for a minute that you have ever considered how this affects us, especially your father's health."

*What garbage,* Lynnie's inner voice told her. *The only one who affects Dad's health is you.*

Her mother's voice was filled with rage and contempt. "Do not fool yourself, daughter. You are nothing but a washed-up housewife hoping for a bit of grace in this world. I don't suppose the New York Times has called you up yet with an offer to join them as a writer?" she scoffed.

"Of course not, because you are satisfied with mediocrity. You lived in a household in which you would want for nothing, and now the shanty you call home is nothing more than a poor man's dream and a rich man's nightmare." Her rage was palpable. "When I'm at the country club and our old neighbors ask what's become of you, I'm mortified to give them details.

"If you want the truth, I'm ashamed and saddened by your life choices, and you have the nerve to walk around so carefree, even being judgmental of your father and me? And don't think we haven't noticed it because we have. We've worked hard, Lynnie, sacrificed everything, provided so many opportunities for you, and you have systematically pissed it all away, your only ambition apparently being to procreate. It's beyond me why you thought that was a good idea."

Lynnie reeled; that was a truly horrible thing to assert.

Elie was an absolute godsend, a blessing, without whom life would be so much poorer.

But her mother had not finished her tirade yet. "So no, Lynnie, please spare yourself and me the embarrassment of pretending you have no part in any of this."

Lynnie had shuddered at the thought of that night, one that would forever haunt her.

Her mother's face had flushed, years of resentment oozing out of her as if from an open faucet. Lynnie had been stunned by her mother's hurtful outburst; she had simply gazed at her mother then, ensuring she finished her rant before making her next move.

And then, calmly, Lynnie walked straight up to her, shoulders back, chest up. She stared her mother in the eye.

"At what cost, Mother?" Lynnie snarled. "Ultimately, you have accomplished nothing yourself. A loveless marriage that produced one child who barely can stand the sight of you, friends who use you for your fancy dinner parties and fine wine, and a husband who will be dead by the end of the year and who is scared of saying a word to you or doing the wrong thing because you beat him up verbally for everything he does or says. You will die lonely and afraid, and maybe at that point, you will look back regretfully and wish you'd lived a life of substance."

Lynnie turned, walking out of the room and slamming the door, sighing in relief.

It was better to have said it, she reassured herself.

Better not to start cowering before this vile woman in the same way as her father did. There was no benefit in staying silent just to keep the peace. When someone was always so vitriolic to everyone around, why even bother trying to pander to her? What good would that do?

The slight problem was that she had mentioned her father, and maybe her mother would now think he must have been saying bad things to Lynnie about his wife.

He had not, but Lynnie knew how her mother's poisonous mind operated.

Lynnie walked through the French doors onto the porch and down the steps to the garden. No regret, just relief, finally freeing herself from her mother's expectations, knowing that her parents harbored ill feelings for her, and there would be no way to unknow that fact.

<hr />

Lynnie looked around the beautiful grounds of her childhood home. When had her mother taken the time to enjoy the smell of the lavish garden surrounding her yard, or to admire the hummingbirds singing to them sweetly throughout the day? She couldn't recall her mother ever gazing over at her when she'd been a child to stroke her soft hair or hug her the way Lynnie did with Ellie. No, her childhood memories consisted of criticism, comparison, and insecurities.

Her mother was hateful of all things beautiful and the more Lynnie thought about it, she was convinced her mother suffered from her own demons of depression and perhaps even bipolar.

As a child, she recalled her mother being moody, dark, and then suddenly cheerful, this strange cycle leaving Lynnie a confused child, constantly blaming herself for her mother's erratic behaviors. Her moods would shift from happiness and excitement to such darkness that she would hide away in her room for days. Lynnie would leave food or tea at these times, but on one occasion, her mother had hurled a lamp at her, barely missing Lynnie's face.

The room would be ransacked and in complete disarray, throw pillows cut open and the stuffing spread throughout the room.

There were broken mirrors, and numerous holes in the walls.

These episodes would last for weeks and one time, a complete month.

Then, suddenly, she would present herself in the kitchen in a pink blouse, black trousers, and perfect make-up as though it had never happened.

Lynnie learned when to steer clear of her mother, but it made little difference to the atmosphere of oppression and fear. Lynnie questioned her father about her mother's behavior, but he would simply dismiss it. "Ah, women. Fickle creatures. I'll never understand them."

Her father's response had been confusing.

She knew other women, none of whom were anything like as fickle as her father proclaimed. Many of them were warm, intelligent, and lovely. Stacy's mother, for example, was a single mom working three jobs, yet she'd also never behaved like Lynnie's mom.

The last time she had been at her parents' house, she'd left that day sobbing, crying the entire way home, defeated and embarrassed by her mother's accusations.

The realization that her parents were ashamed of her stung.

Yet, Lynnie again stood there, this time with her daughter, hoping to form some version of a relationship with her parents. Her father had survived longer than the doctors predicted, and Lynnie felt it was a sign to make amends with him.

Despite his health conditions and gloomy future, her father was unexpectedly grateful for Lynnie's visit and the chance to see his granddaughter, welcoming them both with open arms this time. It was a much better visit than the last, her dad so genuinely happy to see them.

*If only my mother didn't have to be there …*

Sadness flushed over her at the thought of her father's imminent death. He did not have long left on this earth, and he could have been a good grandfather, given a chance.

Lynnie decided to embrace the visit, to do her best to ignore her mother's attempt at sabotage, just enjoying whatever time she had left with her father.

Once they were inside the house, Ellie was soon sitting in front of the same checkerboard with which she had always loved playing as a child. "Dad, Ellie likes to play checkers the same way I did when I was little. Maybe you can play a game with her."

Ellie interrupted. "I love playing checkers. Mom says I'm a pro!"

"Oh, does she indeed? We shall see about that," he said with a chuckle.

The two slowly entered the living room.

Lynnie glanced at her mother and before she could say a word, she quipped, "Not a word, Mother, not a word."

Her mother's eyes filled with tears.

"Look, I know I've been hard on you. I know things have never been easy between us, but I'm glad you are here. And I know your father is as well."

Lynnie held back tears, not pulling away as her mother grabbed her hand and squeezed lightly.

They spent the rest of their time together focusing on Ellie, her parents genuinely happy to get to know their granddaughter. Something between her parents had shifted. A calmness, a respect had come. A knowing that the end would be near, and that life went by just way too fast.

Lynnie caught her father staring off into the distance and when his eyes met hers, he stared at her momentarily and mouthed, 'I love you. You make me proud.'

"Dad, thank you. That means a lot to me. I wish I'd known that sooner though," Lynnie said.

"I wish I'd said it sooner. So does your mother. Believe me, Lynnie, she has a lot of regrets."

Lynnie smiled at him and put her hand on her heart, recognizing this scarce moment in their relationship. She was overwhelmed when she left later that evening, only thinking of the day as a complete miracle—perhaps an intervention from Jessica, who had promised to look over her.

Whatever and whoever was responsible for the day, Lynnie couldn't have felt more at peace although she was cautiously optimistic.

*Lynnie: South Park Nursing Home.*

Lynnie sleeps for a long while, as reading the journals make her uneasy, and she needs rest. When she awakes, familiar strangers—coming to visit often—sit in her room, whispering something she can't quite hear. Then the man who gave her the journals reads from a pink polka-dot book. He smiles and looks over at her. "You lived quite a life, Mom," he says with a chuckle.

"She certainly has been the strongest woman we know," the other man says, sitting by the windowsill, his eyes filling with tears, looking out the window. "We love you, Mom."

*'Mom', there's that word again. Are these my children? They must be. Wish I could remember.*

Once they have left, Lynnie opens the pink polka-dot book and reads some more ...

JOURNAL

I KNEW I WAS RIGHT! RIGHT BEFORE I VISITED MY PARENTS, I HAD BEEN SUSPECTING I WAS PREGNANT. TO MY SURPRISE, THE VISIT WAS AMAZING, LIKE VISITING TWO DIFFERENT PEOPLE, ONES I DIDN'T KNOW. WELL, DAD HAD ALWAYS BEEN LOVING BUT BECAUSE HE WOULD BE UNDER MY MOTHER'S SHADOW AND IN HER CONTROL, HE WAS ALWAYS SUBDUED, NEVER ABLE TO BE HIMSELF. BUT THIS TIME, HE WAS AMAZING, CONFIDENT AND FULL OF LIFE—DESPITE THE OBVIOUS STATE OF HIS DECLINING HEALTH.

THEY WERE HAPPY TO HAVE BOTH ELLIE AND ME THERE, AND AS WE WERE LEAVING, MY MOTHER COMMENTED HOW WONDERFUL IT WAS TO BE TOGETHER. SHE EVEN ASKED ABOUT LUKE. I WAS STUNNED!

ONCE I STARTED GETTING MORNING SICKNESS, I TOLD LUKE ABOUT THE BABY AND HE IMMEDIATELY TOLD ELLIE. THE EXCITEMENT OF A BABY SOON COMING INTO THE HOUSE HAS THEM BOTH OVERJOYED. THEY LOOK THROUGH BABY BOOKS AND, LAST WEEK, HE CAME HOME WITH A SMALL STUFFED ANIMAL FOR WHEN HE OR SHE IS BORN.

Luke's so ecstatic about having his own child, though he treats Ellie like his own anyway.

Being pregnant this time is different. I remember going through it with Ellie, and I still felt so alone despite having the girls around. Though, I can't help but think about Marc. He would have been a great dad. I hate to admit it, but Luke will always feel like my second choice though I am lucky to have him. I wonder if he feels it too.

Sometimes, it feels like Luke is more of a character in my life, a missing piece, rather than a soulmate. That would always be Marc. Of course, I can never say this to Luke, but he surely picks up on it, could that be why he's been drinking so much? Probably not. He's so excited and nervous about the baby that the beers after dinner are just part of the celebration.

Luke is gentle and kind and has exceeded all my expectations as a husband; because of this, I wish I could feel so much more for him than I do and give him what he deserves.

I habitually put perfume on before bed, smoothing my lips with a clear gloss as I nestle beside Luke

BECAUSE I WANT HIM TO ALWAYS FIND ME ATTRACTIVE. I WONDER IF HE NOTICES? OR HAS HE BECOME ACCUSTOMED TO THE SWEET SMELL OF MY SKIN AND THE SMOOTH FEEL OF MY LIPS?

---

JOURNAL

MAYBE I'M EMOTIONAL OR JEALOUS, BUT LUKE HAS BEEN DRINKING MORE THAN USUAL. I'M CHALKING IT UP TO THE STRESS OF HAVING A NEW BABY ENTERING OUR HOUSE SOON. HE GOES OUT MORE THAN USUAL, AND I FIND HIM PASSED OUT ON THE COUCH IN THE MORNING.

I HAVE READ THAT MEN DON'T FIND PREGNANT WOMEN ATTRACTIVE, WHICH SCARES ME.

WE ONCE HAD A VIBRANT AND ACTIVE SEX LIFE, AND NOW IT'S NONEXISTENT. LUKE SEEMS EXCITED FOR THE BABY BUT HAS LOST ALL INTEREST IN ME. I TRIED TO TALK TO HIM ABOUT HIS LATE NIGHTS AFTER WORK, BUT HE DISMISSED IT FLATLY WITH A RESPONSE OF, 'RESTAURANT LIFE. IT'S EXHAUSTING'.

---

# Chapter Twenty

*Lynnie: A Newcomer!*

Lynnie gave birth to a baby boy and was quickly immersed in having a new little one in the house, while Luke instantly fell in love. It had been nearly seven years since Lynnie had dealt with an infant and she had somehow forgotten how exhausting motherhood could be.

But she tried gaining Luke's attention by being more physically attractive. Lynnie was still habitually putting perfume on before bed, smoothing her lips with clear lip gloss before cuddling in close to Luke. But no matter how many diets Lynnie tried or how she dressed, or whatever new hairstyle she experimented with, she had clearly lost her husband's attention.

The only female of importance to him now was Ellie.

Lynnie fell into a depression.

She had hoped the birth of their first child would bring them closer, but obsessing over the new baby was only driving her husband even further away. The tension between them was growing, and Lynnie relied on her children for the love she lacked from Luke.

Despite the distance between Lynnie and Luke, she was happy to have a baby in the house again, in awe of her new child who was giving her life and purpose, caring endlessly for him.

She enjoyed the midnight feeds, his little toes, and tiny cries, immersing herself in motherhood, feeling purposeful and understanding the meaning of unconditional love.

Ellie was ecstatic about the birth of her brother Blake and loved helping to care for him too, always eager to play the part of the big sister.

Lynnie lived for her children and soon didn't notice Luke spending even more time at the restaurant and out of the home, but she even relished his absence, enjoying full access to her children. Despite having spent her childhood in such a lonely way, she could no longer imagine loneliness or isolation, her life now revolving around her special role as a mother.

However, Lynnie worried about Luke. He was missing important milestones in Blake's life.

One night, she decided to try to bridge the gap between them. When Luke arrived home late from work, Lynnie stayed up, awaiting his arrival with a bottle of wine.

Luke was surprised and took an interest in Lynnie that night. They stayed up talking and laughing, eventually making love.

*Why didn't I try reconnecting with my husband sooner? Maybe I was the one at fault.*

The next day, Luke left for work early and didn't come home until the early hours. The cycle had continued between the two, and Lynnie felt the distance between them growing once again.

She was becoming restless, tired of putting forth all the effort in their marriage. Eventually, Lynnie started doing less to impress Luke and more to make her life more manageable.

In late spring, Lynnie became pregnant again, delighted to discover she was having twins. Her growing family was giving her purpose but also less time to focus on herself or her marriage.

Lynnie provided excessive love and devotion to her children, so much so that she wondered if motherhood had taken over her identity. Her days were spent playing endlessly, filled with wonder and joy. She no longer submitted work as a freelance writer either.

In the late nights, though, Lynnie was often exhausted, longing for the company of other adults. Hearing about her friends' blooming careers, jealousy began to grow. She wanted to write again, but by the end of the day and in Luke's absence, she was too exhausted.

Lynnie was growing restless but having two children to care for and two more on the way, her life as a writer had to once again be put on hold.

<hr>

## JOURNAL

I TRY TO KEEP IN TOUCH WITH AMANDA AND MYRA, BUT I'M ALWAYS THE ONE TO REACH OUT.

FINDING A BABYSITTER SO I CAN MEET THE GIRLS IS DIFFICULT, AND WHEN I INVITE THEM OVER HERE, THEY ALWAYS SEEM TOO BUSY. I'M GLAD FOR OUR OCCASIONAL DINNERS AND LOOK FORWARD TO A NIGHT OUT WITHOUT THE CHILDREN. AS MUCH AS I LOVE MY BURGEONING FAMILY OF KIDS, EVERY MOM NEEDS SOME ADULT COMPANY TOO. STRANGELY, I GOT THIS ODD FEELING AT DINNER THE

LAST TIME WE WERE ALL TOGETHER, AS IF I'M MISSING SOMETHING THEY KNOW BUT I DON'T.

IT MAY HAVE BEEN HOW MYRA WOULD LOOK AT AMANDA AS SHE DRANK OR HOW SHE WAS CAREFUL TO OFFER AMANDA A RIDE HOME, JUST CLAIMING IT WAS ON HER WAY.

IT SEEMED STAGED TO ME ... I CAN'T PUT MY FINGER ON IT BUT THERE WAS A WEIRD VIBE.

# Chapter Twenty-One



*Lynnie: A Helping Hand.*

Luke found fatherhood difficult and overwhelming, growing impatient with the noise and concerned with the expense of what four children would mean for their finances.

But at least Ellie and Blake were excited for the babies to arrive.

Lynnie, on the other hand, was exhausted. She had been taking care of the children all by herself while pregnant with twins, but she hadn't complained to Luke for fear of putting more pressure on him. So she did what she had always resorted to, remaining silent.

Inside, she was overwhelmed and lonely without Luke's help.

Outwardly, she put on a brave smile, trying her best to make her home welcoming.

When the twins were born, Lynnie was more tired and defeated than ever, having four children now; two were newborns, and this was too much to handle.

On a particularly bad day, she called Amanda to help.

"Amanda, please, I just need another set of hands," pleaded Lynnie. "Wait, Amanda, are you sick? You sound a little out of it."

"Oh no, don't worry, I was just napping. Work's been hectic. I'll be right over."

Lynnie waited for Amanda to come as promised, worrying when two hours had passed, and she still hadn't heard back from her or seen her at the front door yet.

Just as Lynnie was about to call Amanda back to inquire where she was, there was a soft knock on the door. "This must be her," Lynnie said, rushing to open up. When she did, Amanda stood there, looking as if she hadn't slept in days, her hair matted, and her eyes puffy.

"Amanda? Are you OK?" Lynnie asked.

"I'm great," said Amanda. "Auntie Amanda is here to help!" she said enthusiastically.

Lynnie didn't have time to question her about how strange this all seemed. She quickly said, "Thank you for coming. I'm putting you on diaper duty."

Amanda rolled her eyes but got to work with a smile.

Lynnie was grateful for Amanda coming to the rescue, also ecstatic to have someone to help with the kids. Amanda seemed amused with the chaos and, at the end of the night, said, "Thanks for calling me. It means a lot to feel useful. Can you believe I enjoyed every second of it?"

"Amanda, thank you," replied Lynnie. "You did seem to be getting into it. Maybe I should call on you more often!"

"Your kids mean the world to me, especially Ellie. I feel like I've helped raise her."

Lynnie smiled and said, "You have."

# Chapter Twenty-Two

*Lynnie: A Missing Man.*

Things at home were not getting much better. Luke was coming home less and less while Lynnie was struggling to even find time to wash her face in the mornings. The little ones were a handful, and Lynnie yearned for time alone. The house was noisy, and as desperate as all this may sound, Lynnie was joyful despite it all. She finally had the family she wanted. Although Luke wasn't playing the part, Lynnie made it up in her head.

Frankly, Luke was filled with overall discontent.

Lynnie was thriving in motherhood despite the demands and constant lack of energy for her marriage at the end of the day. By now, since Luke was showing no interest in her anyway, she was finding all the love she needed in her children.

When the day was drawing to a close, she had very little patience for Luke's boring and trivial work stories. She found Luke self-absorbed and starving for attention instead of giving attention to the family. The kids barely knew him, and he hardly noticed. While their marriage wasn't explosive, silent bombs went off passive-aggressively; the once loving couple were now living very individual lives, each looking after their own interests more than sharing togetherness.

They were no longer a unit, merely two people existing in life. The passion had all but evaporated. Alongside the shift, Lynnie had stopped spraying scent on her neck at bedtime.

The ritual seemed silly to Lynnie now. If Luke noticed, he didn't seem interested in it, just stumbling by at some hour past midnight with the smell of alcohol on his breath, a faint aroma of someone else's perfume lingering on his wrinkled clothes. Lynnie never mentioned it; she honestly didn't care anymore. If she ever did notice, she couldn't be bothered with the conflict.

Lynnie carried on quietly adoring Luke from afar.

While her love for him was strong, the commitment to raise her children differently from her own miserable and alienating upbringing was driving her to be overly attentive and nurturing.

As far as Lynnie was concerned, her infatuation with her children was not at all unhealthy; she dismissed it as motherly love. As the children grew, Lynnie couldn't relinquish control, taking it personally that her once adoring children were seeking their independence now.

It was leaving Lynnie with profound sadness and an overwhelming sense of rejection.

She would try engaging them by buying them small gifts, but eventually, they became disenchanted too, barely recognizing their mother's attempts to connect with them in that way.

She should have known better anyway; providing 'things' was not what her children really needed. They were missing out on the closeness of their mother and father, not seeing Mom and Dad enjoying being together anymore. It must have no longer felt like a stable, loving home.

Lynnie slid into depression, losing her way in seeking the love she had received when her children were toddlers. Now, she was badly struggling to connect with others because she had been so invested in her children for so long.

They were school age now, and Lynnie longed to fill the hole inside. Her kids depended on her for rides to practice and afternoon snacks, but Lynnie missed feeling genuinely needed.

By now, Luke had become so absent that Lynnie barely spoke many words to him. His alcohol consumption was becoming more prevalent and while Lynnie was finding her way through the next stage of her life, Luke was sinking further away from his family and from the man who once had been a dependable, loving husband. At one point, Lynnie went to Luke to try and mend their broken marriage. He was drunk, and a fight erupted. Lynnie begged him to go into a program to help with his dependency on alcohol, but Luke refused.

"Luke, please, we have children. They need you," begged Lynnie. "They need both of us."

"The hell they do, Lynnie. They need you. They don't need me!" Luke slurred.

"Luke, you need to leave if you don't think about getting any help. I cannot and will not have you around the kids drunk."

He paused, then made his way clumsily toward Lynnie.

"You mean you can't have *me* near *you*, Lynnie! Admit it, the only room you have in your life is for your kids and your college girlfriends. That immature relationship never grew up. From when you were a kid, you've been permanently dependent on those women. Can't you see, it's time to be my goddamn wife?"

Lynnie stood stunned as Luke wobbled away. He didn't come home for two nights after that, leaving her to worry about where he had gone. On the third day, she got a call from an officer at the precinct; Luke had been arrested for disorderly conduct.

He wanted to know, would Lynnie bail him out?

Lynnie watched Luke as he came out of the building. His hair was messy, and he had a black eye. Opening the car door, he just stared at her for a moment.

"Lynnie, I have a problem and need to face my demons. I haven't been the best father or husband and getting arrested has made me realize how much I have to lose."

Lynnie sobbed in his arms.

"Luke, I'm here. I want the same."

The two embraced, promising to work on their marriage after Luke got the help he needed. Again, Lynnie felt the intervention came from above, hopeful for the first time in years.

She helped Luke register then dropped him off at a facility caring for withdrawals and coping mechanisms for alcoholism. The car ride was quiet, Luke spending most of the hour staring out the window. When Lynnie tried to make conversation, Luke would just nod.

Before he clambered out of the car, Lynnie grabbed his hand and said, "I'm proud of you, Luke. I love you."

Luke nodded, then turned, and opened the car door.

When Lynnie went to walk Luke to the registration office, he stopped her.

"Lynnie, I'm good here. I need to do this alone."

Luke grabbed her hand and hugged her, then disappeared into the brick building, leaving Lynnie alone in the parking lot.

⸻ ◦❉◦ ⸻

Luke had been gone for over three weeks, leaving Lynnie unable to contact him. While she knew he was safe, she still couldn't help worrying about his mental stability at night, also asking herself what he was going through. She started spraying perfume on herself before bedtime again, praying that her husband was recovering. Lynnie felt hopeless but prayed that God would help them find their way back to each other with patience and time.

In an effort to stay sane and calm for the sake of her children, she prayed relentlessly, asking God for guidance while her husband battled his demons, praying for grace. She wanted her family to be whole again and knew this disruption was unsuitable for her children.

She tried hiding her anguish from her children, but it was hopeless; they were perceptive and knew when their parents were in turmoil, no matter how much the adults believed they were hiding the worst of things. it was hidden. Blake would hug her tight when he found her staring out the window. Ellie would be more helpful, and the twins Michael and Christopher would snuggle her more, assuring her she was not alone.

Still, having Luke gone made life even more difficult for everyone, even though he was never emotionally available at home either because he was never sober.

Lynnie's anger toward Luke raged, but she tried to be supportive by learning more about addiction. Despite her resentment and bitterness, she had a new focus, determined to keep her family unified. She knew her responsibility was to her children.

Above all, she needed their father to be sober and alive to help raise them.

If there were something she could do to progress it, so much the better. But she wasn't sure that anything could truly help him.

---

Arriving home three weeks later, things seemed to be going in the right direction. At first, Luke was attentive, vulnerable, and apologetic, helpful around the house, avoided old habits, and genuinely tried keeping the family man persona he had desperately wanted. Lynnie was skeptical but hopeful. Sure, Luke was following the line, but she knew that at any given moment, a trip to town would lead him back into the bar and his old ways. Lynnie encouraged Luke to stay at the facility for over three weeks, but he assured her he was cured. He was ready to return.

As much as Lynnie wanted to believe her husband, she knew better, but she was desperate.

Once the cravings had subsided, maybe she would be able to help him stay sober.

Lynnie blamed herself for his battle with alcoholism, trying to make it right.

"Had I been more attentive or kept the house cleaner, perhaps Luke wouldn't have turned to alcohol. And if I could just lose weight, he might be more interested in me and less in the bar," Lynnie complained to Myra. "My life has been nothing but the kids lately; perhaps he's been feeling neglected and I should have made more time for him.

"Lynnie, this is not your fault. Sometimes, people have demons that only they can figure out. I know something about addiction because of my mother's struggles, and believe me, for years, I blamed myself, but I know my mother was sick, and only she could have gotten herself help."

"I know, I know," whispered Lynnie. "But I just feel so helpless. I don't want my kids growing up in an environment like I did. The most important thing to me is my family."

"Lynnie, you are a great mom, and the only person you can truly be responsible for is yourself. You simply cannot take on the burdens of everyone. You've been doing it your entire life. Aren't you tired of looking after everybody else and neglecting your needs?" Myra asked.

"Myra, I'm so tired. So very tired."

<hr>

Luke had always been a smooth talker, and persuasion was his gift, continually assuring Lynnie that he was fine and committed to staying sober. Still, despite her doubts, Lynnie believed in her husband, offering him every reason and opportunity to succeed. It took Luke seven weeks to wind up back at the bar, and when he failed to arrive home at his scheduled time, Lynnie knew exactly where to find him. The sinking feeling and disappointment were almost too much to bear. She thought about ignoring it, hoping it was a one-time thing, but that would only enable his deception. Luke wasn't the kind of man you could give an inch to.

If you did, he would take the whole damn ruler.

Lynnie called a babysitter so she could go down to Al's bar, where she was sure she would find her husband. However, at such short notice, the babysitter couldn't get there for about thirty minutes, so in that time, Lynnie paced the floors. This one time, she hoped and prayed her husband would shortly arrive home sober, explaining that he'd had to work late.

This one time, there'd be no drink on his breath.

As the minutes rolled on and the babysitter arrived, all hopes of that scenario diminished. He did not show up at all despite the lateness of the hour, and her stomach sank, knowing that the demon drink must have claimed him again. What other possibility could there be?

She headed into the bar, strolling to the booth he would frequent, hearing his familiar boisterous voice telling an exaggerated story to one of the other patrons.

Lynnie could tell by the slur of his words and the tone of his voice that she was already too late, and Luke was drunk again. Approaching the table, she saw a middle-aged man with sunken eyes and the same tired look Luke often had. Next to him was a younger woman who was intoxicated and bleary-eyed, slumped over her drink, half-listening to Luke's story.

Surprised when he saw Lynnie approaching, Luke casually called out her name, "Hey, sweetheart, I came to see some of the boys, ensuring everyone's behaving themselves."

"And are they?" Lynnie asked flatly, then looked at the woman.

Luke could sense his wife's annoyance, immediately getting defensive.

"What the hell is that supposed to mean?"

"I think you know, Luke," Lynnie responded.

"Like hell, I do, Lynnie. I innocently came to see some friends."

"Luke, let's not do this. We can discuss it at home. The kids are waiting to have dinner. Or I should say, the kids have been waiting for more than an hour for their dinner, and they should have been finished long ago. They'll be late getting to bed."

At that, Luke hesitated and stared at Lynnie, knowing she was right. He bid farewell to his audience, left money on the counter and followed his wife out the door.

"Lynnie, please let me explain. I just needed to feel normal again. This had been part of my life for so long and it was about far more than the alcohol. It's a place to relax, to chat and laugh. Everything's been too tense lately between you and me, and I know you feel it too.

"I need you to understand that I'm struggling but still one hundred percent committed. I love you, Lynnie, I do, I just ..." His voice trailed off.

"You just what, Luke? Are you trying to say you just love alcohol more than me? You love alcohol more than you love those helpless children who need their father? Fuck you! It shouldn't be all about you. Luke. We are supposed to be a family in case you've forgotten. And you are supposed to be a father to our children. You used to be such a brilliant dad. But now ..."

She refrained from finishing her sentence, knowing what she'd said was already enough.

The car ride home was silent, Luke spending the time staring out the window.

Lynnie was fuming but kept her emotions bottled up, knowing that this was not the time to address the situation any further. She tried hiding the tears, but the emotions kept flowing.

She focused on the road, controlling her breathing and wishing there wasn't so much traffic on the highway. The silence was deafening, and the tension was high, the fifteen-minute trip passing like a two-hour journey. But she was grateful Luke wasn't belligerent.

Once home, Luke went straight into the shower, spending an hour upstairs, only adding to Lynnie's worry. *What if he's bought a bottle of vodka and is getting drunk up there?"*

The constant suspicion and fear were exhausting, but as usual, Lynnie suppressed her feelings, surprised when Luke walked down the stairs right in time for dinner.

He brushed by Lynnie, gently touching her lower back, and she tried not to cringe.

She was disgusted at his actions these days, smiling sheepishly. She used to love it when he couldn't resist touching her, but nowadays, with the way things were, it made her skin crawl.

There was one good thing though. Lynnie appreciated that Luke had faltered but had been able to rein himself in before it got out of control. In her research about addiction, she learned that the sobriety journey should be considered a lifelong one, and every day would be a struggle.

It meant that once someone had broken the drinking habit, they could never drink again, not even a solitary glass of wine. If they did, they would immediately fall right back into addiction.

Lynnie took a deep breath, quietening the voice deep down.

"One step at a time; be patient," Lynnie muttered, then turned to see her children with their father. She smiled. The kids giggled, and Luke was able to sober up, enjoying their company.

After dinner, Luke offered to read a few bedtime stories.

Lynnie saw his pain and guilt for messing up again, but her anger was getting the best of her. She decided to take a walk outside to clear her mind.

Another good distraction would be to make a call to her friends.

She first tried Amanda but was immediately sent to voicemail. It made sense; Amanda had been busy at work and had mentioned she was on a very stressful deadline for a project.

Serendipitously, the phone rang moments later, and Lynnie could tell by the tone in Myra's voice that she was suspicious. Only then did she remember she hadn't returned the girls' text messages and was immediately regretful.

"Lynnie, is everything good?" asked Myra.

"Fine, fine, everything's good. Just been busy with the kids, that's all ..." Lynnie's voice trailed off. She tried sounding casual, talking about her children, work, and the weather, leaving little room for their regular deep conversations.

"You seem distracted. Are you sure you're OK?" Myra asked.

"Having kids is exhausting, I'm fine. Just tired," said Lynnie.

Later, Myra showed up unexpectedly at Lynnie's door.

Lynnie's eyes widened, tears flowing.

"How did you know to come over?" she asked.

Myra replied, "I just did."

---

*Lynnie: South Oaks Nursing Home.*

"Oh, Lynnie, still reading those journals, are you?" Helen asks. "I brought you some lemon pie, freshly made."

Lynnie looks at Helen for a moment, not recognizing this friendly woman.

She gives a warm smile and takes the pie.

"Are those three young people coming back?" Lynnie inquires.

"No, sweetie, your children left hours ago. They said they'd be back in a couple of days. They sure do love you. Blake said you used to make the best lemon pie when he was a kid. I thought you would like some of mine. Whaddaya think?"

Lynnie approves with a thumbs-up sign.

"So, Michael, and Christopher are twins. That must have been a handful," Helen says as she takes another bite of the pie.

Lynnie just stares. Something is coming to her. "The little girl, where is she?"

"Little girl? There was no little girl here," Helen says, puzzled.

Lynnie sits back in her chair, trying to remember who this little girl is, the one she is thinking of. She isn't able to place her but knows she has gone.

After finishing the pie, Helen says, "All right, love, I'll leave you to it. You seem to be enjoying those journals."

Journal

I invited Amanda over, and she arrived hours after I called her. I was perplexed by what took her so long, but didn't want to seem ungrateful. I was glad to have adult interaction, albeit two hours after she'd said she was coming. I was hesitant to tell her what was going on with Luke because I couldn't bear another 'I told you so.'

But when I opened my mouth, it all came flooding out. Amanda's eyes were wide. "Wow, Lynnie, I am just so sorry," she said. It seemed she was shocked and heartbroken for me.

The dreaded 'I told you so' never came, but instead, a warm hug and an 'I love you' before she stepped forward and enveloped me in her arms. I was so overcome and relieved; what would I have done without her support?

Thankfully, I will never have to be without it. That tender, caring moment made me realize she would

ALWAYS BE THERE FOR ME WHEN I NEEDED HER. THERE WAS NO NEED TO DOUBT HER.

IT FELT GOOD FOR A WHILE, THOUGH AFTER AMANDA LEFT, THAT SAME STRANGE, UNSETTLING FEELING CAME.

WHY HAD I BEEN GETTING SUCH WEIRD VIBES AROUND AMANDA LATELY?

⬦⬦⬦

# CHAPTER TWENTY-THREE

*Lynnie: Running Free.*

After picking Luke up last night, Lynnie was emotionally exhausted. The following day, she did as she was always doing lately and went to a prayer session at church. With a strong faith in family, marriage, and God, her morning mass ritual was important to her.

In her darkest hours, she turned to the church for solace. There was something magical about entering the quiet building filled with illuminating lights, soft music from an old church organ, and the smell of incense burning at the altar. The hushed voices, quiet prayers, and feelings of God's never-ending love encompassing her made her troubles feel smaller.

She had always encouraged Luke to join her, but it was just as well that he didn't.

She never knew what condition he would be in from the night before, and she didn't want his addiction to poison others seeking quiet. It would also be disrespectful for Luke to visit a church under the influence of alcohol, even if it was only from the prior night's drinking binge.

Today felt different for Lynnie, a small, unexpected light falling deep within her soul. It was as if a small switch had been flicked, bringing something warming and reassuring. A minuscule blessing from on high, a glimmer of hope, a need for closure … she wasn't sure.

Later, walking into the house from her morning prayer session, she found a tearful Luke.

"Baby," he said through sobs, "I-I need help. I need *you.* It's time for me to get a handle on my drinking. I'm fully committed this time, babe. Seeing the look on your face when you picked me up last night and then coming home to the kids looking so let down, something inside me snapped. I can't keep living like this anymore. I want to be a better father and husband.

"I can't lose you or the kids, and I also don't want to lose myself. I'll have to go away for a while, Lynnie. I'm checking into the rehabilitation center about twenty-five miles away.

"There can't be any contact with you while I'm there though; you understand, don't you? If we speak, it will remind me of all the drinking back home, and that will hold me back. So, you can't visit me either. I want to do this my way. It's a lot to understand, but I had the strangest dream last night. Lynnie, you were there sobbing at the beach. You needed me, and I needed you, but I saw myself as a wave in the ocean, being pummeled by the rough waters.

"I can't explain it, Lynnie, but it startled me. Gave me a real scare."

Luke was visibly shaken, his reddened eyes showing desperation, and Lynnie felt both fear about how he seemed to be distancing himself, and hope for the future of her marriage.

It was uncomfortable hearing him assert that home was 'a trigger'. It didn't make a lot of sense; he would need to face their home life as soon as the rehab period was over.

But whatever … She had been praying for this moment, and now Luke was making the necessary changes happen. Lynnie stood in silence, unsure of what to say.

Could she believe this? She had heard empty promises from him before, about sobriety.

*I desperately want to believe his words, but I also know the saying that actions speak louder ... He's a good talker, I'll give him that. But when is talk ever enough?*

His actions would be the telltale sign of his commitment to getting sober.

Lynnie was curious about the strange dream Luke said he'd had; it must have been very realistic to lead her husband into a state of panic.

She wanted him to be happy and whole, not caring what it took to get him there.

If she was being honest, there was a slight tinge of anger that all her earlier pleas for his sobriety had gone unanswered, some deranged dream being the stimulus finally driving him into rehabilitation. But she couldn't dwell on small details fueled by her ego.

What she longed to reply was, "Yes, I understand, love. You can go and do that, and of course, you have my full support. Do it whichever way works for you."

Yes, she wanted to say that. But she could not.

Lynnie was confused and exasperated. "Luke, I ... I need a bit of time."

"You need time for what though?" he inquired, his brow furrowing. He refrained from saying anything else, though it was patently obvious that he was unimpressed. Annoyed, even.

As Lynnie was driving down the road, tears flowed, anger and rage resonating within.

"Goddammit, Marc, why did you have to die?"

These unfinished feelings for Marc made everything so damn difficult, but there was no way to escape the fact that he had been her one true love, giving her something she would never be able to replicate with another person. There was no point in even hoping for that kind of depth with someone else; this love only came around once in a lifetime. Most people never had it.

Lynnie did what she always did when she felt defeated; she prayed, asking Marc for strength and courage to continue looking after her family.

Once Lynnie had managed to cleanse all this destructive negativity out of her soul, she took the drive home to her family with a renewed sense of calm.

But when she arrived, Luke was waiting for her on the porch. He looked at her lovingly and grabbed her hands.

"Lynnie, you do know I love you, don't you? I have never been as sure of anything in my life. It's for you and the kids that I'm doing this, and I'll come back a better man. I promise you."

The two embraced and were equally determined to make right whatever was wrong. That evening, they went to bed and made love for most of the night. She hadn't felt as close to Luke in years, the two connecting in a way she thought had been lost forever.

At the time, Lynnie hadn't realized that he was saying goodbye right now, with an intent to leave without delay. When Lynnie awoke with bleary eyes, she watched Luke packing the rest of his clothing into a small suitcase. He seemed frantic, highly impatient as if he just couldn't wait to get out of this place and onto the road. "Luke, you can't just get up and go like that."

He turned, seeming to gaze right through her.

"Luke, where *are* you going? It's Christmas in a week. I thought you meant you'd be going after the holidays," Lynnie said. "Can't you wait a week and spend Christmas here with us? You're going to break the children's hearts. Don't you think you've disappointed them enough?"

"Lynnie, I can't stay and anyway, that's just the point. Don't you see? It's *because* I've broken the kids' hearts that I do have to go right now. It's been long enough, and if I don't leave today, I may never go, and who knows what will happen? Alcohol is going to be the death of me. Please try to understand," Luke pleaded. "If I don't do it right now, my old ways will lure me back in."

What could Lynnie say? Nothing. She smiled weakly. Her heart was fracturing in two at the thought of those poor children and their tear-stained faces on Christmas morning.

Unbeknownst to Lynnie, Luke had woken up that morning, made arrangements right away, and would leave after his farewell to her. He looked tired, scared, and unsure, but she was proud of his decision and still wanted to be supportive.

"What shall I tell the children," Lynnie asked.

He replied, "Tell them the truth, Lynnie. The kids *deserve* to know the truth. I want them to understand that I'm sick and need help, and that there's no shame. I should have done this years ago, but I'm so stubborn. You should've kicked my ass, Lynnie. Long ago."

They made their way down the stairs. It was still early and the children were asleep, not having any reason to suspect their father would be gone when they awoke. As Lynnie stood alone at the kitchen counter, Luke returned with his packed suitcase. Lynnie's head was still spinning; there was no time to understand what was happening, it was all going so fast.

The night prior had been magical, and now her entire world had spun out of control.

She didn't want to be negative, but the timing of this was terrible. He would miss Christmas, and the kids were sure to feel the absence of their father a great deal. She tried not to think about it, focusing instead on the many future—sober—Christmases when they would all be together.

"OK, Luke. I understand. You can rely on my support, and just know I'm thinking of you and cheering you on all the way. I'll take care of things here while you're gone, praying for you and waiting for you to come to us sober and healthy again."

Luke kissed his wife on the forehead.

"Lynnie, I love you. I'm going to make this right. You have my word."

How many times had she heard that?

Countless, although this time seemed different. There was a determination in his manner that she had not seen in the past. She could only hope that his words and actions would prove true, and that Lynnie would finally get the family she had always dreamed of as a child.

JOURNAL

With Luke gone, I'm more insecure than ever. Having four children is a lot to handle, and my constant worry about my future with Luke has my stomach in knots.

My only outlet lately is running. It surprised me too. The weird part was how it all came about! I was so anxious that I went for a walk, and somehow, it metamorphosed into a jog that became a run. It happened that easily. Moving my body, focusing on my breath as one foot raced in front of the other, gave me a sense of calm. It was just what I needed, the release of energy. The feel of the wind, my heart pounding, and my mind's sheer determination made me feel alive. I hadn't felt this way for as long as I could remember, if ever.

Something about the power of my body and soul gave me a newfound confidence. After a hot shower, I was physically exhausted but felt refreshed, even weirdly enjoying all the aches and pains that soon set into every joint! My back, feet and legs were killing me but it had felt good to be free on the

OPEN ROAD, NO KIDS CALLING MY NAME, NO Luke TO WORRY ABOUT.

Just ME, MY BODY, AND THE SOUND OF MY BREATH. AFTER THE SHOWER, I PUT ON PAJAMAS, MADE MYSELF AN HERBAL TEA, AND CLIMBED INTO BED. I THINK I'M GOING TO GO RUNNING AGAIN TOMORROW.

# Chapter Twenty-Four



*Lynnie: Going 'No Contact.'*

Lynnie continued the ritual of running daily, fueling her confidence, and improving her body image. She hadn't heard from Luke in months and had yet to learn when he would come home.

How could she know that he'd even come home at all? He might well just disappear, never to be seen again, just like Marc. She shrugged off the feelings of abandonment; the situations differed, and she had to have a modicum of faith in her husband or why had she married him?

Sometimes, though, she would call the facility to ensure that Luke was still enrolled.

"Is he all right?" she asked the program convener.

"Yes, your husband is here and he's doing very well. I can tell him you called. Unless you would like to speak to him of course. I can go fetch him if you like."

"No!" That sounded terribly rude. Lynnie had been caught off guard.

*We can't have any contact,* he'd said. No way could she go against his wishes.

"I understand," said the kindly receptionist. "Many partners are told not to get in touch when their loved one is in rehab. If that's what your husband has said, please don't worry about it."

Lynnie's head spun to hear that.

"Really? So, it's normal?"

The woman laughed.

"Yes! Perfectly normal! In fact, we advise a lot of attendees to follow that path because it can allow them to keep a clearer head and not get muddled by confusing thoughts of home."

Luke would reach out when he was ready, in that case. Lynnie exhaled deeply, feeling a colossal weight lifting from her shoulders. The woman could not give her any other information due to confidentiality but what she had said was more than sufficient. Lynnie breathed easier, her steps lighter too. Not having contact with Luke was incredibly difficult, but the relief from all his chaos and drunken stupors was a refreshing change. Truthfully, the house was calm, peace reigning when they did not have the worry of Luke's drinking looming over their heads.

<hr>

Looking thinner but healthier, Luke arrived home four months and three days later. He was amazed at the transformation in his wife as well, finding her looking fit and vibrant.

Luke went to his meetings regularly, sometimes attending several a day. He became more present with his children, and although battered and bruised, he and Lynnie committed to making the necessary changes to improve their relationship. They worked tirelessly at having better communication, a greater understanding of one another, and much improved patience.

They were going to marriage counseling weekly and on date nights every Thursday.

The family was healing, the marriage more robust than ever before.

Lynnie was grateful for Luke and his sobriety, vowing to continue healing the wounds.

She was falling deeper in love with him too, seeing the commitment he was injecting into these efforts. He was dedicated to his sobriety, to his children, and to her. It was unfaltering.

Luke had also acknowledged to himself that working long hours at the restaurant contributed to his drinking. He was going to change paths and work only the lunch hours, leaving more time to be home with his family, knowing the importance of being a family man.

To his credit, he succeeded, soon proving he could be there for soccer games and school plays, and to tuck in the kids at bedtime; he even started running with Lynnie, which became an important and fun part of their routine together. But with all that was going well in Lynnie's life, she couldn't shake the notion of trouble on the horizon.

She tried brushing it off, grateful for the small victories in life.

But once again, she ignored her intuition.

# CHAPTER TWENTY-FIVE

*Five Years Later…*

Five years later, Luke had kept to his sobriety. Lynnie's family had healed by now, and the couple were closer than ever. Luke would sponsor others battling the heinous disease of alcoholism or other forms of addiction, saying it would keep him honest and was a way to give back to the rehab center which helped those who, like him, were struggling.

He knew firsthand the battle from within and how addiction affected a person's entire life and all the people around them. He knew how the demon drink could turn a family from being carefree, changing their home into a prison in which everything revolved around the drinker.

In his formerly selfish addiction, the children and his wife had been living no life at all.

Lately, he had found solace and purpose in helping others, knowing the only way to continue his journey was to live clean. Sometimes, he struggled and needed to attend an extra meeting, call a friend, or take a long drive alone. The urge to pick up a drink never stopped, but the desire to stay sober was far more significant now. Luke had too much to lose, and Lynnie's support through his struggles only made him love her more.

Lynnie kept busy with her job and kids, relying on Myra and Amanda for support, the women as close as they had been in college. But it was now infrequent that they were able to get together. Myra had been involved in yet another high-profile case and was more irritable than usual. Still, they met for dinner for an evening to unwind and catch up.

Amanda had arrived before the others, and she was on her third drink. She was slurring her words when Lynnie and Myra arrived.

"Hellooo ladies, what the fuck took you so long? Who wants a drink? Bartender, three dirty martinis straight up, with three olives."

Amanda was unsteady on her feet but smiling widely.

She would often arrive earlier than the others, already being three drinks in before they arrived. Lynnie found it a bit odd but chalked it up to her schedule being more flexible, though she'd also assumed that Amanda had stopped drinking long ago.

Myra exhaled, ignoring the spectacle Amanda was making.

"I can use a drink. I'm exhausted. My workload's never ending, and the stress of the media coverage is overwhelming. I can't leave the office without a gaggle of reporters shoving microphones in my face. It's far too intrusive," Myra complained.

"Myra, fancy lawyers usually like the publicity," Amanda teased. "It's good for business."

"Well, this *fancy lawyer* hates it. It's really wearing on me. I can't sleep at night, and my anxiety's getting out of control."

It wasn't like Myra to admit such sensitive things so freely, and she must have been burnt out to complain about her job. In all the years she had been practicing, Lynnie had never heard Myra talk like this. Was she finally tiring of her job's long hours and harsh nature?

"Can you take on fewer cases?" Lynnie asked sympathetically.

"I'm OK," Myra assured, "I'm just tired and cranky. I'll be fine tomorrow."

"Let's do another round," slurred Amanda.

"Amanda, this is your fifth drink, you can barely stand, and I have work in the morning," Myra said with irritation.

"Yeah, I'm done as well. I'm getting too old for a hangover," Lynnie agreed.

"Ahh, what happened to you two? I'll take one more," Amanda demanded, barely keeping her eyes open.

Apparently, the bartender had become accustomed to Amanda's drunken escapades and knew how to handle her. Knowing she was too drunk to see the difference, he watered down her drinks, advising her politely that this last drink was on the house.

By the time the trio left, Lynnie and Myra were holding up Amanda.

They led her into an Uber. As the car pulled away, Lynnie said, "Do you think she'll be OK getting home and into bed?"

Myra stared at Lynnie for a moment.

"Lynnie, you obviously didn't know but I have been dealing with this for years. I was handling Amanda and her addictions while you were having babies and dealing with your family issues. The truth is, while you think that we weren't all in touch after Jessica's death, I was helping Amanda out of a very dark spot. She battles some heavy demons."

Lynnie stood stunned, knowing her intuition had been right the entire time. The pair had been in contact, and Lynnie had been the one deliberately left out of the loop.

"What, why ..." Lynnie's voice trailed off. "Why didn't you tell me?"

"Lynnie, you had enough going on. I thought I could handle it, and I did for some time, but now, Amanda's going down the same destructive path again. Some people will never learn."

Lynnie stared at Myra, this time really looking at her, noticing the deep dark circles under her sunken eyes, and her protruding cheekbones.

Myra was also thinner than she had ever been, and Lynnie no longer saw a high-profile lawyer. This was but a woman suffering from a terrible burden of anxiety and stress.

"Oh, Myra, I'm so sorry. I didn't know how much you were dealing with. I was so wrapped up in my own life. This must be so stressful for you. What can we do to help Amanda?" Lynnie asked. "I really want to help this time, Myra."

Lynnie had an overwhelming feeling of guilt. The nature of their friendship was that they were all in this together, but Lynnie felt so isolated and shunned by her friends.

"Just because I have a family doesn't mean I don't have time for my friends," Lynnie said, angrier than she intended. "I cannot believe that after all these years, you never knew me."

Myra looked down in embarrassment. "I'm sorry, Lynnie, there was just so much happening simultaneously, and ... Well, I assumed and I'm sorry."

"Promise me, Myra, that from now on, the three of us are dealing with this together. Jessica would want it this way."

"I promise," Myra said, "and you're right." Myra paused, gathering her thoughts. "Here's what's been going on, Lynnie. She's been to the rehab facility already and relapsed, and I'm so disappointed and angry. Amanda promised she would get her shit together, and for a while, she did. Now, though, and as you saw tonight, she's drinking more often, missing work, and falling into the same habits as before. In other words, wasting all our time and efforts."

"It's so sad. I know how hard this is for everyone. When Luke was drinking, it practically destroyed my entire family," Lynnie said. "I don't know what you think, Myra, but maybe Luke can help. I know he helps others and is passionate about his sobriety, so maybe he can get through to Amanda. She's more likely to listen to someone who's been where she is."

"I know they don't have the best relationship, but at this point, we need to try anything to get Amanda back into a program. I'm worried about her safety. She's becoming more reckless and belligerent. The other day, when I stopped by her apartment, it was a disaster, and she looked as if she hadn't showered for days."

"I'll talk to Luke tonight," Lynnie said. "We'll get our friend back." Lynnie took Myra's hand. "We're all in this together, just the way we've always been, Myra."

The women walked separately to their cars, praying they could help Amanda before she did something irreparable to harm herself.

---

The green journal lies across Lynnie's lap as she watches the birds chirping outside her window. She's growing tired, her breathing is slower and her mind slipping.

*I have to finish this last book,* she thinks. *I won't bother with another one after that.*

The red cardinal appears before her as she gives a wave. "Hello, friend," she says. The cardinal flaps its wings once more, then flies off.

---

JOURNAL

AMANDA'S A DISASTER. HER DRINKING'S OUT OF CONTROL, AND I'M CONCERNED FOR HER SAFETY.

THINKING OF IT, MYRA ISN'T GREAT EITHER, SO THIN AND STRESSED OUT FROM WORK. BOTH SEEM SO OFF!

I'LL TALK TO LUKE; MAYBE HE CAN HELP WITH AMANDA'S SITUATION. AS FAR AS MYRA, I'LL BE THE STRONG ONE.

IF JESSICA WERE HERE, SHE'D KNOW WHAT TO DO. GOSH, I MISS HER.

---

# Chapter Twenty-Six



*Lynnie: Sleepless.*

Lynnie went home that night and was unable to sleep.

She had hoped that Luke would still be awake, but when she crept into bed, she could hear the humming of his breath deep in slumber. She stared at the ceiling, replaying the evening's events and trying to find a resolution to her friend's trouble. She had been hoping that Luke would have some answers for her and praying that Amanda would accept the help.

It seemed like a tall order, however, since Luke and Amanda had never developed a great relationship. When Amanda visited, they were cordial, but the past was never out of her mind. Despite Luke's treatment of Lynnie all those years ago in Paris being a distant memory, Amanda never did forget about it. Luke had been trying to prove that he had changed and was committed to being a good husband, father, and life partner, but Amanda never fully accepted it.

Myra, on the other hand, had grown close to Luke. They would talk about football and the stock market when she would come for a visit. The children loved it when Aunt Myra came to see them, delight in the treats she always brought to the home. Myra was a good friend, not just to Lynnie; she was also an integral part of the entire family's lives.

Lynnie tossed and turned through the night, unable to get Amanda off her mind and by early morning, Luke had awoken to find Lynnie staring at the ceiling.

"Hello, beautiful. How was the night with the girls?" Luke's sleepy voice whispered in her ear.

"Eventful, for sure. Luke, I need your help. Well, technically, Amanda does. I know this is a lot to ask, especially since you don't have the best relationship with Amanda, but I think you may be the only one to get through to her," Lynnie said desperately.

"Whoa, slow down, sweetie. Start from the beginning," Luke said, now more awake.

Lynnie explained the situation, feeling she was betraying Amanda but knew it was for the greater good. She had never spoken about Amanda's struggle with addiction to anyone other than Myra, but she felt she could confide in Luke, who understood the battle.

When she finished telling him all the details, Luke sat quietly for a while.

"Lynnie, jeez ... I had no idea. Amanda's crying out for help even if she's unaware of it. She is reckless, careless, and selfish, which addicts feed off to validate the drinking. The thing is, Lynnie, if Amanda doesn't want to get help, there is sadly very little we can do."

"Can you at least try, Luke, for me?"

"Of course, Lynnie, and I'll do my best for her. What's the name of the bar she goes to? It will be less intimidating to her if I happen to show up for a club soda and a bite to eat at the bar than to go unannounced to her house."

Panic ran across Lynnie's face.

"Wait, Luke, you're going to sit at the bar? Do you think that's a good idea?"

"Lynnie, I'm strong enough and confident that I can handle it. There's a good reason to be there, something to focus on other than the drinks. So don't worry, darling. I'll just grab a bite to eat and a club soda and talk to Amanda."

⚬⚬⚬⚬⚬

*Luke: A Friend in Need …*

Luke hadn't been to a bar in years, and when he arrived at the small pub, his palms were sweaty. *Perhaps I'm overestimating myself,* he thought. Still, he walked closer to the bar and saw Amanda flirting with a middle-aged bald man who appeared mesmerized by the attention.

"Hello, Amanda," Luke said softly.

"Well, well, well, look who's fallen off the wagon. I wonder what Lynnie would think about you hanging out at a bar," Amanda said defiantly. "Don't worry, your secret is safe with me."

"Amanda, Lynnie knows I'm here. She asked me to come," Luke replied. "Can we talk?"

Amanda looked at Luke curiously.

"What about? What could she possibly want us to talk about?" Suddenly, Amanda's face changed from antagonistic to understanding that this was about the other night and her drinking.

"Oh, I get it now. Look, Luke, I don't know what Lynnie's been telling you. The other night, I had too much to drink. It happens. You, of all people, should understand that."

"Hey, look, I'll be on my way," the middle-aged man said. "Nice meeting you."

"Sorry, but it's important," Luke said, and Amanda just raised her glass toward the man.

"Amanda, you know I've been where you are. I get it. It's scary," Luke said, moving in closer. "You become accustomed to the fog, the regrets, and the outbursts that you don't even recognize yourself. I have a contact at a rehabilitation facility that worked wonders for me. I've already called and told them about you. They say to get in touch. It works Amanda, it really does—"

"You what?" Amanda cut him off. "Fuck you and your preachy bullshit, Luke. You are the biggest fuck up I know. Why Lynnie stayed with you is beyond me. Now fuck off!"

Amanda was now shouting.

"Bartender, get me another drink," she demanded.

Luke paused for a moment. He sighed deeply, knowing Amanda's feelings. He slipped her a card for the rehabilitation center and said simply, "When you're ready."

As he left the bar, he turned to see Amanda staring at the card, tears rolling down her cheeks.

He walked out, knowing her pain and was grateful not to be in that place anymore.

Luke went home hopeful that Amanda would heed his warning and take his advice.

He didn't think he had got through to Amanda until, at 2 a.m., he was awoken by a text which simply read: 'I'm ready.'

# CHAPTER TWENTY-SEVEN

*Amanda: Rehabilitation.*

Without much ado, Amanda had left, admitting herself to rehabilitation. Luke was the one who brought her, and when he came home, he didn't say much about it. Lynnie inquired about the admission process. Luke was solemn. "Lynnie, she's still in denial."

That was all he said.

He walked out onto the porch and took a long sip of water.

Lynnie could tell when Luke was troubled, and when she inquired about it, he replied, "I do hope Amanda gets the help she needs and stays put for a while."

It was no surprise to Luke that Amanda lasted at rehab for only three weeks. She checked herself out on a Thursday, and it wasn't until Tuesday that her friends realized she was back home. They urged her to finish out the last three weeks of the program, but Amanda was suffocating from the constraints of the facility's rules. Luke tried to reason with her, but she was adamant she could handle outpatient treatment. The meetings—whether inpatient or outpatient—were similar, she said, and there was still a lot of support she could get.

She didn't have to actually reside in the rehab center.

It wasn't long before Amanda started suffering under the pressures of life. Her first sip of Chardonnay went down smoothly, reasoning that one sip, then one gulp, then one glass would never lead her back to where she had been a year ago. Amanda thought she could be the type of person to dabble with alcohol and know when to reel herself in if she felt out of control.

Her sponsor and Luke warned her of these false narratives, but as usual, she didn't listen, keeping her occasional drinking a secret. She made sure never to drink in front of her friends.

As far as they knew, she hadn't touched a drop since before she'd gone away to rehab.

Amanda reasoned that it was easier this way.

She wouldn't complicate things more than they already were.

As the constant pressure of listening to patients' troubles lay heavily on Amanda, her need for a relaxing glass of wine became more frequent at the end of the day. Eventually, the weight fell back on her, depression taking over, a constant reminder of how worthless her life had become.

Her condition now exaggerated the insecurities of her past. She continuously tried leaving her work life in the office but found her job seeping into her personal life. In the evenings, she would relax with a glass of wine and an occasional vodka on the rocks, but 'only to help me sleep'.

Considering her past, this routine was a dangerous road, but Amanda was confident that she was no longer having a problem with addiction. This routine continued slowly, increasing from one glass of wine to three, then a bottle of wine, and eventually, straight vodka from the bottle.

It seemed to have happened overnight. She had thought she had a handle on it one day, but by the next, she was longing for a drink from when she had awoken in the morning.

Without much notice, Amanda once again had little control over her excessive drinking. She would promise herself to cut down in the morning, and this would continue day after day.

"I'll get this back under control tomorrow," she said to herself.

Even in her weakest moments, she would rationalize that she wasn't drinking as much as before, that she could still turn this around. Yet day after day, she continued to binge, then wake up with a hangover, promising that this day would be different, but doing it all again.

The control alcohol had over Amanda wasn't new, but it was becoming increasingly problematic, and she was passing out on the kitchen floor, in the bathroom, and once even outside by the side door. She had no recollection of how she'd got there.

Her memory of the night was always pretty much a blur.

Once again, Amanda relapsed as she'd done many years before, calling in sick from work when her hangover had been too much to deal with. This was despite knowing she was still on probation at her job. The clinic at which she worked was incredibly supportive when Amanda requested time off to seek help for her addiction. But how much more leeway would she have?

Her patients were already complaining about her canceling appointments.

Even at the risk of losing her job, Amanda still didn't stop drinking, the alcohol becoming more important to her than anything else.

It got to the point that without it, she could not function, shaking and sweating profusely from withdrawals if too much time elapsed between drinks.

Drinking did something to Amanda that nothing else could. It made her forget. Forget the pain, the insecurities, and the shame that had been building since she was a teenager and since the time of her brother's football accident. If that hadn't happened to her family, would her life have been different? She also didn't visit her family as often as she wanted because it was a constant reminder that the accident had left Tommy never really the same.

He still walked with a limp and was slow with his words. Her parents still had to care for him in a way that adult children were not supposed to be cared for. Amanda avoided facing her brother's reality as much as possible and drinking was what helped her forget.

She hid empty vodka bottles in her closet, careful not to invite her friends to her apartment, fearing they would discover her secret. Morning coffees had now been replaced with small swigs of vodka. Eventually, the swigs became gulps, and the gulps became glasses.

She had convinced herself that the alcohol took the edge off this terrible stress and anxiety, making her more attentive and sympathetic to her patients.

She saw things from their point of view, she reasoned. In reality, she was failing to realize she was not seeing *at all,* everything marred by a toxic haze. Drink lessened her pain and anxiety for the day, masking her despair with alcohol instead of with empathy.

She spent more time alone, the half-truths she told her friends becoming lies.

Amanda became incapable of telling the entire truth, even details that need not be falsified becoming secrets and twisted lies. Thankfully, Myra and Lynnie hadn't quite figured it out but during a phone call with Myra, Amanda had slipped that she had been home all evening baking.

"I thought you had an appointment for your yearly eye exam," Myra inquired.

"Oh, oh, how could I forget? I meant that I have been home since *after* the appointment." Amanda reminded herself to be more careful when talking with Myra because she was a lawyer, always looking for holes in a story. She also tried avoiding long conversations with either of her friends, fearing they would start questioning her the way they did before.

"Why can't they worry about themselves instead of always going on about me?" Amanda said, frustrated. "I don't pry in their lives and question all their moves, do I?"

Amanda's frustration with her friends was fueled by paranoia and guilt about drinking, and the more she had these feelings, the more she drank. She was tired of keeping up a false narrative of sobriety but had no choice. As a result, she was most comfortable alone in her apartment with a cocktail and Netflix. There, she could be herself, an insecure, shamed alcoholic with nothing to prove to anyone. Having people care was too much pressure, making her feel trapped.

When sober, she would think about her friends with love, but eventually, she always started drinking again, resentful of their overly protective ways.

*The problem with wearing a mask is that it slips off when you least expect it,* she thought.

# Chapter Twenty-Eight



*Amanda: A Sense of Self.*

Amanda's only honest communication was with the delivery person who brought her food. The man was short and balding with kind eyes, and as Amanda would stumble to the door to retrieve her latest delivery, he would try making eye contact, giving her an earnest smile. He knew she was drunk, once offering to bring the meatball sub inside. Amanda declined, but the man rushed into her kitchen when she fell and cut her knee as she walked up the porch steps.

He was clearly uncomfortable, worried, and asked if he could get her a bandage from the first aid kit in his vehicle. "I'm Steve, by the way," he said nervously.

"Steeevvveee," Amanda slurred. "I would have taken you for a Ryan."

The man laughed as he cleaned the fresh cut on her knee.

"I'm Amanda."

"Yes, yes, I know that. It's on the takeout slip," Steve said. "Listen, it's none of my business, but do you have someone you can call, a friend or something? I don't think it's healthy for you to eat alone," Steve added, but what he really meant was he didn't think it wise for Amanda to be alone and drunk. He'd been delivering food during his retirement for two years now and had seen all sorts of things. Amanda, however, piqued his interest.

She seemed so lonely and pathetic, even reckless.

Delivering food for her every day had made him take a vested interest in her safety.

"Thanks, but no thanks, Stevie boy. Anyway, *you* are my friend now. Why don't you stay, and I'll share my dinner with you?"

"Umm … listen, I'm on the clock and still have to return to the shop. I just wanted to make sure you were OK," Steve said, and he left, knowing he'd be back tomorrow, and the next day, and the next. And on each occasion, his customer would be in the same condition as today.

Amanda found solace in food and an immense comfort in alcohol. She started rescheduling patients, then canceling until she missed work altogether. She had already been warned for this behavior ample times, yet she took no pleasure in adhering to her required workload.

During one session with a patient, she looked up from her desk and said, "Are you done? This pity party is getting tiresome. You don't take my advice, and you complain about the same five things each session. When are you going to begin being accountable for these things?"

To the patient's horror, Amanda just stared at her dismissively, but later apologized to her, explaining that she had just been trying to get her to decide about her career and to realize that time was passing by quickly. Sometimes, a tougher stance was required.

She said it was a new method to find a way through to the now distraught patient who needed a push. Lucky for Amanda, her patient never called to report her, so she was careful to hold her tongue even when she wanted to tell them all to fuck off.

She had started drinking excessively by now too, so not even her best friends could reach her. They would continue to call, but each one went straight to voicemail.

Myra was irritated at this, mainly because she was busy with her own life, and Amanda's constant dismissal of her was irritating and to be frank, rude. She was giving the generous gift of her time despite an exceedingly busy caseload, and Amanda was essentially ignoring her efforts.

Lynnie tried to be more patient, knowing the struggles that Luke had endured. Instead of tough love, she'd leave sweet messages on her friend's voicemail, reminding her she was loved and that she hoped to hear from her soon. Amanda hated when either of their names came up as incoming calls, however; it just meant more judgment, yet more lies she had to tell.

She loathed the thought of being pitied, seeing their help attempts as snooping and invasive. She stammered through her day with anger from years of hurt and pain, giving no regard to anyone, especially herself. She was regretting letting people into her life, swearing she would have been better left alone. In her mind, she'd convinced herself she was useless and worthless, every swig of vodka convincing her even more that it was true.

She felt disgusted by her plump body and dark circles under her eyes, the once beautiful woman now looking deranged and haggard.

She startled herself with her reflection on passing the mirror in the foyer. There, she caught sight of a woman whose hair was gray and thinning, cheekbones protruding from her face, leaving her eyes to reveal the damage she had done to her body. Looking down at her hands, the wrinkles from poor nutrition and years of abusing her body showed on every inch of skin.

For a moment, staring in disgust, she realized how sick she looked.

Without warning, she took her glass, threw it at the mirror, watching it shatter.

There was a peculiar sense of release as she did so, a demon let loose.

She walked away acting dignified, ignoring the mess beneath her bare feet, cutting her flesh. Why would she care about bleeding like this? She bled anyway, either inwardly and unnoticed, or outwardly with real blood, her life force. They were both a part of the same thing.

There had been something so cathartic about what she'd just done, and the resultant hurt.

Kneeling, she took a shard of glass and cut her arm, the blood dripping profusely, but she ignored it, the burn from the cut making her *feel* something, bringing her back to life with the pain, so numbed that it seemed only the tearing of her flesh could satisfy her.

The cut was, of course, not a deep one, a mere scratch.

It was just enough not to truly injure herself but sufficient to cause the pain.

By the time she'd managed to stop the bleeding, she was so inebriated that the sound of the wind irritated her, triggering, reminding her of when her brother had been taken away by ambulance. The noise surrounding her that night had played a part in her distaste for overstimulation. Her phone constantly rang from telemarketers, and she couldn't take that noise either, every sound rendering her paranoid. The constant calls from her friends would raise concern and warrant a visit; the last thing she needed was unwelcome guests.

So, there was an obvious solution.

She disconnected her phone and herself from the outside world, lying on the stained couch in the same clothes she had been wearing for the last five days.

Reeking of alcohol, cigarettes, and body odor, she looked around, thinking the most bizarre thought; should she burn the place down?

*So, this is rock bottom,* she thought. *I like it. I think it's making me delusional, but it's some form of escape. And God knows, society and all its interfering and judgment haven't delivered me anything better, not even after all these months of trying to get into my head.*

Darkness swallowed Amanda, leaving little regard for anything but her self-pity. Years of pretending to be happy and whole had exhausted her, and she was ready to be the vile addict she had been since her teenage years. Life didn't matter, and neither did she.

The cut on her left arm reminded her that the pain and blood meant she was still alive.

But that pertained only to her body. As for her poor, tormented mind, she believed that her soul had died. There was no point in taking the help offered, and hopefully, the anger, despair, and guilt would kill her one way or another.

She had lost all sense of self. What was *self* anyway, she often wondered? In her sessions with clients, she was always talking about their sense of self.

But she had never really considered it, what it truly meant.

Myra and Lynnie figured out the trouble their friend was in a bit too late and went to try to reason with Amanda. The first time they showed up, it took fifteen minutes and a lot of pounding on the door before she answered. She did her best to keep it together, which wasn't at all convincing, making excuses of having the flu and only indulging a little in an alcoholic beverage to ease the body aches. Neither Myra nor Lynnie were buying the story.

They tried desperately to get through to Amanda.

"We can go to a meeting right now," pleaded Lynnie.

"Come on. We'll take you," suggested Myra.

Amanda was adamant and said she was fine. She stood at the front door, blocking the view so her friends couldn't see what was behind her.

*They'll surely be worried if they see the state of my home, and then there'll be no escaping their very annoying concern,* she thought.

Begrudgingly, Lynnie and Myra didn't push it further.

But they did promise they would be back to check on her.

"Get your shit together. I'm serious. You're going down a dangerous path," Myra said.

"Fuck off," Amanda said under her breath.

Journal

Myra and I went to see Amanda. She's a mess. We all turned forty and Amanda refused to celebrate our birthdays together, 'refusing to get old', she said.

We know she had been drinking and that her excuse for the flu was bullshit.

It's heartbreaking to watch her wreck her life and to feel so helpless about our limitations.

I pray that God helps her, leading her to a path of security and peace.

# Chapter Twenty-Nine

*Amanda: The Truth of the Matter.*

Amanda had become so crude, rude, dismissive and irritable that even her best friends had trouble putting up with her intolerable behavior. The more they tried to help, the angrier and more disagreeable she'd become. They felt so helpless, also angry and bereft; this was another friend they were losing, though not to death this time, just to addiction. But which was worse?

Addiction was worse by far, they agreed; seeing someone so loved declining at her own hand and by her own repeated bad choices was devastating.

But despite Amanda's objections, Myra and Lynnie would visit her anyway, adamant that friends stuck together. Friends would not go away when times were hard; there was a term for those kinds of people: *fair weather e friends*.

Neither Lynnie nor Myra was willing to be one. They were with Amanda, unconditionally.

Most times, Amanda wouldn't answer the door, leaving them standing waiting outside, growing more impatient with her behavior.

Myra explained, "Amanda has the right to refuse medical attention unless she commits an illegal act. As much as we dislike it—no, as much as we detest it—she is a grown woman, responsible for her own choices even if they happen to be reprehensible ones."

Lynnie's eyes flashed anger at those words.

"This is bullshit. She needs help. Is there really nothing we can do?" Lynnie asked.

"Not a fucking thing," Myra said as they walked back to the car to leave. "If she becomes suicidal, we can take action under mental health laws. Other than that, she has free choices."

Besides worrying her friends to death, she wasn't breaking the law and she also had not expressed that she was suicidal, though didn't drinking herself to death as a means of escaping count as not valuing life? Were they not two different ends of the same continuum?

Bizarrely, Amanda kept her job and appearance while remaining a raging alcoholic. She knew she was out of control yet believed she could control her uncontrollability!

Amanda had come to believe that her life was manageable, and despite her pitiful nights of self-sabotage and foggy mornings of lost memory, she was still OK.

But more and more, Amanda was losing time, cutting off tiny slivers of her life, the clock counting down faster and faster to when her organs might fail or she would lose her job.

Each evening, early, she passed out, not even remember drinking the night before.

She lost time and memory of her whereabouts, and despite trying hard to recall details, she always came up empty. Alcohol had completely controlled Amanda, her physical and mental health both progressively failing. It all came to a head on a rainy day.

When Amanda got in the car on that occasion, the day that would change the lives of so many, she had no recollection of walking to the vehicle, putting the keys in the ignition, or even leaving her driveway. When pressed, she faintly remembered the sound of tires squealing and the strong scent of burning rubber. She remembered the screams, ones that ended abruptly, and the billowing of smoke filling the air.

She recalled her lungs jolting her to witness the destruction that would soon become her life.

Going in and out of consciousness, she would try placing the terrible sounds.

*The screams of someone familiar,* she thought, but in her drunken fog, she was unsure.

Lights and sirens whirled in her mind before she passed out. Then darkness.

When she woke, the only things she saw around her were machines.

Wasn't she hearing faint sounds coming from them? *Beep … beep … beep …* The echoing of voices from a distance was hushed and urgent.

*Am I dreaming?*

The sounds of the machines reminded her of being in the hospital with her brother. Was this what she was remembering? She looked down at her wrists, however, finding them bruised and fastened to the bed. At first, she thought she was still dreaming, but as her vision went from blurred to more focused, she realized she was, in fact, contained by a pair of restraints.

*Why though? Because I'm sick? Is this what they do to people who are just a bit depressed?*

Then it occurred to her.

*Fucking Lynnie and Myra; I bet they reported I'm a fucking danger to myself. And now, I'm in some goddamned psychiatric institution.*

For a moment, she scanned the room, looking for a drink. She couldn't see her vodka; so, she was definitely not at home. She was somewhere she didn't want to be, somewhere strangely familiar but eerily abstract. Trying to make sense of her surroundings, she focused on looking around, assessing the environment.

There was a white-coated man, one with an unimpressed mien.

*Well, dammit. Just shoot me,* she thought. *No need to stare at me like that! Anyone would think I'd just murdered someone!*

He approached her with caution but not gentleness. No, nothing like empathy—or even sympathy. "I am Doctor Sebastian Park. I'm the attending physician and will be running some tests on you. Can you please state your name?"

His voice was deep, and his appearance gruff. She would not have taken him to be a doctor had it not been for his badge. Amanda went to speak, but the words wouldn't come out.

Her voice was weak, the tubes in her nose making it hard to articulate a sentence. Her voice was strained, and all she could mutter was, "Amanda Young."

She noticed in the distance, outside the door, a uniformed police officer. She was tall and stoic in her pose, quickly glancing around the room upon hearing her voice.

*What the hell's happened to me? Someone must have attacked me. That's why I'm here and why they're guarding me. I've read enough crime novels to know this is what they do.*

"I think I'm all right, Doctor," she voiced. "You people work hard enough and long enough hours ... Whoever attacked me, he didn't do a good job because I'm still here. Honestly, you can spend your time looking at a different patient because I think I'm OK."

The doctor grimaced slightly.

Amanda then saw the female talk into her walkie-talkie, still in her position at the doorway.

As a nurse checked Amanda's vitals, the woman made eye contact with her and she noticed a look of sadness and compassion before the older lady quietly left.

Amanda's mind was racing, trying to put the pieces together, but she knew instinctively to say nothing else. Her head hurt, so it was better to keep her eyes closed for as long as possible.

Perhaps the terrible sinking feeling inside her would disappear if she stayed quiet now.

Whatever had happened was terrible and potentially life-altering for her.

However, she had no idea of the extent of it.

Amanda drifted in and out of sleep, occasionally hearing voices getting loud and angry, then a hush would come over, and there was silence. The position was horribly uncomfortable, and the restraints hurt. It made no sense why she would be wearing these, not as a victim. But her mind was awash with confusion, and her body and brain racked with pain.

Within a couple of hours, she felt a nudge; a nurse was once again checking her vitals.

"Sweetheart, you have a lot of people wanting to ask you questions," she said with a hint of deliberately subdued aggression in her tone. "I'm not in the business of law enforcement, and my only job is to provide medical services to you. However, if I were you, I would call a lawyer."

*A lawyer,* Amanda thought, then tried brushing the hair off her face, quickly reminded of the fact her wrists were still bound. *I'm handcuffed, and people need to talk to me, and they're in here every few minutes checking if I am capable of talking, so it seems. And now, there's mention of an attorney. What am I missing? They must suspect me of something. But what? It's surreal!*

"I'm so confused," Amanda said softly. "Can you tell me what's going on?"

Her voice was still weak, the words coming out slower than she had intended.

Moments later, when the officers entered the room, they announced she was under arrest and had the right to an attorney. It was no longer a surprise, only a horrifying shock. After all, the nurse had warned her and must have known what would come within the next few minutes.

She was going to call Myra immediately, although she still had no idea why she was there and what predicament she was in. Myra may not even be the right kind of attorney, but if she knew why she was here, then she could at least ask her friend to point her in the right direction.

But after those words, 'under arrest,' Amanda's mind went blank; she could barely concentrate on anything else, though the two officers were talking so quickly that she couldn't keep up.

The female officer was stoic, the male politely smiling when saying, "As mentioned, you do have a right to an attorney."

*Did someone say manslaughter? Did I really hear that phrase? That's insane.*

"Wait, hold on! *I* didn't kill anyone," Amanda said, now more forcefully.

Her voice had become louder, panic setting in, her heart racing. None of it made sense but she had seen those movies in which someone wound up being framed for a terrible thing.

That was all she could think this was; either they had mixed her up with someone or they were trying to pin a crime on her while she was in this awful state.

Amanda tried to move, but her body was in immense pain, the cuffs stifling her movements.

"Lynnie, I need to talk to Lynnie. Please, let me have just one call. I need to speak to my friend. She can help clear this up," Amanda pleaded. "There's obviously been a big mistake."

"Well, that's what we're hoping too, Amanda," said the male officer, his voice now softer. "The thing is, if you speak to us now, you can tell us your side of the story. It must be a real burden, knowing what happened and now hearing you're up on manslaughter charges. Why don't you just talk to us and *un*burden yourself, Amanda? This is a chance to tell your side."

"I will when I get an attorney," she said, though was thinking, *my 'side' of what? I have no idea what it is you think I've done!*

The officer heaved a heavy sigh; his impatience had returned.

"Once you get a lawyer, we can't hear that same personal account you want to give us, Amanda. Your chance to tell us exactly as it all happened is right now; attorneys only advise you not to speak and usually confuse matters, so as soon as you have appointed one—or we can do it for you if you can't afford one—then your chance to freely tell your side has passed."

*Oh God. I'm so confused,* she thought. *I should call Myra instead of Lynnie.*

But for a reason unbeknownst to her, her strongest urge was to talk with Lynnie.

⸻ ❧ ⸻

Myra rushed into the room. Amanda was so relieved to see her, she started to cry.

There was a look on Myra's face that Amanda had never seen.

She was pale, and her eyes revealed both disgust and sadness.

"Amanda, I need you to calm down and not say another word to the officers; even the most innocuous thing turns out to be incriminating. Please, your life depends on saying nothing. And we're being recorded here too, without a doubt. So even to me, even here, watch your words."

"Officers, can I please have a word with my client?" Myra now insisted.

"Client? Myra, why say I'm your client? You … you're a criminal lawyer. I don't need that sort of assistance. Please, Myra, tell me what this is … all about. I honestly haven't a clue."

Myra stared at Amanda, suddenly understanding she had no recollection of the events.

"Amanda, shut your mouth now," she demanded.

The officers left the room but stood outside the door, protecting it as if Amanda had the strength to try and escape, or even the desire, for that matter.

Myra took Amanda's hand gently, looking deeply into her eyes, revealing that what she would say would change everything.

"There was an accident," Myra explained. "A terrible one."

"What kind of accident?" said Amanda.

"One in which people got hurt." There was a pause, then, "One that was fatal."

"Fatal? *Dead?*" The confusion in Amanda's eyes and the tremble in her voice indicated she was still genuinely unaware of what had happened. "Because of me? But how?"

"Listen to me. I do not say it was because of you, Amanda, but this is the foundation of the charges being brought against you. This is what the police assert, that you'd obviously been drinking, and you left your house in the car. This is bad, Amanda. I need you to trust me and listen carefully to what I'm about to tell you. Every small detail of it, all right?"

Myra's voice was stern but steady. She talked slowly, carefully watching Amanda's face for any clue that she understood what she was hearing.

Amanda's eyes were wide, her chest heaving as if she was scared to death.

"Lynnie's daughter Ellie was driving Lynnie to check on you. Lynnie had just had a root canal and couldn't drive because of the pain medication. In a last-minute decision, they decided to come and drop in on you anyway, to see if you'd like to order a pizza together. She was very worried about you, and you weren't answering your phone. She had been trying for days and finally decided she needed to come see you.

"The police assert that as you were pulling out of the driveway—"

"No, no, no. Please, no, stop," Amanda interrupted before Myra could say the words.

"They say you were going too fast down the hill, and Ellie and Lynnie turned in—"

"Please, stop, no!" Amanda begged, but Myra needed her to understand the severity.

"Amanda, they are saying it was a head-on collision and that no way could Ellie have avoided you. She died on impact, poor Ellie did. Now, bear in mind I do not know any of this is absolute fact. I only know—and am just telling you—what the police charge sheet says."

*Ellie? It was ... Ellie who died?*

The room went black, and Amanda couldn't hear another word.

It seemed she had murdered her best friend's daughter.

Dead. Gone. The infant she had helped to raise was dead because of her stupidity, her selfishness, her thoughtlessness. And now, Lynnie was gone too, for sure.

No way would she still be a friend after this. No way. If these assertions emerged as true, then Myra would also remove herself from her life. What she had done was to kill a young, vibrant, beautiful soul who loved her, and who had not deserved to be hurt, let alone to have her life stolen. And in the process of her ugly selfishness, she had destroyed Lynnie's life too.

There was no sense in Myra even trying to help her. If she had done this, she agreed that she needed the very worst kind of punishment. It was disgusting, heinous, revolting.

Amanda felt as if she was going to be sick.

Her screams echoed down the hall, the uncontrollable sobs of both women enough to make the hospital staff gasp.

—◦◦◦◦◦—

## JOURNAL

HOW COULD THIS HAPPEN? HOW COULD SHE, MY OWN SUPPOSED FRIEND, DO THIS TO ME, TO US? MY ELLIE, MY BEAUTIFUL CHILD, SO GENTLE AND KIND. THAT WOMAN, AMANDA, WITH HER LYING AND DEVIOUS WAYS, HAS STOLEN MY CHILD FROM RIGHT IN FRONT OF ME. AND I WILL NEVER FORGET HOW HER BLOOD, THE FRAGMENTS OF HER YOUNG BRAIN TOO, ADORNED MY CLOTHES WHEN WE WERE BEING CUT FREE ... HER HEAD INJURY WAS MASSIVE,

HER BRAIN AND SKULL SMASHED, BOTH LUNGS AND HER STERNUM PUNCTURED.

THE ONLY SMALL CONSOLATION IS HOW INSTANT IT WAS. MY BABY KNEW NOTHING OF IT.

DEAR GOD, PLEASE HELP ME. I'M HOPING TO WAKE UP FROM THIS NIGHTMARE.

DEATH WOULD BE BETTER, EASIER THAN ENDURING THIS LOSS.

# Chapter Thirty

*Amanda: A Living Hell.*

The utter devastation was lingering within the confines of the hospital room. Amanda tried to will herself awake, believing it was a terrible dream, shaking and thrashing but unable to free herself from the internal and external restraints.

Myra, too, was at a loss for words, needing time to process this horrid reality.

Time stood still as the world around them spun. Myra didn't have much time before the officers were due to return to question Amanda. She had also learned the importance of comforting Amanda before the inevitable unraveling set in. Myra understood the process, and before long, there would be little chance of doing anything on a personal level before it was time for her to be professional, stepping into the role of attorney to legally defend her friend.

For at least a couple more moments, she needed to be not a lawyer, but only a best friend.

The opportunity to be her legal counsel would come later.

Amanda's breath becoming more controlled, Myra gave her one last squeeze.

"Where is Lynnie? Oh God, where is she?" pleaded Amanda.

"I saw her being wheeled down to the morgue to identify Ellie. She suffered facial abrasions, four fractured ribs, and a broken arm. Upon impact, the cars collided on the driver's side, but miraculously, Lynnie didn't suffer any severe injuries. And from what I understand, she's already started making funeral arrangements this afternoon."

Myra choked on the words.

"I've been in touch with Luke. He said the family is distraught but wouldn't say much more."

"Myra, please, take me to her. What floor is she on? I need to see her."

Myra's voice grew stern, and her eyes narrowed. Amanda was still in shock and perhaps didn't understand the legal ramifications she was facing. She simply couldn't see Lynnie. She was under arrest, and as soon as her injuries stabilized and she was released from the hospital, she would head straight to the 42nd Precinct, to be booked for manslaughter.

"Amanda," Myra said patiently. "You may not contact Lynnie or anyone in her family, for that matter. In fact, you may not speak to anyone without my approval or me by your side."

Myra took a long breath. "Anyway, Amanda, even if you could talk to Lynnie, she definitely wouldn't want to talk to you, would she? She has suffered the most horrific loss and is in intense pain. Let her be. The last person she would want to speak to is the one accused of all this."

The reality was starting to seep in for Amanda more concretely.

Her eyes flooded with tears, and her lip quivered, grasping what Myra was explaining.

"Myra, I beg you, please kill me. My life's worth nothing. Never was worth anything. I can't live with myself and don't want to. I'm a murderer. How can I go on living? What will I do?"

"Shh, be quiet now, Amanda. This is no time to be self-righteous. Plus, these are all just allegations at this stage. There will be detailed collision forensics, scene analysis, blood biochemistry, CCTV footage ... a whole raft of evidence to consider before anyone can say for sure that it was your fault alone. For all we know, Ellie was driving badly. We—I—have to examine it all too, from every angle. So, please don't say another word to anyone except me.

"They are all listening and waiting; everything you say to them could be used in court, and anything you admit to me could be used in some other way, even if recorded inappropriately."

Myra took out her laptop, typing fiercely. Her phone continuously rang and she spoke in a hushed voice as Amanda lay motionless, staring off into space.

The next couple of hours passed in a blur.

Amanda wouldn't make eye contact with anyone, especially the nurses, as she couldn't bear seeing how they looked at her. She felt the strain of their eyes in attempting to concentrate on their professionalism. However, many of them were parents themselves and surely had strong opinions about the death of a child at the hands of a reckless alcoholic. She felt the hatred of strangers already eating away at the shame consuming her broken body.

That night, she woke repeatedly from nightmares and horrible palpitations, sweating profusely, reliving the screams and the shattering of the lives of the people she loved most. She envisioned in her mind the blood and the injuries, all the terrible things poor Lynnie must have witnessed.

Half asleep, she would mutter, "No, please, no. I'm a monster. What have I done?"

The sobs continued throughout the night, leaving Amanda exhausted by daybreak.

In addition to the emotional grief, Amanda was going through withdrawals from alcohol.

In some twisted way, she welcomed the shakes, sweats, and all the longings for her desires.

It was the least she could suffer for all the pain she had caused.

Amanda had no visitors, no phone calls, nothing.

Myra had yet to come to visit a second time, and Amanda wondered if she was still willing to take on her legal proceedings or was too angry and distraught for

Lynnie. Probably, much would depend on how Lynnie was behaving and what she was saying to her friend. Maybe she would even be putting massive pressure on Myra not to represent Amanda; after all, was it just and even ethical for her closest friend to choose to represent the woman who had slain Ellie?

And what did 'representing' mean? It meant trying to get Amanda the least possible punishment, and in what kind of a world could that be seen as a good thing?

Six days after the accident, Amanda left the hospital in handcuffs and was on the way to be booked for the death of Ellie. During the drive, she stared out the window of the police cruiser, observing the people walking the streets as they lived their mundane lives with no idea of what was going on inside her world. She had once been one of those people.

Before ... before she had willfully turned her life to shit.

Amanda was fingerprinted, and had her mugshot taken, then stared and followed the directions of the plump officer who spoke in a monotone.

This was routine for the officer, and she barely noticed Amanda.

"Turn left, turn right, now look straight ahead, ma'am," she commanded.

She was stripped of her hospital clothes and placed in bright orange scrubs that were far too tight on her thighs. The material was itchy, smelling of a sterile cleaning solution.

For Amanda, the entire process was surreal and walking down the long corridor, the other inmates were hollering and rattling their jail cell bars.

It was like in the movies, only darker and colder; this time, it wasn't a fictional character being portrayed, it was Amanda's life. Once inside her cell, the door slammed behind her, causing her to jump at the sound of the lock clicking. This was the lowest point of her life.

Standing in a six-by-four cell smelling of dried urine and hopelessness was the finality of her sins caused by far too many bad and ignorant decisions.

The bruises on her face, the bandaged broken ribs, and dislocated shoulder blade reminded her of what she had done. There was no escaping her thoughts or her reality; not even for a moment could she find peace.

"Murderer," one inmate yelled across the way.

Another spat at her cell as she walked past, whispering, "Killer."

Amanda felt a stabbing pain in her heart when her mind allowed her to think about Lynnie. She thought of her tears, her devastation, her feeling of betrayal, and though Amanda would be the last person Lynnie would seek for sympathy, she bizarrely and unjustifiably still longed to be with her friend to console her and wipe away her tears.

Had it been any other circumstance, that was where she would have been, too.

She was the cause of her beautiful friend's insurmountable pain and suffering.

Amanda, the person Lynnie and Ellie loved and trusted, had torn their worlds apart. *Hell,* she thought. *I tore Ellie apart physically too ... her broken body.*

*So young, everything ahead of her.*

*How could I have done this disgusting act?*

"How, how, how?" Amanda sobbed.

Anytime her mind tried to put together the pieces of that fatal night, she became overwhelmed and panicked by the reality. She barely slept at night, rocking herself back and forth, drowning out the noise and anxiety. The prison inside of her was far harsher than the one she inhabited now. For a moment in the early morning hours, she would think that this was some sort of nightmare, almost chuckling at the tragedy of these circumstances.

Then, once again, reality would settle in, the pain and darkness becoming greater, jolting her back, knowing that this hell was the reality of her life.

She had ended a child's life and torn the heart out of her best friends in the meantime.

There was nothing to live for because of the terrible decision she had made, and her fate was now up to the courts. She deserved everything that was bound to come her way.

She was alone. Again.

"Lynnie, my dear beautiful friend, whose greatest gift was her children. Who had already endured more pain than she deserved … How could I have done this?"

These were the questions that kept Amanda up at night, knowing that Lynnie too was probably awake with her heart broken, feeling soul-crushing pain, unimaginable anger.

This was unfathomable and Amanda sobbed as she held tightly to her pillow.

Sometimes, the people with the most love, best intentions, biggest hearts, and brightest light endured the most torment in this life. Unimaginable and undeserving pain, ripping at the core.

Lynnie asked for so little, only wanting to be the mom she'd never had, and now this heartbreak was certain to change her on a cellular level. This was visceral, cruel torment.

Each night, Amanda's sobs echoed throughout the prison, and at some point, she fell silent, hoping that she would wake up and find this wasn't her reality after all.

Still, Amanda lay in her cold cell on a paper-thin mattress devoid of comfort, trying to make sense of her pathetic, hollow life. In the end, there was no sense to make of it.

Time went by slowly, passed in wondering when her court date would be set and what would become of her but mostly, she worried for her friend. Lynnie's love for Ellie was unique; it had been the only part she'd had left of Marc, and now that too was gone, obliterated.

Although Amanda had never married or had children, she'd felt a special bond with Lynnie's children, having been the honoree aunt who brought them lots of candy, spoiled them rotten, then got to go home. She wondered what Blake, Michael, and Christopher were feeling too.

The thought of the pain she caused the siblings was too much to bear.

Time stood still, guilt and anguish swallowing Amanda whole. Life had forever been altered, and there was no possible way out. Amanda finally understood what rock bottom felt like.

⎯⎯ ⁙ ⎯⎯

*Lynnie: South Oaks Nursing Home.*

A tear leaves Lynnie's eye as Helen squeezes her hand.

Helen soon realizes who Ellie is and finds herself fighting back tears.

For a moment, they both look out of the window as a red cardinal reappears. Lynnie reaches her hand out, but the bird flies away.

⎯⎯ ⁙ ⎯⎯

JOURNAL

I CAN'T WRITE, CAN'T BREATHE. WHY MY ELLIE?

MARC TRUSTED ME TO KEEP HER SAFE, AND NOW SHE'S DEAD. MY BODY FEELS BROKEN, BUT MY HEART IS SHATTERED. I KNEW FROM THE MOMENT OF WAKING THAT ELLIE WAS GONE. THE MASSIVE HOLE IN MY HEART TOLD ME WHAT THE DOCTORS CHECKING MY VITALS DIDN'T.

MY FEARS WERE CONFIRMED WHEN LUKE CAME IN, AND WOULDN'T MEET MY EYES. HIS BLUE EYES WERE SWOLLEN SHUT LIKE HE HAD GONE NINE ROUNDS IN A BOXING RINK

HIS SHOULDERS SLUMPED AND VOICE LOW, HE SLOWLY APPROACHED THE BED, TOOK MY HAND, AND SOFTLY PLACING HIS LIPS UPON IT.

HE STOOD THERE HOLDING MY HAND, ONE WHICH HE HAD HELD MANY TIMES BEFORE. HIS HEAVY BREATH TRIED DESPERATELY TO HOLD ONTO HIS MUFFLED SOBS, UNABLE TO SAY THE WORDS.

WE HELD EACH OTHER AND SOBBED SOUNDS THAT COULD ONLY BE DESCRIBED AS ONES YOU WOULD IMAGINE FROM WILD ANIMALS IN PAIN.

⸻ ❦ ⸻

Lynnie spent most days in bed. Luke couldn't reach her and was taking control of all the parenting and household chores. The boys kept busy with sports, but a sadness was consuming the house. They missed Ellie and despite seeking therapy, there was no resolution of her absence.

The family had endured a terrible loss, and the trial and publicity left them fractured.

Lynnie felt more alone than ever, although for the first time in her life, her mother was showing up to support and care for the family.

"Mom, thank you for coming. This is just so much to deal with ..." Lynnie said.

"I will be here, helping Luke to take care of things. Luke really is a good man, Lynnie. He loves you and those boys," Marylou said softly.

"I know, Mom, and he loves Ellie too. He raised her and this loss is something I don't think any of us will get over."

"I know, Lynnie. But we're all here and in this together. Somehow, we'll manage day by day."

Lynnie could have never imagined having such a vulnerable and transparent relationship with her mother, and now that her father had passed away, Marylou was alone too, needing her daughter and her family. Time had passed and her mother had become softer and more loving.

Finally, Lynnie had the mother she had wanted, though under the worst circumstances.

---

JOURNAL

I NEVER THOUGHT I WOULD SAY THIS, BUT MY MOTHER HAS SHOWN UP FOR ME IN A WAY I ALSO NEVER IMAGINED POSSIBLE. THESE DAYS ARE LONG AND HARD, AND MY GRIEF IS ALL CONSUMING. I APPRECIATE HER LOVE. MORE THAN EVER, LUKE'S BEEN MY ROCK. I'VE NEVER BEEN SO GRATEFUL FOR HIS LOVE TOO.

THE BOYS ARE COPING BY DISTRACTING THEMSELVES WITH FRIENDS AND SPORTS. I JUST WISH MORE THAN ANYTHING I HAD MY DAUGHTER BACK, MISSING HER SO MUCH I CAN BARELY BREATHE.

---

# Chapter Thirty-One

*Amanda: A Well of Shame.*

The shame Amanda endured for killing another human was unbearable and the fact that the human had been her best friend's daughter was unfathomable. Amanda felt that she had no right to enjoy life, suffering tremendously, making it a point to absorb every negative emotion and never allow her body or mind to have any peace. This was causing her great anguish, and her mental health was suffering. She would wake in the middle of the night sweating, reliving the screams and the sound of her tires screeching. For a moment, she would be comforted that it was only a dream, then realize that she was reliving that fateful night.

She was sullen and withdrawn, her eyes staring without focus, barely hearing any noise around her. She lived inside herself, a place she loathed, a person she despised.

As part of the program offered within the jail, a grief counselor visited Amanda.

The woman, in her late fifties, carried herself with authority but had a soft smile and compassionate eyes. Her thick figure made the long black dress she wore seem more casual than she would have expected. Amanda wondered if the visitor dressed this way usually or because she was seeing her patient in jail and that it seemed better to wear smarter attire.

Jody Bloomberg was a top-rated therapist who helped the inmates who'd caused accidents to deal with their trauma. Jody approached Amanda as she just stared ahead.

"Hi, Amanda," she said softly, but Amanda didn't even acknowledge her presence until Jody sat and touched her arm. Before a guard could come and reprimand her, Jody said, "Amanda, I'm here to help. You can trust me."

Amanda stared at Jody briefly. "Can you bring back that little girl and have me die instead? If not, then there's nothing you can do for me."

Jody wasn't surprised by Amanda's reaction, having previously dealt with this sort of thing.

"Amanda, this was an accident. A terrible, horrible accident. Bad choices, yes, but not filled with malice. You will have to forgive yourself at some point or be swallowed up with remorse."

"Do I deserve anything better than that?" Amanda snapped back. "My life is over. Ellie's gone, so don't even let me think about Lynnie or her family. Their lives are forever altered, and the police say it's all because of me."

Tears welled, and saying the words out loud only made her predicament more surreal.

"All of those facts are true," explained Jody as her light brown bob haircut fell softly on her face. "But there is nothing you can do to change that night's event. They happened. It's over and done and the best you can do is live and learn from it. You living every day in self-torture will not rectify a thing, will not do any 'right', will it? So why not make a difference, dammit?

"You'll be going to prison more likely than not. Heal when you're there, become a better person. Find a purpose. You must still find a way to live, even confined behind cement walls."

Her tone was more aggressive than Amanda was expecting, startling her a bit, and Amanda moved uncomfortably in her seat. Oddly, it reminded her of her own harsh words to that woman who'd been attending her therapy sessions. She had also told the woman that she had to stop feeling so sorry for herself and move on with her life. It was surreal to hear it coming back now.

"Accident or not, every day, I wear a suit of shame," said Amanda. "It's a part of me, tattooed on my soul, permanent ink that will never fade no matter how sorry I am. I just can't make it better." Amanda's voice cracked slightly, but she caught herself because she wanted Jody to understand the guilt's fortitude.

Jody nodded slowly. "I know, Amanda, I really do. But are there no better ways to deal with it? Ways that could help to do good, maybe even in honor of that young girl's life? Can we recognize that guilt but still find a way—develop a way—to live a productive life?" asked Jody.

"I don't know," Amanda said quietly, a tear dripping down her face.

Jody suggested that Amanda look into being a guest speaker within the prison or, perhaps when she was released, to help underprivileged kids know the dangers of drugs and alcohol.

If she told her story, owned her shame, and could help others make better choices, it would perhaps facilitate Amanda's recovery from the vat of toxic shame from which she ate daily.

The taste was more wretched than anyone could imagine, burning her throat and forcing her to gag with every spoonful. Amanda willfully ate it daily as a reminder, as a punishment for the life she'd once lived, the pain she had caused, and the death she had brought about.

It would be not only for Ellie but also Lynnie.

Amanda couldn't think of that now; there was still the trial and so much time before it could ever be possible.

# CHAPTER THIRTY-TWO

*Myra: In Defense ...*

Myra's dark hair was loosely in a bun as she scoured the law books, hoping to find just cause to have the case dropped against Amanda. The bags under her eyes were becoming darker and heavier, but Myra was determined to do the only thing she knew how, to practice law.

The problem was that she was a prosecutor, not a defense attorney, and would have never considered defending anyone for a crime. She always walked around with an air of arrogance reflecting upon enough people roaming the world, and she didn't want to contribute to the garbage walking the streets. When it came to criminals, Myra was harsh and unforgiving.

Perhaps her past had something to do with her resistance to find redemption, or maybe life had been so jaded for Myra that she could no longer see the good in people until they *proved* good

Myra was an action person.

She had learned that people would tell you what you wanted to hear, most being inauthentic. She had witnessed firsthand how her own mother had promised to stop drinking so many times, and as she'd lain passed out drunk, sprawled on the living room couch, her mother's actions had told a different story.

She'd claimed to have love and devotion to Myra, but after the child was hauled off to foster care, where she'd been neglected and abused, it proved words meant nothing.

Myra's hard outer shell was a defense to protect herself from more hurt, insisting that the only way to survive as a woman and lawyer was to be tough, tougher than any man.

Myra tapped her pen against the thick brown desk impatiently.

Looking around the room, she felt the air's heaviness, and the furniture's darkness filling the room. Getting up to open the window, she suddenly felt faint.

She steadied herself against the chair and took a deep breath.

*When was the last time I ate?*

Perhaps she couldn't remember yesterday morning. The days seemed to mesh and meld into one, and she kept time with her court appearances. She went to her large work bag and dug around to the bottom, where she found an oatmeal granola bar and a meager bag of nuts.

She returned to the window and opened it, feeling the breeze on her skin and noticed the oak tree right outside for the first time. She observed a cardinal making a nest, happily preparing for its new home. As Myra watched in awe, she wondered ... When had been the last time she had allowed herself to appreciate life? She couldn't recall when she'd walked in the park or even taken the time to enjoy her surroundings.

She remembered her time at Delaware University, frolicking through the campus, pointing out the different flowers and lying in the grass as the sun warmed her body. Those times in her life were peaceful and full of hope, a camouflage against the scars she tried to hide.

Awaiting the trial made the time go slowly. Amanda was humiliated and riddled with guilt over everything. She constantly received hate mail, and the other prisoners were brutal.

"Killer," they would chant. "Child murderer!"

One mother incarcerated for killing her ex-husband for abusing their child was merciless to her. "I'm in hell because I'd die to protect my kid. You are here because you recklessly killed a girl just getting her life started. You deserve everything you get! There's no justice in this world.

"We all know your white ass will be out well before I ever will. But believe me, I'll be here to remind you every day that you killed a child while I protected mine. Make no mistake, bitch!"

For a moment, the vitriol dumbfounded Amanda.

She didn't even react to the hateful words being screamed at her in a fit of rage, but just as the stranger started walking away, she turned and spat in Amanda's face.

Amanda stood motionless, the other inmates cheering with delight.

The women were ranked by attitude and swagger, so most of the inmates' behavior was acting, each attempting to outdo the others with bold acts. It was a contest to discover who was the baddest bitch in the unit and who would risk the most to prove their hierarchy.

To survive, Amanda quickly learned that there'd be a drama if there was any kind of an audience. Part of this behavior was out of boredom and pride, but mostly done for survival.

Amanda would look around, often thinking, who would these women be if they were not confined to these four walls? It was surreal thinking that, at one time, these women had been different, maybe even happy at one point in their lives. Amanda knew better than to spend too much time having emotions for anyone else, simply focusing on surviving the day.

For Myra, the isolation of defending Amanda was almost as lonely as being in a cold jail cell. In some ways, she, too, was a prisoner. She couldn't leave her office or apartment without the media chasing after her, asking questions and demanding answers. Defending her friend, she knew, was a gamble. It could be considered a potentially harmful move that might backfire on Myra herself too. Even though she wasn't in the cell, she felt imprisoned anyway; the bars were invisible, but the feelings were the same. Myra felt just as trapped as Amanda.

As Myra rounded the block to the courthouse, approaching the swarm of news cameras, she could feel her heart beating fast. She knew how this would go, but she had always been on the other side of the law. She knew very well that acting as a defense attorney, the circus gathering outside the courthouse, the chants, insults, and calls for justice would all be overwhelming.

This case had been on national news, everyone talking about how the cold-hearted lawyer was defending her friend, soon to be imprisoned for the killing of their best friend's child.

Regardless of the verdict, Myra would forever be a prisoner in her own mind, and knowing that Lynnie's child died and she'd betrayed her to defend Amanda was hell anyway.

Lynnie immediately stopped talking to Myra once she found out.

Her last words were simple, through a torrent of tears. "How could you?"

At that, she walked away as Myra stood with her head down in shame, but she had to defend Amanda since there was no one better for the job. Lynnie had family and could heal, and Myra knew if she let Amanda rot, her life would be over for good.

Either way, Myra was stuck in the middle, and there was no easy answer.

Myra exhaled, preparing herself for what was to come. The cold February breeze stung her face as she briskly passed reporters awaiting her as she exited her dark blue Mercedes.

Hoping there would not be any overzealous reporters sticking a recorder in her face as she arrived, she was careful to keep her head down.

She glanced back momentarily, noticing the bare trees lining the street like soldiers guarding the courthouse for justice. She wondered briefly what really would constitute justice in this case.

How could justice be served when there was no 'justifiable' way to rectify this situation?

She nodded briefly and kept making her way past the reporters, knowing there was no time right now to have doubts. The time for these was long gone.

A short woman with a light complexion and dark hair kept screaming over another tall thin woman, trying to be the first to get a response.

Myra couldn't understand the urgency of their questions. She nodded their way.

"Ms. Nali, is it true that you have a relationship with the defendant?" one reporter shouted. "Will this have any influence on the prosecution's case?"

A man's voice interjected, "Can you be fair and just?"

Myra stopped dead in her tracks, seeking out the voice asking the question.

As the other reporters kept screaming questions at her, she looked straight at the man who asked about fairness and justness.

She replied, "Sir, I'm this state's top lawyer. As in all other cases, this will be fair and just."

The tall man looked confused and surprised that Myra had responded to his question, the other reporters present feverishly jotting down notes based on what they had heard.

Under a further barrage of questions, Myra noticed Amanda's parents and brother Tommy approaching the courthouse, somber and zombie-like, walking almost as if in a trance.

Tommy's eyes met Myra's in desperation as they approached the reporters.

Amanda came from the courthouse's side entrance, walking briskly as officers surrounded her for protection. When the reporters noticed her and her family, they quickly jockeyed their way for a position to bombard the next set of questions.

"Have you spoken to Lynnie or her family?"

"Did you intentionally run over your best friend's daughter?"

"How does it feel to have been so drunk, you mowed down a girl just at the start of her life?"

"Will there also be a civil lawsuit?"

Before there were any responses, Amanda escaped from the barrage of questioning and continued through the chaos and into the courthouse. She glanced back briefly at her family and saw Tom glaring at her with an uncomfortable and uneasy sympathy.

Through the noise and havoc, Amanda tried desperately to meet the eyes of Myra for comfort, but she wouldn't meet her gaze. Myra was stoic and would not even acknowledge anyone familiar in the courtroom, especially Amanda. The intentional avoidance of meeting Amanda's gaze was her way of politely saying, 'Fuck off and let me do my job.'

Myra watched Amanda in the standard orange jumpsuit, her ankles shackled, and her wrists uncomfortable in handcuffs. She had seen this many times before and didn't react to other prisoners but watching her own friend shuffle her way to sit beside her, the pain was so deep she could feel her heart racing uncontrollably.

Amanda was pale, withdrawn, and looked shocked and despairing.

The prosecutor had the same look of disgust and judgment that Myra had worn so many times before. She had sent many people to prison without even a second thought and when the convicted got the harshest sentence, she often found herself with a glass of Chardonnay.

Myra wanted to scream about the injustice to her friend, longing for everyone to know that the woman she knew was good, kind, loyal, and responsible.

How could the court not understand this one event didn't define who she was?

Later, the prosecution would describe how Amanda's blood-alcohol level had been twice the legal limit. "Some may call it poor judgment," said the prosecutor in his opening statement. "And others would say it was a hideous and unforgivable criminal act, committed with intent."

Yes, she had got behind the wheel of her car and was culpable, whichever way.

The jury would surely subscribe to that theory and see to it that Amanda would be hauled off to prison for a long time. She knew how this story would end. She had seen this story, had lived this story, and in fact, she had *written* this story for many others countless times.

Even her pull at the district attorney's office couldn't help to soften this blow, begging the prosecution to reach an agreement and to make this go away. One night, staying late at the office, Myra tried one more last-ditch effort to save her friend and call in a favor.

Jack Thomas was the leading prosecutor, hungry for a top-ranking position.

He would be hard to persuade. Still, Myra desperately tried to have him give leniency.

"Come now. You know better than that. You know I can't do it, Myra," Jack said.

"Jack, please, I will do anything," Myra pleaded. "This was an accident, and you know it."

"An accident that killed a young girl, your best friend's daughter, isn't it? I do my homework also, Myra. Why would you protect the piece of shit who slaughtered your best friend's daughter, Myra? She was way over the legal alcohol limit. If you prosecuted this, you'd go in hard too."

"You know why I'm begging you, Jack," Myra desperately pleaded. "Amanda's like a sister. She's not how you portray her. Jack, please, I beg you. Let Amanda enter a plea deal."

Jack hesitated momentarily, and for a brief second, Myra thought that maybe Jack would entertain the thought of a plea deal instead of a trial.

"Myra, let me ask you, what would you do if this wasn't your friend being tried for murder right now? Would you go easy? Do you not think your friendship is blinding you to the sordid realities of this case? This young girl, bright and intelligent, full of life, has been taken."

Myra bowed her head and silently wept, knowing the answer.

*Yes, he is absolutely correct. This is an appalling crime, fueled by alcohol and ignorance.*

Jack showed shock at Myra's outward emotions. He had never seen Myra show emotion in all the years they had worked together. Jack wouldn't meet her tearful gaze, headed for the door.

As he placed his hand on the door handle, he called back, "Anyway, this is a highly publicized case, and I'm up for a promotion. We both know a conviction's precisely what I need to get that. Soon, I'll be on my yacht, taking a three-week vacation and celebrating my new partner status.

"In fact, I hear they are redecorating my corner office."

Jack smirked, put his hand on Myra's shoulder, and walked out.

Myra's stomach turned, her body ached, and her heart was ready to fall out of her chest.

She had been on the other end of the law her entire career and never once imagined what it was like being on this side. She thought back to the mother of the teenage girl who had been caught stealing at a department store. When the verdict was read, her mother had set off weeping uncontrollably, screaming to hear the guilty verdict being announced.

She thought about the twenty-five-year-old in a boating accident, convicted because Myra had pushed for first-degree manslaughter despite the proof of no intent.

How could she even look Amanda in the face, knowing that she had convicted many other people in the harshest way to promote her career? In fact, Myra would often brag that for each criminal she got off the street, her bonus checks increased and her shoe collection became more extravagant. Once, she had taken all the girls out for an expensive meal at an extravagant steak house, celebrating that she had prosecuted and won the most cases in her firm.

She was the one winning the harshest sentences ever in her firm's history.

And now Jack was essentially doing the same, leaving no room for retribution to secure his spot on the board for another conviction.

Myra was torn between doing what was right and what was just. She couldn't possibly watch her friend go to prison, but could she look in the mirror daily if she did the unthinkable?

She was a woman of morals, values, and integrity, but at what cost? At what price would she put her values before her best friend's life? She spent many sleepless nights wrestling with a no-answer solution. Either way, people would be hurt, she could lose her career, and her life would never be the same. So, either way, she was fucked.

Frankly, she had no obligation to do anything, but she just knew she had to do something. There was no good answer to whatever she chose.

At night, she would stare out her window, hoping for guidance from a higher power, hoping for a sign from the universe to help her make this decision. Nothing ever came.

She cried herself to sleep most nights at the thought of Amanda alone in a cell rotting away. During the day, she would scour through law books and previous cases, hoping to find a loophole to exonerate her friend on some technicality. If she could find a way to get her out of this legally, then it would be up to the court to decide her best friend's fate.

She spent hours studying, researching, and seeking advice, turning up with nothing every day, at least nothing with any real hope of dismissing the trial.

Overturning the conviction would be far more complicated if they lost the case and Amanda was found guilty. As much as Myra hated being in limbo, her best chance was to delay the trial for as long as possible. Myra was both determined and discouraged by the entire case.

Myra felt enormous shame, thinking about Amanda being prosecuted. There was remorse and sadness that the legal system could be so harsh, regretting the years of prosecuting to the fullest extent of the law and now 'seeing' the person inside the crime.

Sometimes, good people made poor choices and there was a gray area when it came to life.

The victims were not only the people affected by the crime; the circle of loss went way beyond to include the accused and their family. In retrospect, she saw room in the legal system for rehabilitation and leniency. There was now a clear difference in killing another between someone with no malice or intent and someone premeditating the crime. She thought back to all those cases she had tried with no compassion or understanding of the person.

It had never occurred to her that her intense need for a conviction and the harshest penalty the law could provide would have major consequences for real people and their families.

She had always slept soundly at night, having got another lousy guy off the street, one fewer scumbag to hurt innocent people.

Although her intentions were good, she now understood how her actions affected many others. Sometimes, a first offender could have gotten off with probation and a fine. Still, she ensured they would spend three years in a maximum-security prison that only hardened the seventeen-year-old kid, forcing him into a life far worse than if she had gotten him community service.

How many lives had she taken away from people because of her need to avenge the crime from her own past? It was the crime of having an alcoholic mother who'd forced her into foster care, leaving scars more profound than the physical abuse she could ever have endured.

Amanda had her own demons to work through, but Myra was on the brink of changing the course of history by either actions or inactions. It was a terrible spot to be in, and she would have to jeopardize her law license and maybe even her freedom to help her friend.

———◦❈◦———

Journal

When will they stop plastering Myra's face all over the news? I knew her job as a high-profile attorney would get publicized, but it just makes her betrayal hurt more.

Amanda's in prison, and I can't get myself to even think about her or, frankly, to care; she had every chance to get help and instead, chose to murder my daughter.

I will never forgive her!

# CHAPTER THIRTY-THREE

*Myra: Is there Any Way Out?*

Lying awake at night, Myra thought of every and any scenario she could to get Amanda off on a lesser charge. Without the prosecution willing to make a plea deal, it was impossible to do it legally. Myra would lie awake with the reality of her choices, contemplating secretly walking into the prosecutor's office with a satchel full of hundred-dollar bills.

The prosecutor was a crook, and everyone knew it so perhaps he could be bought. No, she knew the answer already; he *could* be bought but was this a viable solution?

It was clear he could make the evidence disappear, also tamper with the evidence. Jack Thomas could be bought, and Myra was desperate enough to sell her soul.

It seemed to be the perfect storm. Myra had to make a move.

She left Jack Thomas's office without the satchel, hoping he would hold up his end of the bargain and the damaging evidence would disappear.

He knew how to do it, and it had been rumored he had done it before. Myra thought she would feel some relief from the transaction, but instead, the pressure was too much, guilt eating away at her. Her thin frame was getting smaller by the moment, and every bone in her body hurt from depression and stress. She was dead inside. She sat in her car thinking of all the people she had prosecuted and persecuted for breaking the law, and now she would rank among these criminals.

And soon enough, she did, news of a huge blaze spreading, a blaze that had broken out in the storage vault where the files had been kept. The deed had been done, and by all accounts, it had all gone perfectly to plan. Yet still, she was in turmoil and if ever this were to be uncovered, her life as she knew it would be over. Would she have freed Amanda only to incarcerate herself?

Besides, how could she live the rest of her life knowing she was responsible for letting Ellie's murder be in vain? How could she ever look Lynnie in the eye?

There was technically no case against Amanda Young anymore, because all the evidence had been devoured by those avaricious flames. How convenient. Sure, the prosecution could amass the witness statements afresh for an adjourned trial, but all the forensics were gone.

And Jack, of course, showed himself in favor of not trying the case, citing the huge tax burden to the state; it was not worth it for an unintentional act, however deviant. But it was not his choice; the wheels of bureaucracy continued to turn, looking at alternatives, and Amanda remained locked up. Only if a judge dismissed the case or a settlement were reached would this all draw to an end. Jack and Myra waited long enough for those wheels of the law to be seen continuing to turn; voting that there could be no proof would point straight to nefarious acts.

And so, Myra's dream of a settlement was about to happen.

After the investigations had been declared at an end, and months had passed, Myra knew a plea deal would be coming. Since much of the physical evidence had been destroyed, it left room for Jack to make a plea deal without anyone suspecting. No one questioned Myra, her reputation as a cutthroat lawyer both universal and unwavering. No one would ever suspect what she had done, and Jack would never indict her for keeping his indiscretion secret.

JOURNAL

IT IS CLEAR WHERE MYRA'S LOYALTY LIES. DOES SHE EVEN CONSIDER ME? DOES AMANDA? IN WHAT WARPED WORLD IS THIS FAIR AND JUST?

I WANT TO HATE THEM BOTH, BUT THE TRUTH IS, I DON'T. I'M IN PAIN AND MISS MY DAUGHTER.

I WOULD DO ANYTHING TO SEE HER AGAIN EVEN FOR ONE SINGLE, MINUSCULE SECOND, TO HOLD HER IN MY ARMS, TO FEEL HER YOUNG HEART BEAT AGAINST MINE ... TO BURY MY FACE IN HER SOFT HAIR AND TELL HER HOW MUCH I LOVE HER, TILL THE END OF TIME.

# CHAPTER THIRTY-FOUR

*Myra: The Unthinkable.*

Myra couldn't reconcile who she had become. Her strong work ethic, fierce beliefs, unbreakable integrity, and respect for the law had been broken, making decisions she never imagined. And now, she had done the unthinkable. She contemplated confessing to destroying the evidence, admitting her crimes, taking responsibility. Still, in the end, none of it would matter; her career would be over regardless, the news reporters eating her alive.

Myra became more depressed, paranoid, and withdrawn and would lie awake thinking of a way to save her beloved friends from pain. There were no viable answers.

In a way, they were all victims of circumstance.

Although she tried to help Amanda by destroying some evidence, she had left enough of a trace that Amanda would suffer *some* consequences. This was no longer a slam dunk case, and the prosecution would have to work harder to get a conviction. Therefore, Jack would make a plea deal, and Amanda would get out earlier than had there been a full criminal trial.

Did Lynnie know what she had done, and had just never mentioned it?

Lynnie surely would be aware that Myra would not stand by and allow Amanda to spend her life in prison, and it was beyond coincidental that a substantial part of the evidence had been destroyed just days before pre-trial. There had already been speculation at the headquarters that Myra had something to do with the documents' odd disappearance. She'd been questioned relentlessly, and as she had learned to do all of her life, she kept a stone-cold face as she lied.

No emotion, no guilt, no way to link her to destroying anything.

After the plea deal, Myra had more time on her hands, thinking back to the many nights of being sexually abused, also to her mother's alcoholism and neglect, and how she would put a smile on her face the next day, feigning that none of that had happened.

She would still show up for school too.

In short, Myra had become accustomed to wearing a mask, fooling people into thinking she was OK and that life wasn't nearly as hard as her reality. Even as a child, she'd known how to beat the system by excelling in classes, making firm friends with teachers, and being involved with school mostly to cover up the horrific abuse she endured daily. It was her way of escaping the reality of her childhood. Was it any wonder she had become a fantastic liar as an adult?

The gift of lying had benefited Myra throughout her career and certainly now that she was under such scrutiny regarding the case. The media frenzy had gotten out of control, and Myra found no respite from the chaos surrounding her. In desperation, she took a trip into the mountains, trying to escape all the chaos in her head. Everywhere she went, there were whispers about the case, about her, about her friends that she had known for decades, and plenty of speculation of what would become of all of them.

It was just too much for Myra to handle. The overwhelming noise, the unknown and the fears for her future, and the incredible guilt brought her to utter despair.

Thoughts of suicide were now plaguing her daily, and as much as she tried to hush those voices, they were always there, becoming louder and louder. Often drifting off to sleep, she would reminisce about a simpler time, a time of four beautiful young girls filled with life, laughing and dreaming about their future. No one could have known how their lives would intertwine and end up in such a perilous situation.

It was tragic. A friendship had been severed, lives destroyed, and hurt and shame overtook every cell in Myra's body. She cried tears of regret, grief, and sorrow, praying to God that somehow, all that had transpired could be resolved. However, Myra was no optimist. Her reputation would forever be tainted. She suspected that it was only a matter of time until an investigation against her would proceed, potential criminal charges coming her way too.

The life she lived would forever be altered in the most traumatic way.

Her days of ruling the courthouse with her charisma, power, and ability to shun negotiations would no longer be valued. Most of her colleagues had already dismissed and shunned *her*, and it wouldn't be long before she would have to defend her law license and possibly her freedom.

The probability of being disbarred was significant, and she had absolutely no idea or purpose in her life without practicing law. Who would she become without being a lawyer?

The very concept of needing to secure a new career was just too much to bear.

She glanced in the mirror. Her shallow eyes were sunken so deep into her face, and her cheekbones were gaunt, her hair thin, and her soul no longer the reflection staring back at her.

Myra was gone in every way that mattered, her form akin to an empty shell.

Myra fought back the tears and gasped at the sight of herself. No longer able to stand her reflection, she violently threw the empty bottle of vodka at the mirror. Its glass shattered, leaving a small cut on her cheek, blood dripping down her face and mixing with fresh tears.

It was at that moment Myra decided to end her life. She wasn't physically tired but was beaten, fractured and exhausted in every other way possible.

She couldn't go any further and had no will to live.

As much as Myra had given up on herself, her friends, her future, and her life, she wanted the choice of ending her life to be her own.

It was the least she could do to have control of her final farewell to this earth. Myra knew when she visited Lynnie that it would be the last time of seeing her. She felt she owed it to her to say goodbye, even if Lynnie had been unaware of what was coming.

Never would she have anticipated that Myra, the strong one, the one who'd always had an answer and a solution for every circumstance, would take this terrible way out.

---

JOURNAL

MYRA CALLED, WANTING TO SEE ME AND THE KIDS.

LUKE REFUSES TO BE HERE OR HAVE ANYTHING TO DO WITH HER, AND WHO CAN BLAME HIM? HE THINKS IT'S A MISTAKE TO LET HER INTO OUR HOME. DOES SHE NOT THINK I REALIZE SHE HAS SOMETHING TO DO WITH THE FIRE DAYS BEFORE THE TRIAL?

I THINK ABOUT WHAT I WOULD HAVE DONE IF I'D BEEN IN HER SHOES. I DON'T KNOW, JUST CAN'T SAY. I WANT TO HATE HER, WANT TO HATE AMANDA, BUT I DON'T. MY FAITH HAS HELPED SAVE MY SANITY.

THE TRUTH IS, I LOVE THOSE WOMEN SO GODDAMN MUCH, WAY MORE THAN THEY DESERVE. MOSTLY, I CAN'T LIVE THE REST OF MY LIFE WITH A NEED FOR VENGEANCE BURNING INSIDE ME.

MY ELLIE, THAT KIND AND GENTLE, FORGIVING SOUL, WOULD NEVER HAVE WANTED THAT.

---

# Chapter Thirty-Five

*Myra: A Fond Goodbye.*

When Myra arrived at Lynnie's house, she was nervous. The two had barely spoken since Ellie's death, and Myra was surprised that Lynnie was willing to see her but grateful that she had taken her desperation seriously. Lynnie offered her a lemonade and asked Myra to walk down a small path in her backyard to where she'd planted a tree and made a memorial for Ellie.

They both shed tears and held hands, Lynnie recounting her favorite things about her daughter. While describing Ellie's infectious giggle when her toes were tickled, a bright orange butterfly landed right on Lynnie's shoulder. The two remained still momentarily. It was Ellie, visiting them, they thought. The two friends laughed and cried, holding on tightly to one another.

As Myra wiped away Lynnie's tears, she said, "You know your beautiful little girl will always be with you, just like I will always be by your side. And I do know that you feel I am letting you down, letting your Ellie down. It is not what I want, but I also know you do not hate Amanda."

Lynnie's demeanor seemed to say, *and how can you possibly know that? How dare you!*

But she bit her lip and said nothing, evidently unwilling to break this moment.

As Myra walked down the path to return to her car, she looked back at her friend one last time.

Lynnie had grown older, and the lines on her face had made her seem older than her age.

But beneath the wrinkles and frown lines, Myra saw her friend as that same beautiful college girl she had met many years ago. Myra had been the cocky, cheeky one, and Lynnie so shy.

She walked away smiling, knowing Lynnie would be OK and eventually find peace again.

Later that day, Myra removed the necklace she had been wearing since her mother's death.

She gently put it in an envelope.

Once sealed, she wrote Lynnie's name on the front, and held it to her heart knowing that eventually, Lynnie would receive it, knowing she was the last person Myra had thought of.

⸺⟐⸺

A fisherman discovered Myra's lifeless body floating south on the bay, three days after she jumped off the bridge. People speculated if it had been an accident or suicide.

The case, just like Amanda's, remained unsolved.

Journal

What has she done? I thought Myra's visit was to make amends, not say goodbye. When I learned that she'd taken her own life, it made sense.

I never wanted her to kill herself, never would have wanted any of this.

Helping to empty her apartment, I was stunned to find the envelope with my name. It was the necklace Myra had worn since her mother died. She must have been hurting so bad to go to these lengths, and all I can think of is to wonder how she was feeling and what her thoughts were as she quietly took off that precious chain and decided to give it to me.

My heart breaks for you, Myra. But you'll be all right, you know? You will be fine because my girl Ellie will meet you and look after you. I know that she will. And strangely, there is no right or wrong anymore in all of this. You were in no way to blame for protecting your friend.

No, not 'your' friend ... 'Our' friend.

Myra, I can't fathom the guilt you felt or the immense sadness. What happened to us once young girls? How could we have imagined that we would end up like this?

# CHAPTER THIRTY-SIX

*Amanda: Life in Hell.*

If there was hell, Amanda was confident of being in it. The coldness of the place went further than the temperature, and she wasn't sure how she could survive her sentence, also unable to fathom being in prison. Whatever had happened to her and how had she got to this place?

Why hadn't she just listened to her friends and got help for her addiction?

Her self-loathing, regret, and remorse overcame every cell in her body.

She had no idea what the future had in store, but she needed to change.

While she was grateful for the lesser sentence, time went by far too slowly.

Her hair was matted from a previous scuffle with an inmate; she'd held her own, but the clumps of her hair, missing from her bald scalp, said otherwise.

Dried blood across her left eye, and a slightly swollen lip offered evidence that her reality was now in the dwelling of this cement building.

It was hard to forget that Amanda was incarcerated; there was no escape from that reality, but often, Amanda would gasp at what had transpired, wondering how her life had traveled down such a tragic road. Her mind still couldn't reconcile how she'd become inmate 628.

She'd once had a privileged life, and even though her teenage years had been challenging, her family loved her, and seeing them when they visited was more traumatic than being left alone to rot inside her prison cell. She felt enormous guilt for putting them through this ordeal, also worrying about Tommy and his sobriety.

Everyone's swollen, tired eyes and defeated body language were too much to bear as they sat across the table during the visiting hour. One moment of time had destroyed so much, and now, Amanda would pay the price along with so many others.

She didn't feel sorry for herself, though, deserving her punishment, only feeling worse for her family, and unable to even think about Lynnie.

Her parents had looked forward to retirement, but now they were in a financial pinch because they had withdrawn all their life savings to help with legal expenses.

They spent every moment worrying about Amanda, which consumed their lives, and their dream of driving across the country in a Winnebago was now ruined.

Her parents were the ones to break the news about Myra's death. Amanda didn't react upon hearing the information. She just sat and stared, knowing the depression and anxiety that Myra had endured had finally overtaken her life.

Amanda was blaming herself for it, especially after hearing the whispers that said Myra had been responsible for destroying the evidence of the accident.

It made no sense. Myra had loved her, that much was obvious, but she had loved Lynnie too.

More than that, she loved practicing law. There would be no way Myra would have risked it all for her, no way at all! She grieved her death as a suicide because of her mental health, not from the guilt of having carried out a crime of arson to destroy evidence for a friend.

No, that concept was too ludicrous, too impossible.

At first, Amanda had no real recollection of the accident, but over time, it came crashing back.

She tried erasing the scene from her mind, the blood-curdling screams from Lynnie, and the thump as the cars collided forever etched in her mind. At night when trying to sleep, she replayed the visions, wishing the entire situation away.

Even hearing alarms in prison, it would take her right back to that dreadful night, to hearing the sirens, having the police question her, and the chaos that ensued after.

She relived feeling Lynnie pounding on her body relentlessly, screaming, "How could you do this? I hate you. I hope you rot in hell. You are a despicable person and I hope you get what you deserve. You have ruined my life, murdering my poor daughter, Ellie, Ellie, Ellie ..."

Amanda tried desperately to block out that fatal night, but it was no use. This would scar her for the rest of her days, and she would spend every day reliving the pain she had caused.

Every day felt like an eternity, waking in a fog, unsure if this was a reality or a nightmare.

The noise around her became overwhelming, the clanging on the bars, disputes between inmates, cries for help, cries for mercy ... Her senses were on overdrive.

The smell of vomit, blood, and urine was enough to make anyone dizzy, but Amanda kept her head down and barely looked anywhere other than the floor, counting the tiles as she walked, carefully noticing every crack in the old flooring. It kept her focused and occupied, decreasing her chance of getting into an altercation with another inmate.

She learned that if you looked an inmate in the eye, you were either confident or crazy. On the other hand, if you showed any weakness, you had a death wish. It was a balance and one that was never easy to decide. Some days, keeping your head down kept the peace, while at other times, it was construed as a sign of disrespect that would cause a riot.

Amanda tried to work the vibe of the room, minute by minute. She didn't have the edge over many other inmates and knew she would crack if pushed too far. Her body ached everywhere, and her soul was empty, but the only way to survive this ordeal was to keep calm and show no sign of weakness. Her previous jubilant life was over, and she had to be steadfast, needing to think on her feet and be prepared for every situation. It was impossible to have her guard down even for a moment, leaving her anxiety high and her senses always on full alert.

As the months passed, and the season changed, so did Amanda. She learned the ropes and was no longer a meek inmate waiting for her demise. This place was beyond merciless, but she now walked with an edge, the once swaying of her hips and gracefulness of her legs replaced with a trot of urgency. The smile that used to meet strangers now met them with a stone-faced glare and the glimmer once sparking in her eyes was now empty behind her pale green eyes.

She was now a shell of a person whose poor decisions had led her to prison. Prison. She could hardly believe it. She felt like a walking zombie, not even noticing her ligaments move. Her mind could barely hold a thought, and she was in true survival mode. At night, she would hear the sobs of other inmates and shove her head under the pillow, trying to muffle their cries of hell.

The only way to survive her reality was drowning out her thoughts.

She would think about when she'd first got to prison and how she would obsess over things she could not control. It would drive her mad, but now, she understood that her survival meant keeping her wits about her and playing a part she wasn't comfortable with but was necessary.

Amanda settled into the role of an inmate, picking up the others' walk, talk, and attitudes to fit in far more than in the beginning. She would force herself to go into a place far away from the grim walls and steel bars where she could think of happier times, times of her childhood, and when she was brave, would let her mind stray to those dear friends from the University of Delaware. She would remember moments once forgotten and smile briefly at her youth.

With Jessica and Myra gone, Lynnie was the only one left and was no longer truly alive.

She lived in her own special hell, and the once laughing girls were, for all purposes, now skeletons, some living and some dead. All those years ago, she had never known how intertwined and complex the girls'—now women's—lives would become.

Amanda fondly remembered grabbing coffee, taking hikes, gossiping, and the closeness they had all once shared. How could life turn all that love into such great heartbreak?

A cool shiver took over Amanda's body, and she shook uncontrollably. Was it another panic attack, a chill? Had she gotten ill? She wasn't sure. As much as she had adjusted to life in prison, she would still get tremendous anxiety and sometimes suffer from panic attacks.

There wasn't much she could do once that happened, except use the skills she had learned on a yoga retreat with the girls many moons ago.

Breathing, tapping the third eye, envisioning calm, and counting; those were the techniques. She would do this continuously, repeating each like a mantra until she was calmer.

On one particular night, these methods just didn't help and as much as Amanda tried, she couldn't control her thoughts or her breath. Her heart was racing, her palms sweaty, and the world around her spinning. She felt colder than ever, and the scratchy thin gray wool blanket was barely helping. Amanda tried desperately to gain control of her thoughts and emotions, hoping to calm her now trembling body, hoping for it to grow warm.

She tucked her knees up to her chin the same way she'd done as a child, hoping to feel safe, burying her head in her hands to block out the sound of her thoughts. Nothing helped.

She rocked herself back and forth, trying to hold back tears, but they began flowing.

She wept through the night until she observed the faintest peek of light coming from the window into her otherwise dark cell. There was suddenly a woman's voice, "Inmate 8873?"

Not recognizing the number, Amanda didn't move. With more agitation, the woman spoke louder. "Inmate 8873. I see you lying there. You answer when I roll call you."

Still, Amanda, unaware that the correction officer was talking to her, hesitated to move. *Perhaps she'll go away and leave me alone until breakfast,* she thought for a second, but soon realized she had no choice but to respond. Amanda quickly complied, knowing that if a correction officer wanted your attention, you couldn't simply wish them away.

You were now the state's property, basically belonging to them.

Amanda perked up immediately, knowing full well that she could no longer ignore the demands of the short, stocky woman outside her cell.

"Yes, ma'am. Inmate 8873 present," Amanda announced, groggy and stoic in front of her cell.

She noticed the correction officer looking at her with disdain and a bit of familiarity.

Amanda couldn't quite place her, but momentarily, she saw a look of satisfaction come over her piercing blue eyes. Amanda brushed it off, assuming this was just one step closer to losing her mind and having a lack of sleep, edible food, or sunlight—she just couldn't trust her own senses. The woman simply stared at Amanda and slowly walked away.

*I don't know what that was all about,* Amanda thought, and slowly crept back into her bed, confused about that interaction.

It seemed strange; had she already found an enemy on cell block 628?

God knew, she had enough problems and didn't need this.

She had a rightfully hard time adjusting to prison life, her depression so out of control that she thought she was losing her mind. In prison, no one cared about mental health, and the lack of treatment or recognition was a tremendous problem barely addressed.

At best, most inmates were heavily medicated or punished for 'out of norm' behavior, and Amanda quickly returned to her psychology expertise, realizing that if she ever got out of this place, she would help inmates dealing with mental health issues while incarcerated.

This thought brought along with it a realization.

That was the first time Amanda had dared to think about her future, spending most days dwelling on the past, making her life at the penitentiary even more miserable.

During her career, she often told her patients to switch perspectives and note how their attitudes changed. Amanda desperately wanted to find a way to survive this ordeal and make a difference, but she most often found it challenging to make it through the day.

The days were brutal, and the nights unbearable, every twenty-four hours seeming like weeks. There was no way of knowing how she would survive years in this element.

Amanda kept a journal, hoping writing her fears and anxieties on paper would help her mental health. She would often write about other inmates, the food, and even one time, about hearing two birds in the distance, chirping. Had it been a sign from Jessica and Myra, trying to assure her she was not alone? The singing of the two birds brought a smile to Amanda's face, imagining her friends outside free, singing a duet in the early morning. She missed them and her old life, waking every morning hoping to hear more chirping from her feathered friends.

Most days, she didn't, but when they did sing, she noticed them flying around her window, even getting up on a chair to try and steal a peek.

Although she could never catch a glimpse of them, she heard them, which was enough.

Two days later, the same correction officer arrived at her cell in the early morning hours. Amanda felt she was being watched. Opening her tired eyes, she saw the same woman standing outside her cell as if she was going to say something.

Amanda jumped to attention, unsure of the visit's purpose, curious as to why this correction officer had taken such an interest in her. Amanda's stomach squirmed at the uncertainty, but by now, she knew not to exhibit any fear openly. Stepping up, she was about to call out her prison number, but the woman on the other side of the bars shushed her.

"Was I speaking to you, inmate?" she snapped with overzealous authority.

Amanda went to open her mouth but knew better than to respond; she'd found out the hard way that prison was a cluster of rhetorical questions.

It had been confusing to learn, and only through two days in solitary confinement did she finally understand that there were more unwritten rules than written ones.

When she'd first arrived in prison, she had made the dire mistake of answering a question not meant for a response, immediately realizing her folly when the inmates around started hissing and heckling her. "Oh, snap," one quipped. "The little lady is about to find out she isn't in Kansas anymore." The others laughed.

A woman with long black hair and a strong Latina accent said, "Bitch is about to get fucked up, pretty girl. You are about to discover what ugly means."

Two correction officers roughly dragged her out before Amanda could even understand her mistake. Unbeknownst to Amanda, her casual demeanor had been taken as a sign of disrespect. She wasn't aware of the ramifications of this infraction at the time. She soon understood.

They threw her into a dark cell for ten long days, and the only light she saw was when a male guard would bring her food and be sure to first masturbate in front of her, vile and frightening.

Amanda knew she could have been raped at any time and tried to keep her fear buried in her soul. She watched him until he finished, then he gave her a sly smile, licked his fingers, and casually walked away.

Amanda was terrified but kept her eyes straight ahead, not showing any emotion. By now, she knew better. It was a learning curve. She wasn't prepared for this kind of life, and had never imagined this would be her fate and hadn't understood that this life existed.

She had heard Myra talk about cases, always assuming the person convicted deserved the harsh treatment, but she had never comprehended the roughness of the system.

Many of the other inmates weren't completely bad. Often, they were just people who had made terrible mistakes, getting caught up in a world of trouble. One woman named Linda had killed her ex-husband after discovering he had been molesting their three-month-old daughter.

Another woman, who had gone by the name Vivi, had been forced into prostitution and got hooked on drugs. When her 'John' was choking her, she had taken the knife out of her bag and stabbed him fifty-six times. She had to serve five years in prison, despite saving her own life.

Outrage from many community leaders came out on the war against women.

Vivi had been kidnapped and pushed into a life as a sex trafficker, also being forced to take drugs, and still, the legal system found her guilty.

Because Vivi didn't have family support or financial backing, she couldn't get an adequate defense to keep her out of prison. So many women fell victim to gender and economic inequality, and the prison was packed with women who simply had not been left with many choices in life. Many of the stories were similar, their lives turning upside down before they had been forced to take drastic action, then to grasp the consequences of their actions.

With the harsh circumstances, Amanda couldn't claim the same innocence as some of the other inmates. She had played a big part in why she was behind bars and took responsibility for it. Justice for Ellie needed to be served. Amanda had made a decision to drink and drive.

She had every opportunity to have a legal defense, the love and support of her family, a quality education, and great legal representation. Still, she was paying her dues to society just like every other inmate. She knew she deserved each and every day she served. It didn't make it easier, though, didn't make time go faster or cause guilt to ease.

She was guilty. She had taken a life, but not just any life, her best friend's daughter's life.

Yes, it was an accident, but was filled with negligence and stupidity, and she deserved every day of torture that would come her way. One thing prison certainly provided was time to reflect.

The days were long, especially in solitary confinement, but bizarrely, a small part of Amanda enjoyed the silence the confinement provided. Though she was often placed in solitary for minor infractions, the one officer who kept visiting always found a way to throw her into the darkness. Still, Amanda became accustomed to it, able to sit still with her thoughts without distraction.

It was painful, and she shook with remorse, but it was necessary.

Amanda would beg God for forgiveness and pray that Lynnie could find peace in her heart one day. She knew better not to pray for her own forgiveness.

She had done the most unforgivable thing.

# Chapter Thirty-Seven

*Amanda: Happy Birthday.*

On Amanda's sixtieth birthday, she spent it thinking about the many birthdays she had spent with her friends. It had been years since the accident and each day, she found herself thinking about life before she had made that terrible decision. As her prison sentence was coming to an end, Amanda would often reflect on Myra. As time passed and clarity revealed itself, she often wondered if Myra did have something to do with the destruction of the evidence.

Did she kill herself because of it? It seemed likely.

What other reason would there have been for her suicide? With no objective evidence, she tried not to dwell on it, continuing to live her life the best way she could by helping others.

If her suspicions were correct, and Amanda was pretty sure they were, Amanda felt as though she 'owed' Myra to make something of herself. Her story could not end as Prisoner 8873, and the pain Amanda had caused to many motivated her to be better. Was this not exactly what her counselor had advised her to do so long ago? It was true; it was the best way.

"I'll not let all of this be for nothing," she told the parole officer. "I have a lot of life to live and a lot of good to do. One day, you'll open a newspaper and see me in it for my achievements, not my mistakes."

The crack in her voice was quickly replaced with confidence.

"I want to help others before they make the mistakes I did," she said quietly.

Through the prison system, Amanda obtained her certificate as a public speaker. She worked hard drafting speeches and spent much time with other inmates who needed inspiration.

She remembered years back when the social worker had come to visit and suggested she take part in this program. At the time, she couldn't even have imagined doing something so bold, yet here she was, making a difference, paying retribution, even beginning to heal.

⬦⬦⬦⬦⬦

JOURNAL

I feel so alone. For most of my life, the only friendships I have had were Myra, Jessica, and Amanda. I focus on my children and my writing, but I miss the friendship we enjoyed.

Funny, my friend Stacy called out of the blue. We hadn't spoken in ages; it was nice to hear her voice again. We caught up on life. She had heard about Ellie and was genuinely heartbroken for me.

WE LAUGHED ABOUT OUR CHILDHOOD AND HOW WE'D BEEN EACH OTHER'S ONLY FRIENDS. WE ALSO TALKED ABOUT HOW WE LOST TOUCH WHEN I WENT AWAY TO COLLEGE AND HOW SHE WOULD LOVE TO SEE ME AGAIN SOMETIME.

IT WAS GREAT TALKING WITH HER; IT'S BEEN TOO LONG. BUT THEN AGAIN, I NEVER HAD TIME FOR HER WHEN THE GIRLS WERE AROUND, DID I? AM I JUST USING HER NOW I HAVE NO ONE?

# Chapter Thirty-Eight

*Amanda: Freedom.*

By the time she was released, Amanda knew what she was supposed to do—she wanted her story to not be in vain and to give hope to others around her. For the first time in years, she had something she hadn't known for almost a decade. Hope.

Gathering the last of her belongings to prepare for her release, the same guard who had spent years harassing her awaited outside Amanda's cell.

"So, you're finally getting released. Too soon if you ask me. Poor Lynnie never deserved the heartache your actions caused, and she'll have to live with it for the rest of her life. I have known Lynnie since childhood and the pain you have caused is unforgivable."

Amanda stood there stunned. It had finally clicked.

This woman seemed familiar because … she knew her. This was Lynnie's best friend from childhood. She remembered seeing pictures of her throughout the years, and they'd even met briefly at Ellie's first birthday party. It all made sense.

Officer Kurt was otherwise known as Stacy, Lynnie's lifelong friend. This revelation explained the officer's animosity toward her for all these years.

Amanda opened her mouth to speak, but no words escaped her quivering lips as Stacy's glare haunted her. There was nothing to say. 'I am sorry for killing your friend's reason for living' would sound heartless, even if true.

All these years, Stacy had been watching her, presumably reporting right back to Lynnie.

The hatred was palpable, but Amanda had no time to consider it.

The day she was finally free to leave prison, her now elderly parents waited outside the gates with open arms. It had been so long since she'd felt their embrace.

She moved in with them as she settled back into society and looking around her childhood room as an adult—an adult ex-convict at that—was surreal. Inside her closet, she found a box tucked away in the far-right-hand corner of her old high school memorabilia.

Rummaging through it, she discovered her acceptance letter to the University of Delaware, and as her fingers brushed the dusty pamphlet, she sighed.

This time seemed so very long ago, and so much had changed.

After her release from prison, she completed three hundred hours of community service, deciding the best way to make an impact was to become a public speaker regarding drug use and alcoholism risks. Visiting schools and youth groups, she was honest and open regarding her struggles. She held back tears, recounting the awful night she had claimed her best friend's daughter's life. She spoke in depth about her time in prison, the loneliness, the fear, the self-recriminations, and the incredible remorse and regret. She missed her friends and the friendship and love that they provided, hoping that her story could change the trajectory for many others.

Within the next three years, Amanda became the top motivational speaker in the country, visiting schools across America, talking to the youth about the dangers of substance abuse.

She spent her time writing self-help books and became a revered source, an expert, making it to the bestseller list many times. She learned to tell her story confidently instead of being shameful, exhibiting hope instead of guilt. She knew her story would impact all who encountered her, deeply desiring to spend her life making a difference.

After all the hurt and sorrow that life had thrown at her, this was the only way for Amanda to make amends with her past.

At the end of every speech, she would say, "There is a vast difference between accepting your past and moving on from it; once you can decipher between the two, you can be truly free."

After years of touring the United States, Amanda decided to return to the University of Delaware, where she was asked to attend a conference titled 'Alumni Who Make a Difference'.

At first, she was hesitant; wouldn't her past only cause grief?

She was older now and growing tired, and it had been three decades since returning to campus. She was accompanied by her healthcare worker, who'd been there only to help her with the mundane things of traveling. Still in good shape, Amanda could make her way around, and the Friday night of the event, she wore her favorite blue dress with gold sparkles on the front.

She felt good and was ready to discuss how second chances were possible.

Making her way down in the elevator, she noticed the magnificent ballroom. *I certainly never had these accommodations when I attended the university,* she thought.

Helping herself to hors d'oeuvres, she sensed the stare of someone a few feet away, and before even looking up, she knew. *Lynnie! It's Lynnie.*

It wouldn't have occurred to Amanda that Lynnie would also be invited to the event.

But of course, she had been.

*How is it possible for the university to overlook the connection between us and invite us both?* She surmised that after thirty years, people tended to forget the details about others' lives. The room stood still as the two locked eyes, and Lynnie gave a nod to Amanda and a small smile. It appeared Lynnie had found peace after all, still so beautiful inside and out after all these years.

The calm look and approval of Amanda's presence told her all she needed to know, and Amanda instinctively approached. But in a split second, Lynnie was gone.

Amanda scoured the room looking for her, but she had disappeared.

She had been hoping to have one more encounter, even if brief, but clearly, Lynnie wanted no part of it. Out of respect, Amanda didn't search further for her old friend, though she had been grateful to have taken one more glance at the woman who had once meant the world to her.

But after all, sometimes, things were better left unsaid.

A day later, Amanda returned home from the conference more tired than anticipated.

The pain on her side was becoming more bothersome, so she decided it was time to seek medical attention. Even before the news came out of the doctor's mouth, she already knew ... pancreatic cancer. She had Googled her symptoms one evening.

Within weeks, she was in hospice, slowly watching her life disappear.

Taking her last breath, she saw herself as a young girl, with Lynnie, Myra, and Jessica all laughing so many years ago. She felt at peace and was ready to go.

Closing her eyes for the last time, her friends from long ago stood waiting to welcome her into the gates of heaven. They were happy, whole, healthy, and ready to spend eternity together.

After all, life on earth was just a series of lessons. Love and friendship never died.

Only the body did, the soul continuing for eternity.

Luke had passed away many years ago, leaving the boys to care for Lynnie. They now had their own lives but stayed close to their mother, doting on her regularly. Even though they had lost their sister, the boys remained close too. The loss, although paralyzing for some time, had made the family draw together, the loss of Ellie bonding the family. They had spent many years celebrating their lives and their love for Ellie and for one another.

If nothing else good came from the tragedy, Lynnie was grateful that Luke and the boys stayed close, and even in Lynnie's darkest moments of despair, the boys gave Lynnie a reason to smile.

She also knew that Ellie watched over them all, her presence surrounding the family.

*Lynnie: South Oaks Nursing Home.*

"Baby, you doin' all right? There are only a couple more pages in this journal. You read through all of them today. You must be tired." Helen nudges Lynnie slightly.

"Oh yes, I'm good. I'm tired. I want to finish these last few pages, then I can go."

"And where you think you are going, Lynnie?" Helen says with a chuckle. "You be staying right here; I will be bringing you your medicine."

Lynnie smiles, not quite sure who this woman who cares for her is, but she is deeply grateful for the companionship. Lynnie is happy almost to be done with this last book.

She hopes to rest, eagerly concluding the final pages.

---

## JOURNAL

I saw Amanda for the first time since the accident. Even though it has been over thirty years, I would recognize her anywhere. She saw me too, but nothing was left to say.

What was I to do? I had to do what was best for me, and that was to be secure, knowing there were no words to make it better, nor was it my responsibility. I have endured a lot of loss, Marc, Ellie, and Luke, and it's taught me to love while I can because nothing lasts forever.

Sometimes, words aren't necessary. Sometimes, closure isn't needed, and sometimes, life happens as it is supposed to but, in the end, we are securely insecure doing the best we can.

---

# Chapter Thirty-Nine

*Lynnie: South Oaks Nursing Home.*

Lynnie sets down the pile of journals. She is tired. The tiny bird soon appears at the window again and Lynnie reaches for it, knowing it is almost time to say goodbye to this life.

She barely recognizes her own reflection, looking into the mirror, and the deep creases in her cheeks and dark circles under her eyes make her unrecognizable.

She looks intently at herself, desperately searching for the once-young girl who was filled with love and hope. Slowly, she is slipping.

One gentleman calls her *Mom,* and she never has understood why.

She often sees the tearful stranger begging her to recognize him, and Lynnie says nothing and only stares out the window, returning to her own world.

By now, Lynnie is mostly living inside her own mind, recounting a different place and time, also trying to place the people who seem to know her. They all want her to recognize the importance of their existence, expecting something more than what she has been able to give.

Although she tries to accommodate them, she becomes frustrated and scared at all the talking they always do. Their memories are never hers, though they desperately tell her they are.

Familiar strangers these are to her, but with fragments of some faint, fleeting recognition.

Sometimes, she recalls the smell of baked apples and remembers children baking a pie with her in the kitchen, but whose children, she cannot know. Only that the soft apples and sweet butter smell used to make her feel a sense of home and safety, but she just isn't quite sure why.

Some days have seemed longer than others lately, days on which Lynnie has been stuck in her own head, sometimes trying to recognize her face in the mirror.

Her features are still soft and beautiful, but the lines covering it make it difficult to see.

She has sometimes looked down at her old hands, wondering what work she has done to make her fingers so stiff and fragile.

Each line tells a story but the trouble is, she doesn't know what story.

Often, she has tried to make herself remember, an effort only leading to panic and shame.

A young, vibrant woman once accidentally appeared in her room looking for her grandmother, and Lynnie called out, "Ellie, is that you? I have been waiting for you."

The girl just smiles and runs off, looking for her rightful relative. It feels the same now.

Lynnie now knows she is eager to leave this life because someone is waiting for her somewhere special, but she just can't recall who, or where.

The feeling eats away at her until she has finally exhausted herself to nap.

As she closes her eyes to rest, a beautiful angel of a girl appears with soft blue eyes and light skin, her warm smile mouthing, 'Soon, Mama. I will see you soon.'

Lynnie goes off to sleep, soon waking more confused and agitated than before, longing for that girl to return. She feels safe in her presence, craving to hold her tight.

All she remembers is that the girl will be waiting for her to arrive somewhere, soon.

Closing her eyes, she drifts, soon seeing some beautiful young women laughing on a college campus, filled with love, life, and friendship. Just as when she was a child, she stands on the sideline, watching, eager to join in. But why do they seem so far away, so unreachable?

She feels so much love for these women who dance around in her mind.

She's unsure why, only certain of the fact her heart beats with joy, yet barely beats at all, remembering only faintly a true life, one that once was.

Her heart is full, her life complete, and her time here on this earth is done.

She smiles faintly, knowing that she is going home.

Lynnie's last book ends with this passage:

---

WE ARE ALL ON OUR OWN DESTINATION, A PATH UNKNOWN.

PLANS ARE MADE BY COWARDS. TO LIVE FULLY, WE MUST LIVE FREELY, WITHOUT KNOWING WHO WILL COME INTO OUR LIVES, WHO WILL STAY, WHO WILL OPT OUT, AND WHAT WE WILL LEARN FROM THEM. IT IS PART OF THE HUMAN EXPERIENCE, THE FEAR AND THE ASTONISHING TRUTH OF BEING HUMAN. TO FULLY LOVE AND BE PRESENT IS TO BE VULNERABLE TO THE UNEXPECTED JOYS AND TRAGEDIES THAT OUR LIVES WILL BECOME.

THE DESTINATION NEVER ENDS, THE LEARNING NEVER CEASES, AND THE PAIN IS INEVITABLE, BUT THE ULTIMATE PLEASURE, IF YOU ARE BRAVE ENOUGH TO SHOW UP FOR IT, WELL, THAT IT IS IMPECCABLE. LIFE IS BOTH TRAGIC

AND FRAGILE. IF YOU SIT WITH IT, YOU WILL APPRECIATE ALL THE BEAUTY IT HAS TO OFFER.

LIFE WILL GO ON. IT ALWAYS DOES.

***

*Lynnie: South Oaks Nursing Home.*

Lynnie goes in and out of sleep, her old body ready to rest, and her soul excited to find its way home. She looks out the window, seeing a light snow falling and a red cardinal chirping on the sill. Her breathing is getting shallower.

She looks around the room, her eyes searching for someone.

Her eyelids close, and she reaches toward the sky, quietly uttering something.

"There you are."

# Acknowledgements

*Securely Insecure* has been a work in progress that has taken time, patience, and immense tenacity. While writing the manuscript, there were many ups and downs, but I believed in the story and felt compelled by the characters.

This story needed to be told so people would relate to the issues and understand the heartbreak of the characters.

Special thanks to my mother, my biggest supporter and champion, Franny Parisi. Without you, I would have never come this far. You have been my rock, inspiration, and hero. You always believed in me and for that I will forever be grateful.

To Joe, thank you for treating me like your own. I appreciate you always.

Thank you to my siblings and best friends, James, Marissa, Phyllis, Andrew, Victoria, and Tim; you have always been there when I needed you the most.

Thank you to the people who continually inspire me to be my best self: Suzanne, Aimee, Christine, and Helen, and to my Roger Williams University friends who have taught me much about friendship, sparking the idea of this manuscript.

Thank you to the kind souls at Sacred Space Hot Pilates Secret for giving me a place to heal, grow, and be inspired.

Thank you to Sophia, Rocco, Gloria, and Jim for welcoming me with love.

Thank you to my friends and family, all of you who support and love me unconditionally.

Thank you, Anelie Parisi, for your marketing expertise and dedication. Thank you, Betty Withrow, for helping me with the character development in my story, and a special thank you to my editor, Annie Jenkinson, and her team for the unbelievable transformation and incredible understanding of my story.

To my beautiful children, William, Emma, Benjamin, and Matthew, who have watched me struggle but understand how important this project is to me. If nothing else, I hope you have learned from me to follow your passions in life, believing that all things are possible.

To my soul mate, Marc Ferolito; I will never be able to thank you enough for loving me honestly, profoundly, and authentically and for inspiring me to chase my dreams and believe in them. You are everything I wished for and so much more. You are my person. I adore and love you with every fiber of my being. You are the best thing that has ever happened to me.

# About the Author

Donna Lynn Lito will graduate with her master's in creative writing in May 2024. She currently creates thought-provoking podcasts and blogs on her website, www.donnalynnbooks.com. Deeply passionate about issues affecting women and openly discussing the emotional pressures of womanhood, Donna Lynn encourages readers to reject the societal expectations that attempt to cage them instead of allowing them to live as their authentic, best selves.

Lito's work helps promote a community of self-loving healers who better understand finding happiness by being Securely Insecure.

When not working on her writing, Donna Lynn enjoys Pilates, being out in nature, and spending time with her family. She looks forward to the second half of her life unapologetically, following her passions and living her truth.